Codename Charming

BY LUCY PARKER

Codename Charming

LUCY PARKER

AVON

An Imprint of HarperCollins*Publishers*

CODENAME CHARMING. Copyright © 2023 by Laura Elliott. All rights reserved. Printed in the United States of America. No part of this book may be used or reproduced in any manner whatsoever without written permission except in the case of brief quotations embodied in critical articles and reviews. For information, address HarperCollins Publishers, 195 Broadway, New York, NY 10007.

HarperCollins books may be purchased for educational, business, or sales promotional use. For information, please email the Special Markets Department at SPsales@harpercollins.com.

FIRST EDITION

Designed by Diahann Sturge

Flowers © lisima / Shutterstock

Library of Congress Cataloging-in-Publication Data has been applied for.

ISBN 978-0-06-304010-6

23 24 25 26 27 LBC 5 4 3 2 1

In loving memory of Nana, Uncle Ken, and Kate

Prologue

Months (and many minor calamities) ago

Most people went viral on social media because they pulled off a successful joke on Twitter, posted a particularly hilarious photo of their cat, or deliberately provoked an entire fandom so that thousands of people felt compelled to prove they were wrong. Going out on a limb here—or a scalp, to be strictly accurate—Pet was guessing she would be the first person to trend at #1 after being accidentally catapulted off a conference stage by the soon-to-be newest member of the British royal family and ending up wrapped around his bodyguard's head.

The sights and sounds of the Oxford Green Eighty environmental conference faded into a blur of white noise and gaping faces as she clung to Matthias Vaughn's massive shoulders. She was balanced tummy-down as if they were attempting a see-saw acrobatic act, his closely shaven head was surprisingly slippery, and it was entirely possible that her knickers were on display to photojournalists from seven major tabloids. It was a good thing she'd abandoned her circus dreams at a very young age, because if she'd ever had delusions of flexibility, they'd just fractured. Along with what felt like several ribs.

She wasn't quite sure what to do now. She'd landed at a precarious angle, and Matthias couldn't let go to lift her off him without unceremoniously dumping her on the floor. Tentatively, she shifted her weight, shot forward, and would have landed headfirst if he hadn't gripped her tighter.

"This is unfortunate," she observed, as the blood immediately rushed to her upside down head.

He didn't immediately respond. Apparently, even in these circumstances, he wasn't inclined to waste words. If Pet could collect every syllable that had ever left his lips in her hearing, it would add up to a paragraph shorter than her average text message. His shoulders shifted beneath her as he exhaled. Very gustily. Very long-suffering. Very understandable when wearing a fully grown woman like a snood.

One of his hands slid up her arm, until his strong fingers were wrapped around her wrist. "Don't move."

His voice was crisp and efficient, but edged with a gravelly undertone, like someone had gone to town on his vocal cords with sandpaper. Matthias was ex-military and used to giving orders. He was also about nine feet tall, built like an absolute weapon, and unsurprisingly, most people were inclined to follow those orders.

As a personal assistant, Pet made a career out of fulfilling wishes and making sure people had everything their little hearts desired, but she also had a strict policy of not working for mannerless pricks. Authoritarian orders made a rebellious devil appear on her left shoulder and cock a brow.

This evening, however, she quite literally was in no position to argue.

She could see nothing of his face from this vantage point, and he probably couldn't see anything at all, with her breasts resting on his brow bone.

This was very awkward.

And it had all gone wrong so fast.

Twelve seconds ago, she'd been standing on the central dais next to her boss, Johnny Marchmont, extremely earnest fiancé of Princess Rose of Albany, the king's least favorite granddaughter. She'd handed him the speech notes he'd absentmindedly left on the dessert table, and he'd cast her a grateful glance and tripped over the microphone cord. His flailing left arm had sort of . . . *scooped* her, right across the back. He'd heaved her into the crowd like he was throwing a tennis ball for Rosie's pit bull. If she delved back into her memories of school physics, there was probably a handy series of equations that would explain the height and velocity she'd reached in point-five of a second.

Unfortunately, Pet was pretty sure she'd left her brain back on the stage, because her mind was just an echo chamber of four-letter words right now—although for some unholy reason, she'd retained enough muscle function to starfish her arms and legs as she flew. Like a bat.

Luckily for her, and extremely unfortunately for him, Matthias had been doing his laser-eye sweep of the crowd directly beneath the stage. He'd managed to break her fall. With his skull, but still. He must have moved like lightning, but he was used to reacting quickly, especially in this security detail. As much as she liked her incredibly well-meaning boss, she hoped Matthias and the rest of the bodyguards were getting hazard pay.

Just this morning, Johnny had attempted to pick a bunch of flowers for Rosie from the palace gardens and set fire to a wheelbarrow.

After kissing him on the cheek, his fiancée had calmly filled an antique chalice with pond water, extinguished the flames, and continued speaking into her work phone. The royal couple in a nutshell.

Still dazed, Pet twisted her head sideways and looked up at the stage. Johnny's cheeks were crimson, and he appeared to be frozen to the spot. The ludicrous dismay in his expression snapped her brain back into its correct location—and it finally sank in exactly how far away she was from the ground. If Matthias dropped her at this point, she'd crack like an egg.

"High," she squeaked brilliantly, and her breath rushed out as he moved his big hands again, lifted her a few inches, and did some sort of flipping maneuver. She landed squarely in his arms, her hands instinctively fisting in his crisp black shirt. Blinking, she met his inscrutable gaze.

"Hi," he said, deadpan, in that deep, level voice. As usual, his harsh, uneven features were set in imperturbable lines, and people had been giving him slightly wary glances all night.

Admittedly, his body language did emit a general aura of "fuck with me at your peril," but when they'd first met, in fairly traumatic circumstances, he'd been kind to her, in his gruff, monosyllabic way. She'd been looking forward to already having a friend on the palace staff when she started work. Overly optimistically, as it turned out.

In the ten days since she'd officially joined the team as Johnny's personal assistant and troubleshooter, this was their longest one-to-one encounter. She might as well add "part-time magician" to her résumé, because hey presto, she could make a fully grown, big bear of a man disappear with a single "good morning."

Renewed self-consciousness washed over her as he set her carefully back on her feet. As a young child she'd been quite shy, a perfectly valid personality trait she'd nevertheless thought she'd outgrown until this past week. He scanned her for visible signs of injury, closely and thoroughly, but with his usual professional detachment.

"Are you hurt?" he asked, and there was a fractional edge to the words.

To be fair, she'd probably put his neck out.

He was very subtly rolling one shoulder, and she detected a lightning flicker that might have been a suppressed wince.

Pet smoothed down her dress, very aware of the many faces and cameras pointed their way.

"I'm fine. Thanks to you," she said, flushing, and he made a short, dismissive gesture with his bearded chin. She cleared her throat. "Just . . . not *exactly* how I'd pictured my first big function on the job."

She jumped violently, then, as a loud, strange noise traveled around the room, stretching out above the excited hum of voices. It was hard to describe, but if pressed, she'd have to go with the dying throes of a drunken raccoon. "What the hell was—?"

On the stage, Johnny was holding the shrinking remains of an enormous inflatable green creature. The Green Eighty Task Force mascot let out one final plaintive wail before it shriveled into a pile of wrinkled recycled plastic. Not a raccoon, but . . . not far off the mark.

Johnny stared down helplessly at the dead mascot.

Pet looked at Matthias, who ran his fingers over his jaw. His closely cropped dark beard made a cozy little scratching sound.

"Welcome to Team Marchmont," he said dryly. "I suggest you invest in a portable fire extinguisher, a lock-pick kit, and a crash helmet."

Chapter One

Amidst a suffocating cloud of wisteria perfume, the director of the new Fine Arts Museum leaned forward, her lips parting in a tight smile, revealing a large piece of spinach stuck to her protruding front teeth. As Pet tried very hard not to watch, it fell off and landed on the tip of her shoe.

"We're so delighted to have Mr. Marchmont with us this evening," the director murmured, and Pet upped the wattage of her own, equally forced smile in return.

The poor woman didn't look delighted. She looked like a person who'd spent weeks brandishing a shiny, exclusive-looking parcel, bragging about its contents to everyone in earshot, only to belatedly discover that it contained a ticking bomb.

It was an expression Pet had seen often throughout the past months, since she'd started working for Johnny.

"I'd just like to extend our apologies again about the DeWitt sculpture," Pet said, trying and failing not to pause slightly before she finished that sentence.

She considered the arts one of the saving graces of humanity. A vital form of expression and communication. Frequently the last speck of hope and beauty in a world overrun with tax-dodging billionaires, politicians, murderers, and friend requests on Facebook from apparently amnesiac school bullies. She was an artist of sorts herself, although the paper silhouette portraits she snipped when she was stressed or bored were child's play compared to most of the exhibits in the museum.

Most of the exhibits.

But, frankly, "sculpture" was a very generous word for Brooklyn DeWitt's *Orgasm*—a warped, writhing mess of metal pipes, clay, and tin cans, which had looked a literal load of rubbish even before Johnny had lost his balance and sat on it.

She glanced anxiously over at him again. Having finished destroying the ugliest artwork in the foyer, he was talking to a rep from the museum's executive committee. His fuzzy blond curls were all but crackling with nervous energy, and one hand was moving rhythmically in his pocket.

Either he was fiddling with his speech notes, or he'd taken the relaxation breathing techniques they'd practiced to a *whole* other level of public stress relief.

"These incidents happen," the director said with another rigid curve of her mouth, and Pet couldn't help an ironic glance around at walls laden with millions of pounds worth of Old Masters and contemporary classics.

She certainly hoped they didn't happen often, and she suspected that if the culprit arse in question didn't usually dwell in a palace, it would find itself hauled into court and landed with a massive damages bill.

"Anyway," the other woman added in a slightly more natural tone, "fortunately Brooklyn places a lot of faith in serendipity. He believes the work has now advanced to its next natural stage of existence. He just said . . . let me get this right . . . ah! 'The splayed, somnolent lines of the crushed metal represent the moist limbs of the sated female, her state of being molded by the force of the male. Nature at its most vivid and elemental.'"

Pet couldn't hide her expression, and very briefly, the director lifted an eyebrow as they exchanged looks.

"Ah!" Pet repeated agreeably, and unfortunately had to complete the rest of her response silently in her head: "The random bullshit of the absolute pillock."

The director's posture had relaxed, but when she spoke again, both her words and her gaze were very direct. "It was a great coup for us to secure a royal presence at the opening, and for Mr. Marchmont to give the keynote address." She, too, cut a sidelong glance at Johnny, whose Adam's apple was visibly bobbing, even at this distance. It was never a good sign when he started the compulsive swallowing. "Her Royal Highness Princess Rose's husband currently reminds me of my son on school sports day. Wobbly knees, sweaty brow, and about five seconds from faking a sudden case of laryngitis. Is he going to manage this? The press presence is very heavy this evening."

Yes, Pet had noticed that. Members from the standard royal press rota had woven themselves throughout the room, like a tapestry of cameras and shrewd eyes, interspersed with the usual nose-twitching rats from the more sensational tabloids, and a few royal bloggers.

She was used to an occasional paparazzi encounter when she was out with her brother, Dominic, and his wife, Sylvie, who were both judges on a very popular TV baking show, but the typhoon of media attention on the royals was an entirely different league. At times, it was terrifyingly intense, overwhelmingly intrusive, and she couldn't imagine ever getting used to it. The fact that Johnny had voluntarily signed up for it, for his entire life, was testament to how much he loved Rosie. By nature and inclination, he ought to be a nursery teacher in a sleepy little village somewhere, or holed up in a room designing his favorite console games, not making awkward small talk and facing public pillory on a daily basis.

It was her primary task to help him manage all this—go through the briefings with him while they did their homework on whom he was going to meet, organize his schedule, accompany him on these trial by fire engagements. Play her part in keeping the cogs running smoothly. This was her wheelhouse, and it sounded very simple on paper.

In practice . . .

Well, her boss was *Johnny*. Adorable, enthusiastic Johnny with his heart of gold and his two enormous left feet, one of which was usually lodged squarely in his mouth. E.g., when they'd arrived at the museum this evening and been introduced to the current Member of Parliament for Chelsea and Fulham, Mr. Simon Winger. Johnny had cast a quick glance at the "S. Winger" on the man's name tag and said cheerfully, "I know the House of Commons is l-legendarily full of f-fuckers, but I didn't realize things were quite *that* exciting."

He was going to kill her stone dead, any day now.

Despite the pulverized priceless artwork, *some* sort of angel was watching over them, because in a room stuffed to the gills with reporters and phones, not a single soul had heard him except Pet, the blinking MP, and Johnny's personal protection officers.

Although even ultra-professional, ever-expressionless Matthias had been unable to repress a tiny cheek twitch at that one.

Pet opted for overall truthfulness now. "Mr. Marchmont isn't a natural public speaker, but every person in his position grows into their role over time. He has a genuine passion for the creative industries, and he's equally honored to be here this evening."

The director looked at Johnny with a shade of sympathy. "Not an easy role for a shy person."

"No." And Johnny *was* shy. Behind his disastrously candid comments and surprisingly dirty sense of humor, he was a shy man—and a kind one. Despite the frequent mishaps, he was by far the best boss of her career to date.

He was due to give his speech at exactly seven o'clock, in a few minutes' time. Excusing herself, Pet skirted tactfully around the perimeter of the room, automatically returning a quick smile when a handsome guy in a perfectly tailored suit cast her an interested glance. He winked at her without breaking off his conversation. She'd noticed him come in earlier and had him pegged as one of the mega-rich City investors. Definite merchant banker aura. Clothingwise, they all looked like they'd come straight from a funeral.

Brooklyn DeWitt might be a pretentious con artist, but at least his fuchsia overalls were livening things up a bit.

On the other side of the large reception space, a massive figure, also in head-to-toe black, stood against the velvet-draped wall.

Looking straight at her.

A rare occurrence, since unless they were having a brief, blunt discussion about the correct care and feeding of a new royal, Matthias usually treated her like a veritable superhero.

Invisible Woman.

Pet immediately returned his gaze in full, staring back into irises of the palest, clearest green. Those sea-glass eyes belonged in the face of an absentminded country vicar, or a young ingénue in a play, or—somebody like Johnny. Somebody openhearted and friendly, maybe a little naïve.

There was nothing naïve about Matthias Vaughn.

Or particularly friendly.

In his remote, cyborg-y way, he did genuinely care about Johnny, however—demonstrating that you could always find at least one point of common interest with a person. She appreciated Matthias's dedication to his job and Johnny's safety, even if he was about as bendable and open to negotiation as a titanium plank.

He was still looking at her, his lips disappearing into a familiar grim line. It was the same expression he'd pulled last week, after she'd proposed the idea of a game of laser tag in the palace gardens. Anyone could see that Johnny—and Rosie—needed a regular burst of fun and sheer silliness, or they'd never cope as well with the public side of their lives. Several staffers had confirmed that the princess had been withdrawing into herself before she'd met Johnny. He was the love of her life and soul, the person who embraced every inch of her for the caring, snarky goth she was. Apparently, they'd giggled their way through a night of beer drinking and video-game troll-bashing on their first date. The following day, Rosie had engineered a fund-raiser for chronic illness support, adeptly prying millions of pounds from the wallets of Whitehall clout-chasers, the same MPs who'd systematically stripped away vital health-care funding in the first place. Exactly the life balance of badassery, chill, and poetic justice Pet was aiming for.

If only Matthias would stop vetoing every suggestion on the grounds of safety violations and failure to follow advance protocols.

What she called spontaneity, he considered a grievous insult to his precious digital clipboard of schedules and red tape. Yesterday, he'd caught her *barely* leaning over a second-floor balcony to retrieve the game controller Johnny had accidentally thrown out the window into a trellis; he'd behaved like she was stringing a high-wire from the sixth-story turrets.

The man had probably laminated his copy of the protocol manual and carefully sponged the fingerprints from it every night.

Obviously, she wasn't suggesting anything that would actually endanger Johnny. Security was a legitimate and constant issue. Their boss had joined a family who'd had targets on their backs from the cradle, and he'd attracted dangerous, overzealous attention of his own before he'd even walked down the aisle. Pet's mind immediately tried to flinch away from that memory playing out again, but she gritted her teeth and dragged it back, like pulling reluctant performers onto a tiny stage.

Rosie's twenty-fifth birthday ball last year. Beautiful, opulent, full of famous faces—and the only one Pet had seen was her brother's. She'd had an argument with Dominic that week, bitter words and hurt, and had wanted desperately to make it up. She could still hear the sounds of that night, the live band, the hum of voices, her heels tapping as she crossed the ballroom, the beads on her favorite vintage dress dancing and clicking against her legs—and then the flash of movement as a blonde woman emerged from the crowd, her eyes fixed on the royal couple, her face blank. Just blank. When the woman had raised her arm, the overhead lights had twinkled with incongruous gentleness on the knife in her hand.

It was still a blur of adrenaline, that cluster of surreal minutes. Pet didn't really remember lunging between Johnny and that first downward stroke—and only fragments of what followed, including the slice of burning heat as metal cut through her skin.

Almost unconsciously, her hand went to her forearm now. She'd had the best surgeon in the city, thanks to Rosie. The scars were neat and had progressed through an ombre palette of colors, moving progressively down to the lighter end of the scale. Most of the time she forgot they were there, until nerve pain skittered through every cell from elbow to fingertips, sparkling and terrible until it faded.

Another spike of memory—a big hand folded around hers, a tight squeeze of comfort. Drifting in and out of consciousness that night, she'd been only half aware of the stranger crouching at her side. His black clothing had blurred into the darkness edging her vision, her eyes skating over his uneven features, unfocused and fuzzy. He'd seemed somehow both substantial and ephemeral, and in her confused mind, he'd been a sort of dark angel. It had been a startlingly intense shock when Matthias had later turned up at the hospital with Johnny and Rosie, like coming face-to-face with a wistful fragment of a dream.

Across the room, his gaze slipped down to where her thumb traced the line of the largest scar.

He was always so still. Even in the rare, glorious hours when Pet had absolutely nothing to do and nowhere to be, she needed something in her hands. No double entendre intended.

It was fascinating to watch him at work. Physically, he was not someone who should ever be able to sink into the background— and yet, when he needed to, the man might as well have a supernatural cloaking device. Just shimmering into the shadows, his eyes all intent like a cat.

A ginormous, humorless cat.

She could still sense the disapproving vibe even at a distance. She could fully admit that for all his personality quirks, Captain Risk Averse was very good at his job, but the sentiment was not mutual—and if she were brutally honest, he did have reason to consider her more of a liability than a team asset so far.

Reasons such as the fact that she kept landing on top of him in public.

Four times now, she'd been the unintentional victim of Johnny's malfunctioning limbs.

And four times, Matthias had been in her trajectory, forced to catch her.

Four times.

She was trapped in a vaudeville nightmare.

At least she usually landed in his *arms* these days.

Right on cue, a middle-aged man wove through the crowd with a cocktail in his hand and did a slight double take when he saw her. His eyes narrowed as he obviously tried to place her, then the confusion cleared. "Ah," he said with a smirk, chuckling loathsomely to himself. "The Green Eighty conference girl."

The Green Eighty conference girl.

Absolutely fuck her life.

It had reached a million views on YouTube now, the clip of her clinging to Matthias's head, and every time she thought about it, a little piece of her soul chipped off and died.

It had been like she was a slightly too-snug shirt, she'd told Sylvie gloomily on the phone that fateful night, and he'd got stuck halfway through getting her off.

"Do you want to rephrase that?" her sister-in-law had asked with a soft snort.

She knew Johnny couldn't help it. It seemed to be coded into his DNA, but she'd never been into the damsel-in-distress act. She was one of the best PAs in the city, bloody good at her career, with no hesitation in saying so. Prior to this contract, she'd been sitting, standing, and walking without catastrophe, all on her own, for over twenty-seven years.

Several guests walked past her toward the bar, and the fit merchant banker winked at her again. Matthias's laser focus briefly switched to him. His career centered around protecting clients from dangerous people, but it also seemed to be an ingrained personality trait for him, looking at everybody as if he were a human X-ray machine, capable of seeing through flesh and bone to their worst qualities and innermost thoughts. Pet wondered what judgment he'd formed of the winker. Not a favorable one, by the look of it. His frosty demeanor suggested he'd excise the first vowel of "winker" and insert a different one. She found herself instinctively averting her gaze when the guy turned to look at her once more. She did tend to use Matthias as a gauge of trustworthiness. If someone passed his silent tests, they were probably a good egg; if not, steer clear.

She couldn't help an envious glance at all the people ordering drinks. She'd consider sacrificing a limb right now for one of those cocktails, especially with Johnny's speech still to come. If he were anyone else, she'd suggest a very small shot of liquid charisma for him as well, but even stone-cold-sober Johnny was unpredictable. Tipsy Johnny was a daunting thought.

"Champagne, ma'am?" A waiter appeared at her side, tray in hand, and it was probably time to stop staring tragically at the cocktail menu like an unrequited lover.

Regretfully, she shook her head with a polite no. Over his shoulder, she saw the faintest twitch of Matthias's eyebrow, as if it wanted to lift in a mocking arch but had belatedly remembered its owner didn't do frivolous expressions.

His bearing really was particularly militant tonight.

Pet didn't even have the excuse of booze that she suddenly found all that upright sternness very provoking.

They were on the clock and his was a very serious, important job, but they were still in a stunning building surrounded by beautiful things, and there was a huge cake on the food table. As a novelty, they were all being given slices to take home in seriously cute little containers, like the poshest kid's birthday party she'd ever attended. Free cake! In boxes shaped like tiny houses, decorated with miniature versions of the museum's most popular artworks. He could relax the facial muscles just a bit. He was a bodyguard, not a Beefeater.

Before his gaze traveled on its way, Pet narrowed her eyes, rapidly scrunching up her face into an exaggerated, prune-like scowl. Within two seconds, she'd smoothed out her expression again.

Not so much as a blink in response.

"Have to bring bigger guns than that, honey. He once managed to guard a client through an entire screening of *Bringing Up Baby* with nary a titter," a voice murmured in her ear, and Pet glanced sideways at Benji, Matthias's co-lead on Johnny's protection detail.

"I'm baffled how you two ever became friends." For someone who could literally have people's lives in his hands, Benji lived his own in a state of languid amusement. The two men existed at totally opposite ends of the personality scale.

"Shame the Duchess of Clarence isn't here tonight." Benji's tone was musing as he made a few unnecessary adjustments to an already immaculate tie. His black curls were cut ruthlessly short, and his brown skin was clean-shaven as usual. Pet had never seen him with even a scrap of stubble. He stuck even more stringently than Matthias to the no-nonsense grooming of their military days, which had initially seemed out of character, until he'd informed her—cheerfully and entirely unprompted—that it would be criminal to conceal such glorious bone structure. And had she ever seen such a godlike scalp? He thought not. "She'd pull out her soothsayer cards and provide a vivid explanation of how Matthias and I complement each other. Opposing energies twining together, emblematic of the connected universe."

"Careful. Brooklyn DeWitt and his cohort will think you're usurping their territory. They've got the market cornered on pretentious dickery." Pet lifted her brows at him. "And I don't think the duchess actually claims to predict the future."

When Rosie's aunt wafted around the palace with a cocktail in one hand and a romance novel in the other, her vague comments did often hit on an element of truth, but Pet suspected that had more to do with a canny network of informants than actual clairvoyance.

"Unless you count the time you decided to tightrope-walk the perimeter of the courtyard fountain after staff drinks, and she accurately predicted what would follow." Pet checked her watch and looked across at Johnny. He'd stopped fidgeting, at least. "But in that case, slap a crystal ball in front of every other person there that night and call us Nostradamus."

The amusement in Benji's dark eyes turned into a flashing grin. He nudged her affectionately with his elbow. "You know, if she's right and opposite energies do draw together, you and Matty ought to be lifelong best buds."

Only Benji would get away with calling hard-faced, impassive Matthias *Matty*. There was no way that man had ever been a sweet little Matty, even when he was little. She could see him as a businesslike baby, already five feet tall and grimly handing out safety infringement notices to any kids who moved too quickly with scissors.

"Once upon a time, I nearly became an astrophysicist. I used to daydream about being part of an exploratory expedition into the great unknown beyond the observable universe." She tugged at the button on her silk fringed dress. She'd burned off nervous energy with her silhouette portraits from a very young age—she'd have been one of those children annoying Matthias with her improper handling of stationery—and her hands were suddenly itching for paper and scissors. "I think there's more chance of that still happening than there is of Matthias curling up on the couch with me to eat Jammie Dodgers and binge-watch K-dramas."

Benji brightened. "Is that an open offer?"

"Yes, but I should warn you that I accept happy endings only, become far too emotionally invested in people who don't exist, and seem to have gone through a hormonal upheaval since my last birthday. Last week, I was watching the news and I cried at an ad for loo roll."

"Platonic soul mates, you and me. Next night off. I'll bring chocolate Hobnobs." As he spoke, his eyes were scanning over the room and its occupants. He was a stark contrast to Matthias physically as well as in temperament, leanly built and a much more convenient height for Pet's neck. For all their differences, however, both men were at the top of their field, and very little got past either PPO. Johnny was at ease in Benji's happy-go-lucky company, but he was also in secure hands.

Benji shot her a sudden glance. "Odds the speech will come off without incident?"

Pet couldn't hold back a fractional grimace. Johnny was even paler than earlier, and he looked deceptively small and fragile with Matthias in proximity. "He managed a clean run-through this afternoon, so fingers crossed."

Before she'd finished speaking, the museum director ascended to the central dais for the long-winded introduction of their royal patron.

Pet held her breath when he took his place at the podium, straightened his notes and his bow tie, and began to speak.

"Good evening, and th-thank you all for coming tonight . . ."

He faltered momentarily, but most of the faces around Pet were relaxed and warm. She'd like to think that only the tabloids and a tiny handful of small-minded people would give a shit about someone's stutter or shyness. Even as the words formed in her mind, she noticed a couple of women by the bar whispering to each other and exchanging looks. The older of the pair turned her head, seemingly sensing herself under surveillance. She met Pet's stare, and the disdainful curve of her mouth deepened.

Pet's jaw tensed.

"The arts have always been an important part of my life and I look forward to working with you all in the coming years . . ." As Johnny continued through the speech he'd painstakingly constructed, his shoulders went back, and he even managed a few genuine smiles. Pet didn't realize she was clutching Benji's arm until he leaned over and whispered that he was happy to be a support prop any time, but her fingernails were about to sever a vein.

She murmured an apology, letting go. Her eyes returned to the dais, her gaze skating over Matthias. He was looking at her with faint disapproval yet again.

Now what had she done? She leveled her brows at him, and he became more expressionless than ever.

To her tremendous relief, Johnny was nearing the end of his speech. When he wrapped it up without incident, she wasn't sure which of them was more thankful. The crowd applauded politely, several people casting furtive, longing looks at the cocktail station, and Johnny took a step back from the microphone.

The director mounted the stairs to join him, with the head of the museum's fund-raising committee at her side. "Thank you so much, Mr. Marchmont," she chirped, also with transparent relief. "Now, if you would do us the honor of continuing tradition by cutting the building's Christening cake with the ceremonial Carolingian sword—"

Pet had been so focused on Johnny that she hadn't even noticed that the committee chairman was holding a massive bloody Viking sword. Obviously, neither had Johnny.

The blade caught the light as the man spun it jauntily in his hand, showing off and preparing to offer the weapon handle-first. Everything went into motion very quickly: first and foremost, Johnny's feet. She was already rushing forward as he went sheet-pale and backpedaled away from the sword.

He slammed into the microphone stand, which hit the wooden platform with an almighty crash, and he fell, landing awkwardly on his side.

The director and chairman froze where they stood, appalled.

In stark contrast, most of the journalists in the room looked like kids on Christmas morning. Even the ones who were decent enough to have some concern for Johnny's well-being couldn't hide the furtive gleam of yet more impending headlines.

It didn't help that from this angle, with the chairman still holding the outstretched sword, it looked like Johnny had stabbed him in the chest.

Matthias and Benji were at Johnny's side in seconds, helping him up as Pet hurried up the stairs to join them.

"I didn't mean to—" the chairman began in bewilderment, but the director had caught on, too, and flushed.

"I'm terribly sorry," she said in a low voice. "I didn't think." The chairman's frown redirected to her, and she gave him a pointed, exasperated look. "Mr. Marchmont was the victim of an attempted knife assault at a function last year. Of course, he—"

Crimson-red patches streaked into Johnny's cheeks. "Actually,

Ms. De Vere was the v-victim of the *successful* knife assault at the f-function last year," he said stiffly, with an almost pleading look at Pet, "and I'm afraid I am still a bit . . . j-jumpy, apparently. I apologize for—"

Pet's heart was beating so hard that it was almost painful. She pressed her palm against her breastbone for a second, then she stepped forward and took the sword from the chairman. "No harm done." Her voice was very, very calm. She paused to make sure her hand was steady before she passed the sword to Johnny, who took it automatically. "Shall we carry on? The cake looks delicious. Our compliments to the chef."

"I believe your brother's bakery provided the cake this evening, Ms. De Vere," the chairman said hurriedly, with a grateful glance at her. "We've used De Vere's for all our functions, for many years. If you'll come this way, Mr. Marchmont . . . ?"

Johnny had managed to regain his outward composure, she was pleased and proud to see, but their eyes met briefly as he passed her. There, she saw bone-deep mortification and a hint of a totally unnecessary apology.

Fleetingly, she touched his elbow in reassurance, and a little zap of pain went through her forearm, snaking down almost to her wrist.

She heard Benji release a short breath and caught the faintest wince from Matthias.

They'd almost got through an entire function without providing a single arrow of ammunition to the *Digital Star* and its ongoing vendetta against Johnny, Rosie's "incompetent, lecherous, serial cheat of a husband," she believed had been yesterday's offering.

So close.

Chapter Two

Johnny was staring glumly out the tinted window, slumped in the back of the limo. As they were only traveling a short distance and didn't have Rosie with them, they'd skipped the full cavalcade and only employed a subtle escort for this event, so few curious faces peered back at him from the pavement when they stopped in traffic for the eighth time. Matthias had been working protection details for high-profile clients for years, but even the most self-important celebrities—usually the musicians, collectively the most excruciating pricks he'd ever met—hadn't moved around with the level of fanfare accompanying senior royals. Coming from a background in covert ops, it went massively against the grain to court unnecessary attention, but he couldn't deny the transport procedures were a well-oiled machine.

There were at least a dozen levels of protections for even the simplest outing, and a contingency plan for every action. The protocols couldn't align more with his own instincts if he'd written them himself. It was probably annoying as hell for Johnny most days, being treated like a cross between a priceless diamond in a steel vault and a newly hatched chick. Unfortunately, it came with the job description when marrying the fourth in line to the throne—and the man's golden-hearted, dangerously naïve temperament under-scored the need for extra care. He made a bloody Care Bear look cynical and streetwise.

When Matthias had joined the palace staff, it had been with a great deal of underlying cynicism. He'd been prepared for the usual self-serving bullshit and fakery, but nevertheless committed to protecting his boss's safety to the full extent of his ability.

Within twenty-four hours of taking co-lead on the protective detail for the princess's then-boyfriend, he'd seen every preconception and precedent smashed into dust. There was nothing artificial about Johnny Marchmont.

Kind, generous, a better man than Matthias would ever be, he approached life from one minute to the next with an open and honest heart, and a haphazard unpredictability.

It was both endearing and a complete bloody nightmare.

Usually, within a very short space of time, Matthias could anticipate his charge's reactions and movements, but Johnny's limbs seemed to act independently of his brain. He moved straight from thought to action without a moment's reflection. He would smilingly accept everything he was handed in public. Bunch of flowers? Handknitted scarf? Envelope of anthrax? Who knew? A fun lottery of potential hazards at any time, with a boss who possessed the survival instincts of a dazed moth.

And then the de facto prince had acquired a human sunbeam for an assistant, and Matthias's daily trouble quota had increased a hundredfold.

After the close call at the ball last year, he was taking no chances.

His jaw tight, he glanced at the woman sitting next to Johnny on the soft leather seat opposite. Pet was crossing and uncrossing her legs every thirty seconds, her big brown eyes sneaking surreptitious, concerned glances at Johnny. She seemed to be biologically incapable of sitting still for more than a minute.

He'd developed a very specific sixth sense where she was concerned, and he already sensed an incoming—

"The speech itself went really well," Pet said, with determined pep for a woman who'd been on duty all day and hadn't even got the fancy booze she'd been staring at so longingly. She tucked a shining strand of black hair behind her ear. "Someday soon, all this will be commonplace, and you'll be running on muscle memory at every event. I think you have natural ability in public speaking—the rest is just understandable nerves."

Sugaring the pill a little too strongly there. Johnny was becoming an entirely adequate speaker, solely because of natural warmth and empathy, but he wasn't the modern Cicero. Pet wasn't just propping him up with well-intentioned bullshit, however; she lived her life in a similar state to Johnny—and even Benji, for all his shit-stirring. Perpetual, determined optimism and a genuine belief in people.

It was a beautiful, fragile lens through which to view the world, but when a significant percentage of the population were proven dickheads, such an indiscriminate level of trust left them all intensely vulnerable.

"That's right," Benji piped up next to Matthias, when Johnny didn't look particularly cheered. "The incident with the sword could have happened to anyone. You recovered quickly." He hooked an indolent finger around his glasses and tugged them off. Cleaning them with the end of his black tie, he added, "And you didn't yeet Pet across the room this time, so you know, progress."

He glanced up, encountered pointed looks from Pet and every member of the team on the side seats, and blinked.

The tips of Johnny's ears pinkened, but his upward glance was self-deprecating. "Well, that's f-fucking tragic, isn't it, when you tumble head over arse because someone wants you to cut a sponge cake, and it's the most uneventf-f-ful outing of the month." He looked guiltily at Pet. "Is your elbow still bruised?"

At last week's state funeral in the Abbey, he'd tripped on the perfectly smooth stone floor and accidentally sent her stumbling. Fortunately, he seemed to have an internal failsafe and had once again flung her toward Matthias.

Matthias had been able to break the bulk of her fall, but not before she'd whacked her arm against a massive Gothic column.

He also shot Pet a piercing look, and she caught the tail end of it and flushed. In a self-protective gesture, she cupped her elbow. "It's fine."

Their eyes held for a second. Two. Three. He saw a flicker of something that looked definitely mutinous, and his gaze narrowed as suspicion grew.

Her teeth sank into her upper lip as she looked again at Johnny's unhappy face. That little underbite gesture always preceded—

"Maybe we could do something to salvage the day," she ventured.

—the attempted upheaval of a schedule that was locked in well ahead of time for good reason.

She turned her wrist, looking at her small gold watch. "It's only half past eight. One of my friends has started an escape room business in Kensington. There's one in a cellar where you have to solve a murder in the Jacobean royal court. Johnny can hang with the ghosts of his historical in-laws—"

"No." One of only a handful of words Matthias had spoken for hours. Silent vigilance was a key requisite in this career. Unlike

Benji, not one he'd ever found challenging, but his voice was more graveled than usual from disuse.

Pet's chin lifted. "It'd be perfectly safe. Vic knows what he's doing." Warmth hummed through the words, her expression suddenly fond. "He's very security conscious, and he's used to high-profile clientele. Nobody would even know Johnny was there."

"As we roll up to a central London celeb hotspot in the armored limo." They'd had some variation of this exchange at least twice a month since she'd joined Johnny's team. It was becoming almost a part of the routine now, but a low thrum of irritation was suddenly buzzing through his gut. "And take Johnny into a locked chamber in the cellar of an unfamiliar building, with no easy means of retreat."

"Obviously, the staff would open the door in an emergency." Pet loftily ignored his flat tone. "And I wasn't suggesting we *all* go in. I didn't really have you down as a murder mystery bloke. Even if you're happily imagining throwing me into the traffic stream right now," she muttered, just audibly. "I have no doubt you'd be keeping a close watch outside."

She crossed her legs again, smoothing the filmy-looking fabric of her dress over her knee before reaching for her phone. Her hands were ridiculously small, like the rest of her. Matthias was used to walking into a room and feeling like Gulliver arriving in Lilliput, but that feeling now magnified.

After years of training and fieldwork, he viewed and treated his body as just another tool in his arsenal to get the job done, but there'd been moments lately when he was acutely conscious of his own frame in a way he hadn't been in years. At the Marchmonts' joint staff meeting last week, Pet and Rosie had been standing directly in front of him, the petunia and the rose with their heads together, conspiring, both of them about half his size. He'd felt like a fucking monolith in danger of accidentally crushing the whole team's favorite flowers.

Pet tapped into her phone. "Plan B, then. It's been a busy week and Rosie deserves a treat, too. Murton's isn't far away, they're open until nine, and I got an email this afternoon that they've received early stock of the game Johnny has on preorder. If we swing by, I'll collect it, and pick up takeaway drinks and desserts from the Midnight Emporium a few doors down." She grinned at Johnny. "You can kick off the anniversary week of your first date with a recreation of events. Extreme sugar consumption and vicious troll annihilation. Fun for all the family."

One look at Johnny's expression and it was obvious that "Plan B" was going ahead. The prospects of gaming and baked goods were hanging in a glowing golden halo over his naïve, cheerful head. Veto this one, as well, and it'd be like walking up to Winnie-the-Pooh and yanking his prized pot of honey straight from his unsuspecting paws.

Resigned to the diversion, Matthias turned to inform Stephan, Johnny's favorite driver, while Benji spoke into his earpiece mic to update their escort on the new route. Out of the corner of his eye, he saw Pet's tiny smile.

Murton's Games was surrounded by popular restaurants, so there wasn't a chance in hell of getting a parking spot anywhere near it. Stephan dropped Pet off as close as he could get, intending to circle back.

Matthias eyed the growing food and drink order she'd jotted into her notes app, and the darkening sky outside, and grimly followed her out of the car. Johnny was in good hands with Benji and the team, and there was no way they were just chucking Pet out to wander the streets by herself at this time of night.

"It's only one tray of drinks and a couple of bags of food," she protested mildly, slipping on her coat in the cooling evening air. "I can manage."

"Getting dark," Benji returned with equal lightness, tossing Matthias his own coat. "If the rumors are true that this part of the city is haunted after twilight, his face will scare off the ghouls." Matthias gave a low, brief snort, and Pet looked at him. A small frown etched between her brows. "And I got my wallet nicked a block from here. He hasn't got much chat, but nobody's stealing your stuff with Matthias around. I won't go anywhere after dark without him now. He's the human equivalent of activating invincibility mode."

About two seconds after those sentences left his mouth, his teasing grin vanished, replaced by a gleam of genuine apology in his dark eyes, and Matthias's own amusement dropped away.

He shook his head slightly in response to Benji's obvious regret. It was meaningless, light commentary, that just happened to jab at a very roughly stitched wound.

Pet had noticed the sudden change in the mood. Her frown deepened.

Seeing an opening in the traffic stream approaching, he shut the car door, tapping the roof to give Stephan the all clear. As the car pulled away from the curb, he shrugged into his coat and inclined his head in a brief gesture. "We'd better move if it closes at nine."

In the oddly tense stillness, she continued to study him, her teeth sinking into her dark red lip, then she turned away, tucking one hand into her coat pocket. They walked in silence, Pet fidgeting with the strap of her handbag and showing an inordinate amount of interest in shop windows.

A group of women walked toward them, a couple of them doing exaggerated, tipsy double takes when they saw Matthias. One visibly flinched; the other looked quickly from him to an oblivious Pet, with a gleam of speculation and what looked like recognition.

Behind them, a businessman barreled along, moving like a human bulldozer, nudging people aside with his briefcase. His keys were in his hand and his focus on a Maserati parked farther down the street.

Pet's faked interest in the windows had now become genuine absorption in a display of balls of wool. She wasn't the only member of Team Marchmont to frequently demonstrate that total disregard for her surroundings, and it never failed to make Matthias's skin itch.

Eventually, she dragged herself away from the yarn balls and blinked a small smile at him. "Sorry, rapid onset of pretty-wool haze. I was overcome by a sudden image of myself in a new pink mohair jumper."

He'd never been good at small talk at the best of times, but as she was looking at him with a slight air of expectancy, he said stiffly, "I didn't know you knit."

Pet's usual method of occupying her restless fingers was to cut incredible silhouette portraits of whoever crossed her view or mind. For a full week after she'd first moved into St. Giles, she'd left one next to his coffee cup as she'd walked past him on her way out of the Albany wing staff lounge. She'd unfortunately captured the jut of his brow and nose perfectly, but every time he'd tried to leave them on the table, he'd found himself closing them carefully inside his work folder. He'd always appreciated true art.

When there were no scissors or paper to be had, she stroked buttons, constantly fiddling with the fastenings on her clothing, and he wouldn't be surprised if she regularly had to sew them back on. However, he'd never seen her with needles and wool.

Blithely, as if she hadn't just spent a full minute mentally assembling a nonexistent jumper, she said, "Oh, I don't."

He restricted his response to a small grunt, as they resumed walking toward the flashing signage of Murton's. Even six storefronts away and over the traffic noise, he could hear the high-pitched *pew-pew* of simulated shooting coming from the gaming shop. He wasn't a fan of video games. Once you'd experienced the reality of violence, the sound of it, the smell of it, virtual warfare and combat for entertainment lost much appeal.

It was a busy street, the flow of cars heavy and punctuated by horns and occasional shouts, but every other minute, the chaos seemed to pause to catch its breath. In a few seconds of strange quiet, Matthias could hear Pet's high heels tapping against the concrete. The sleeve of her coat brushed against his hand, and he was caught by the unexpectedly smooth nap of the fabric on the back of his fingers. He looked at her properly. The coat, old-fashioned in style like most of her clothing, was a cream-colored velvet, fastened at her throat with a pearl clasp. It was probably the most impractical piece of clothing he'd ever seen for navigating the crowds in beautiful, rainy, dirty London, but when she turned her head under the light of a streetlamp . . . just for a moment, it was like one of the misty oil paintings in the small gallery behind her had cracked open, spilling its scene out into the street. A strange, disorienting sensation.

Lightly shaking out his hand, he crossed the remaining distance to the neon-lit gaming store, keeping his pace shorter than usual to match hers.

She suddenly raised her head. "I'm aware you'd much rather have escorted Johnny straight home, but everyone will know about tonight's hiccup by now. He needs a distraction and a breather to get his mind back on an even keel, and they both need some fun tonight." Her expression took on a note of blandness. "And at least it's not an escape room, right?"

Matthias reached out and pulled the door open, standing aside to hold it for her. He looked down at her with the faintest lift of his brows. "And of course you always intended to take him to an escape room. You didn't simply introduce that suggestion first, to make 'Plan B' seem a comparatively minor schedule adjustment."

That hint of mischief returned to Pet's eyes. Framed by the cream velvet, they looked very dark in the disappearing twilight. "Matthias. How very—"

"Correct?" A reluctant smile lurked as he followed her inside.

She collected the game Johnny had ordered, handing her work credit card to the staffer behind the counter. The lanky, spotty teen was the full stereotype of an amateur gamer, down to the pungent cloud of supermarket body spray wafting around him. The kid puffed out his chest and put back his shoulders, and Matthias suspected he'd mistaken Pet's age because of her short stature.

Romeo managed to drag his infatuated gaze away from her face, but his initial disinterested glance at Matthias became an openmouthed gawp, then he adopted the body language Matthias was used to from strangers, averting his eyes and making such a point of not staring that it conversely became a lot more noticeable.

"Thank you," Pet said, taking the receipt and bag from him. Her tone was suddenly so frosty that the kid went scarlet.

As they left, the blushing teen picked up a cleaning cloth and made a beeline for the rear aisle. With a flicker of dark amusement, Matthias wondered which of them had sent him scurrying to hide.

A short distance down the road, the Midnight Emporium was located in one of the winding side lanes. The dessert and cocktail bar didn't close until nearly dawn, targeting the sweet teeth of customers wandering out of restaurants and cinemas. They were hit with a warm wash of sugar-scented air the moment they walked inside, and as Pet placed Johnny's order, Matthias looked up and around the low ceilings. It was a slightly claustrophobic space, decorated in a steampunk theme with navy blue walls and fittings. Bronze pipes and cogs spun and hissed over their heads. Very low over their heads. These buildings dated back to the sixteenth century, when the average human had apparently been the size of a mouse. There were several interesting tunnels winding away, lined with display cases of prepared desserts and drinks, but he didn't venture any farther. One minor catastrophe for the evening was enough; he'd prefer not to end the night wedged inside a steampunk burrow like a stuck cork. Wouldn't be the highlight of his career to date.

"With two bakeries in the family, I feel guilty," Pet said after she accepted the order. Matthias took the bags from her, and she tucked the tray of drinks under her arm. "Giving money to a competitor of sorts, but Notting Hill would be a bit too much of a side diversion, and it's not a good idea to visit De Vere's or Sugar Fair while I'm still on the clock. I don't know if I've ever spent less than an hour in either."

She shivered a little as they stepped back out into the lane. Typical for this year's summer, there'd been a sliver of sun earlier in the day, but the night was beginning to feel borderline wintery. He moved to her left side to block a bit of the wind, but it was the insidious sort of chill that wound down necks and up sleeves, and her legs and ankles were bare beneath the hem of her dress.

He tapped a quick message into his phone, suggesting that

Stephan collect them around the corner behind the New Pantheon Theatre, where they'd be able to shelter while they waited.

They kept close to the buildings, skirting the crowds. A scrolling billboard across the street was advertising the stage adaptation of a famous detective novel, opening soon at the New Pantheon. Rosie and Johnny had invitations to the premiere, but Benji was heading up that shift, so Matthias would have to wait for the next theater outing to hear a few snatches of dialogue and see absolutely none of it.

Pet had followed his glance. "That's one of my favorite mysteries, but it's already fully booked until November. As much as I love Rosie and Johnny, you couldn't pay me to live in their positions most of the time, but I might *consider* the princess life just for royal-box tickets." She scanned the traffic, shaking her head as they walked through a caustic-smelling fug of steam outside a restaurant. "Sometimes I get really tired of the queues, the traffic jams, the pollution, never seeing the stars. The ridiculous rent on an ugly concrete box of a flat, before I got to move into the staff housing at the palace. I think, living here all year round, it's easy to forget the parts of London I adore. The museums and the theaters. The art."

She nodded at the imposing eighteenth-century building coming up on their right. "Did you know there used to be popular assembly rooms in there?" He hadn't, but his gaze flickered over the intricate façade, switching to her face as she continued, "The ballroom was huge, the full stretch of the first floor. A few hundred years, in the ultimate scope of things it's an infinitesimal blink—it might as well have been yesterday that this road was full of carriages and lantern-lit."

The fingers of her free hand smoothed the fabric of her coat, taking a handful of her dress below the hem and rubbing the silky fabric, as if she were imagining the skirts of long-ago dancers at a forgotten ball. He'd noticed before how tactile Pet was, always choosing silks and velvet and lace for her clothing, always the first to hug a member of the team having a tough time. She reached out for people with the ease of someone who'd had a happy childhood, used to affection, confident of her welcome. At the museum earlier, she'd clearly found it difficult not to touch the exhibits, even the godawful piece of crap Johnny had squashed. At one point, she'd actually tucked her hands under her armpits to stop herself from prodding a strange squishy ball hanging on a pendulum.

Matthias enjoyed most art, but some of the curator's choices tonight had been . . . questionable, to put it mildly. And if an oversized ticking stress ball was considered a museum-quality piece, at least let people squeeze it.

They were passing the former ballroom, and a window opened, classical music spilling out into the street.

Steam from a grate swirled around Pet's feet, fluttering the hem of her dress. Her shoes were sparkling, light catching on what must be tiny crystals, and the music twining around them on the street twanged hard at Matthias's memory.

It was a Kovalenko symphony. This same piece had been recorded and remixed as a rock song a few years back, by the band who'd headlined at Rosie's birthday ball. They'd played that song right before the knife assault. He stopped walking abruptly, looking down at the beading on Pet's dress. He had a vivid recollection of the bead strands all over her gown that night, shimmering as she walked, twinkling under the lights the way her shoes were now. Her eyes had been nervous but determined, fixed on the small group around the royal couple. His whole body had come alert in that instant, every nerve alive and thrumming. It was a feeling he'd had only a few times in his life. A sense of— He didn't know how to put it into words. A prescience. Shadowy knowledge. Raw, reflexive reaction.

And the absolute, primal certainty that shit was about to hit the fan.

Less than sixty seconds later, Pet had shoved Johnny into the arms of a white-faced Rosie, and fallen to the hard floor of the ballroom, those dark brown eyes open and staring dazedly up at the chandelier overhead. Blood gushing down softly freckled skin, pooling under her short fingernails, seeping through antique lace and little amber beads. For a sickening, gut-tearing moment, he'd thought she was dead, until her hand had moved, fingers curling, chest lifting in a shuddering sigh. A tiny whimper of sound that had ripped through him.

Benji and their team had taken the assailant into custody, but the woman had been frozen and still by then, like an empty husk with her anger drained away.

He remembered kneeling at Pet's side, his heart a hard, heavy knock in his chest, a shake in his legs that hadn't been there for years. He'd applied pressure to the worst of her wounds as they all waited for the ambulance, one of his hands covering her firmly, trying to stop the flow. With his other hand, he'd held her fingers in a featherlight grasp, hoping it might offer some inadequate comfort as she drifted in a state of shock. Afraid to hurt her more.

It had been déjà vu of the worst kind, crouched in someone else's blood, their cold fingers limp in his.

Too distracted. Too slow. Too late.

"Matthias." Pet's voice was jarring, shaking him free of the icy grip of the past.

He lifted his head, frowning, realizing he was standing still in the middle of the pavement. The foot traffic was thinning out significantly, only two people walking past on his left, then his right. The symphony was still playing.

Apparently, he needed a few refreshers, himself, on staying alert on a public street.

"Are . . . you okay?" The hesitancy was clear in her voice. She'd moved nearer to him, close enough he could see that her diamond earrings were actually tiny playing cards. A fleck of gold in her right eye that looked exactly like the geographical outline of Italy. A small patch of dry skin where makeup was wearing off her nose. He seized on the small details as he'd learned through dozens of career-mandated therapy sessions, pulling in a slow breath until the buzz of sound in his ears cleared.

He had no idea what to say to her, but any necessity for speech was eliminated when a sudden scream slammed through the air. It was a sound that wouldn't have been out of place in the dispelled memories, but it snapped him back to the present like nothing else. At the fear and anger in that shriek, his mind and body were ice-clear and working in smooth cohesion.

They were near the entrance to an alley. He took one look down the narrow space and moved immediately, already scanning the street for further threats. Pet had also spun to see what was going on, and he gave her the shopping bags. She took them automatically, her eyes huge.

"Keep going, get away from the alley, find a safe space in a shop with other people, and call the police." He fired off the words calmly, but he could already feel his blood pulsing as adrenaline kicked in. She was understandably freaked, but he saw instinctive rejection slide into her expression after that curt series of instructions.

Without thinking, he reached out and cupped his hand around the back of her head, lowering his own to look straight into her eyes. Another weird jolt went through him as he did so—although there was no basis for any type of déjà vu now. Apart from the night they'd met, or the times Johnny had repeatedly shot-putted her at Matthias's head, they didn't touch. And never so intimately. Their breath mingled as he said strongly, "Secure yourself first. Do *not* follow me."

Despite her determination to fuck with his schedule, Pet was extremely good at her job. The woman could tick off tasks with an efficiency and ingenuity that should be bottled and distributed in Parliament. However, in situations like this, she'd already set a horrific precedent. He knew exactly which way her instincts were likely to go, the moment she snapped out of her shock.

And it was not toward quiet safety in a shop.

With a final pointed glare, he let her go and disappeared into the alley.

Chapter Three

Pet's breath was sawing in and out so quickly that her chest hurt. She stood there, totally bewildered by how rapidly it had all happened, clutching a video game about street monsters that suddenly seemed way too real.

Until the attack at the ball, she'd never seen real violence in person. She'd grown up with a man who'd been emotionally abusive as a parent, a pathetic, sneering, miserable excuse for a human being, but Gerald hadn't been physically violent; even on nights out in London, she'd never witnessed more than an occasional boozy shouting match and thrown drink. But Benji wasn't her only friend who'd been mugged or robbed, and obviously she'd read about random stabbings in the news—the papers seemed to report them with absolute sordid glee.

She knew exactly how it felt when a blade slashed through skin and tendons—burning heat and intense shock preceding the actual pain—yet somehow it still didn't seem real as she stood there and watched Matthias move into an alleyway to face three men with weapons.

None of them could have been much out of their teens and even the biggest looked like a scrawny beanpole next to Matthias, but one had a knife and two were holding metal bars at their sides. They'd already knocked a middle-aged man to the ground, and blood was running into his eyes as he tried and failed to get up. His wife was screaming, that terrible noise of primal fear, trying to cover his body with her own as the biggest of the thugs pulled back his leg to kick him with his heavy bootcap. The smallest had already dragged the woman's bag from her shoulder, and the third ripped a necklace straight from her neck. They were getting ready to run, when they turned and saw Matthias.

Absolutely identical *Oh shit* expressions, as they all realized they'd made very poor life choices tonight.

It was like watching a scene from a film, especially when Matthias disarmed one man within seconds, whisking away his iron pipe with the same effort she'd expend plucking an eyebrow hair with tweezers.

Pet inappropriately almost cheered aloud when another one went sailing backward with poetic ease—and somebody *did* cheer. It didn't help the surreal, cinematic feeling when she realized a small crowd was gathering behind her. Thankfully, somebody else was already talking to the police on their cell, since she was being no help at all.

Matthias had taken control of the knife now and handcuffed its owner. She had no idea where he'd gotten the handcuffs from; she supposed he carried them for professional reasons, unless he was into sexual role-play and planned to meet up with someone after his evening shift. Her teeth sank into her lip with a sharp bite.

He didn't really seem the kinky type, but sometimes reserved Type As were the ultimate bed-breakers. She'd once dated a tax accountant who'd looked like a solicitor in a detective novel. He'd turned out to be a card-carrying member of an infamous Mayfair sex club, with an interesting penchant for smacking his own balls with a kitchen spatula. Quite a surprise when he'd invited her around to cook a meal together.

Spiraling thought fragments were popping up and colliding, slamming into each other in a panic. A sharp sound of warning came from a girl filming everything on her phone—the unstoppable app generation, even at a time like this—and still in that strange daze, Pet snapped back around. She'd heard people say that dramatic trauma often played out in a type of slow-motion, but it was the opposite. More like she'd hit fast-forward; she could see what was about to happen with deadly precognition.

As Matthias crouched at the side of the injured man and spoke to the shaking woman, the smallest mugger—the one who'd been knocked down first—suddenly rose like a snake uncoiling. In one sinuous movement, he drew a wicked-looking serrated blade from his boot.

Nausea was a powerful, overwhelming bite in her throat.

Matthias started to turn, and the man darted in with that creepy cobra-like swiftness.

And Pet acted on total, utter instinct.

Which was to propel herself into the alley and launch through the air, straight onto the swearing fuckhead's back. For reasons known only to her reflexes, she did the starfish-limbs, swooping-bat thing again. It did seem to make her more aerodynamic.

Her legs coiled around the kid's skinny waist, and she squeezed— very tightly, with muscles earned the hard way, through years of stiletto-wearing. She did the same with her arms around his neck and sank her teeth into his earlobe for good measure, which was both unplanned and disgusting, but netted excellent results.

The little shit howled like a banshee and foolishly dropped the knife to swat at her.

He got in one small blow on her cheek before he was grabbed by the scruff of the neck like a misbehaving kitten. In a series of short, efficient movements, Matthias tucked her gently under one arm and chucked the mugger the full length of the alley with the other.

The crowd cheered once more, with great enthusiasm.

His chest heaving with fractured breaths, Matthias spun her back to her feet, clutching her upper arms. His eyes were fiery green chaos, spitting sparks. He very rarely lost his cool, but right now he was patently furious. "Are you hurt?"

Her cheek was slightly numb, but it had been a negligible knock. She'd once accidentally punched *herself* in the face harder than that, trying to comb a particularly bad knot out of her hair. "N-no. I'm okay," she managed, her heart pounding. She felt a bit sick and slightly light-headed.

One of his hands released her. When she looked down, it was a spike of shock to see his big fingers shaking as he curled them into a tight fist against her arm.

She was absently conscious of how loud her breaths sounded in the still air. Everything seemed to have frozen around them. Swallowing on a dry throat, she lifted her head and met his turbulent gaze. That look deep in his eyes—just for a moment, it was almost . . . tormented. Far more so than she'd have expected, after the ease with which he'd dealt with the situation. She reached out, lightly touching the lapel of his jacket with concern. His head moved in a rough jerk, and his own breath touched her nose and mouth.

His hand turned to grip her arm again—and a flare of awareness returned to his eyes. Awareness, and . . . was that a hint of confusion? Matthias abruptly released her, stepping away, and the sounds of the alley rushed back in.

Her hands trembling harder than his, Pet slipped an arm across her body, wrapping her hand against her neck in a reflexive supportive hold.

Even with the shouts and swearing and chaos around her, and the twinges of pain in her cheek, she was still drifting on the very edges of that dream state, where it all felt quite unreal.

His face set and pale, Matthias reached up and gripped his tie, jerking it free as he strode to the side of the stirring thug. She heard that hissing sound again, this time interspersed with vicious swearing as the guy regained his wits and found his wrists being bound inexorably behind his back. A lot less gently than he'd handled her, Matthias dragged him upward and passed him into the hold of several members of the public.

Apparently, their audience had decided to contribute more than cheerleading and social media footage. Quite a few people were helping to restrain the men, while an off-duty nurse knelt by the injured couple.

One elderly lady added a frankly welcome farcical note by shuffling very slowly down the alley and hitting Snake-Boy over the head with her umbrella. He had the nerve to look offended.

"That was *wild*," the teen with the phone gushed. "Did you see their faces? I totally thought he was just going to, like, *smash* them."

Noticeable disappointment in her voice that Matthias had refrained from actual smashing.

She looked at Pet curiously, pushing a handful of pinkish hair behind the multiple piercings in her ear. "And . . . I *know* you guys, don't I? You're the little flapper girl, and he's the big bodyguard. You work for the royal family."

At that, a slice of alarm broke through the weird fog, rousing all Pet's impulses of professional discretion. "No—" She barely got out one syllable. The girl's expression was increasingly eager.

"Yeah, I've seen you!" It didn't take any kind of psychic skill to predict what was coming this time. With resignation, Pet almost recited it with her. "You jumped on him in that YouTube video."

That was going to end up on her gravestone, wasn't it?

Hopefully not Matthias's, also, if it continued to be a regular occurrence.

"Wild," the teen repeated, shaking her head, and Pet supposed that summed things up well enough.

It seemed like forever before the emergency services arrived, but it had probably been less than ten minutes. Pet stood with her arms crossed and her hands tucked into her armpits, watching as the police carted away the sullen, seething thugs. She was relieved to see the injured man conscious and talking to the paramedics. He took the hand of his sobbing wife as she stumbled alongside his stretcher, holding it to his stubbled, bloodstained cheek. As the ambulance doors closed behind them, he was rather wildly demanding they tuck her under the covers with him, and a thread of softness broke through the hard chill in Pet's body.

Matthias spoke tersely to the police, and she wasn't surprised that he seemed to know a few of them. During major state events, the internal security team had to liaise frequently with the Met. Every few seconds, he looked over at her, his jaw visibly tight under his beard.

When she gave her own statement, she tried to keep it as crisp and professional as his, but things went downhill from the moment she accidentally used the sentence "threw them like bowling balls."

A policeman with steel-gray hair and uncompromising eyes swept Pet with a censorious look. "Not particularly wise to intervene when weapons are involved."

In his deep, gravelly baritone, Matthias made a noise that was neither snort nor scoff yet communicated his feelings very clearly. Apparently, he found the copper's observation something of an understatement.

"Brave, though," the man added unexpectedly, and Matthias's jawbone shifted so disapprovingly that Pet was surprised he didn't shatter a few teeth.

She appreciated that he at least waited until the officers left before he broke his smoldering silence. That simmering wrath clearly wasn't directed solely at the muggers.

When the last police car had reversed from its haphazard parking spot in the entrance to the alley, his chest expanded with a long breath, and she cleared her throat. "I think if we look at this rationally, we can agree it was a perfectly natural reaction."

His parted lips sealed closed again, and he simply looked at her.

She assumed a succinct, brutal safety lecture and several unflattering remarks were brewing, but after a good ten seconds, he'd neither blinked nor moved. She might have been addressing one of the sculptures that appeared every winter in Hyde Park.

"I know you said to leave, but he had a knife," she said, and that statement of the obvious acted like a whack from a chisel. The ice didn't so much crack as explode.

"*I know he had a fucking knife.* They all had weapons. Which is why you shouldn't have been anywhere near that alley. I told you to get to safety. You already damn near died once. Did you *want* to end up in the hospital again?"

He wasn't shouting—she'd never heard Matthias raise his voice to that extent—but the barrage of harsh-bitten words fired at her like bullets. Shivering internally, she spoke as evenly as she could. "I'd rather not, no. I'm sorry. It was instinct. Nobody could just stand there when someone's about to get hurt. He was going to hurt you."

"I'm trained for this. You're not." Another acerbic rasp, bitten out. "It was dangerously reckless. As usual."

She knew it had been reckless. Stupid, even, but by nature she was neither rash nor irresponsible. Impulsive, yes; protective, sometimes; irresponsible, no. But—in her mind, she saw it again, the knife sliding out of the scuffed leather boot. A different knife, lifting in the air, glinting under the lights. Pain. Fear. "Trained. Not invincible."

Her voice cracked slightly on those words, against her will, and he cut off his next response.

That strange expression flashed back through his eyes—something so . . . *haunted*, was the only word she could think of to describe it, that her breath caught.

The emotion was gone, covered, in a blink, but it had been there. Any further words dried in her mouth at the intensity of it.

Looking down at her, that muscle leaping in his jaw, he ran one hand roughly over his head and clasped the back of his neck. The gesture was jerky and frustrated, his biceps straining the fine wool of his suit jacket, and she finally noticed his dishevelment.

Despite her argument that he wasn't invulnerable, she'd still half expected him to have come through that experience with barely a shirt wrinkle. It was somehow grounding to see the dirt and grime on his hands and trouser legs. His shirt was torn open under his tie, revealing an expanse of bulky muscle and chest hair. And—she winced—an angry red patch where it looked like some had been ripped out.

"You *are* hurt," she said, stretching out a hand, and he stepped back so swiftly that a surge of renewed heat flooded her cheeks. Her fingers hovered uselessly for a second or two before she tucked them against the front of her coat. "Sorry."

The air was thick with strain; she was breathing it in like smog, like a million little droplets of regret.

Curtly, Matthias shook his head, glancing dismissively at the graze on his chest. "It's nothing," he said, rearranging and smoothing the fabric of his shirt to cover it.

"Well, not life-threatening, no," she found herself agreeing candidly. "But as a person who regularly gets waxed, having an awkward conversation with a man who clearly does not, I bet it hurt like a bitch."

Oh god, had she actually said that? Outside of her head and everything?

The silence stretched.

A hundred million droplets of regret.

To her eternal gratitude, he made the firm decision to ignore the past thirty seconds of their lives, simply saying after a moment, "I've alerted Benji, but they're still waiting for us at the New Pantheon."

Full awareness and brain function was returning with a vengeance, and she looked sharply down the alley. "Hell, I dropped everything."

Flung everything would be a more accurate description. The bags were upside down on the pavement, where she'd left them in her *reckless* lunge forward, and the drink containers lay in a spreading puddle of liquid.

When she bent to salvage what she could, she was relieved that the game appeared to be safe in its box, but the inside of the cake bags was an icing massacre.

Licking away a smudge of the buttercream she'd just smeared all over her thumb, her gaze lit on the storefront across the street. "Be right back."

She replaced the ruined treats with a bag stuffed full of sweets from the small express market. Fortunately, both royals were easy to please when it came to empty calories.

When they made it to the theater without further incident and rejoined the team in the limo, she expected at least a few ribbing remarks from Benji about their inability to complete even minor errands without running into a full-scale crime scene. To her slight surprise, he was solemn after checking that neither of them had been hurt in the fray—and the glance he shot at Matthias's uncompromising profile was taut and . . . worried?

It had been horrible—frightening and violent, but ultimately a far worse time for the poor couple spending the night in the hospital, and now that the shock had dissipated, she was quite sure that both Matthias and Benji had faced down much more dire situations.

When Stephan passed through the guarded gates and stopped outside the private west entrance of the palace, she slipped out of the car after Johnny, murmuring a thank-you to the staff member who'd moved forward to open the limo door.

She was walking into the plush atrium when she heard Benji speaking behind her. A very soft murmur. "Y'all right, mate?"

A slight rumble in response, a few short words from Matthias that she couldn't hear. Without stopping to think that it was none of her bloody business, she turned her head and saw the two men exchanging a look that was again . . . odd.

Benji spoke again, most of it unintelligible, but she definitely heard the word "mugging."

She saw the way Matthias's already expressionless face hardened before his body language shut down further.

And she wondered.

As she turned to leave the atrium, she heard her name, a bitten-off syllable. She looked back. Matthias speared her with another lightning-fast sweep of her face and body. There was nothing intimate or inappropriate about it. She felt as if she'd stepped in front of a sci-fi anatomy scan.

His succinct "Sure you're okay?" was equally impersonal, but that he bothered to ask at all—it was nice.

She nodded silently. When her gaze collided with Benji's, the other man was still unusually somber, but he shot her a small smile.

Pet hoped Johnny didn't get waylaid for too long on his way up to his and Rosie's suite, because his wife looked shattered when Pet took the shopping bags to their rooms. In the large, comfortable lounge, the princess was half buried in the couch cushions, discussing next week's outfits with her stylist, Elodie. However, neither tiredness nor a busy schedule would prevent her from taking up cudgels on his behalf if anyone tried to give him grief about the minor disaster at the museum.

Not wanting to interrupt the late-night meeting, Pet lifted a hand at both women and went to put the treats on the coffee table, but Elodie lowered her tablet and Rosie scooted forward to peek into the bags, smiling.

"Not that you're not welcome any time, especially if you come bearing enough sugar to give the entire palace diabetes, but why are you still on the clock?" The princess's tone was stern. She was aware that many of her staff worked odd hours and didn't like to infringe on their time any more than necessary.

As she plucked out a bag of Smarties and ripped the corner open, she glanced up and her gaze sharpened. "What happened to your face?" She dumped the sweets back down and swung her legs to the floor, leaning closer to examine Pet's cheek.

Pet was aware of continued dull throbbing over her cheekbone, but she'd surreptitiously checked in her phone camera before they'd rejoined the team in the limo, and there'd been no visible sign of injury then. She quickly touched her cheek. "Is it bruised?"

"And swelling." Rosie stood up and disappeared into the kitchen, returning with a tea towel and a bag of frozen beans. Wrapping them in the towel, she gave the makeshift cold pack to Pet with an uncompromising stare. She would never acknowledge any points of similarity with her mother, but there were times when Pet definitely saw the Duchess of Albany in her daughter's implacability.

Meekly, she accepted the beans and held them against the swelling. "Thanks." She nodded at the second bag on the table. "We picked up the new game you've had on preorder. Johnny was hoping you might want to kick off your first-date anniversary with a few snacks and games, but to be honest, I think he's going to take one look at you and order you straight to bed."

"One can only 'ope so," Elodie piped up, her Parisian accent taking on a mischievous lilt, and Pet had to suppress a smile.

"I meant because you look so tired," she said, successfully moving from innuendoes to insults. Knocking it out of the park professionally tonight. She could put the cherry on the disastrous sundae if the amateur paparazzo from the alley decided to share any of the footage she'd darted away with. The last thing any of them needed were more gossiping headlines.

Rosie's expression softened at the mention of the anniversary, but she wasn't so easily deterred. As she scanned Pet for any further injuries, she winced. "Was there an incident at the opening?"

"Yes." There was no point beating around the bush on that topic. There *would* be at least a few articles about Johnny's stage tumble. "I'll let Johnny fill you in on that, but it was understandable, and he recovered perfectly." Firmly, she added, "He wasn't the one who hit me."

Rosie had looked torn between a groan and laughter, but her expression hardened dangerously at that last assurance. "Somebody *hit* you? On purpose?"

Judging by her tone, Snake-Boy was fortunate it was no longer socially acceptable for royals to roll out a guillotine.

Elodie's fuchsia lips parted, her hand lifting to touch the frill of lace at her throat. "Oh my god. It wasn't . . ." Her voice trailed off, and both Pet and Rosie turned to look at her. A faint flush rising beneath her freckled skin, she ventured, "Not ze *grand garde du corps* . . . ?"

With a sharp jolt, Pet realized what Elodie was hedging at, and her reaction was immediate and intense, flooding into her. Shock, anger. Dismay. "It wasn't Matthias!"

At her forceful snap, Elodie's blush deepened.

"*Pardon!*" She lifted her hands in apology. "I just thought . . ."

Rosie shook her head, as much in disbelief as anything. "Elodie— *Matthias*. I know he looks . . . the way he does—" She stumbled slightly, and Pet's sudden extreme irritation grew.

Yes, Matthias was . . . tough-looking, and he'd been even more so as a stranger. If he were an actor, he'd be in strong demand for henchman roles and heavyweight boxer biopics. He might not be fluffy-haired and baby-faced like Johnny, and he wasn't traditionally handsome like Benji or Dominic. But they didn't have perfectly symmetrical features, either, and nor did she. Her nose turned up, her ears stuck out, and several of her teeth were crooked. She had stretch marks all over her breasts and hips from a fast but very short-lived growth spurt that had still failed to lift her much higher than five feet. And who cared about any of it?

A single sneering comment to a waiter could turn the best-looking man in the world into an ugly prick.

"He's the *last* man who'd ever hurt an innocent person. And he especially—" Rosie cut herself off with a scoffing sound. "Just, no. Ten thousand times no."

"I'd probably have been hurt much worse if it hadn't been for Matthias." It was Pet's turn to flush as she related a curtailed version of events, and both women's brows rose swiftly.

"He had a knife." Rosie had progressed from disbelieving to incredulous. "And you jumped on his back?" She rubbed at her nose. "I don't want to be ungrateful, when your alarming instincts around armed offenders probably saved my husband's life, but . . . what the fuck, mate?"

"Trust me, I already got an earful from the *grand garde du corps*," Pet muttered, and the princess snorted.

"Jesus Christ. Matthias has been around actual war zones, gang violence, drug cabals, international espionage—and between you and Johnny, fifty quid says he'd rank this as his most stressful position yet."

Loftily choosing to ignore that, Pet frowned, remembering that fleeting, haunted look in Matthias's eyes and Benji's strange reaction. "Has Matthias—" What? Been on the receiving end of a knife wound himself? Seen horrific violence that would give anyone flashbacks when confronted with the scene in the alley? Of course he'd witnessed the latter; Rosie had just described the breadth of his career herself.

As her mind returned to those surreal moments in the immediate aftermath, she bit her lip. Rosie cocked her head curiously, and the discomforting clutch in her stomach tightened its grip. With the other women looking at her so expectantly, she murmured, a little reluctantly, "There was this moment right afterward. He . . . The look in his eyes, it was like he was—" *Somewhere else.*

She shook her head abruptly. "It doesn't matter. I'll leave you to it." She gestured with the defrosting beans and shot Rosie a faint smile. "Thanks for the anti-swelling device."

Lifting her hand at Elodie, she walked swiftly to the door, but as she opened it and briefly turned her head, Rosie was watching her with a rather odd expression.

Chapter Four

There were many downsides of living in a four-hundred-year-old building, even when it was the bloody palace, but one of the advantages was St. Giles's natural soundproofing. Matthias didn't enjoy any kind of apartment living, but he wouldn't have shot down rent-free accommodation even if his position didn't make it mandatory for him to be on the premises, and at least he didn't hear a peep from the occupants on either side. The walls in his last flat had been tissue-paper thin, and he'd been wedged between an amateur bassoon player with very limited musical talent, and a guy who snuffled and grunted like an animal nosing through a bin during both sex and Arsenal matches. The staff wing here was quiet and peaceful—but there was one thing he imagined hadn't changed much over the centuries. Rats. No matter how many times the maintenance staff tried to get rid of the building's smallest tenants, they inevitably returned, stubbornly resisting eviction.

He barely noticed the scratching presence in the wall behind his bed, but it absolutely enraged his flatmate. Miriam had spent the past month plotting and carrying out various assassination attempts, all of which had failed. The cat had now resorted to periodically standing on his head, loudly swearing revenge on her tiny foes. At least it had perked her up in her middle age. Everyone needed a hobby, but he wished she'd sing the song of her vengeance at a more reasonable hour.

Not quite awake, he rolled over, gently dislodging her from her perch on his neck. As a bead of sweat ran through the hair on his chest in the overheated room, stinging faintly on the patch of abraded skin, he shoved the covers to his waist, and Miriam jumped off the bed. She stalked out of the room indignantly, tail waving in the air, and he slid back into the darkness, the familiar shapes and shadows fading, reshaping into a moss-stained court-yard, dusted with falling golden leaves . . .

Through the growing mist that crept along the cobblestones, sinking over ancient stone like the fogging breath of invisible spirits, Matthias could see an old clock marking time above a crumbling arch. He rarely visited Cambridge, but he could see the appeal of both the city and the campus. There was something—settling, oddly grounding about stand-ing on a spot worn rough and dusty by hundreds of years of traipsing feet and wandering souls.

At his side, Padraig McCarthy tossed the remains of his early dinner in a nearby rubbish bin and rubbed his hands together, keeping warm. He'd been oddly twitchy all afternoon, so Matthias wasn't surprised when he at last came out with it. "I'm going to propose to Jenny."

His eyes crinkling, Matthias turned his head to meet Padraig's slightly sheepish gaze. "Yeah? About time, too."

"Says the bloke who barely looks at a woman unless she's an imminent security threat."

It was getting dark quickly, and lights were turning on in the sur-rounding buildings, creating a gentle, cozy glow in the chilled air. There weren't many people around.

At the sound of light footsteps and soft murmurs, they turned and watched a pair of students stroll around the perimeter of the courtyard, holding hands. A pretty girl with her pretty boy, totally oblivious to their surroundings. Lost in each other.

"We've done a lot of scary shit, you and me," Padraig said suddenly.

Matthias remained still and watchful in silent acknowledgment.

"Never been so terrified in my life since I met her." Padraig spoke very softly. "She could do a lot better. She's . . . good. Sweet. Gentle." His jaw shifted. "But Christ and the Mother help anyone who tries to take her away."

"No," Matthias said. "She couldn't do better."

His friend raised his head, and for an instant they might have been kids again. That bone-deep hardness in his face—it was still there, but it battled and finally merged with something else. Something Matthias hadn't seen there for a long time. Peace.

As the fog swept in more sights and scents of the approaching night, he reached out his arm, and Padraig clasped his wrist. Briefly, their foreheads touched, the echoing gesture of their years with the Guard. The oath of loyalty and trust from one officer to another.

"Congratulations, dearthair."

Brother.

Padraig's grip tightened on his. In that moment, his face was grave and unfamiliar in the shifting light. With jarringly explicit certainty, he said, "It'll happen for you, too."

That was about as likely as the corporate crook they were guarding tonight having a crisis of conscience and donating the contents of his numerous bank accounts to the nearest soup kitchen. Matthias made a low sound in his throat of mingled derision and amusement, but Padraig shook his head.

Padraig, who never interested himself in anyone's personal life, even his closest friends, and whom had always been a brutal realist.

"She's out there. Trust me." His wink was a swift slice of devilry. "And Lord help her when she finds you. Your overprotective instincts are going to go through the motherfucking roof."

Matthias rolled his eyes, but despite the light devolution into nonsense and his genuine happiness for his friend, a strange feeling was swirling up like the mist. It wrapped around his legs and chest, cold tendrils like trailing fingers and a tight fist in his gut—

He couldn't put it into words. Just . . . an insistent drumbeat of dread, slowly getting faster. Louder.

His work phone beeped, shattering both physical quiet and internal turmoil, and Padraig backed up, with another quick flash of his usual grin.

"Ten quid says that's the boss. If you field that one, I can dash back and grab a bottle of water before we need to be back inside. My throat feels like a stripped cactus after that muck. You want anything?"

"No. Thanks. But—" Automatically, Matthias drew the phone from his belt. Yeah, it was their immediate boss. More unnecessary reminders about the meeting the following morning, to begin briefing their next assignment. The man had the memory of a tadpole, not uncommon with the bureaucrats.

"Be right back," Padraig said, while Matthias was still scanning the screen.

Lifting a casual hand, he jogged lightly away, cutting a left around the corner.

When the screaming started, Matthias was tapping out a quick acknowledgment, half listening to faint music and the trilling of a sleepy bird in a nearby tree. It sliced through the night, sudden, vicious, and violent, jarringly out of place in these pretty, hallowed walls of books and dreams.

His hand tightened around the phone, his head snapping up in an al-

most wolflike movement—and he ran. His boot soles slammed against the cobbles as he sprinted around the corner, retracing Padraig's casual, peaceful steps, his own heavy and urgent. His heart was beating so hard it hurt; it felt as if it were slipping, falling, tearing free of veins and ligaments to sink into the pit of dread in his stomach.

He swung around a stone wall, splashed into a puddle, and water flew up to soak his trousers. A biting smell of iron and copper. Lifting his hand, he looked down at his clothing. Not water.

Blood.

He woke with his heart pounding, the back of his neck damp with sweat, and his phone beeping with increasing persistence on the bedside table. Sitting up with a swift crunch of slightly sore abdominal muscles, he ran his hand over his face and head, exhaling in a harsh rush of air. Swallowing a few times to clear his dry throat, he shook his head as if he were physically dispelling the remnants of the dream. Already, most of it was hazy, as if it had slipped back into that Cambridge mist, but the feeling it left manifested as a physical chill, sloughing off his skin like the trailing touch of icy fingers.

As it dissipated, he became aware of the golden glow in the room, a strip of sunlight passing through the crack in the drapes to skate across the carpet. He'd pushed off the quilt in the night and grabbed it now before it slipped all the way to the floor, running the backs of his fingers over the neat stitches binding together each square of fabric. Fionnuala, Padraig's grandmother, had made it by hand for Matthias's eighteenth birthday, when he'd graduated out of the foster care system. She'd used pieces of old sports jumpers, cuttings of colors he liked, a piece printed with text from a favorite novel, interspersed with squares representing the McCarthy family. In a rare moment of insensitivity for a boy profoundly protective of his family, Padraig had snorted over the gift, scornful and embarrassed that his Mamó would give his mates *blankets*. He hadn't understood what it meant then. Fionnuala had.

She was gone now. A fiery, strong, kind woman who'd received life's last great blessing and slipped away peacefully one night in her sleep. Almost ten years ago already.

"*Mrrp*." Miriam jumped up to perch on the end of the bed, daintily licking her toes. When their eyes met, she repeated that purring, pirriping sound, which deepened when he reached to scratch behind her ears, one of the forms of affection she allowed. That sweet little coo would quickly become a pissy yowl if the soft approach failed and her breakfast didn't immediately materialize.

He'd been a woefully unprepared cat dad, having never had a pet in his foster households and no intention of adopting one as an adult, so he'd caved into every demand from the moment he'd tucked her into his jacket and brought her home. He was reaping what he'd sown, and now shared a home with the feline equivalent of Angelica Pickles.

She butted him with her patchy, misshapen head, and he felt a bit more of the tension slip from his body. His phone vibrated with another message alert, wiggling impatiently, like the department gossip itching to share usually unwelcome news. As he stretched to grab it, he felt the satisfying pop of his muscles and a renewed twinge in his ribs. One of those little fuckers had got in a single hit yesterday, and unerringly caught him right on the site of a past fracture. It played out in his mind again, that slinky shit going for his knife—and Pet gliding through the air like a flying squirrel with a death wish.

Jesus. His heart did a renewed somersault just thinking about it.

"Going to drive me up the wall," he muttered, flicking his thumb against the screen, and Miriam gave another loud "*mrrp.*" That one sounded distinctly disapproving, bordering on scolding. "If you knew her, you'd get it."

He was tired. He couldn't remember the last time he'd had a full eight hours of uninterrupted sleep, a homecooked meal, or an orgasm even by his own hand. And now he was arguing with the only direct member of his family.

Who was a cat.

Belatedly, he saw the time and his brows shot up. After eight. He wasn't on duty today, but it'd been weeks since he'd slept this late. Throwing back the covers, he swung his legs out of bed and stood up, appreciating the cool morning air on his bare skin as he read the message that had hauled him out of a private hell. His frown deepened.

It was from Ji-Hoon, Rosie's PA, unusual in itself. The other man was part of the Marchmonts' inner circle, a genuinely nice guy—although a well-intentioned bloodhound when it came to the staff. As well as possessing an encyclopedic knowledge of who was sleeping with whom in every branch of the Royal Household, he kept a notebook record of everyone's birthdays, and insisted on filling the staff lounge with balloons and cupcakes every time one rolled around, which felt like at least once a week. Only the two diabetics on the admin team were able to refuse a serving. Ji-Hoon baked and decorated them himself, in his own time. He would offer them with such a hopeful expression that it was like being confronted with a lost puppy, and either picking it up or booting it in the face.

Despite that soft-hearted interference, Matthias couldn't remember Ji-Hoon ever texting him directly, on either a professional or personal basis. The message was succinct and to the point. With sincere apologies for the short notice, Rosie was requesting a nine o'clock meeting. In the Marchmonts' personal suite. Any staff who weren't officially rostered on this morning would be compensated for the overtime.

No less odd. Joint staff meetings were scheduled well in advance, and they sure as hell didn't take place in Rosie and Johnny's private home.

He texted back a brief confirmation of receipt and attendance. Miriam's demands for her breakfast were reaching a level where she sounded less like a cat and more like the siren for the Westminster volunteer fire brigade. Before any poor bastard leapt out of bed and went running for their hose, he filled her food bowl, and went to shower and dress.

Bypassing his usual off-duty clothes, he pulled a crisp white shirt from the wardrobe, shrugging into it and fastening the buttons with one hand as he flicked through yesterday's unopened mail on the table. Mostly bills, but one card that had come through the internal system, a notification from the mail room that a delivery was waiting for pick up. He flipped it over.

Wrong mailbox. It had been intended for Suite 202, not 302. Which was apparently occupied by Petunia De Vere.

He ran his thumb over her name, and that strange feeling brushed lightly along his spine, the odd prescience of something approaching.

So far, it had led only to disaster.

In a small concession to the warm weather and the fact that he wasn't technically working this morning, he left off the jacket, rolling his sleeves up his forearms. However, despite occasional teasing comments from the inhabitant of Suite 202, it would take more than a hopeful streak of sunshine before he'd walk around his workplace without a tie. The planet would have to be on a direct collision course with the entire goddamn sun.

Before he left the flat, he lifted a pointedly yowling Miriam to the high perch he'd erected next to the TV. She was fully capable of climbing up there herself, but Rosie wasn't the only princess residing in this building.

They looked at each other and he lifted his hand, palm facing outward. Last month, Benji and a few others from the team had come around for a poker game. Ignoring Matthias's exasperated reminder that Miriam was neither a dog nor amenable, Benji had insisted he could teach her to high-five. Irritatingly, he'd proceeded to do so, in less than ten minutes. Even more annoyingly, she would only do it for him.

As expected, she simply stared at Matthias scornfully.

He departed with his ego sufficiently squashed.

Johnny and Rosie's apartments were in the western end of the palace, in the Albany wing, although far enough from her parents to preserve everyone's sanity. Running late for the first time in months, he cut down the rear staff staircase and headed to the basement kitchens. It was the quickest shortcut to the west tower, as the catering lift offered direct access to the floor beneath the Marchmonts' home.

The lower hallways were organized chaos, with a palace garden party scheduled for the afternoon. Eight hundred members of the public were attending the event on the south lawn. Voices shouted back and forth, people pushed past with massive trolleys stacked with bread and sandwich ingredients, and trays constantly clattered into place.

A caterer Matthias knew by sight nodded to him politely, looking harassed as she darted past with a small crate of cucumbers.

He diverted to a back passageway to keep out of their way and almost ran straight into a tiny elderly woman arriving for work. Under a light coat, she was wearing the uniform of the tea ladies, her gray hair neatly wound into a bun at the nape of her neck. He apologized, stepping back to let her pass, and she craned her neck up—and up—to peer at his face.

Her mouth literally dropped open. No intelligible words fell out, but she managed a sort of gasping squawk. She sounded so much like a startled hen that if she squeezed herself into one of the garden coops, the chickens would make room without question.

Matthias grimaced. He possessed a mirror—he'd been looking into it ten minutes ago, to trim his beard and brush his teeth. He was under no illusions about his appearance and most people's reactions to it. His face had been ugly as hell even before he'd joined the workforce, and being whacked with an iron bar twice throughout his career hadn't improved his profile. However, few people went so far as to actually squawk.

Faint, derisive amusement swiftly soured when the woman glanced down at her handbag and clutched it to her chest. Did she really think he was going to—what, knock her down and take her bag? All else aside, he was wearing at least six items that identified him as internal security, including the clearly marked lanyard around his neck.

"Ma'am," he began crisply, as she looked around wildly. Despite the ridiculousness of this, and the unwanted flicker of humiliation that coiled low in his gut, he didn't enjoy frightening the elderly.

The woman gave a shrill little laugh. "Excuse me, I have a meeting with—" Lifting her chin, still cuddling her bag as if it contained the bloody crown jewels, she hurried toward the nearest door with the decisive stride of a person with an urgent appointment. Scuttling inside, she closed it behind her. A strip of light appeared under the frame as she found the light switch.

And presumably realized she'd just marched, with great purpose, straight into the cupboard where the under-gardeners stored spare rakes and fertilizer.

Things had descended into enough of a farce without hurtling a pensioner into cardiac arrest, so he decided against opening the door and attempting blunt reassurance. He kept going, idly wondering how long she'd feel compelled to lurk in there.

He arrived at the long corridor in the western wing with a minute to spare. The space was almost empty—except for the woman standing outside Rosie and Johnny's front door, trying to catch her breath. With that smooth curve of hair falling forward, Pet propped her hands on her hips, puffing out her cheeks as she exhaled.

His mind and body still a bit taut from both the restless night and the encounter downstairs, he walked to join her, clearing his throat a couple of times to warn her of his presence. When he'd reached the door and she still hadn't looked up, he waited for a moment, and was about to speak when she took a sudden step back and slammed straight into him.

Her head shot up, eyes rounded, cheeks still full of air. Without opening her mouth, she emitted a high-pitched shrieking sound from her throat, like a bird warning off a predator.

He froze.

Chapter Five

"Jesus, Mary, and Joseph." Pet had never met her maternal grandmother, Aoife, but she'd read the incredibly romantic letters that had once passed between her grandfather, Sebastian De Vere, and the feisty Irish girl. Dominic had given them to her so she could know them better through the legacy of their own words, since she'd rarely had contact with Sebastian, either, before his death. She could probably recite every word of those love letters, she'd read them so often, and apparently, she'd started channeling Aoife at moments of intense stress.

Like when men the size of heavy artillery tanks managed to appear in corridors without a single solitary footstep to herald their presence.

And caught people with their cheeks blown out like a puffer fish.

"Sorry." Matthias stepped back very decisively. He was typically composed and immaculately groomed, with a perfectly ironed shirt and a neatly knotted tie. Unusually casual, though, for him. She couldn't remember the last time she'd seen him without a jacket, or with rolled-up sleeves. For an embarrassing few seconds, she found her gaze caught on his thick wrists and the silky-looking hairs on his arms. She doubted if her fingers would wrap even half-way around the heavy muscles there.

As his own big fingers moved, lightly curling and then straightening as if he'd relaxed them by force, she continued to stare at him in silence—mostly because she was attempting to force her heart out of her throat and back into its correct home in her chest.

He lifted his hand and ran it over his head in a quick, uncharacteristic gesture. They were standing right in front of a stained glass window, and as the sun shone through a pane of green and blue, it cast a tinted haze across his scalp. Over his ear, in a long patch where no hair grew, the greenish glow made the jagged scar there look deceptively purple, as if the wound were still fresh. "I didn't mean to scare you," he said, a bit stiffly. "I did warn you I was here."

She finally regained the ability to voice more than old curses. "*When* did you warn me you were there?"

"I cleared my throat while I was walking behind you."

Actually, maybe she *had* heard that, but she'd thought it was the faint echo of the western wing air-con, which was prehistoric and regularly rumbled through the walls like an angry T. rex. It seemed politer to keep that to herself.

"It's fine," she said, and in fact, she felt a little champagne sparkle of lightness and humor cut through her fatigue. "I expect jumping out of your skin is good for the circulation."

"My good deed for the day twice over, then, and it's only nine o'clock in the morning."

She looked at him questioningly, and he said crisply, "I just passed one of the tea ladies near the basement level and apparently startled her as well." His tone became the definition of sardonic. "Although she didn't so much jump as clutch her handbag closer and pretend that she was already planning to turn off through the nearest door. Unfortunately, that led to her walking into a garden-ing cupboard, but she at least committed to the error. She's prob-ably still in there now."

"You're joking." When he simply raised his brows, she stared at him, that sparkle of amusement fading into genuine ire.

Jesus Christ.

Someone had actually jumped into a fucking cupboard to get away from him?

Between that and Elodie's supposition last night—did he put up with this kind of stuff all the time?

"I hope she steps on a rake every time she turns around in there," she muttered.

She thought she saw a flash of . . . something in his eyes—perhaps surprise—but if he'd intended to reply, it was lost when she moved and the sunlight fell on her other cheek. His whole body stiffened as his gaze went straight to the bruise, which was still peeking through despite her hasty efforts with a concealer bottle.

He didn't touch her, but he was suddenly close enough that she could smell his cologne. A muscle twitched in his jaw. "You said you weren't hurt."

"I'm not. I can barely feel it today. I just bruise easily." She couldn't help glancing again at his scar, as she wondered . . . Matthias was clearly protective by nature, for all his gruffness, but the intensity of his reaction in the wake of the mugging and even now—

"Were *you* hurt in a mugging once?" The question tumbled out impulsively, gracelessly, without consideration. If she'd thought his body was already tense, it was nothing compared to his reaction now. It was like watching someone physically ice over.

He said nothing, but his breathing had quickened, ever so slightly, and her stomach clenched.

"I'm sorry," she said.

They both flinched when the study door opened, and Layla Woodward blinked at them in surprise.

"Oh, good," Johnny's assistant private secretary said, rallying quickly. "You're here. Come on in."

Pet hesitated, her eyes still fixed on Matthias, but his demeanor didn't encourage further conversation even if there'd been time. He stepped back, waiting for her to precede him inside.

She followed Layla into the room, quickly smoothing a stray wrinkle from her midi skirt, a favorite piece she'd thrifted from a store specializing in items from the '40s. She just bit back a sneaky yawn—not a good look to succumb to boredom before a meeting even began, but she'd slept poorly. Despite her assurances to everybody who'd stopped her on her way back to her suite last night, the palace grapevine having moved as quickly as ever, her dreams had been dark and twisting. She'd briefly woken herself by crying out, before slipping restlessly back into the shadows. She'd only settled when illusory arms had wrapped around her, pulling her back into a tight cuddle; she'd run her fingers over scarred, hair-dusted skin and corded muscle, and felt—safe. *Home.* It had been utterly disorienting to wake up alone in her tangled, sweat-clammy sheets, the sensations so real she'd reached out for that warm body before she'd opened her eyes.

She had no idea what this gathering was about. There hadn't even been time for a proper breakfast after she'd got Ji-Hoon's message. She'd stuffed down a stale croissant as she jogged through the back corridors to the western wing, slowing to a slightly more decorous pace whenever she crossed paths with another member of staff. At one point, she'd almost collided with Rosie's aunt, Lia, the Duchess of Clarence. The royal had beamed at her and continued on her dreamy way down the hall, with a large antique vase tucked under her arm. God knew what she was doing in the staff corridors before nine in the morning—rearranging the palace décor, apparently.

Pet sank down on a couch, inhaling deeply with pleasure. The room smelled strongly of the white tea and jasmine candles Johnny was always burning everywhere.

Rosie was curled up next to Johnny on the couch opposite. The princess's hands were resting lightly on the closed case of an iPad. Her short, functional nails were painted black, but since last night, she'd added a little red teardrop—blood drop?—to each thumbnail.

"I just ran into your aunt hauling antiques around the basement corridors," Pet said. "Should I ask, or—?"

Rosie looked preoccupied. It took a moment for her words to register, but then the princess simply nodded. "It's all right. She's just nicking stuff."

Pet was startled into a giggle. "Sorry?"

"She sells off some dusty old vase or painting a few times a month. Gives half the money to charity and squirrels the rest into a private bank account. I think she's planning to ditch Uncle Frederick when she has enough." Rosie sounded serenely unconcerned by the prospect. "She loves Venice. I imagine she'll go there."

Layla came out of the kitchen with two cups of coffee, handing one each to Pet and Matthias. Pet just about dove into hers in gratitude. As she sipped, she studied the other occupants of the room.

Besides the royals, Layla, Matthias, and herself, Ji-Hoon was sitting in a rocking chair, and Benji was lounging in an armchair. Members of the palace PR team were perched on wooden stools, with earnest, concerned expressions. This was a highly edited version of the couple's joint staff, pared down to the people they trusted most.

Rosie was up to something.

If they were about to attempt a coup d'état and wrest the throne from King James by force, Pet hoped she had time to finish her coffee first. She reckoned she'd be quite good with a bayonet, but caffeine improved her precision.

Fabric rustled behind her as Matthias took up a watchful stance near her sofa. He remained standing, ever vigilant. When she turned, she saw him exchange a glance with Benji, who subtly lifted one shoulder in a small shrug.

Rosie and Johnny swiveled their heads toward each other in unison and did their spooky telepathic communication thing, having a full conversation with their eyes in five seconds flat. It ended with Johnny inclining his chin with obvious resignation and Rosie looking determined.

Ominous.

"Well, good morning," the princess said then, her gaze skating over all of them, lingering on Matthias, and coming to rest with a great deal of focus on Pet. "Thank you very much for coming, especially those of you who aren't rostered on this morning."

As she was being stared at, Pet assumed she was nominated to reply. "That's all right," she said, with a shade of uncertainty, before she decided there was no point in hedging. "What's gone wrong?" She almost but thankfully did not add "this time."

A trace of humor lightened Rosie's serious expression. "I do like you, Pet." The words were spontaneous, like the impulsive honesty of a child, and Pet felt a bit chuffed.

That didn't last long, as Rosie opened the iPad and turned it to show her a tabloid headline.

Inwardly groaning, she leaned forward to look, expecting to see images from the mugging last night. She'd fully assumed that the pink-haired teen who'd recognized them would cave to the temptation of some easy cash. When she realized what she was looking at, however, her chest went scarlet down to the neckline of her blouse.

The *Digital Star* had published a photo from the museum opening, the scene on the dais in the aftermath of Johnny's tumble. Not unexpected in itself, but the camera lens had zoomed in on *her*. Incidentally, with her boobs pushing halfway out of her bodice after the breathless dash up the stairs. She'd mistakenly thought that dress was quite demure. The photographer had captured perfectly the moment when she'd reached out to touch Johnny's arm in simple reassurance, and he'd looked down at her with apologetic mortification in his eyes. From this angle, only the side of his cheek was visible, shielding their true expressions.

Oh, Jesus.

Not *again*.

She'd thought the tabloids were giving up on this particular brand of bullshit. Desperately hoped they had. The stories had started within a month of her employment here, just the odd bit of innuendo now and then, but humiliating even when it had just been hints.

Benji groaned before she could speak, not that she had a single inkling what to say.

So sorry the whole country thinks my job description includes shagging your husband silly, thanks to the absolute fuckwits of the gutter press?

Benji had been sitting with his right ankle propped casually on his left thigh, but he lowered his leg and sat up straight now, leaning forward. "Look, I'm sorry. I know she had genuine issues, but that woman from your birthday ball has a lot to answer for. It was that bloody photo last year that kicked all this off. Implying that *Johnny*, of all people, is fooling around with any woman close to him. I highly doubt the internet would have turned him into Don Juan all on their ownsome. No offense, sir," he added, hastily.

"None taken. And please don't call me 'sir,'" Johnny rubbed his fingers between his brows.

It was telling that in this company, his stutter had all but disappeared, but Pet was momentarily more preoccupied with the pit of her stomach sinking toward the carpet.

Helena, Johnny's former stalker, was a woman from his village who'd been obsessed with him and genuinely believed he'd betrayed her with Rosie. In her desperation for revenge, she'd managed to sneak into the ball. She hadn't really known what she was doing in that whole debacle, but Pet was fully responsible for her own part in it.

A couple of days before the knife attack, Helena had ambushed Johnny in the palace gardens and forced a kiss on him. A photograph of that assault had ended up plastered on front pages across the globe, and it was resurrected basically every time Johnny left the house. The tabloids would likely still be printing it as evidence of his serial infidelity when the couple was in their eighties. It was so ridiculous it would be almost laughable—if it weren't for the pain and annoyance it had caused on all sides. And unfortunately, scores of otherwise intelligent people believed everything they read online, especially if it fit their preferred narrative.

Nobody would have known a thing about that incident if it

weren't for that photo—which Pet had taken, snapping it so very casually when she'd stumbled across the scene in the grounds. She'd been tagging along to St. Giles with Dominic and Sylvie that day, helping them with the designs they were drawing up for the royal wedding cake. Treating the whole thing lightly, as if it were a game.

Playing with people's lives.

If she'd never taken the photo, it would never have been stolen off Sylvie's phone and sent to the papers, and Johnny and Rosie could be having the bog-standard beginning to a royal marriage.

Which would still be insane by normal people's standards, plagued by rumors and lies, but without *this* kind of bullet for the tabloid gun.

"We can't do anything about that now," Rosie said with pragmatic crispness. "That whole experience was horrendous"—for a moment, shadows carved lines into her face, and Johnny reached for her hand—"but Helena is getting the care she needs, and eventually it'll lose most of its impact, since that photo is all they'll ever have."

"They should never have had it in the first place," Pet blurted, not for the first time. "It's my fault. If I'd never taken—"

"The only people who ought to be ashamed of themselves in this situation are the staff of the *Digital Star.*" Matthias spoke abruptly, firmly. She twisted in her seat to look up at him, and his eyes connected with hers before redirecting over her head. He stared stonily at the unlit fireplace as he finished, "The reputable news media stopped printing that photo once the context was known. The gutter press knows full well they're profiting off the breakdown of somebody's mental health, and they don't give a damn. Pet acted on an impulse, with no malicious intentions."

More than a bit disconcerted by the sudden vocal support, she sat back with her fingers tucked against her stomach, toying with one of the buttons on her blouse.

"Of course it isn't Pet's fault," Rosie and Johnny agreed, again with the perfect synchronization. The goth princess and her earnest, fluffy blond husband. All those post-engagement headlines about opposites attracting, but really, they were incredibly alike in the ways that mattered. Give them another year or two of marriage, and they'd be able to hit the road with a miming double act.

"But now all *this* rubbish—" Pet gestured at the iPad. She was genuinely mortified, and beneath that, aware of simmering anger. She took her job extremely seriously, and she always adhered to a strict code of conduct. She wouldn't dream of having a sexual or emotional affair with an employer, and certainly not a married man.

Besides, anyone with an eighth of a brain ought to see that Rosie and Johnny were devoted.

It was for their sake, but also her own professional credibility, that she said with reluctance, "Quite seriously, do you want me to step down from this role? These articles—"

"Absolutely not." Rosie was obviously taken aback. One black-tipped finger came up and shot out for emphasis. "*Nobody* in this room is going to be driven out of their job by those . . ." A dire-enough term for the tabloid journos failed to emerge, and she simply shook her head. "If you ever choose to move on for your own reasons, we'll be very sorry to lose you, Pet. But I hope you'll be with us for a long time." Her eyes lasered around the room and its occupants. "We're all here, and we all stay. And we all know our own worth."

Her gaze landed and lingered last on her husband.

Johnny was gazing at her in his transparently besotted fashion, but his head dipped in very subtle assent.

Pet conquered the urge to applaud.

It really was a pity Rosie wasn't a bit higher up the line of succession. Pet would be quite happy to one day see that pugnacious chin on her postage stamps.

"However." Rosie cleared her throat, and one of the PR team shuffled from side to side on his stool. "I'll be honest here. Johnny and I are very busy at the moment. We still have several projects in the pipeline for this year."

Correct, and the last thing they needed was this sort of malicious gossip diverting attention, but—

Rosie's left eyelid was twitching. Pet's mood took a swift turn into renewed apprehension.

And suspicion.

"Yes," Pet said warily. "I totally agree that you don't need to be dealing with this"—*total bullshit*—"entirely false press speculation. How do you want to address it?"

She looked at the fidgeting row of PR professionals. Technically, this fell under their purview. It was their job to at least suppress this sort of lying crap, and if possible, stamp it out.

When Rosie nodded at them, the most senior member of the team straightened her glasses. Despite her shifty body language, her voice was calm. "When there's zero factual basis to it, it's fairly simple to subvert this type of thing." She lifted her pleasingly bushy brows at Pet. "One method being redirection. For instance, Person A is very unlikely to be involved with Person B, if their affections have already been won by Person C."

Pet absorbed that for a single second. "Noted. Unfortunately, I'm not going to be much help there. I can't produce a Person C. I'm currently not even getting casual D."

That last slipped out before she could stop herself, her hand flying to her mouth, and Benji choked on his laugh.

Even Matthias gave a short cough.

Rosie controlled the leap of amusement in her eyes. "I realize you're not dating anyone at present," she said, much more classily, and Johnny, Ji-Hoon, and Layla all nodded knowingly.

Pet barely suppressed an eye roll. Honestly, even the best fictional detectives had nothing on the palace grapevine.

"But the thing is—" Rosie was looking a shade awkward again.

Her husband came to her rescue. "While the t-tabloids are making up nonsense about you and me, social media has a very different idea. You're a ship on Twitter."

He beamed at Pet cheerfully.

She considered that comment and was extremely displeased about every possible interpretation. "I'm sorry?"

Up came Rosie's iPad screen again, and Pet leaned forward.

Under another press photograph—this time a godawful, unflattering shot of her body draped over Matthias's head like a dropped pancake—a stream of strangers had written things.

Like "*omfg, how cute, his tiny assistant and the massive bodyguard.*"

"*Hashtag toll and smoll.*"

"*They're so fucking.*"

"*It's like real-life Beauty and the Beast.*"

Despite the growing knot of apprehension in her stomach, irritation spiked over that last one. She'd better be the "beast" in that comment, which would be apt at certain moments, because otherwise, fuck right off.

Forgetting herself, she snatched the iPad from Rosie and scrolled down. *Oh god.* There were dozens and dozens of similar posts about them. Hundreds.

She objected to being reduced to a cutesy "smoll," but obviously she was a very short woman. Whereas Matthias . . . There was a photo of him flanked by five Met policemen. He looked like he could pick them up in one hand and juggle with them.

The two of them were frequently seen and photographed behind Johnny at events, and they were a startling contrast in the images. She hadn't realized how much, until now.

Apparently, that was enough for some people to assume there were beautiful, medium-sized babies in their future.

The back of her neck stirred. Matthias was looking over her shoulder, and she held the iPad to her chest. The posts were embarrassing, but it all boiled down to typical internet nonsense. However, she didn't want him reading the scattering of vile comments about his looks, especially after the morning he'd had.

There were reasons she'd seriously culled her social media use lately, one being discretion over her new workplace.

The other being that people were total twats.

She couldn't look at him.

This was the man who'd once visited her in the hospital—a complete stranger to him, then—and pressed a tiny teddy bear into her hand when she was hurting.

He was also a man who could only tolerate her company in short bursts, who barely said a direct word to her.

A man about whose personal life she knew almost nothing; even Ji-Hoon had charmed very little info out of Matthias. He must be incredibly private about his family, a fact Pet respected. She'd become good friends with many people here, but she rarely talked about her own family. Dominic would hate to be the subject of gossip, especially when most of the staff watched *Operation Cake*, his baking show, and knew who he was. He was even more protective of his wife's privacy, and when it came to their other relatives—what was there even to say?

But if Rosie and Johnny, and this entire room of watchful people, were about to suggest what she thought . . .

It was Ji-Hoon's turn to beam enthusiastically at her. His smile was so infectious that she automatically returned it, despite her screaming apprehension. "That's where Codename Charming comes in."

"Codename Charming," Matthias repeated. His tone reminded her of a stormy night, that ominous quiet right before the deep roll of thunder.

"Because of this article," Johnny clarified helpfully. "Very sarcastic references to Pet as a scheming femme fatale, worming her way into the p-palace, trying to hook a P-Prince Charming. Me," he added unnecessarily.

Super.

She scanned their hopeful expressions. "And 'Codename Charming' would involve—"

"We were hoping you might play up to the less damaging online rumors for a while," the PR lady confirmed, with totally inappropriate perkiness, "and let people think that you and Mr. Vaughn are romantically involved. Just until the other speculation dies down."

This was a very tragic turn of events.

She was going to have to quit after all.

Matthias had a mate who'd worked a security detail in New Zealand. Beautiful country, apparently. Nice people. He'd once offered to hook Matthias up if he ever fancied a short-term change of scene. Right now, he could see the attraction. Solid working conditions, spectacular scenery, and about twelve thousand miles from the palace and its present occupants.

As Johnny's naïve, hopeful gaze fixed on him, he allowed himself the brief luxury of pressing his thumb and forefinger against his eyes.

All his previous clients had been capable of pulling similarly winsome expressions, producing whatever façade would benefit them most at any given time.

In Johnny's case, it was—of course—purely genuine.

He dropped his hand to his side and his jaw flexed.

With one exception—the woman currently looking at anything *but* him—every person in the room was now watching him expectantly, waiting for his agreement to this biggest bout of absurdity yet.

The whole thing would be laughable if it weren't fucking excruciating.

He looked down at Pet's glossy black head as she continued to hug Rosie's iPad into her stomach, hiding both her face and the screen from him.

She was obviously embarrassed about the ridiculous online romanticizing. So was he. But when she'd sensed him behind her, in the instant before she'd rolled into herself like a spooked hedgehog, her fingers had instinctively moved to cover a particular tweet.

He'd already scanned the badly typed words with zero interest.

He didn't give a damn what a bunch of anonymous strangers on the internet thought about him. The prospect of spending your limited spare time trolling people you'd never meet, who'd forget about you in seconds, was so pathetic it wasn't even worthy of conversation, let alone reaction. Pet's attempt to protect his feelings was unnecessary, but it was also very . . . sweet.

Despite his extreme distaste over the turn this meeting had taken, warmth touched his chest, but it was fleeting.

He lifted his head and his gaze collided with Rosie's. He had a great deal of respect for the princess. She possessed solid street smarts for a woman who'd been born on the highest bough of the privilege tree. A protective and savvy human being.

Also a spoiled one, perhaps unavoidably given her circumstances. When she wanted an idea actioned, it usually came to fruition.

So, she was about to get a short, sharp shock.

He could still see little of Pet apart from one crimson cheek. She probably didn't know which was worse, the affair accusation or the proposed remedy.

This was their solution to the tabloids' shit-stirring? Play up to it, fake up a hot little romance; just swap out the clumsy prince consort and sub in his gargoyle bodyguard.

No harm, no foul, no feelings. Simple.

It was a suggestion from the dregs of Hollywood, a mainstay of C-grade films and PR showboating. The team had no business asking it of her, and he wasn't jumping with joy on his own behalf, either. If he wanted to send his life tumbling farther into chaos, he *could* make a public arse of himself playing the besotted and very unlikely boyfriend of this woman, but fortunately he had a decent sense of self-preservation.

"Absolutely not," he said, and what he'd intended as a calm refusal emerged as more of a growl. "We'll implement a Plan B."

As Pet had demonstrated last night, there was always a Plan B, all the way through to Z, if need be.

Johnny caved immediately. "Oh, well, quite. I suppose it is a bit of a cheek to—"

The PR spokeswoman was made of sterner stuff. She tempered her interruption with a sweet smile, and she was shrewd enough to focus her attention on Pet, whose empathetic personality was going to be a rank liability here. He'd heard about her tearing up over a toilet paper ad. Her heart would bleed all over the royals if she thought they were unhappy.

"But this would quash the other rumors very quickly, and so simply. Of course, we would never ask you to do anything you're uncomfortable with. Absolutely not." The woman sounded suitably horrified. There was a distinct air of caution hovering around all the PR team. As visions of awkward questions before the Human Resources tribunal danced in their heads. "We aren't suggesting anything drastic—"

"You don't need to throw down and shag in the middle of Trafalgar Square," Benji translated helpfully. He'd already been looking far too amused by this whole situation, and his grin was growing. They'd been friends for years, and right now Matthias had never liked him less. "Maybe rub shoulders and hook your little fingers together near the press pen. A soppy lingering gaze or two." He reached out a foot and nudged Pet's ankle with his boot tip, and Matthias's own boot twitched. "If you really need to seal the deal, just suction onto his head like cling film again. Worked well with your cute little Twitter fans last time."

Pet stopped trying to disappear into the couch and turned to look at him.

Matthias couldn't see her expression, but Benji retreated with the haste of a man who'd just been metaphorically separated from at least one testicle.

With a faint blush, the PR exec tried again. "You're frequently on duty in close vicinity, and you don't need to make any sort of manufactured scene." A minatory glance at Benji, who winked at her. "When you're with Johnny, you're by extension in the paparazzi firing line, and as we've all seen, you've managed to attract rather a lot of online attention for—"

She didn't finish that sentence and didn't need to.

For two people who were supposed to be the professional equivalent of background scenery.

He wasn't offended and doubted Pet would be. In normal circumstances, people flicking through pap shots of the royals would pay no more attention to hovering protection officers and assistants than they would to a park bench or stray tree. Who in their right mind would *want* strangers zooming in on them and making weird cooing surmises about their sex life?

Matthias inwardly swore.

In this career, it was frequently an asset if people found his size and demeanor intimidating. It was the main reason he'd got his first leg up in the industry at all, before he'd earned his stripes with his service record.

His appearance was less helpful during occasionally necessary stealth maneuvers . . . and when he clocked out for the day and still had people crossing the street to get away from him. Or diving into gardening cupboards.

If he'd thought that unexpected trickle of humiliation with the tea lady had been bad, he'd almost been cut off at the knees outside the door just now, when he'd walked up to join Pet and she'd nearly hit the ceiling. For one stopped heartbeat, and however irrational it was, he'd thought the intolerable flash in her eyes was genuine fear, not simply startlement.

His lips thinned as multiple faces continued to stare at him encouragingly, underlining the main point here—

That it was fucking unfortunate looking like the enforcer of a biker gang when it turned him into one half of a circus act: the amazing St. Giles Odd Couple.

On the couch, Pet's hands were clasped in her lap. She was very still for once, all that irrepressible energy contained, a taut rubber band waiting to snap. Sitting there with her neatly bobbed hair and long lashes, she was an old photograph come to life, a flapper girl who'd tumbled out of a sepia print into a twenty-first century shit show.

He understood why they might have attracted some passing notice, even before Johnny had sent her sailing directly into his face multiple times.

Side by side, they looked almost cartoonish.

Like a joke.

He fixed the PR rep with a renewed and very hard stare. "With all due respect," he said, with a shade of sarcasm that he felt was both warranted and restrained, "may I point out the pertinent phrase there? On duty. Where there are press cameras, there are people. Crowds. Cars. Windows. I assume you're not suggesting I continually break surveillance to bat my eyelashes at my colleagues. Curiously enough, I'm a little more concerned with snipers than . . . shippers."

Benji snorted loudly. "It's ruined your entire week having to add that term to your vocab, hasn't it?"

Well-practiced at ignoring those interjections, Matthias addressed Johnny without a pause. He'd seen the other man flinch.

"Serious threats are extremely unlikely, and while anyone in your position needs to take security precautions and exercise common sense, there's no need to let it preoccupy your mind." Evenly, he added, "Because you have a vigilant and experienced protection detail, who are focused on the task at hand when on duty."

Pet moved in his peripheral vision, her shirt shimmering under the light as she reached to return Rosie's iPad. The satiny fabric was the same crimson red as her lipstick, so glossy it looked almost liquid, and a jagged flash of his nightmare sliced into his mind.

Blood trickling into cobblestones.

And blood smeared across a parquet ballroom floor.

He inhaled slowly. Exhaled.

Ji-Hoon spoke up in his typically levelheaded, reassuring murmur. "I don't think you need to be publicly canoodling on the clock. That would be inappropriate in *any* workplace." He beamed at them. "I'd reserve that for the dates."

The dates.

"And we all know you can convey a lot with the most subtle of gestures," Layla chipped in, because apparently their whole bloody Scooby-Doo gang was in on this. "Nobody can read more into a single look or lip bite than an internet fangirl. Or boy or enby. Anyway, Ji-Hoon's right. You can still throw cold water on the Pet/Johnny speculation outside of work hours. Unfortunately, Pet's now well on the paps' radar, and they'll likely be watching even when you're not around Rosie and Johnny. It doesn't help that there's the added news element of a famous brother."

Pet had been listening in continued silence, but she looked up then. Her natural exuberance had clouded over, her mouth turned down. She was entitled to darker moods like everyone else, but her visible unhappiness made him even more exasperated with the whole thing.

"Oh, yeah, the silver fox judge on *Operation Cake*," the most junior PR advisor interrupted with a lustful purr.

"The sexy, mean one?" her manager asked with interest.

"Mmm, he can frost my buns any time."

It took Pet a good five seconds to finish being openly revolted by that, by which time Rosie had taken over again. The princess had been quietly observing Pet and himself, with a shade of something he couldn't quite read.

When she spoke, there was an undeniable bite to her voice, which wasn't surprising. She'd faced down the public and her peers with an iron spine this year, but it hadn't exactly been the ideal honeymoon period. Nobody would enjoy seeing made-up headlines about their new spouse's lack of loyalty every time they opened a news site. "I'm afraid that they're really cottoning onto this," she said to Pet. "A photographer followed you to Tesco yesterday. They ran an entire article featuring sixteen nearly identical photos of you walking home with your shopping."

A sudden spike of fury worked its way down Matthias's spine. "They've deployed somebody to stalk her at the supermarket? What, hoping she's going to rendezvous with Johnny in the biscuit aisle?"

Another glint in Rosie's eyes, but she looked at Pet with genuine apology. "I hate that you've got caught up in this bullshit, Pet, especially after all you've done for us. But I really think we need to nip it in the bud fast. If we can subtly get it out there that you're happily involved with someone else, even just in the beginning throes of infatuation, that should end the pap intrusion in your private life. You and Matthias might still get some comments on Twitter, but the newspapers want scandal. They don't give a damn about budding romances between our employees. No offense," it was her turn to add hastily.

She paused, then let out a long breath. "I'm super sorry, folks. I know how inappropriate this is to ask. But for the next few weeks while Pet's still on their radar, *could* you spend a little time together in public? You know, just hang out. Try to look . . . friendly."

On that last word, her voice slipped. She failed to fully hide a note that made Matthias's eyes sharpen, but her features were carefully blank.

She kept talking, but like her PR advisor, had enough slickness to direct most of her persuasion at Pet. "I don't think you'd have to keep it up for long. News moves quickly, and attention spans are short. Especially as we get closer to Uncle Alexander's wedding."

The heir to the throne's wedding *should* give Rosie and Johnny a big press reprieve, but Matthias cynically suspected it would be a very temporary ceasefire.

Prince Alexander had finally hung up his bachelor hat and popped the question to his longtime lover last year, an attractive, kind-eyed microbiologist. They were an intelligent couple, fit and active, in their prime. Mutually very keen on intense cardiovascular exercise. Mostly between the sheets, according to the relentless palace grapevine.

To the youth-oriented media machine, they were almost in their dotage. The papers would still go mad for months over their state wedding, but the future king and queen consort probably wouldn't even be back from their honeymoon before the paps' attention would return to the younger generation.

Until Rosie's older brother stopped fucking around, found a serious relationship, and provided some new clickbait, Rosie and Johnny would remain the prime real estate for the tabloids.

She was correct, though; without fresh gossip, Pet would be discarded as a dead end by the journalists. He made a slight sound of agreement on that score.

"Oh!" Johnny reached over to the side table for an envelope. He held it up, grinning at them. "We've even organized a date."

"Have you?" Matthias heard the dangerous note in his voice, and Rosie briefly scrunched her nose. She was carefully not looking at her husband, and Matthias suspected Johnny was jumping in a little prematurely with that part of their plan. The man in question was unfazed by his tone, however, and continued to beam around.

"We thought you might like to join us in the royal box for the theater premiere." He finally clued in to how far the atmosphere had deteriorated, and his hopeful smile faltered. "Er—maybe you don't fancy murder mysteries, but the seats are very comfortable," he assured them earnestly. "And there's plenty of champagne."

The resulting silence extended, everybody looking at somebody else.

As much as Pet had wanted to see that play, it hadn't been under these circumstances. Her hands curled in her lap, and she turned slowly to look at him.

Their eyes met. He saw mortification there, a clear apology as she took on the blame for others' misdeeds again . . . and the smallest hint of something that might be stirring entreaty.

Similar grim resignation was creeping into Matthias's blood.

When it came down to it, he wasn't just concerned with Johnny's bodily safety. He did care about his boss's mental well-being. Ditto for his wife.

And there'd be serious consequences for Pet if these rumors became widespread and stuck.

Every royal couple put up with affair speculation for the full stretch of their marriage, whether there was a speck of evidence or not. It had probably been the same since the Middle Ages, just gossiping courts and marketplaces then, instead of nasty comments on Twitter. It was something the Marchmonts would have to accept and ignore, and he'd thought Rosie had been relatively sanguine about that fact. Johnny's unlikely reputation had to be galling, but there was only so much material damage it could do to *them* with no substance behind it and no further "evidence" forthcoming.

But Pet— If people really started to believe she was the secret mistress of a royal, a goddamned *newlywed* royal, for Christ's sake, it would dog her steps forever. It was potential career detonation. Especially for a woman. This was one arena in which double standards had dug deep trenches.

If all this had already progressed to creeps following her in the street, it bloody well did need to be nipped in the bud. Now.

Finally, Pet spoke, in a pinnacle of understatement.

"Oh, damn," she said, faintly.

Chapter Six

As usual, the rain began half an hour before the palace gates opened
for the garden party. Pet always wondered if there was a supersti-
tion attached to the tradition. Perhaps the Duke of Clarence had
once insulted a modern-day witch, or she'd picked up a terrible
case of food poisoning from a cream scone and ensorcelled all future gatherings into sodden misery. It had absolutely poured at the
last one, turning the south lawn into a muddy slip-and-slide. More
than one person had splatted into the grass in their best clothes
and had to meet the king with mud dripping off their ears and
lashes. In the aftermath, Pet and Ji-Hoon had found someone's fas-
cinator floating in a fountain, an unknown story that had likely
begun with too many glasses of complimentary champagne.

So far, it was only a drizzle, but the St. Giles events team had
passed out colorful plastic parasols to every arrival. It was quite
pretty, really, especially when she peeked out an upstairs window
before joining the others—a series of pink, lilac, yellow, and mint
circles, clustered together like pastel honeycomb. Or long, winding
caterpillars from a children's story.

Her mind was desperately taking refuge in absurdity.

She stood in the reception room by the glass doors leading out into the south portico, waiting as Rosie and Johnny prepared to move amongst the crowds. All the royals were rostered on for periodic garden party mingling, but the higher somebody sat on the line of succession, the more meet-and-greets they had to attend. The other Albanys were away, but she'd seen Prince Alexander and the Clarences heading outside earlier. The king had cried off this one, and fair enough at his age. If Pet lived to be eighty, her grand plans involved books, art, pets, enough yoga to ensure that nothing snapped off during sex, and otherwise doing fuck all in her theoretical garden.

Elodie straightened Rosie's dress, a simple white shift overlaid with antique lace. The princess wore a dainty anklet above her left sandal. From a distance, it looked like a daisy chain; up close, it was a series of interlocked skulls-and-crossbones and had cost two pounds. Johnny had won it for her in an arcade game during their engagement, and she'd also worn it under her couture wedding dress.

Johnny unsuccessfully attempted to flatten his blond curls, which were looking particularly floofy in the humidity. Rosie still looked a bit tired, but the body language of both was relatively relaxed. They enjoyed joint engagements when they could spend time together, and the garden parties played to Johnny's strengths. This was absolutely where he came into his own, connecting with people in person. As individuals, the real human beings rather than the figureheads, the couple were strangers to most of the country; face-to-face, people could form their own impressions. And most people who met Johnny liked him, when they weren't being guided by the tabloid narratives that had somehow flung Pet into a real-life pantomime.

She sensed Matthias before she saw him. He came into the room with Benji, and they stopped next to her. She shifted, rubbing the insides of her knees together in an old nervous gesture. Those occasional threads of shyness had suddenly become ropes of platinum, binding her limbs and stitching her lips shut.

Benji reached up and playfully tweaked a leaf on the towering ficus above her head. "You look like you've taken root," he murmured, in highly amused tones. "Most of the paps out there have a distinct lack of both brains and morals. I don't think it'll take a RADA-level theatrical performance to redirect the malicious chatter. However, I suspect you *may* have to move, petal." He lifted his arms and wiggled his fingers. "Unless you want to kick things off with a page out of your usual playbook, in which case climb aboard and I'll heave you at Matthias's head."

The sheer normality of the teasing started to loosen the knot in Pet's chest, but at a signal from a staffer by the doors, Benji touched his earpiece and activated his mic with a low crisp murmur, all traces of levity disappearing.

The security team moved into formation and the royals headed out, and she felt Matthias tense at her side. He wasn't rostered on this afternoon, but Rosie had wheedled him into attending the party for a short time anyway, so he could put on a little tabloid show with Pet without endangering anyone. She was only on duty for a very short time herself, just to see Johnny settled into the event and bat her eyes at his bodyguard.

"Maybe if you just—you know, move around the lawn with the serial killer face," Johnny had suggested brightly, when they'd set up the plan.

"The serial killer face," Matthias had repeated flatly.

If Pet hadn't been roped into many games of charades and "Who Am I?" with their boss during long car trips, she might have been surprised by the alacrity and skill with which Johnny had immediately blanked his face of all expression, his eyes becoming hard and opaque. He was a sad loss to his local amateur dramatic society. Without changing his appearance at all, he'd been almost unrecognizable—and yes, the look could be described as serial killer. Or dead fish.

She'd had to hastily scratch an itch between her brows; when Matthias had slid her a look of his own, the rising giggle became even harder to swallow.

"And then when a t-tabloid journo is watching Pet, you can stand near her, and look at one another. Pet, if you touch the t-tip of your t-tongue to your upper lip, it's a sign of sexual attraction, and smile just s-slightly, like you're holding a silent, secret conversation—" Johnny's increasing enthusiasm had broken off as he looked around. "What?"

"No, no, you carry on, babe." Rosie had spoken first. "We're just taking a moment to appreciate the heights you could have climbed, directing period dramas."

At that point, the inherent awkwardness and embarrassment had faded into pure humor—and Pet realized she could still be amused by it now, if it weren't for the silent man at her side.

And by "her side," she meant at a solid three-foot distance and staring straight ahead like a man on his way to the gallows. She could spontaneously sprout an extra four limbs and waddle along the parquet flooring like a human octopus, and Matthias would probably still find her exactly as appealing a companion as he did now.

Stoic, clipped-voiced, occasionally grunty Matthias, her shiny new fake boyfriend for a bit.

Quite honestly, with most of her mates and a few genial acquaintances, she might have gotten a kick out of this in the past, partaking in an honest-to-goodness fauxmance. She'd been glued to a fake-dating storyline in a brilliantly terrible soap last year, but obviously she'd never expected to be part of one. She didn't have the slightest desire for any kind of fame and this situation with Johnny had reinforced that with a vengeance, and unfortunately, no eccentric relatives had recently penned a legally questionable will, requiring her, with odd specificity, to be married by twenty-eight in order to claim her millions.

So, well—it was an experience, wasn't it? A one-off. With anyone else, it would have been a silly laugh, and they could have salvaged some basic entertainment from it.

But with Matthias, who barely seemed to tolerate her company some days . . .

And she felt awful he'd been dragged into this. She bore some responsibility here, but he'd literally done nothing but save her a few concussions.

"Matthias." She touched his arm as he moved to follow the team outside. They were alone, the room having vacated in a swelling rush after the royals' exit.

Had he just flinched from a featherlight elbow tap? Jesus, this was going to go well, wasn't it? If they managed to convince even the most half-witted pap that they were in the midst of a heart-fluttering, wall-banging affair, she'd submit their BAFTA nominations herself.

He turned, his face a mask of professional indifference as he waited politely for her to speak.

Despite the unwanted gravity of her mood, it was so exactly like Johnny's impression of him that she smiled. Letting her own expression ice over, she leveled the look back at him—and he snorted softly.

"If I needed confirmation that the editor of the *Digital Star* is a brainless twat," he said unexpectedly, "suggesting you and Johnny are romantically involved would do it. I've never seen such an obvious sibling dynamic."

It was a new thought, but—not inaccurate. She did think of Johnny as almost a brother. The sweet, clumsy little brother she'd never had, to balance the stern, workaholic older brother she did have. "If it were possible, I'd swap out my sister for Johnny any day," she murmured, and Matthias's brows lifted a little.

As she doubted he actually wanted any further information about her older sister, and she preferred to allow Lorraine minimal space in her brain anyway, she steered them back on course. "I'm really sorry," she said bluntly, "that you got dragged into all of this."

She couldn't stop fiddling with a button on her silk dress. "Prevent someone from crashing headlong into the floor a few times and be turned into an internet meme for your trouble. I know how seriously you take your job—and how little you must want this attention. Let alone being forced into intimate situations with someone you—I mean, not *intimate* intimate, but—"

Please, merciful god of all Socially Awkwards, kill her now.

Thank God—*thank God*—Matthias intervened before she buried herself any further. "Pet." God, his voice was deep. "This isn't your fault. Stop shouldering responsibility that isn't yours to own." Her hand stilled against her middle. "It's not an ideal situation, but the potential consequences are too serious if we let those rumors run amok."

Despite the calm words, he gave away his underlying disquiet in the smallest of staccato movements, the flex of a shoulder, the fractional narrowing of his eyes. There was a short silence. "It's a security assignment," he said. His mouth twisted, just a pinch of

movement at the very corner. "An extremely out-of-the-box one."
Or under the table, she thought, with the amount of subterfuge
involved. "But an assignment. Objective stated, method determined, timeline in place. We're on the same page, with a common
goal. We'll manage," he finished succinctly.

As speeches went, it wasn't exactly Captain Wentworth declaring his undying devotion, but on considering the matter, Pet was
slightly alarmed by the flutter of response in her middle. Who
knew she'd find somebody speaking like a futuristic police-bot a
bit . . . sexy?

He frowned at her. Communication was key in any situation,
and probably very important in maintaining a healthy relationship
with your fake lover, but she decided against sharing her thoughts.

She nodded solemnly instead, and twiddled her button again. It
fell off, and Matthias bent to pick it up. She had no pockets in her
dress, a major failing on behalf of the designer, so he slipped it into
his own pocket to look after it for her.

An attendant approached to offer umbrellas when they stepped
outside, and Pet gratefully accepted a pink one. The light drizzle
was already dampening her hair; she could see the black strands
out of the corner of her eye, gleefully expanding into frizz. Without
her straightener to keep things under control, things got very verti-
cal, very fast. She gave it four minutes before her head looked like
a startled sea anemone.

There were twenty stone steps down from the patio to the
lawn, and Matthias glanced at her high heels and silently offered
his arm. Tentatively, she took it, feeling absurdly like she *was* in
a Johnny-directed period drama. With his instructions in mind,
she held her breath, lifted her head to meet Matthias's unreadable
gaze, and touched the tip of her tongue to her top lip.

Somebody immediately took a photo of them.

Her choreographed "slight smile" was perfectly genuine as a dash of amusement returned, and Matthias's gaze brushed over her mouth. His eyes caught and held hers. She swallowed, and her fingers tightened on his arm, neither action premeditated.

He looked away as they moved, restricting the length of his steps to match hers as they headed down to the lawn.

Pet released an oddly uncomfortable, pinched sort of breath.

She'd had low expectations of Matthias's acting ability in this assignment, but that had been almost Shakespearean. Another camera flashed when she snuck him a glance.

Through a parting in the crowds of chattering, excited guests, Benji winked at her in passing. A few people were looking at her speculatively, presumably having read the papers today, but she maintained a bland, friendly smile.

Rosie and Johnny were moving down an assembly line of VIP guests, mostly young children connected to their foundations, and it was a relief to see everything going smoothly so far. Johnny bent to solemnly admire a small boy's doll, shaking hands with both child and toy.

A little girl farther down the line wriggled with excitement, clutching her dad's hand tightly as she waited for their turn. She was beaming, stretching out her arms for a hug, but clearly overwhelmed. Pet wasn't surprised when she dissolved into tears. Her dad murmured quietly to her, trying to comfort her, and a horrified Johnny started clucking like a grandmotherly hen. He attempted to cheer her up by doing a makeshift puppet show with his handkerchief, which successfully confused her enough that some of her sobs did falter.

Before Pet could move to help, Matthias was slipping quietly past her. He knelt at the child's side, and she blinked up at him, gulping down her tears, visibly fascinated. Without a word, he produced a sealed packet of tissues and a wrapped sweet from his pocket, like a boy scout magician, or a very overgrown Pippi Longstocking. The wee girl took the tissues and sweet, smiling bashfully, and the rest of the meet-and-greet continued without incident.

"Handy bloke to have around in a crisis," Layla murmured at Pet's side. She was holding a leather document file and a sky-blue parasol and had swapped out her usual tailored corporate wear for a pretty floral dress. The crisp white linen made her dark brown skin glow, although she was probably regretting the color choice in this weather. Thankfully, the drizzle did seem to be lightening, so they might avoid the lawn transforming into a bog this week. "Everything going smoothly otherwise?" She sighed. "The weather excepted."

"So far." Pet dragged her eyes away from the reception line. Keeping her hand at midlevel where nobody else would see, she held up crossed fingers. At a smarmy chuckle beyond Layla's shoulder, she said in a low voice, "I see Frederick's in his usual form."

Rosie's uncle, Prince Frederick, was officially styled as the Duke of Clarence, but most of the staff privately attached a shorter and more explicit arrangement of letters to that "C." The king's third son lived up to every condescending stereotype of both spoiled youngest children and entitled toffs. If life were fair, and souls and bodies perfectly aligned, he'd have been born a wasp, not a human being with a guaranteed lifelong income.

"They've lost another two staffers this month," Layla said, lifting a brow. "The only long-termers are there because they're loyal to Lia. They'll definitely go with her when she leaves."

Like Rosie, Layla was blandly unconcerned by the prospect, and spoke similarly as if it were a foregone conclusion.

"You really think she'll go?"

"Would *you* want to shag the duke into your dotage?"

Fair point.

"I'm surprised she's stayed this long," Layla said. "If she's set on raiding antiques from the family members she dislikes, just stage a heist and take the lot in one night, then scarper. I guarantee it would be years before any of them noticed." Her head tilted consideringly. "Maybe she's planning to do him in." She brightened at that cheering prospect. "She's the type to use poison and stand a good shot of getting away with it."

"Murder mystery fan, by any chance?" Pet inquired, and Layla grinned.

"Just a macabre optimist. But speaking of fictional murders, here are your passes for the New Pantheon royal box. I am awash with jealousy and may or may not take a leaf out of the duchess's theoretical book and slip cyanide in your tea."

Pet took the passes and tapped them lightly against her palm, her extremely mixed emotions clearly showing on her face.

"I know it's going to be a bit of a strain," Layla said sympathetically, "having to make small talk for hours with Matthias. Hell, it's like finding the Holy Grail just getting twenty consecutive words out of the man, but at least you get free tickets. The press previews were very positive. And there's endless booze in the posh seats."

"I suspect that where painful small talk is concerned, you're offering sympathy to the wrong half of the equation." There was still legit discomfort lurking beneath Pet's forced lightness. "Matthias is probably submitting an application for hazard and irritation pay as we speak."

"Actually, his attention right now is all on you." Layla directed a quick smile over Pet's head, just as she felt a tingle of awareness on the back of her neck, a quick warning that the topic of conversation was now within earshot. "There's also a photographer working his way over here, so I'll leave you to your next round of Play the Players. Or should that be Play the Paps?"

Pet swung around, intending to look at Matthias's face. That odd self-consciousness was twanging at her again and her gaze made it as far as his hand, tracing over short nails and a blunt, callused thumb, which twitched under her rude stare. His skin was evenly tanned, no sign of a one-time wedding ring. She didn't need to wonder or ask if he was currently in a relationship. He'd never have agreed to this if he'd made real commitments elsewhere.

He could make her toes scrunch up with frustration, but she'd never for a moment doubted his integrity.

More than one pair of eyes was on them, including the journo, whom Pet had been trying to ignore. Hard to believe some people actually *wanted* this sort of attention, actively courted it.

Matthias's abdomen moved with his breath, then he interrupted her intent study of his hand by extending it toward her. It was an efficient movement, performed with all the underlying enthusiasm of someone pulling out a fingernail with pliers and hovering their bleeding hand over a shark tank.

She looked down at his fingers a beat too long. As they began to curl, she hastily slipped hers in to join them. The slide of their bare skin was baldly explicit. It felt far more intimate than the light, practical clasp of his arm. They were only holding hands, but for some reason she felt incredibly exposed, as if the watching eyes and cameras had reached out and stripped away a layer of her clothing.

His grip tightened on her—and she audibly squeaked when he tugged her closer, simultaneously turning his body and taking the parasol from her, lowering it behind their heads so their faces were completely blocked from any nosy view. They might be doing anything back here—kissing, discussing global events, seeing who could touch their nose with the tip of their tongue.

"Excellent panache," she whispered after the initial surprise, grinning up at him. "Gene Kelly *wishes* he'd been that suave with his brolly. I feel like I'm in a 1940s film."

She thought his mouth tipped up very slightly. "You're dressed for it, too."

She touched the nipped-in bodice of her shirtwaist dress, running her hand over the fabric. "I sometimes think I was born in the wrong era. Although—I covet the fashions, I idealize the romance, but for multiple reasons, I wouldn't really want to go back into the past. I would not function well in a world without modern medicine, to start with. If one of Sylvie's potions at the bakery has unexpected consequences and I'm suddenly booted into medieval times, I'd last about ninety minutes. The moment it sank in that I couldn't even buy a packet of ibuprofen, I'd march straight to the docks and sign up for a short-lived career as a human cannonball."

"Going out with a bang?"

"Always."

"You've had a bit of practice since you started working for Johnny." There was a definite suggestion of a smile in his eyes now.

"If the words 'green,' 'eighty,' or 'conference' are about to leave your mouth, I strongly suggest you reconsider." In the strange bubble of umbrella-intimacy, sheltered against his body, they were talking almost with the ease of longtime friends—a fact they seemed to realize simultaneously, since something changed in his face.

He lowered the parasol, his shoulders straightening.

"Well, well. It's social media's favorite new couple," an abrasive voice said. "The Beast and the Side Piece."

Pet's fingers tightened on Matthias's as the muscular man with a goatee and a pugnacious mouth abandoned all subtlety and just took a photo right in their faces.

"Or should I say 'convenient' new couple?" the guy added, with an unpleasant smile.

She recognized him by sight, although she'd never bothered to look up his official byline. The PR corps referred to him as the Bulldog. He worked for the *Digital Star*, so he wasn't part of the official royal press rota. Usually, he was only able to shout vile provocation at Rosie and Johnny from public areas.

This kind of thing was his standard modus operandi and Pet always counseled Johnny to ignore whatever the gutter press threw at them—a reaction was exactly what they wanted, the more violent the better—but at the reemergence of the "beast" comment, her hackles went straight up.

She opened her mouth, and Matthias pressed the pad of his thumb warningly to her wrist.

Very calmly, he said, "You're at least twenty meters out of bounds. I strongly suggest you return to the gutter line of your own accord." At the dispassionate reference to the tabloid boundaries on palace grounds, the other man's taunting smile faded. Matthias's own lips moved in a taut curve. Pet didn't like to be dramatic, but if she were in the pap's shoes and on the receiving end of that "smile," she'd probably wet herself. "If you don't keep your eyes and your filthy insinuations away from her, I'll happily remove you myself. You won't enjoy the helping hand."

"Keep up the threats," the Bulldog encouraged. "It all makes for good copy."

He couldn't hide a note of uneasiness, however, and as Matthias secured his grip on Pet's hand and they turned away, she saw him scowl and retreat.

"Dickhead," she said darkly.

"Ignore them." Matthias moved his thumb again, returning it to its original position. "I know it's difficult, having that shit directed at you, but it seems to be an occupational requirement in his field, being a total prick."

"He can call me what he likes," she muttered, cupping her wrist with her free hand as if she could apply pressure and stop the light tingling sensation there. "It was the other thing."

It was a breath or two before he looked down at her, a little sharply, but Rosie had just left another group of children and was coming over. She lifted her brows when she noticed their entwined hands, but didn't comment except to ask, "Taking off?"

"We've positioned ourselves in proximity for the circling vultures," Matthias said coolly, "and Pet worked through her break earlier, so yes, we're leaving now."

"Good," Rosie said. Her voice was very mild. She cocked her head at him. "Have I fallen irredeemably out of favor?"

"Probably not irredeemably." He'd resumed his poker face. "Call it temporarily. Check in again next week and we'll see if the situation has devolved any further."

"My, my. That was almost a joke, and Pet's looking a bit militant. You're rubbing off on each other already."

Despite her arch amusement, the lines of fatigue were deepening around Rosie's eyes and mouth. She was usually a human dynamite stick, full of repressed energy. She'd been so happy right after the wedding, and she'd literally danced with sporadic bursts of joy since her chronically disapproving private secretary had retired, announcing that he was too old to deal with the fallout when Johnny inevitably burned down the palace.

Right now, her whole vibe was off. Those visceral signs of returning stress were a stark reminder why they were doing this. Pet's strengthened resolve was underlined when she walked with Matthias back toward the stone portico and hesitated, looking at the locked iron gate to their right.

Beyond the gate was a trail, which wound through the gardens in the far west corner of the palace grounds, one of the few parts of the property that were solely the family's private domain. An oasis of calm in the middle of central London, it was patrolled by guards, and accessible to the staff and public only by invitation. As a thank-you for her actions at the ball, Rosie had given Pet her own key card for the garden gates and automatic security clearance whenever she wanted to go there.

It was the scene of one of Pet's biggest regrets, where she'd snapped the photograph of Johnny and Helena, but ultimately, those gardens had brought her luck as well. She'd entered a collision course with fate there, setting in motion the series of events that had finally reconnected her with her brother. And led to her new career path, and . . . all of this.

She rarely returned there, not wanting to infringe on the family's space, but it was a shortcut back to the staff wing, and that serene peace away from gossiping mouths and insulting paparazzi suddenly seemed very attractive.

Making a swift decision, she reached for the key cards clipped to the lanyard around her neck—and realized that the gate key was currently on her sideboard. She'd taken off the nonessential passes last week and forgotten to reattach them.

"Damn," she murmured.

Matthias released her hand and took out a key card of his own. He was senior security; of course he'd have access to almost everywhere on the property.

As she played with her fingers, rubbing her thumb over her palm, he unlocked the gate, holding it open for her to pass through. Closing it firmly behind them, he returned the key to his pocket and withdrew a small piece of paper. "Almost forgot," he said, holding it out. "This is yours. Mix-up in the mail slots."

Frowning, she scanned it as she walked. It was a notification of a large package delivery, to be collected as soon as possible from the mail room. She wasn't expecting anything, unless she'd been doing middle-of-the-night stress shopping again. When she'd been trying to get up the nerve to contact her brother for the first time in years, she'd bought two pairs of shoes at three in the morning—and for some reason, several items of dollhouse furniture. They were beautifully made and very sweet, but she'd never owned a dollhouse in her life and had no idea why her night-self had purchased tiny armchairs and bookcases.

"Thanks," she said. "I'll stop by the mail room."

With the scents of roses, hyacinth, and damp grass thick in the air, they crossed over a small wooden bridge, and Pet peeped over the side, looking down into the beautiful clear water. Still no fish. Disappointing.

To their right, behind gently waving flowers, was the stone structure where the infamous kiss had occurred.

"I do hope you're not still blaming yourself for that tabloid debacle," a new voice said lazily, out of absolutely bloody nowhere, and she almost tumbled off the bridge. If she ended up at the bottom of the royals' fishless pond all by herself, she could never think another judgmental word about Johnny and his incurable left feet.

Swearing, Matthias grabbed her waist, his hands almost spanning her entire rib cage. "Jesus, but—" He cut himself off with a curse. "I've been blaming Johnny for constantly hurling you across rooms like a tiny missile. Don't join in giving me a fucking coronary."

She steadied herself against the railing and looked back at him ruefully. "If you ever feel like a career change, let me know. I think we could pitch ourselves to the Whitechapel Circus as an acrobatic act. We've covered most of the basic skills. If I add some sequins and a few twirls, we're golden."

His gaze redirected over her shoulder toward the owner of the voice.

Underneath a towering oak, the Duchess of Clarence was sitting on a white curlicued bench. There was a felted board beside her with jigsaw pieces on it. Feeling just a little like Alice wandering into the Mad Hatter's tea party, Pet bobbed a curtsy, and Lia blinked at her over the rim of the biggest cocktail glass she'd ever seen.

"You aren't going to collapse, are you?" the duchess queried, sipping her drink. She was supposed to be at the garden party with her husband. Instead, she was just out here in the private garden, knocking back a margarita the size of Birmingham—complete with novelty umbrella—and casually doing a jigsaw. "Because I would wade in to save you, but I'd rather not. This dress is pure silk, so I'd have to remove it, and my husband was cross for months the last time I was photographed swimming in the nude. It was extremely boring."

"I was curtsying."

"Oh, were you?" Lia asked with interest, as if she didn't have people bobbing and dipping in front of her 24/7. She studied her jigsaw and set another piece in place. "I'd prefer you didn't."

Examining her drink approvingly, she swallowed some more of it.

And that was definitely an X-rated puzzle. Even from this distance, Pet could see a cock.

"I think I was actually starting the process of forgiving myself," she said, with equal frankness.

"Good. Martyrdom is such a tedious quality," the duchess murmured. "Especially with everything you're doing for my niece and nephew-in-law now."

Pet exchanged a guarded glance with Matthias. "You mean . . . as Johnny's assistant? I enjoy working for him, and I'm well compensated."

"I should hope so." Lia crossed her legs and set her glass down at her side, with no apparent concern about the uneven surface of the bench and her pure silk dress. Pet tried not to find that extremely stressful. "No, I mean pretending to partake in a passionate affair with the absolutely enormous bodyguard in order to squash the pervasive gossip about your pretty self and my nephew-in-law." She made a thoughtful noise. "Very unique face."

It wasn't entirely clear whose unique face was under discussion, Pet's, Johnny's, or Matthias's, and she didn't elaborate.

Matthias cleared his throat.

The duchess lifted her head and smiled at him. "Oh, there you are."

Apparently, she'd previously missed the absolutely enormous bodyguard standing protectively over Pet, directly in her line of sight.

She flicked another puzzle piece into place, completing a transversus abdominis muscle. "Perhaps you're disciples of Millicent Mugsworth?"

Pet was now well enough acquainted with this woman that very little should surprise her, including the duchess being fully versed on a confidential plan that had only been in place for a few hours. Yet she still found herself stumbling for speech. She managed one word, a faint "Who?"

"Spiritual philosopher." The duchess thankfully picked up her drink again before it spilled. "A great believer in manifestation through visualization." She hummed. "Turning desire into reality." Lia finished her cocktail. "Well, when life opens a door, darlings . . ." Her voice trailed off as she frowned into the middle distance. She was silent just long enough that Pet assumed she'd lost interest in the conversation, then announced with satisfaction, "Henry Biggles!"

Not for the first time lately, it did occur to Pet that she might have accidentally crossed into some sort of parallel existence.

Where duchesses made weird and unsettling comments and did dick jigsaws.

"Who?" she said again, helplessly, because it seemed she was part owl in this alternate world.

"It's Henry Biggles who's the spiritual philosopher. Millicent Mugsworth is my hairdresser." Lia eyed her empty glass and stood up. "I need another drink."

Holding the glass stem between two fingers, she walked off without another word, simply pressing two fingers to her mouth and blowing them a kiss over her shoulder.

Pet stared after her, then walked off the bridge to look at the jigsaw, just in case her current sexual dry spell was making her see erotic imagery in commonplace—

Nope. Bunch of cocks.

Matthias joined her, leaning forward to complete another puzzle piece. She'd actually been all right *not* seeing the illustrated bollocks in full. "Maybe it's a subtle allusion," he murmured, "as to what she really thinks of her husband and his family."

He straightened, and she caught another hint of his cologne or beard oil as he brushed against her. Whatever the scent was, it was profoundly delicious, and it was provoking an extremely unsettling urge to lick it.

She was mentally composing a very strongly worded email to the manufacturer.

"Being inside the duchess's mind must be similar to taking a trip on Willy Wonka's hallucinogenic boat," he said, blissfully unaware of the state of her brain, "but she's a handy person to have around if you need a mental distraction. It's like a conversational A-bomb, just an explosion of random words firing off in all directions."

"Should we be concerned that she apparently knows all about Codename Charming?" Unenthusiastically, Pet tried out the team's cutesy moniker from the newspaper slander.

According to the PR exec, stealing a quote from the writer's bullshit was a subtle takeback of power. Which was one perspective. Another perspective was that multiple people in this building had been reading too many spy novels and were enjoying all this a little too much.

Matthias didn't hide his equal distaste for the name. "If it were anyone else, maybe. But I think everyone's accepted that the duchess knows things she shouldn't, and in many cases logically and logistically *couldn't*. If it doesn't affect my cha—client, I've given up wondering about her sources."

He'd definitely been going to say "charge," probably out of habit. Pet bit back a reluctant smile. She wondered how many high-profile politicians and celebrities had been unknowingly reduced to the status of foot-stomping babysitting charges by their security teams.

"Theories abound on that subject," she said, and he lifted his brows.

"Which one is your money on?"

"I'm torn between 'bribing someone in the CCTV room' or 'immortal witch who married Prince Frederick as a step toward turning humanity into her puppets, but forgot that in this century the royals have limited governing power, and is realizing she should have magicked herself into the role of billionaire magnate instead.'"

"Might explain why she's looting the palace valuables. Building her empire."

Movement flashed in Pet's peripheral vision, and a small tuxedo cat leapt nimbly from the oak tree to land on a stone wall. It lifted a paw and began to clean it vigorously, eyeing her with aloof disdain.

"All this hotshot security," she teased softly, "and a trespasser's still managed to sneak in."

"He does the rounds. He's engaged in an ongoing feud with my cat, who can't stand him. It's a long list, Miriam's grudges," Matthias added sardonically. "She thinks she's human and resents association with any creatures she considers lower on the food chain."

Pet's smile was growing. "Miriam," she repeated.

"I came across her on an assignment. She was small enough to fit in my boot then, ribs sticking out, wounds all over, none of them healing. She'd been kicked, multiple times. Half starved. I couldn't leave her there." He pushed one hand into his pocket, his expression darkening, but he gave her a faint smile as their eyes met. "A then-workmate's little girl insisted on naming rights. She named her after her nan, because apparently both Miriams have 'lovely wonky teeth.'"

She'd been listening in sick disgust to the reminder that some people were just straight-up human garbage, but that startled her into an unexpected laugh. "I don't know that Miriam Senior would be all that chuffed about the great honor bestowed on her."

"I met Miriam Senior once." The inflection in Matthias's voice made laughter bubble up inside her again. When she giggled, the harsh lines of his face seemed fractionally softer. "It turned out to be an apt choice. They both have the soul of a pantomime grande dame."

"Must be a clash of like-minded souls with this little guy, then." Even though the cat's stare wasn't encouraging, Pet couldn't resist the possibility of a cuddle and approached carefully. All she got for her trouble was one appalled yowl, and Miriam's furry foe shot out of sight, rustling through the trees.

"I think he belongs to the head gardener," Matthias said, and she snorted.

"I reckon *he* thinks he belongs in the Throne Room." As they moved down the path, heading in the general direction of home, she said philosophically, "Could have been a worse reception. I had dinner at Dominic and Sylvie's a couple of weeks ago. Their feline demon-child, Humphrey, knocked a bottle of industrial cleaner into my tea in his latest murder attempt. I hope and pray for the day he just legs it the minute I arrive—or lurks upstairs and sulks in his bedroom until I relieve them of my presence."

Matthias made a low sound of amusement in his throat as he held back a branch for her to pass under the tree. It wasn't quite a laugh, but she still felt a flicker of pleasure. "'His' bedroom?"

"Dominic gave the hellspawn his own room in their flat." Pet rolled her eyes. "And that was *before* he got together with Sylvie, so he can't even claim it was just because they wanted privacy. Which

I would totally understand. The flat is perfect, all antique wood and bookcases and a spiral staircase, like something off a Christmas card, but it's pretty cozy for two people and a cat Humphrey's size. Nobody wants to get frisky under the beady eye of homicidal Bustopher Jones."

They ducked between the thick, gnarled trunks of two fairy-tale-esque trees and came out by the exit gate.

As Matthias unlocked it, he glanced back at her. "And are these homicidal tendencies specific or widespread?"

"He particularly despises me," she said tranquilly, although was compelled by honesty to add, "I think he took lifelong offense to being nicknamed Boggart." She hugged herself as she passed through the gate. That single streak of gold in the sky wasn't doing much warmth-wise. She should have worn a dress with long sleeves. "But his attitude to all the De Veres has been grudgingly tolerant at best. It's only Sylvie he loves. He took one look at her and lost his shriveled black heart." Boggart had *some* good taste. "He first lived with Sebastian, my grandfather, before Dominic inherited—" She broke off as Matthias shrugged out of his jacket and held it out for her, her eyes moving from the fine wool to his face.

Slowly, she slipped her arms into it, pulling it close over her chest. It swamped her, but it was warm, and the lining was soft and silky. "Thank you," she said, and he glanced at her.

"Sebastian founded the patisserie, didn't he?"

She took the hint. Matthias had made it quite clear he disliked being thanked for thoughtful gestures. He'd been considerably more comfortable with a mugger punching him in the ribs than he had with the creep's victims crying with gratitude.

"Yes, my grandfather opened it decades ago." She didn't hide the pride in her voice. Between them, Sebastian and Dominic had created more than a financially viable business—a significant feat itself, especially in London. They'd built a legacy, fostered moments and memories for thousands of strangers. People who'd bought De Vere's chocolates in the earliest days were still buying them now, for themselves and their children and grandchildren. The king himself had frequented the bakery as a young man. Every week, every day, people cut into Dominic's cakes to mark engagements, weddings, birthdays, all the happiest times of their lives.

"And it's right across the road from Sylvie's bakery?" Matthias asked the question slightly stiffly. This was probably the first time in ages he'd forced himself to make small talk, but when she glanced at him warily, very conscious of not annoying him with endless chatter, he did seem genuinely interested.

He'd at least met Dominic and Sylvie a few times, so it wasn't quite as tedious as someone rambling on about total strangers.

She nodded. "Both on Magnolia Lane in Notting Hill. When Sylvie was looking for premises to open Sugar Fair a few years back, the most suitable vacancy was in the building across the street from Dominic."

"Reasonable business decision." On the pebbled path, Matthias's footsteps were out of sync with the tapping of her high heels, and she liked the rhythm of the two sounds. "The street already had an established flow of customers and a proven business record, then, and it sounds like the aesthetics of each bakery are different enough to intrigue newcomers into visiting both and establish their regular clientele. Sound economics."

"Fate," Pet corrected firmly, as they rounded a hedge. This was usually one of the public areas of the gardens, but it was closed for the party. "And don't roll your eyes at me. It's rude."

"You weren't even looking."

"I'm developing a very specific sixth sense."

For some reason, that generated a hint of a genuine smile. As she failed not to stare, he started rolling up one of his sleeves again, obviously feeling the cold a lot less than she did. "It must have been fun as a kid, having a grandad who made chocolates for a living."

"I—" She hesitated. This was edging into territory that sometimes made her button up, in the same way he did when anyone dared think he was nice sometimes. "I didn't visit De Vere's when I was little."

She looked down at the path but was conscious of his sharpened attention. "I never knew my grandfather well. I lived with my parents and sister." She didn't have to wonder if he'd heard the infinitesimal pause before the word "parents"; Matthias missed nothing. "Dominic left home at thirteen, when I was just a baby, and Sebastian raised him. There was very little contact between our households. I didn't even see him again until I was eighteen."

And she'd pushed him away harshly at that time, unable to deal with the ructions it had caused with Gerald and their mother, Lana.

When she lifted her head, Matthias's eyes were steady on her, a muscle jumping in his jaw, and the sudden urge to reach out for him was so incredibly strong she couldn't breathe for a moment.

Shaken, she tore her gaze away—and caught another flash of movement. Across the grass, a man in a suit and tie had just turned away from them, toward a bush. He was holding something in his hands. Her heart beating hard, she strained to see if it was a camera—and released another abrupt, pinching breath when he started walking again. Not a camera. A giftbag. Just a guest from the garden party, leaving the grounds.

The press presence had always been a necessary irritation,

but right now, the whole thing made her feel incredibly exposed and . . . vulnerable.

"You don't need to be nervous." The words and his tone were businesslike, but when her eyes jumped to Matthias's face, he was looking back at her with steady reassurance. "It's unsettling to be under surveillance, especially when they're trying to push a false narrative, but nobody's going to hurt you again."

Taut implacability in that last statement.

Again, he'd said. Somehow, she didn't think he meant the tiny bruise on her cheek from the mugging.

"Matthias. You don't still blame yourself for what happened at the ball. Do you?" She searched his face anxiously—and saw the answer there with crystal clarity before he closed it off.

She bit on the inside of her lip. The noise she made wasn't quite a laugh. Shaking her fingers free from the enveloping sleeve of his coat, she ran her hand over her head, smoothing back her fluffing hair. "I'm starting to think you and I might have more in common than just our connections to high-maintenance cats."

He made a short sound of his own in his throat. "Veritable twins."

She ignored the satirical bite. "If I have a bit of a martyr complex over my role in the Johnny and Helena debacle, as I'm constantly being informed, then so do you." She was suddenly caught and dragged into penetrating, almost transfixing green. "And if I have to forgive myself and—stop," she said, slowly, "so do you."

Without thinking—an increasingly common state of affairs in this undertaking—she reached out and touched his arm. The feel of his bare skin was again a tactile shock and her fingers flexed. That intense pale green seemed to darken with almost violent swiftness. Her breath catching on the slightest indrawn hitch, she was irrationally aware of her own pulse, as if she could physically feel the blood pumping at the base of her throat and down into her fingertips.

They stood there, looking at each other, and then, with an explicable entwinement of hyperconsciousness and detachment, she withdrew her hand, tucking it back into the warmth of the coat sleeve. She was somehow excruciatingly mindful of every tiny movement and changing expression, yet also felt as if she were observing herself—wondering—from a distance.

He turned from her with a crunch of his boot sole on the pebbles. "You barely knew Rosie and Johnny when you took that photo." There was none of the lingering strain she was feeling in Matthias's voice; it was very flat. She'd have thought she'd imagined every one of those heart-thudding seconds if it hadn't been for his left hand, fisted so tightly at his side that the tendons were standing out in his forearm. As she watched, he released it. "You acted spontaneously; if anything, probably out of concern for Rosie. There were no ill intentions. It's not the same. The night you were hurt—the night you could have been killed—it was my responsibility. I was point person on that team. I fucked up. Again."

At that second "again," she lifted her head sharply, concern swamping her own preoccupation, but he'd well and truly slammed an invisible gate shut.

"Matthias—"

"I'll come with you to the mail room." He started walking toward the stone walls and beveled windows of the staff wing.

After a moment, she followed.

The mail room was in the basement, and it ranked amongst both the best and worst parts of living in St. Giles. For some reason, even the architectural style of that floor was different, the most dramatic excesses of Gothic gloom. Combined with practical linoleum and lighting straight out of a horror film hospital, it was a long and creepy stroll to check mailboxes and collect parcels, and Pet went as infrequently as possible.

She wasn't ashamed to admit she was grateful for Matthias's presence as their footsteps echoed unnaturally loudly in the otherwise silent corridor.

Even with the taut, brooding vibe stretching between them like twanging wires.

After successfully navigating the long hallway without being murdered or possessed by rogue spirits, the mail room itself was bustling and busy, overseen by a plump, pretty woman named Nell, who was a sunflower in human form. Pet always thought there was something mythical about it—navigate the dark journey through flickering lights and eerie sculptures of malevolent creatures peeking around iron fixtures, and arrive in a land of sunshine and freshly baked biscuits.

Nell greeted them with her usual exuberance and offered a plate of her latest baking experiments. Pet took a piece of shortbread. She was a De Vere to her bones. When times were hard and her sex life imaginary, she turned to sweets. She bit in and the buttery crumbs melted on her tongue. The Royal Household ought to include the mail room biscuits in their job advertisements. Pet would rate them over most official work benefits.

Matthias started to refuse but took one when Nell's face fell a little.

There were quite a few children living in the family suites upstairs, with one or both parents working on staff. When they had sweets to sell for school fund-raising, Pet bet they all made a beeline straight for Matthias's door with their hopeful, plaintive smiles. Fifty quid said he caved immediately and bought multiple boxes.

Digging into his coat pocket for the collection card, she passed it to Nell.

"There are three boxes, I think," the other woman said, without even looking at it. "Give me a sec. I'll bring them out."

Three?

Jesus, how many pieces of tiny, superfluous furniture had she bought? As cute as they were, if she were going to blow her discretionary income on pink armchairs and mahogany bookcases, she'd prefer to be able to *use* them. Neither her books nor her arse were appropriately thimble-sized.

Nell's footsteps echoed from the back rooms, and she reappeared holding two large boxes, stacked in her arms. "The first two," she said cheerfully, setting them down by Pet's feet with a little *oof*. "I'll just grab the last one."

When Matthias offered a hand, she waved hers at him. "Thanks, but it's arm day. This'll save me a trip to the gym."

Pet crouched, taking hold of the first box and turning it, looking for the sender. Her name and address were written in block capitals, but there didn't seem to be—

She found the customs sticker pasted haphazardly on the far side, and inwardly groaned as she read the contact details.

Bloody hell. What a week.

"I'll carry them up for you, but if the third is the same size, you might have to act as navigator." Matthias looked at her more closely. "Problem?"

"They're from my sister." Pet tried to decipher Lorraine's unintelligible scrawl on the description of contents. Did that say *lettuce*?

Why would she send vegetables across the Atlantic? And what was with the sudden arrival of mass gifts?

She hadn't heard a peep from Lorraine in months, since her older sister had loudly disowned her for daring to get back in touch with Dominic, which she'd assumed would last until Lorraine wanted something or ran out of people to complain to in her home circle. Pet was surprised the silence had extended this long, but she'd be perfectly happy to make the break permanent.

In almost every way, Lorraine was her father's physical, moral, and temperamental duplicate, and putting up with one Gerald for over twenty years had been more than enough.

It seemed very unlikely that her sister had decided to post garden produce all the way from her home in the United States—but it was extremely out of character for her to send Pet anything at all, especially if she'd had to pay for the postage. She'd also shared Gerald's greed and tight-fisted attitude toward money. Pet swore inwardly at the cost printed on the postage slip, for which she fully expected to be invoiced.

Letters. Not lettuce. Letters. And documents, photographs . . . a word that might be ceramics . . .

She remained there, crouched on the floor, looking down as her fingertips gently stroked the box.

"Pet?" Matthias came down on his haunches, glancing shrewdly from the customs label to her face.

She slid her palms along the top of the box until the sides of her index fingers touched, as if she were subconsciously creating a barricade with her hands against whatever lay beneath. "These things. I think they're my mother's."

Chapter Seven

If Matthias had walked into this suite without knowing the owner, he'd still have guessed it was Pet's. In layout, it was identical to his own—a small lounge and attached kitchen, a compact bedroom and bathroom—but it was light and bright, despite the overcast sky outside, and he felt the increase in temperature warming his skin as he followed her inside. On the terms of the residential contract, they could paint walls and make cosmetic changes if they returned the rooms to their bland default setting on moving out. He'd never bothered, but Pet had taken full advantage. Her lounge was a rich, calm blue, she'd replaced the blinds with proper drapes, and there were cushions and fluffy blankets everywhere. The walls were covered with framed paintings and prints, her shelves crowded with books and random objects. It was all immaculately clean, but slightly askew, comfortably untidy. She'd lived at St. Giles less than half the time he had, but she'd created far more of a home for herself.

Carefully, he set the stack of boxes down on the floor beside her coffee table. He straightened, feeling a creeping return of that gut-gripping self-consciousness. He'd navigated many tight spaces in his career, both literally and figuratively, but he felt as if he'd take a single step in this pretty, cluttered room and one of her treasures would shatter against the floor.

As she turned on the kettle in the kitchen, he forced his stance into artificial relaxation, trying not to stand quite so much like a peach-fuzzed new cadet in an assembly line. He'd disliked more than he'd enjoyed about his time in regimental service, but he hadn't been out of place there. He hadn't felt like an invader in someone's personal space.

His usual instinct would be to excuse himself and go. He had no business here. No tabloid scum would bubble to the surface in the staff wing; there was no excuse of perpetuating the myth of their unlikely romance.

But he couldn't bring himself to leave. When she'd seen the delivery from her sister, and when she'd realized the provenance of the contents—

He'd seen similar expressions many times throughout the years, usually on the faces of people standing beside rubble or behind police cordons. Alone. Bereft. It was something to be witnessed and addressed with sympathy, with empathy, but with emotional distance, or the burden of other people's grief would quickly become insupportable.

But seeing it momentarily flicker across Pet's face . . .

It was entirely foreign to everything he'd ever associated with her. *Assumed* about her. Exactly how much had he not let himself see in Pet De Vere? Another legacy of his military years—his defensive instincts had sharpened to a fine point.

She had been busying herself taking cups and tea bags from cupboards, probably equally uncomfortable with his presence here, but she returned to his side now. She stood still, looking down at the boxes, then huffed out a breath.

When she reached up to a shelf for a retractable box cutter, he glanced at the framed photo next to the jar of stationery—a wedding photo, of a beautiful, smiling bride and a groom with deeply happy eyes. Pet's brother, Dominic De Vere, and his wife, Sylvie Fairchild. Matthias had indirectly attended their ceremony and part of the reception, on duty with Johnny and Rosie.

It had been a reasonably small wedding, surprisingly so, considering both bride and groom were public figures, albeit reluctantly. Most of the guests had consisted of the pair's various workforces, whom they seemed to have collected into a sort of eclectic, patchwork family. Rosie and Johnny had stayed for half the reception, but eventually made a tactful exit after the cutting of the cake, aware that their presence was inhibiting to many of those present. They'd all left with slices of cake, even the security team.

As the head bridesmaid, Pet had rarely left the dance floor, twirling in the arms of both Dominic's good-looking sous chef and Sylvie's business partner, who looked like he belonged in the pages of a nineteenth-century vampire novel. He'd watched her coaxing dances and smiles out of single guests of both sexes. She'd even tried with Matthias and Benji. If Benji hadn't been on duty, he'd have been on the floor with her in seconds. The fact they had a job to do hadn't prevented him from winking flirtatiously at anyone who looked at him twice.

Benji and Padraig had been peas in a fucking pod when it came to their love lives, until Padraig had turned in a crowd one day, seen Jenny, and never looked away. Matthias's gut twisted as he looked again at Dominic and Sylvie in their wedding clothes, their hands entwined, the pink and purple gems of Sylvie's engagement ring glinting in the light.

Padraig hadn't chosen a traditional diamond, either. He'd bought a pearl ring because his girl loved the sea. Jenny's father was a retired naval captain, she'd told Matthias, when in the end, he'd been the one to take the small velvet box to her. Watched her open it with violently shaking hands. Watched her cry. A warped version of what the scene ought to have been. A keepsake now, a fading memory, not a promise. Not a future.

Time was the only force that could pry open the bite of grief, slowly lessen its grip, but the mugging yesterday, seeing someone else he— The dark echoes, the similarities, had grabbed him by the throat, sinking in with sharp fangs.

Pet had followed his fixed gaze to the photo. She touched it affectionately. "That was a good night. Even if you did turn me down flat for a dance and crush my poor little feelings with your totally reasonable excuses."

Wrestling emotion under control so he could respond, he doubted he'd have been able to match her lightness of tone, but he suddenly saw what was perched on the other side of the wedding portrait.

He groaned aloud. "You actually kept that."

Lifting her brows at him, she immediately reached out for the little teddy bear on the shelf. She held it against her chest. Exactly as she had when he'd given it to her in the hospital—after an agonizing few seconds that had felt like a fucking year, in which she'd stared at him wordlessly. A full story of reaction had played across her expressive face, running the gamut from blank shock to the natural confusion of being presented with a cheap kids' toy by a total stranger. And then her smile.

There'd been no question that he was going to her that night in the hospital, although it would likely have taken longer to get in without Rosie and Johnny's regal influence cutting through all protocols. The only time he'd appreciated and actively encouraged rule-jumping. He'd fully expected her to be surrounded by visitors—friends, family, a besotted boyfriend or girlfriend; anyone who walked into a packed ballroom of shining wealth and seemed to glow from within, as if they'd caught all the true light inside, would draw love and attention like a warm, flickering flame.

But he knew what it was like, lying in an unfamiliar hospital bed in the small hours, and he'd felt compelled to take something to her.

Some latent instinct, maybe, left over from long-gone days. He had a slight memory of visiting a foster parent in the hospital when he was very young, being given a few quid from her husband to buy flowers for her. They'd been decent people, as far as he recalled. He'd lost contact with that household after they'd left the country for work, and either been denied permission to take him with them or hadn't asked. He couldn't remember their names now.

The streets had been dark and glittering with ice, the night Pet was hurt; the hospital gift shop long since closed. He'd found a twenty-four-hour newsagent on the corner. Their flowers had been sad, drooping bundles, all life departed, and they'd been sold out of chocolate boxes. All they'd had was the one little teddy bear. It had obviously been sitting forgotten on a high shelf for months, its fur and waistcoat sprinkled with dust.

He'd cleaned it off as best as he could and taken it up to the ward, strongly regretting the impulse with every step. He probably wouldn't have given it to her at all if Sylvie's curious gaze hadn't locked onto it like a sniper's bead the moment he'd entered the room. As much as he'd felt like someone was scraping a razor blade over already abraded skin, standing there like a total prick with all their surprised eyes locked on him, it hadn't seemed a step up to just leave with it again like it was his damn mascot.

"Excuse me," Pet said now, smoothing gentle fingers over the toy's ridiculous miniature pocket square. "This is my best little buddy you're scowling at. We do not disrespect Hercule in this palace."

"Hercule," he repeated evenly, his eyes traveling down to where her smile was twitching to life.

Some of the tension was leaving her body. She held the bear and the cutter in both hands, looking down at them. "He kept me company that night. After Dominic and Sylvie left. I— Reaction caught up with me. I was shaking like a leaf. Although that's a silly expression, really. Leaves are either still, or waving in the wind, turning to the sun, drifting to the ground. They're elegant, leaves. There was nothing elegant about me that night."

She kept her attention steadfastly on the toy—on . . . Hercule— and Matthias stood, just as still.

"The room was dim and beeping incessantly, and I could hear sounds all down the corridor, but I felt totally alone for a while there. And—I was scared. Even though I hadn't been afraid at the time. There'd *been* no time. You know?" She lifted her head in a twisting gesture, and he nodded once. Her lips quirked ruefully. "At four o'clock in the morning, I decided his name was Hercule Poirot. He'd once been the most feared detective in Teddy Land, before he'd ended up on the shop shelf in his retirement, because generational culture and government policy treat the elderly with appalling indifference."

Matthias cleared his throat, and her almost-smile returned, this time coming to full bloom.

"Vast quantities of morphine have an unfortunate effect on my brain," she said. "A couple of hours later, I was absolutely convinced that I'd missed my calling as a prima ballerina, and that if I showed up at the Royal Opera House the next day, some casting director would take one look and twirl me onto the stage for my immediate debut."

She made a sweeping gesture at her body. "I enjoy *going* to the ballet when I have time, but—well. Short, hips, zooming up on thirty, never taken a dance class in my life. Unless they need a stand-in for a background mushroom in the *Giselle* forest, I don't foresee an imminent career change. Fortunately, I'm happy where I am. Even if Johnny's giving me premature white hairs and the tabloid press sucks balls."

Short-lived amusement flickered through his preoccupation, and then with it, a reevoked memory. "My first year in the private sector, I did a very brief protection gig for a dancer in the Royal Ballet. They were doing back-to-back performances of *The Sleeping Beauty* at the Opera House."

Pet didn't hide her curiosity. "Why would Sleeping Beauty need a bodyguard? Overzealous fans?"

"She'd just ended a relationship with an abusive partner and was justifiably concerned he might retaliate. Fortunately, the bastard tried his hand at robbery a few days later, made a suitably shit thief, and got a long custodial sentence." He remembered haunted eyes and a bruised face. His gaze moved to the purple mark high on Pet's cheek. She'd tried to cover it with makeup. Renewed anger stirred low in his gut. "He should have got longer."

"Poor woman," Pet said somberly, and he saw with regret that the laughter had left her eyes.

"She was dancing as the Lilac Fairy," he said. "I'd forgotten all about it until your brother's wedding."

Caught off guard, she snorted. "Because of the wedding in the third act? I know Dominic got shockingly fancy about the decorations—for a man who acts like edible glitter is culinary sacrilege, he got his hands on a wedding catalogue and briefly turned into a cross between Liberace and a sergeant major. It was bizarre—but I didn't think it was quite Opera House swanky."

The decorations at the reception *had* been fancy. Given Sylvie's obvious delight in all things embellished and excessive, it wouldn't have been his first guess that famously ascetic, minimalist Dominic De Vere had unexpectedly run amok with rose sculptures and foliage.

He'd had a very happy bride, however.

And bridesmaid. He saw again Pet making sure everyone was enjoying themselves, flitting through fairy-lit trees in her frothy lilac dress, a crown of flowers in her black hair.

He made a noncommittal noise.

She stroked Hercule's waistcoat. She was quiet for several quick, thudding heartbeats. Then she lifted her chin and speared him with a very direct look, her brown eyes serious. "I'm going to say something, and you're going to dismiss it and shrug it off like it's nothing, and just—don't. Please. You don't have to say anything; you don't have to—care, but let me say it."

He looked back at her. Gave a very slight nod of assent. An odd sensation tugged as she exhaled a quiet breath through parted red lips.

She held up the bear. "I know you think this was a silly gesture. But it meant a lot to me. If I were sent back in time, I wouldn't change anything about that night because we're all here, we're all . . . we're all okay, but it was one of the most disorienting, frightening experiences of my life. A lot of it is a blur now, but I do remember—I think you held my hand. And then, even though you didn't know me, you brought me this bear, to—to make me feel better. It did." She swallowed, and that complicated feeling tightened its grip. "Twice, you gave me something to hang on to that night. You were kind, and I don't think I've repaid you well."

He shook his head, a short, abrupt movement. "Repayment doesn't come into it." The words came out low and gruff. "There was no question of some sort of debt incurred."

She was silent again, before she spoke emphatically. "On either side," she said. "You owe me nothing from that night. It wasn't a mistake on your part. It certainly wasn't negligence. It just . . . was what it was." She pulled her gaze from his and returned it to the toy. A strange frown passed over her brow. "Things happen the way they have to happen."

He was not a believer in fate, destiny, or any of the pretty lies people frequently told themselves to avoid personal responsibility. Yet, in that moment, there was nothing light and frothy about that statement. It landed and sank into him with unexpected weight and gravitas. He couldn't so easily dismiss his role in what had happened, but something within him did alter, ever so slightly.

Very carefully, Pet set the teddy bear back on the shelf. She turned back to him. A small smile had reignited in her eyes, but she said gravely, "Thank you for my bear, Matthias."

She returned to kneel beside the boxes without waiting for a response, verbal or otherwise, probably not trusting that he'd do as she'd asked and not brush it off. As she sliced open the tape on the first carton, she added, apparently inconsequently, "He's my first teddy." She coughed. "Of the *toy* variety, anyway." That last was a low mumble.

His mind having turned inward, there was a few seconds' delay

before those comments registered simultaneously. The unexpectedness of the first just managed to override the inappropriate flare of
heat colliding with the second. "You never had a teddy bear when
you were little?"

Even he'd had soft toys. They'd been standard gifts in the system, especially from well-meaning strangers plucking labels from
charity Christmas trees and buying for an unknown "Boy, aged 6."

He ripped off a piece of tape that had caught on the side of the
box, frustrating her attempts to open it.

"Thanks." She paused with her hands on the top flaps, but her
mouth had set into a thin line. He recognized the face of someone who'd rather be almost anywhere else, but sure as fuck wasn't
letting themselves be defeated. Tugging open the box, she looked
down at a jumble of bubble-wrapped items, typed correspondence
and old bills, and stacks of photos. "No," she said, and he looked
up. "I never had a teddy bear."

Matthias had a hell of a lot of faults and failings. They didn't include an inability to admit when he was wrong. Or a betting habit.

But as he watched her pull out a battered notebook with trembling fingers, he'd wager a substantial sum about his assumption
regarding Pet's happy childhood.

It had landed far wide of the mark.

As she began removing items from the box of her mother's belongings, laying them out on the rug beside her, Pet's lips twisted,
pulling in at the corner. It was a quirk of dark humor, no real
amusement behind it, simply a nod to the perversity of whichever
universal force was having fun at her expense. If she was going

to end the week as a renowned homewrecker with an imaginary lover, why not throw in a gold-digging sister and the figurative ghost of a neglectful mother?

Automatically, she unwound the bubble wrap from a mystery object. It was a ceramic piece, a vase that had originally belonged to Gerald's mother. Pet didn't remember her well, just faint recollections of a meek woman who'd been glad to move into a care home and forego her son's company.

The vase was Art Deco in structure, painted with a bright splash of color. A couple danced around the smooth curve, their hands outflung and entwined, the woman's dress flowing behind her. It was very much Pet's personal taste, but its inclusion wasn't likely to be a thoughtful gesture on Lorraine's part.

After their mother's death, Lana's will had divided her estate among her three children. A surprise to all of them, since she hadn't spoken to her son in over twenty years. Dominic had immediately and unceremoniously chucked his share at Pet and Lorraine. Pet hadn't wanted it, either, but in the end, she'd invested it into De Vere's. Lana had starved her father of her company for decades; she could at least posthumously contribute to Sebastian's legacy.

Lorraine had lived up to a lifetime of hypocrisy by avidly accepting Dominic's check, even as she veered between ignoring his existence or badmouthing him at every opportunity. She'd arranged for the family house to be sold before Lana was even buried and had shipped most of the contents to her home in America. Pet hadn't given a damn. Her life was a million times better now; she had no desire to look back, and very few warm, fuzzy memories that needed propping up with mementoes.

Belatedly, she spotted the piece of paper taped to the inside of the box. In typically passive-aggressive tones, the sickly little note expressed Lorraine's wish that her little sister have some "special memories" to keep—even if she *had* been so ungrateful recently.

Loosely translated: this was all the stuff that had no monetary value but had been cluttering her sister's garage.

Quite a bit of it looked like paperwork from Lana's various careers and old bills. Not exactly *awash* with nostalgia.

Pet carefully tipped the vase to its side and lifted her brows at the signature painted on the bottom, still perfectly legible after so many decades. If Lorraine had a clue who Clarice Cliff was, she'd be kicking herself right now. At least one misstep with her valuation.

Matthias had been standing quietly, a far too reassuring presence for a man who was only here because of his platinum-plated sense of honor. He lowered to sit on the couch, his foot just brushing her splayed knee. "Is that a Clarice Cliff?"

"Yup." She set it on the coffee table and admired it. "Lorraine should have had a London dealer do an appraisal before she stripped the place. She wouldn't voluntarily hand over anything worth more than a tenner. There's a reason most of this is photographs and letters."

"Your sister's not especially sentimental, I take it."

"There are rabid wolverines with more emotional depth than Lorraine. And probably better temperaments." She leaned forward with her hands propped on her thighs and surveyed the remaining contents of the box. The other two were presumably more of the same. A complex mix of emotions twined together, and she felt a bit overwhelmed. Exhaling again, she looked at Matthias.

His eyes studied hers. Quietly, he said, "Your mother's passed on?"

"Mmm." She pushed her hair back behind her ear, cupping her neck. "A few years ago." The discarded bubble wrap was draped across her leg. Setting it aside, she reached into the box and lifted out a small stack of photos, holding them on her lap. "These are the last keepsakes and physical reminders of her life. She held these things. Saved them."

She ran her thumb over the top photograph. Lana glinted back at her, her cheek propped against her hand as she reclined on the edge of a stage. She'd never been an actress, but she'd worked for a few theaters during her PR days. Pet thought she might also have done a stint as a dresser. Her mother's crooked smile was light and lazy. One long leg was bent at the knee, mimicking a pinup pose. She looked about twenty-five, so had probably been a decade older.

Pet looked into those intense eyes. They were Dominic's eyes, down to the differing shades of brown in each iris, but the expression, and the heart and the soul behind them, were so different it was hard to recognize the similarity.

She wondered how it felt, looking at your child and seeing an exact copy of your own eyes.

She wondered how it felt to betray and abandon that child.

"My primary instinct probably shouldn't be to bin the whole lot, should it?" She let go of the photos and they fell, scattering across the rug. Several of the snapshots landed against Matthias's boot.

"It's just . . . stuff," she said, almost to herself, a soft persuasion of something that was true in the literal sense. Emotionally, more complicated. "Just things."

Lightly, he reached out and touched the vase. "Art always captures a bit of the creator's soul," he said, and she twisted, just far enough to see him. "And an object that somebody loved, a photograph, a scrap of handwriting—it's all tiny pieces of them, their history. Scattered bits of their story. The lingering echo of their presence."

Not so long ago, Pet would have rated Matthias another of the completely unsentimental personalities in her life.

She watched him now with a tight feeling in her throat.

"There can be meaning in something that belonged to somebody significant. Comfort." Matthias held her gaze as firmly as if he were reaching out physically. "But if it's just—pain, it's not worth it. If you need to bin everything, do it."

She nodded, very slightly.

She'd taken off his loaned coat in the warmth of the room, and her hair was a sensual, shivery brush against her bare neck and hunched shoulders.

That intense awareness of her body, her skin, was a shot of warning. She'd always been quite a physical, tactile person, always appreciated the feel of silks and velvets and the touch of someone's hand. But when her workload was heavy and the daily routine was chaotic, her mind tended to operate on a practical surface level. Focusing on schedule details and speech edits, not on dust motes swirling in pretty patterns in the air, or light through a stained glass window changing the color of a man's scar, or the tingling sensation of her hair stimulating tiny nerves.

When she started paying close attention to the scents of flowers, and cologne, and the light scratch of fine wool trouser fabric against her knee . . .

All hazard lights on.

She'd thought she'd outgrown indulging in futile attractions.

And obviously, she had found Matthias attractive when he'd entered her life so dramatically. Or when she'd literally thrown herself into his, depending on the viewpoint. It would take a stronger woman to avoid at least a small initial crush on a man who turned up out of nowhere with a tiny teddy bear in the palm of his huge hand. A teddy bear wearing a polka-dotted waistcoat with a minuscule pocket square.

It wasn't something she'd consciously dwelled on. It was a recipe for disaster, letting herself fall into a fully-fledged infatuation with a man who didn't like her and showed no interest in even friendship.

Also, he'd sometimes been bloody annoying when it came to Johnny.

She could shut herself off from the cinched-tie, flat-eyed, grim-mouthed bodyguard.

But the Matthias who reached out with gruff comfort even to strangers, who crouched down on a muddy field to help a crying child, who'd agreed to put himself farther into the tabloid lens even when he must be loathing it—

Despite his size and demeanor, he had never seemed physically intimidating to her, but right now he was exuding a very different type of danger.

Before, she wouldn't have even entertained the prospect that the physical attraction might be mutual, but she didn't think men's eyes dilated from sexual indifference. It made that shyness flow through her in a deep flush, the thought that Matthias Vaughn might—*want* her, a little, at least in that way.

She could see it now, even as he tried to slide it back into concealment behind the mask, that flickering glimpse of interest, that very specific intensity.

However, she wasn't kidding herself. In every other way, his guard was still up, and he hadn't exactly jumped at the prospect of spending more time with her. He'd have shot down the whole idea of Codename Charming in an instant, if his protective instincts hadn't been triggered. She wasn't the only one who couldn't just stand back and watch someone take a hit. He'd clearly keep the whole world safe if he could.

They'd been working and living in the same building for months. If he'd ever wanted to see her outside of work hours, it wouldn't have been difficult. Instead, he'd left rooms soon after she entered them, and consistently looked at her with either disapproval or . . . nothing.

If someone thought you were pretty, that was nice. It was also ultimately meaningless.

Fleeting. Temporary.

In an abrupt motion, she pushed aside useless thoughts and reached blindly into the box, lifting out an old, scratched leather notebook. Absently opening it, she thumbed through to the first page of writing.

In her mother's familiar neat, looping handwriting, it was dated at the top.

"It's a journal," she said huskily. "From when Dominic was little, a couple of years before I was born. I don't remember my mother ever keeping a diary when I was growing up."

This one hadn't been a long-term endeavor, either. Flipping through it, the lines of violet ink barely filled a quarter of the pages, and the dates encompassed only a few months before the entries stopped. Lana had always gone through fads, picking up things—and people—for a while before losing interest.

Pet had no idea what sort of journal her mother might have been inspired to try, whether it was a detailed account of her daily activities, the places she'd gone and the people she'd met, or a stream of consciousness and random thoughts—which would be far more in keeping with her personality—or a Bridget Jones–esque calorie count and internal whinge.

Fortunately, she could rule out even the slimmest horrifying possibility that it was a saucy boudoir memoir à la Lady Chatterley; for all her mother's airiness, charm, and general ineptitude as a parent, she'd been an intelligent woman, who'd lived with a suspicious and deeply petty man.

Lana's extreme dislike of confrontation hadn't prevented her multiple extramarital affairs, but she'd never have risked recording any details on paper.

"She wasn't an especially literary person," Pet said, turning another page. The words there were blurred; her eyes were only skimming over the surface, not focusing on any specific sentence. "Although I do remember her going out in the evenings to a book club."

Or had it been an art club? Either way, looking back as an adult, she assumed that the "club" had met in a hotel room and involved very few members and even fewer clothes.

It was a strange feeling, holding something into which her mother might have poured private thoughts and feelings. Even just everyday opinions. Any snatches of inner self, which Pet had hardly known, despite sleeping under the same roof for eighteen years.

Given the date on it, she wasn't sure she wanted to read any of it—and she was worried about it stirring up bad memories for Dominic. Things had been bad enough for him at that time that he'd already been hoarding any money he could find to buy a train ticket to London. Eventually, when she'd come along, he'd managed to buy two. She'd only discovered that last year, that he'd initially taken her with him, that Gerald had tried to have him charged with kidnapping when he was still just a kid himself.

She knew her mother had harbored at least some regrets where Dominic was concerned. She'd once found a photo of him hidden in a bureau drawer, and Lana had cared enough—or felt guilty enough—to include him in her will. But ultimately, she'd let it happen. She'd chosen to be unfaithful, and she'd let her husband punish the innocent child conceived in that affair with relentless neglect and disdain, and eventually complete alienation in his own home.

And then she'd done it all over again twelve years later with Pet. When Gerald's carping criticisms and impossible standards had turned on her daughter, she'd once more turned her back.

Pet's phone buzzed, loud and startling in a room so silent she'd been listening to Matthias's quiet breathing.

Dropping the journal, she unclipped the phone from her belt and checked the name flashing on the screen—Ji-Hoon—while Matthias bent to pick up the scattered photos that had fallen against his foot. He shuffled them together and moved to set them aside for her, idly glancing down at the top image.

"I'm sorry to interrupt your break," Ji-Hoon said in her ear. "Just a quick note. Rosie and Johnny have decided to throw a dinner party for friends next week, and they'd like to purchase desserts from Sugar Fair for the occasion. I was going to phone the order through as usual, but Rosie thought you could be visiting your brother and sister-in-law this afternoon and, if so, might not mind dropping it off in person."

Pet was listening, but her attention was caught on Matthias's expression. He'd looked down at the photo in his hands with a flicker of a smile—which faded as his eyebrows lifted. She wondered what had caused Mr. Unflappable to do a small but genuine double take. From what she could see of the upside down picture, it was a posed shot of a group of people and looked like a work function. Not earth-shattering.

Wryly, she inquired, "And did Her Highness by any chance suggest that Matthias might like to accompany me on this family visit, where I'm quite likely to be photographed going in?"

"Well . . ." Ji-Hoon hedged, with gentle amusement, and she cast her eyes up.

"I'll let him know he's been summoned for Codename Charming Phase Two. And *if* he wants to come, he can. Thanks."

Ending the call, she reclipped the phone. "You heard?"

"That Her Royal Puppet-Master is tugging a few more strings?" Matthias's response was equally dry. "Orders received."

He nodded down at the photograph. "Your mother had strong genes physically. Other than identical twins, I've never seen such a vivid family resemblance. I thought it was you at first. Although the clothing is the wrong era." He quirked a brow at her. "Not nearly vintage enough."

She frowned, reaching for the photo. "Really? I don't think I look much like my mother at all. Dominic has her eyes, but—"

The words caught in her throat as shock hit her like a physical collision.

She stared down at the snapshot. It was probably several decades old, and it *was* some sort of gathering or celebration. About twenty people stood in a group under strings of bunting, a few holding champagne glasses, the rest posing with the usual awkwardly placed limbs and self-conscious smiles.

"No." She moved her thumb, her pink-polished nail stopping just short of the woman who stood neatly at the side of the gathering, her hands clasped at her waist. "No, that isn't my mother."

It was—Pet.

For a moment, she thought so, as well. That she'd somehow been photographed in a place she'd never been, in clothing she'd never owned, with people she didn't recognize.

After the initial heart-jump of astonishment, she started to notice the differences as well as the similarities. The woman's face was narrower, and her hair was shorter than Pet had ever worn her own. She also stood a good head over her immediate companions, so unless the rest of the party attendees were Lilliputians, she was quite a bit taller than Pet.

But otherwise—almost a doppelgänger.

And Pet had never seen her before in her life.

Chapter Eight

It was more than a little disconcerting, realizing that the face she'd looked at in the mirror for twenty-seven years had belonged to someone else first.

That physically, she was basically a human photocopy.

It would have occupied a lot more of Pet's thoughts on the taxi journey to Sugar Fair if Johnny hadn't sent a perky, chatty text informing them that, as expected, they'd left the palace with a tabloid tail, and maybe—if it wasn't asking too much, obviously a cheek and all that—they could, you know, up the ante a bit regarding a public perception of affection.

I.e., could Pet kiss Matthias when they got out of the car?

Not too much, Johnny added hastily in a second message. They didn't want it to look like a performance. Just a *little* kiss.

Wordlessly, she tilted her phone, and Matthias leaned over to read the messages.

They looked at each other in perfect unison.

Christ, Rosie and Johnny's synchronized double act was contagious.

Matthias really had absolutely nailed the art of the non-expression.

A+ example. They could use his photo in the dictionary under "I" for impassive.

"It's an interesting sensation," he said. "Being moved about like a human chess piece."

"I suppose it's how they frequently feel themselves," she said, and was quite impressed with herself for the light normality of her tone, when mentally she was digging a large hole and twirling herself dramatically into it.

"Generous of them to share the experience," he muttered, turning sharply to scan the street behind them.

The edge to his words was both unflattering and totally relatable.

As she saw the lights of Sugar Fair and De Vere's approaching, her stomach turned over in a ridiculous heart-jump of nerves.

She'd had a lot of kisses in her life. Some good, some . . . all right, and a few charged with sparkling sexual chemistry. She'd even *acted* a few snogs in the past, in am-dram at school.

And she'd planted kisses in spicier locations than the pavement and a man's mouth, so there was absolutely no reason to start behaving like a cross between a teenage virgin and a literary spinster. She still couldn't help joining him in a darting check for obvious cameras. It wasn't surprising they'd been followed. They'd taken the taxi because there wouldn't be a hope of finding parking anywhere near central Notting Hill at this time of day, but it had meant departing from a visible exit rather than the underground carpark.

For once, the whole point was that they *were* photographed, she did realize that. The sooner that multiple images of her "actual" St. Giles romance appeared on social media, the quicker the malicious speculation about Johnny would be—not completely stamped out, there were too many people who'd rather believe the worst, but at least dampened.

Therefore, they just had to keep going and ride out the storm.

And all she had to do was pay the driver, get out of the car, stretch up on her tiptoes, and press her mouth to Matthias's. A quick gesture. The natural affection of two people who kissed and touched all the time.

Spontaneous. Not at all forced. She didn't feel incredibly self-conscious in the slightest as she stood on the pavement and contemplated her entire existence.

"Do you think people are really going to buy this?" She spoke close to his chest, under her breath. Nobody seemed to be paying them much attention, but the street was busy, and she was pretty sure that, yes, there was at least one photographer scuttling about on the other side of the street, six cars down.

Either that, or an inexperienced burglar was scoping out the adjacent jewelry store and making a woeful job of casing the joint.

At least it wasn't the prick from the garden party again.

"It's all very well as a plan, but it's not exactly subtle, is it?" It was feeling a hell of a lot *less* subtle right now. "The bullshit about me and Johnny ramps up, and suddenly, out of nowhere, you and I are snogging in the streets." She hesitated—then slipped her hand into the crook of his arm and smiled up at him. He managed not to noticeably flinch this time. Miracles abounded. "The *Digital Star* won't be the only ones to question the timing. Even the most die-hard romantics have got to be a little suspicious."

"It should be the miracle of the fucking century if *anyone* finds this plausible," he said, just as quietly and more than a little de-risively. "But this had the potential to make your life hell. If the tabloids stop testing the waters with idle shit-stirring and become legitimately convinced that you're sleeping with Johnny, they'll invade the bakeries to question your family. They'll ambush your friends, bug your phone, contact every person you've ever worked with or for." She shivered, and his mouth firmed.

"And significantly," he continued after a moment, locking into cool professional mode, "in this scenario, what can they do? If they follow you and Johnny around twenty-four seven, they'll be a fucking nuisance, but they're not going to get any genuinely compromising images. Meanwhile, the . . . *shipping* shite is flooding social media. The PR team isn't wrong. There are enough people who do believe what they see to create an impression. Ultimately, that's all you need. Enough doubt and diversion to upset the narrative, it won't become fixed, and eventually it'll be swept away by the next scandal."

As Benji had noted with such enjoyment, Matthias's body language when he had to voice the word "shipping" was like someone having their teeth extracted without anesthetic. The reluctant giggle that bubbled in Pet's chest warred with a deep-buried pang.

She was only skeptical about the timing and how it would be perceived. Clearly, from his perspective, the entire idea of them as a couple was not simply implausible, but almost laughable.

Internally, her smile had faded, something inside her quietly withdrawing, but she kept the laughter on her face.

Before she lost her nerve, she rose on her tiptoes and lightly touched her palm to his cheek. She'd been wondering what his beard felt like, whether it would be soft or scratchy against her skin. It was both.

She counted her heartbeats—one, two, three, four, thudding under her ribs—as Matthias looked down into her eyes. Searching his face, she couldn't read anything there, certainly not a reflection of her own anxiety. Only the change in his breathing, quickening perceptibly, betrayed a crack in his iron control—and gave her some comfort that she wasn't entirely out on a ledge here by herself.

Just a quick kiss. It's only a kiss.

Achingly slowly, he brought up his hand, the side of his finger resting just under her chin. Pet's free hand jerked, curling, and her toes dug into the soles of her shoes.

Very, very gently, he nudged up her chin and lowered his head. He was so much taller that he was almost doing yoga just to reach her, even when she stretched up as far as she could. It was so physically awkward that she couldn't help smiling, her sense of humor rising through her spiraling nerves, and she saw the faintest flash of reciprocal wryness in his eyes, so close to her own.

She teetered, and he put his hand on her back in a supportive hold, his long fingers curving around her waist. His thumb accidentally brushed over the cutout in her dress, stroking the incredibly sensitive skin over her lower spine. His expression shuttered. Her indrawn breath was quick and shallow.

Any incipient laughter dried in her throat.

They just—froze there, a tableau of coiling energy and slowly building tension. Caution and some deep sense of self-preservation gripped her arms and legs, holding her back; the tingling in her core and chest tempted her forward. An invisible, shivery feeling was crackling through her body, raising the fine baby hairs around her temples, sparkling against the pads of his fingers where they held her.

In tumbling thought fragments, her heartbeats starting to come too quickly, she almost wished she could paint, that she could glory in a frightening rawness of sensation and pour it into oils, and brushes, and canvas. Or some Brooklyn DeWitt–esque sculpture of velvet and ink, silk and iron, and a few crushed cans for nostalgia. She'd call it *Prelude to Just a Little Kiss* and nobody would buy it because apparently that would be *the miracle of the fucking century*, and maybe if she could expel even half the inner trembling heat, it would drop back to something familiar and safe.

She hadn't realized her mind's propensity to shelter behind nonsense when she was nervous, embarrassed, experiencing the strongest sexual attraction of her life, and getting a crick in her neck, because he was all-the-way-up-there and she really needed a footstool. It would be taking their budding circus act a little too far if she stood on the nearest fence. Or started carrying portable stilts.

His other hand shifted to cradle the curve of her neck. He'd seen her slight wince of discomfort, and his movement then was swift and sure, in contrast to his earlier reticence. He never let anyone suffer physical pain in his presence. Once, she'd had a headache on an engagement, and a packet of ibuprofen had been slipped into her hand in passing.

The blast of a car horn made her jump, a dash of cold reminder as to why they were here—and who was watching.

Matthias's fingertips pressed into her skin. His eyes were darker than usual, but she watched the sharpening of awareness. She could almost *see* resolve sliding over his body like a suit of armor, before his mouth met hers.

Despite the artificiality of motive, there was nothing slick and practiced about it; instead of the smooth peck of two sophisticated faux lovers, their noses bumped, and she drew in another steadying breath through her mouth at the wrong time and just about inhaled him.

Seemingly driven by the same pure instinct, then, he slid his thumb under her ear, along her jawbone, angling her head into the right position, and she gripped his tie, pulling him into her as their lips returned for a second attempt.

He was warm and solid against her, over her, and she had about two seconds to enjoy the sheer physicality of him—his scent, his touch, the very slight clumsiness of his big hands, unexpected and endearing—before she found herself parting her lips, his own plump lower lip catching hers, with just a hint of his taste.

For head-spinning seconds, their tongues touched, teased, sinking into each other as her hand fisted in his shirt, and she forgot . . . everything . . . that—

A door slammed nearby, and she jerked back, still braced on his supporting palm.

Her chest was moving jaggedly. The sensuous slip and glide of her clothing felt abrasive on sensitized flesh.

His blunt cheekbones were flushed.

Just a little kiss.

The moment stretched into excruciating silence, but when he went to speak, she half put a hand up, a sheer reflex, desperately not wanting him to—to rationalize or sweep aside, or, oh god, *apologize* . . .

Across the street, beyond the passing cars, the photographer had moved level with them, brazenly snapping photos, even cheekily waving when Pet met his avid stare, momentarily too dazed to feign pap-obliviousness.

"Not even trying to be subtle." Matthias's voice was a little thick, and that deep husk rasped over her skin like another physical touch.

No. *Subtle* was not the word she'd use for the past few minutes.

She had to forcibly keep her head from turning back to the street. As disconcerting and invasive as it felt, knowing strangers would be dissecting every angle of her body and change in expression, the pap was a tangible anchor.

Sugar Fair's door opened with its familiar joyful tinkle. A woman came out, holding a box with the bakery's insignia, a pink and gold whisk standing tall amidst laurel leaves, a culinary tree for Sylvie's enchanting city woodland. She gave Pet an absent-minded, polite smile, but did a double take when she saw Matthias, which effectively knocked Pet further out of her preoccupation.

God, some people were so bloody rude.

Matthias caught her fingertips when she stepped toward the door—and it wasn't a flirty little tingle that shot up her wrist that time. Full-on zap.

She turned, and he lowered his head again as he tugged her close. For an embarrassing moment, she thought he was going in for another kiss and every nerve in her body nodded enthusiastically and stretched out eager arms for him. She clasped hold of herself before her actual arms joined suit.

If he'd felt even a tenth of that bewildering head rush, he'd recovered his composure with humiliating ease.

His breath stirred the tendrils of hair above her ear. "We were distracted in the car. If your sister-in-law is inside, are we privately fronting up or keeping up the charade?"

The word "charade" was being murmured in her ear, even as her stomach clenched every time his breath touched her skin.

A needle of almost panic went through her, sharp enough to stop her own breath, and she ducked her head against him for a second.

Then, ruthlessly steeling her mind, she swept him a glance through flirty lashes, nudging along the *charade* that she was a woman so seductive her man couldn't resist pulling her in to nuzzle against her skin.

"I'm so used to ironclad nondisclosure agreements," she whispered, clearing her throat. "And even though this isn't an official assignment, confidentiality is key. I'd trust my brother with my life, and that extends to Sylvie, but—we probably ought to keep up the . . . the act even with them."

The bell jangled again with more departing customers, who annoyingly decided to stand and chat right next to them. In a rapid movement, Matthias lifted her slightly with his arm, backing her past a display of fairy-lit foliage, her feet doing a tiptoeing backpedal like a ballerina en pointe.

Despite the swiftness and his strength, he was so achingly gentle with her.

The customers' murmuring glances turned their way, but perhaps naturally, the people moved off a short distance to give them some privacy. Or to tut about the PDA.

He braced one arm against the brickwork beside her head, blocking anyone's view of her face, and she felt as if she'd suddenly been enclosed back in that warm bubble. She couldn't see or feel anything but his body, and it was the farthest feeling imaginable from claustrophobia or dislike. She could understand why Johnny felt so secure in Matthias's care. Somehow, when you were the center of that intent focus, it was difficult to believe that bad things ever happened anywhere.

"You don't want to," he said, with calm perceptiveness. "Pretend with your family."

The words left her in a rush. "When I was eighteen, Dominic asked me to meet him for lunch. It was essentially the first time I saw him in person. I was too little to remember him before he left home, and my . . . my stepfather had forbidden him contact with me. When Gerald found out that we were meeting up, it kicked off a huge row. I couldn't deal with it. I told Dominic to leave me alone. I told him I didn't want to see him again." She'd crushed something inside him that day; she'd seen it as clearly as she'd felt the same shriveling pain in her own abdomen. The stamping out of hope. "He respected my decision. I didn't see him again until they died." Matthias waited for her to continue, his eyes on her face. "I finally have him back in my life, and things are—getting good. I don't lie to him. Not anymore."

The lingering customers outside the door finally hugged and departed, heading off in opposite directions, and Matthias straightened away from her. It wasn't overly cold now, but she rubbed her arms.

"Then we won't," he said. "You've vouched for them. They'll keep it to themselves."

It was a straightforward statement of fact and intent, as if there were no question about it. She'd said it, so he believed her, and they would do it.

The feeling inside her, then, was hard to describe. But after a moment, she shook her head. Regretful, but decisive. "We gave our word to Rosie. Dominic would understand and respect that."

Having said that, it was quite possible he'd guess the game plan, anyway. This *was* the man who could spot a mistake in a cake batter from right across a steaming kitchen, and he was a bigger cynic even than the Bulldog. Very little got past Dominic, and he'd been furious earlier in the year when Sylvie had showed him the malicious stories about Pet and Johnny. It wasn't only in his cake decorating that he was good at connecting dots.

On the other hand, she doubted if either of them knew how much things had ramped up this week. Sylvie only used social media for work, Dominic would have to be lobotomized before he'd spend his limited free time scrolling the *Digital Star*, and business was booming for them. They'd just come home from Paris last night, after snatching a few days for themselves; they'd barely had time to sit down lately.

Even if he did guess—it wasn't in Dominic's character to pry into people's personal lives. He respected her privacy, so unless he thought she was at physical risk, he probably wouldn't interfere.

She touched her lower lip. If there was danger here, she didn't think it was physical.

They were going across to De Vere's after this, and hopefully, her brother would be much more interested in the mysterious photograph in her bag than in her love life. Although "love" was a bit of a misnomer when it came to her romantic history. Pet had found and inspired many things in many people—liking, lust, friendship, fleeting fun—but it never dipped far below the surface.

Very quietly, she said, "Anyway—it's not for long, is it?"

She kept her gaze fixed on the knot of Matthias's tie, still neat and tight despite that demanding tug she'd given it, which already felt a bit dreamlike and surreal.

She absolutely did not want to wiggle that stodgy knot open, undo the top buttons of his shirt, and press her nose there.

It was his work tie. Uniform black. Stark, severe, and crisp. Because even off-shift, even with wild, overwhelming bursts of sexual chemistry, he was doing his duty.

"No," he said. "It's not for long."

Above the Sugar Fair entrance, a hidden machine was sending out occasional bursts of iridescent bubbles. They rippled and burst amidst the noise and exhaust fumes, the fairy tale colliding with harsh reality.

When Pet pushed open the door, they were immediately hit with a hot rush of caramel-scented air. The patisserie smelled even better than the Midnight Emporium, which was now permanently tainted by the memory of Snake-Boy pulling a knife out of his sock.

Sylvie had cleverly designed her shop floor so the first thing in shoppers' eyeline was a display of bottled sweets. Row after row of colorful balls and ribbons, chocolates and sherbets. Pet always watched with interest as people instinctively searched out their favorites.

Matthias's eyes traced along the inviting lineup and stopped on the white chocolate mice.

Along one wall behind Sugar Fair's iconic chocolate fountain, floor-to-ceiling bookcases contained boxes of handmade bonbons and truffles, packaged as vintage books.

The door to the kitchens swung open, and Mabel Yukawa, Sylvie's senior assistant, walked out with a big bowl of sugar syrup. She barely spared them a glance before she sat down at her little worktable, immediately plucking an *amezaiku* lollipop from a silicone rack. The candy was intricately sculpted as always, although for some reason she'd chosen to mold that one into a portrait bust of Prince Frederick. With just a few strokes of her brushes, she'd truly captured the characteristic expression of blustering condescension.

If most people walked in now, they'd look at tiny Mabel, serenely painting her sweets, her short legs swinging as she hummed along to music in her head, and they'd look at Matthias, and zero odds on whom they'd find more intimidating.

Those poor sweet summer children.

"Hi, Mabs," Pet said, and the other woman gave a critical "Hmm," of acknowledgment. "This is Matthias."

Mabel finally deigned to look up from her work, her extremely spiky lashes flicking up and down like spiders' legs as she gave Matthias a once-over. In Mabel-language, her grudging nod of greeting signaled mild approval. "Sylvie's in the annex, colluding with the competition."

"Dominic's here?" That would save some time, although she'd been hoping to exploit her shareholders' perk and stock up on her favorite De Vere's truffles.

"They're collaborating on a project," Clara said helpfully at the till as Pet handed Rosie and Johnny's dinner party order to the young sales assistant.

"Those Team Marchmont crash helmets might come in handy," she muttered, as Matthias followed her toward the swinging doors. "Sylvie and Dominic's joint commissions are usually gorgeous at the end, argumentative at the beginning, and fireworks in the middle."

She had her palm on the left door when Mabel murmured with complete indifference, "I used to flat with a fellow shorty who dated a heavyweight boxer. Much taller than she was. The size difference was never an issue."

Pet hesitated, very aware of the silent, watchful man behind her. Her skin was still prickling with awareness, and they weren't even touching now. "No?"

Mabs changed brushes and applied a tiny fleck of detail to her lollipop. "She just spent most of the day sitting on his face."

Pet was not looking at Matthias.

Possibly ever again.

Pushing open the door with more force than necessary, she hooked a finger in the neckline of her dress and peeked down her chest. Apparently, a person could blush all the way to their nipples. Life: a never-ending education.

The kitchens smelled even more delicious, pots of sugar bubbling on the stoves, cakes in different stages of assembly on the counters, tray after tray of chocolates being hand-painted, and everything overlaid with the scent of buttercream.

She returned the staff's greetings on the way to the newly built annex, an addition Sylvie's business partner and best friend, Jay, had contracted. She did her delightful mad scientist act there, testing out each brainwave. It was equipped with a kitchenette, a drafting table, comfortable chairs, and a large amount of counterspace.

Assuming that her brother and sister-in-law would be bent over sketches or steaming pans, Pet didn't wait after knocking, barging merrily on in to find them bent over the table instead.

She copped one eyeful of Sylvie sprawled backward on top of scattered sketching paper, Dominic's face tucked into her neck, their clasped hands sliding up the table above their nestled heads.

Thank Jesus everyone was still fully clothed, although she saw a hint of purple bra lace.

"Ack." She backed up several steps, crashed into Matthias, and in a jumbled movement, went way up on her tiptoes, trying unsuccessfully to cover his eyes with one hand while she blindfolded herself with the other. "Sorry! Sorry. We're not looking. We're leaving. And it's not even five, fam. I'm scandalized."

She heard Sylvie give a horrified giggle as she kicked the door shut on them. For a moment, neither she nor Matthias moved, then he gently peeled her hand away and returned it to her.

"Presumably not what you meant by 'fireworks,'" he said, and she found herself giggling, too.

Despite the extreme awkwardness and—everything else, she couldn't help loving these peeks into that unexpected streak of wry humor.

She turned as the door reopened and shook her head at Sylvie in mock censure. "And I thought you put a lock on that door to protect your professional secrets. You might want to snick it if you're going to jump the neighbors during work hours."

Sylvie's cheeks were pink, and she was still hastily tucking her shirt back into her skirt. "On heart rate alone, I think that just maxed out Dominic's Fitbit for the rest of the week."

The wall clock ticked through three long, painful seconds.

"Congratulations," Pet said. "You haven't just crossed the border into the land of Too Much Information, you've won the mayoral election."

Sylvie's blush had turned into more of a firestorm. "Oh my god, I meant because he moved so quickly when you opened the door—"

Pet took pity on her. "And moving equally quickly to a new subject, for all our sakes, how was Paris?"

Amazing, obviously. Her sister-in-law's face instantly went all soft and gooey. She was just about radiating animated love-hearts.

Dominic appeared over her shoulder. The silvered black hair above his left ear was slightly ruffled, but otherwise it was like he'd pressed a reset button and instantly restored himself to factory settings. Even his tie was military straight. He and Matthias could start some sort of nattily attired club.

He barely hesitated before he reached forward and kissed Pet's cheek, and a stranger would never realize how momentous the simple gesture still was for them.

"This is a nice surprise," he said, in the voice so many people found ice-cold. Stroking the back of Sylvie's head, he nodded at Matthias. "Vaughn. Good to see you. Does Johnny have an engagement in Notting Hill today? If you two are together, he's usually close by. Creating accidental havoc."

"We're not on duty this afternoon," Pet said—and as simple as that, Dominic's eyes sharpened, cutting a scalpel line from her to Matthias's inscrutable face.

Despite her mental readiness for that exact reaction, her boob-flush was already spreading up to her hairline—which in turn drew Sylvie's attention, pulling her out of her Parisian love-haze.

Pet had barely said a word yet, and her sister-in-law had snapped to alertness like an eager meerkat, while her brother's extremely expressive left eyebrow was on the rise.

"We did have an order to drop in for Rosie," she added, reminding herself that she was an experienced, fully adult woman, and trying to will away the blush through sheer obstinacy, "and I have something I need to show you. And—"

She glanced at Matthias, floundering slightly. Sylvie and Dominic had met—in passing—one or two of her dates, but those occasions had just been casual introductions and hadn't involved a man they already knew. What was she meant to do, sweep her hand in front of Matthias like a game show host and announce, "Boyfriend"?

The triple threat—awkward, a blatant lie, *and* objectifying.

"And then we're going out for dinner." Matthias moved to stand at her back in his familiar, vigilant stance. It was a profound relief, just the sheer normality of having him looming over her, skewering everyone with a penetrating glower. "It's been a long week, with a load of bullshit, and Pet needs a break."

"Where are you going to eat?" Dominic asked unexpectedly and totally irrelevantly, his eyes just as watchful.

Since Pet was actually going home to three-day-old leftovers of a very average casserole, and she had no idea what either of the men were doing or thinking, her brain immediately blanked on every one of the literal hundreds of London restaurants she'd booked and quality-checked for her bosses.

"We'll find somewhere in Little Venice," Matthias said, and added simply in those low, deep tones, "The canal makes her happy."

Little Venice and the canal *did* make her happy. It was her recharging spot in the busy city, her place of solace in the same way Rosie loved the private garden at St. Giles. She'd mentioned that once, months ago—in her very first few days at the palace, when she was still trying to engage Matthias in casual conversation. Still thought of him hopefully as her first, and at that time only, friend on the staff.

"I didn't know you'd heard that," she murmured, too surprised to monitor her answers in front of the others. She twisted to look up at him. "Honestly, I thought you just tuned me out when I was annoying you with the newbie chatter."

His expression didn't change much, but the faintest line appeared between his heavy brows. "I don't like small talk myself," he said, with a definite stress on that last word. "It's not my forte. But it's an occupational habit to watch and listen." That was expectedly impersonal, but after a pause, his jaw jumped. "And you never annoyed me, Pet."

Once again, it wasn't exactly a romantic declaration for the ages, but the statement was so bluntly candid—a handful of words that seemed totally outside of the playacting and pretense—that to her, it might as well have been a bloody Shakespearean sonnet.

"With the chatter," he added. "There are several other things you do that piss me the fuck off."

He was still poker-faced, but there was a glint in his eyes. It deepened into silent laughter as Pet pressed her hand to her chest and said with delighted fervor, as if they were exchanging the most fulsome of compliments, "Matthias, I feel exactly the same about *you*."

Sylvie had been watching them avidly, her smile growing. She couldn't contain herself any longer. "So, you two are—"

Pet had been reluctant to lie. Matthias saved her from having to commit herself aloud. He answered, short and gruff. "Yes."

She barely had time to blink before Sylvie pounced. Her sister-in-law flung her arms around her neck, and Pet staggered back a step under the force of the hug. A large hand touched the base of her spine, steadying her.

"I'm so happy for you," Sylvie said, lowering her voice to a whisper that wasn't as quiet as she obviously thought it was. "It's a lot sooner than I— Honestly, I didn't think he'd— And I didn't know you were— But this is so nice." She pulled back and beamed, the warmth of her personality cushioning that absolute jumble of half-formed sentences.

Pet managed to smile back, but guilt was fierce and prickly. There hadn't been time to form many expectations about any of this, but she hadn't anticipated quite so much enthusiasm.

Sylvie was not only eyeing her like a proud mama bear, but she looked about ten seconds from heading out to buy a hat for the wedding. She was an intelligent, shrewd woman, but there wasn't a shred of suspicion or doubt in her expression. And she was so *pleased*.

She turned her congratulatory hug on Matthias, then, and he reacted as if he'd been embraced by a koala. Could be a warm, fuzzy cuddle; could be the prelude to having his face clawed off. He stood frozen, before touching the fingertips of one hand to Sylvie's upper back and giving her a tiny, sad little pat in return.

Pet looked at Dominic. He was observing her in silence, but she could see it in his eyes—he knew something wasn't right.

It hovered in the air between them, and she waited tensely, but they *were* beginning to know each other well. His narrowed gaze communicated volumes. However, as she'd thought, he was reserving judgment for now.

When he did speak, it was merely to ask mildly, "What was it you wanted to show us? Presumably not Matthias."

Sylvie had apologetically released Matthias from the enthusiastic cuddle, and Pet felt the return of his protective warmth at her back. Reaching into her bag, she withdrew the doppelgänger photo and held it out.

Lifting that mobile brow once more, Dominic took it, scanning it with idle curiosity—and stiffened.

Matthias stood against the wall of the sweet-smelling annex, having declined Sylvie's offer of a chair and refreshments. His eyes were fixed on Pet's face as she spoke to her brother. He'd watched the man's cool, ascetic features closely, but there'd been zero signs of recognition. Dominic didn't have a clue as to the identity of the mystery look-alike. He was genuinely taken aback by the uncanny resemblance, baffled as to whom the woman could be.

Privately, Matthias had been concerned that Pet's brother might be concealing something, that she'd stumbled on an inevitable skeleton in the De Vere family cupboard. In his professional experience, most families—no matter how close—had buried secrets and betrayals. Dominic was obviously important to her, but if they'd only reconnected last year, the bond between the siblings was relatively new and fragile.

And—Matthias had never been able to tolerate seeing her hurt.

Shoving one hand into his pocket in an aberrant, restless motion, he felt something small and cold. The button that had fallen off Pet's dress. Absently, he ran his thumb around the pearlescent curve, playing with it.

"How old do you think this is?" Sylvie asked, studying the image with fascination.

"Judging by the clothes—thirty years, maybe?" Pet drank a

mouthful of tea and lowered her cup. "She looks around my age. So presumably my prototype is now—midfifties to midsixties?"

Sylvie grinned. "The return of Petunia De Vere, Baker Street's lost apprentice. I've missed her."

"She's like Sebastian," Dominic observed, a glimmer of humor cracking through his brooding caution.

Matthias didn't know the chef well, but he suspected they were on a similar wavelength right now, centered on growing concern for the woman seated at the small table, her hands tense around her teacup.

"Inquisitive, optimistic, and almost painfully intelligent?" Pet asked sweetly, and her brother's reluctant smile deepened.

"Nosy as hell."

Matthias snorted, and Pet scrunched her nose at him.

Christ, she was cute.

Her teeth sank into her lip as she stared back—and for a moment, he was back out on the street, lost against the silken softness of her mouth, the addictive sweetness of her elusive taste. The demanding clutch of her fingers fisted in his shirt; the sensual, playful touch of her tongue, teasing his own. An aching pulse in his blood. Raw desire, in its most pure form.

For fuck's sake.

His grip tightening around the button, he jerked his gaze away, staring at the array of decorated biscuits on the counter. He was one more heated glance and memory away from taking the Guard's motto of "outstanding and upstanding" to an entirely too literal level, six feet from the censorious eye of her older brother. Just to truly gild that gold-standard display of inappropriate thoughts and impulses.

He'd never been in a situation like this in his life.

Sex had always been something practical; physical and usually quite empty mutual pleasure—and once, years ago, a source of deep-buried degradation, realizing that the person in bed with him was attracted to his body and his uniform, but couldn't look at his face. He'd only been about twenty then. He'd recently taken the first disfiguring blow to already decidedly unpretty features and was young enough to still care about stares and snickers. That night had resulted in about three years of celibacy.

He no longer gave a damn what most people thought, but on the extremely infrequent occasions he slept with someone, it did lurk wryly in the back of his mind that his face was probably being mentally replaced with something a bit more appealing.

It all made for an experience he could easily forego—and it was all light-years apart from what had happened outside.

Just one kiss. A fucking *kiss*.

His skin was still almost—*vibrating* with tension, so sensitized that if she reached out and touched him now, he'd probably purr like his damn cat.

He'd spent over a decade honing his reflexes, wielding steely control over his body and mind. From the moment he'd realized where that bloody staff meeting was leading, he'd been formidably aware of the challenge ahead.

What he hadn't factored in, what would never have crossed his fucking mind, was the mutual desire in Pet's dazed eyes as she'd clung to his tie.

There'd been earlier moments, snatches of indrawn breath and quick glances, when he'd thought—he'd written it off as a combination of acting, projection, and Pet's naturally affectionate personality. She was touchy-feely with all her friends, and she'd made it clear from the beginning she wanted friendship from him. Before they'd butted heads over Johnny, at least, at which point she'd probably cut a new silhouette of his face and started throwing darts at it.

In the hot, pulsing seconds when that kiss had briefly deepened—tingling, heady, wet—it hadn't felt remotely fake—or tidily *friendly,* what had flared and sparked between them.

However, this wasn't a natural environment, and subsequently, reactions and impulses were likely to be heightened and influenced. There was always a buzz of adrenaline in a covert operation, even an unofficial, farcical one. A coiling energy that gathered in the spine and thrummed through the blood. Pet was likely feeling the same rush of nerves and epinephrine, possibly caught up in the elicit thrill of pulling off a con job, getting some subtle revenge back on the press who'd dragged her name through the mud.

If she weren't having to actually put it into practice with her killjoy colleague, he suspected that in theory, she'd get a kick out of the whole showmance deal. And if *he* weren't bound by continuing NDAs and professional ethics, he could tell her about several high-profile mock-relationships he'd witnessed firsthand. He knew of at least one full-on marriage that was entirely for show and always had been, and how vicariously fascinated she would likely be.

The atmosphere was lending itself to ideas of danger and sex. He didn't want to unintentionally take advantage of it or have her come out of this with regrets. Even the idea of it clawed nausea into his gut.

But when Pet cleared her throat, and his eyes returned to her face, he still had to clamp down every muscle against a tangible pull.

Her cheeks were slightly flushed as she said, with forced sound-ing lightness, "A babysitter did once say I was born with a magni-fying glass in one hand and an encyclopedia in the other. On the bright side, I look forward to the day I retire to a chic country cottage with a dozen guinea pigs and a hundred vintage dresses, and evolve into a higher-tech, better-dressed Miss Marple, peering at the neighbors through my telescope."

Sylvie laughed, but the seriousness had returned to Dominic's face. When he spoke, it was with a clear warning. "I have every respect for your abilities, Sherlock, but unless those boxes can magic up a birth certificate and current address to go with the photo, it may be difficult to find out who she is. As far as I'm aware, nobody in the family was much of a scribe, and we're a little short on living branches of the tree to fill in any genealogy gaps. And if it was taken decades ago, she may be dead." The addendum was both gentle and brutally blunt.

"I know," Pet said soberly, but as her gaze narrowed speculatively on the photo, Matthias could see various avenues playing out in her mind, flitting through her changing expressions. As a skilled researcher, she knew how many searches hit dead ends and were ultimately scrapped; real life unfortunately didn't play out as neatly as detective novels. As an incurable optimist, she'd try regardless, and her sister-in-law wasn't so easily discouraged, either.

"I wonder if it's a work function or some sort of community group," Sylvie mused. "Disobliging of them not to pose under a sign, isn't it?" She touched her fingertip to the photograph, peering more closely at it. "There is something on that bunting. In the middle. It looks like—"

"A crest," Pet said. "I think. Which does suggest an organization, but the only detail I can make out is the rose in the bottom left corner. I'll run a search on institutions and corporations using heraldic symbols and rose imagery tonight." She glanced at her brother. "Obviously it might not be much help even if we could identify the gathering—especially if it's just a small community group, thirty-odd years ago, in a fairly nondescript setting. It's probably not even still running."

There was a small silence.

"I did look into our genealogy," she said tentatively, as if she were venturing onto a conversational minefield. "Long before this. Aoife and Sebastian were both only children of only children."

Dominic nodded once. His eyes were still very watchful. He was playing with his wife's hair, sifting his fingers through it, rubbing and smoothing colorful strands with a distracted reverence, but his intent gaze didn't leave his sister.

"And in turn, they only had Mum." Pet didn't need to wait for her brother's confirmation this time. "That woman—we *must* be related, at least distantly. Even if it's true that we all have a doppelgänger somewhere, the photo was with Lana's things." Her fingernail found a loose sliver of wood on the tabletop, worried at it. "But—exactly. Biologically, it's just you and me. And Lorraine." She and Dominic made the same gesture with their mouths and brows, and momentarily looked extraordinarily alike. She seemed to have been trying not to look at Matthias, but those conflicted brown eyes flittered back toward him now. "There *are* no distant relatives. No extended family." She swallowed. "Not on the maternal side."

There it was. In light of those facts, the obvious implication hung over the small room like a specter, invested with years of unknown history. The scraps of information about her early life that she'd laid bare so far—they snicked together into the beginnings of an ugly picture, and Matthias was grimly wondering just how bad those missing pieces were.

When Pet had referred to her deceased stepfather, her clipped words had been imbued with so much disdain that he'd felt his hackles rise. Padraig had given him repeated shit about his protective instincts, and at this point, he couldn't deny it. He had little more than a name, he considered violence a last resort in all situations—and if it were possible to punch a poltergeist in the face, he'd still take five minutes alone with the prick whose memory alone could extinguish the dancing light in her eyes.

What she *hadn't* mentioned, what everybody seemed to be skating around in this tense, stop-start conversation, was a father. By the look on her face now, the whiteness of her knuckles as she clutched the photo Sylvie had returned, that absence was more than just verbal. In the face of that visceral, painful anxiety and—*hope*, Matthias compartmentalized his own preoccupations and reticence, his full focus on her.

Of course, technically, this was none of his business. A mocked-up romance and one kiss didn't entitle him to be privy to deeply personal revelations. He sure as hell didn't have the right to instincts that pressed him to both protect and comfort. Pet wasn't Johnny; Matthias wasn't her bodyguard, and she had at least a dozen people in her life she could turn to for any comfort required. His professional and personal creed for years had been to keep his nose out of other people's dramas and complications if it didn't relate to work—and bluntly, there'd been few people in whose lives he *wanted* to be involved.

He was satirically aware that none of that mattered a damn to his body and at least part of his mind, and he turned his head to encounter a renewed stare of calculated speculation from Dominic.

After a prolonged stare, the other man returned his attention to Pet. He seemed to be weighing his words. "It's been a while since you even mentioned your biological father, and you've never spoken of seriously seeking him out."

The silence returned as Pet said nothing for several moments. "When Gerald died," she said at last, slowly, "and Lorraine and I had the genetic tests to make sure we wouldn't get sick, too, I was genuinely shocked when I found out he wasn't my biological dad. So damn *relieved*, but I honestly hadn't expected it. I don't know why, really, considering he treated me and Lorraine very differently, so *he* may have known, instinctively if not for sure."

Something very dark crossed Dominic's face at those words, and Sylvie stood to slip her arm around him. Their bodies turned into each other automatically, in such an ingrained sense of support, an almost primal bond. Matthias ignored the rare jab of something a lot like envy.

"It gave me an entirely different level of closure over those years, that I could break that last link with him." Pet's mouth twisted. "I used to fantasize, when I was little, that he wasn't really my dad, that someday my real father would come. Yet, when I realized that there really *was* a 'real' dad out there, or had been, suddenly it wasn't even a factor. I doubted if Lana had known who he was. There was no chance of finding him, so there was no point even going there."

Her thumb moved on the photo, sliding to rest under the disconcertingly familiar face. "I probably won't be able to find her," she said. "But I have to look." Her eyes met Dominic's shuttered gaze, then—in a strangely natural movement that made something tighten in his chest, hard and fierce—she again turned toward Matthias, as if they really were the lovers they claimed, as if it were instinctive for her to seek comfort with him. "If there's a chance she's connected to my bio dad, that she might be able to tell me who he was, that I might have even a *name*, I have to try."

Chapter Nine

It was a reasonably quiet evening in Little Venice, but Pet could hear the clinking of plates and cutlery, and sporadic bursts of laughter from nearby restaurants. Lights were turning on in the narrow boats that berthed end to end along the stone embankment.

Walking at Matthias's side, she plucked a steaming-hot chip from grease-spotted paper and blew on it. Somehow, they *had* ended up at the canal to eat together, although they'd looked at the busy restaurants and simultaneously suggested takeaways from a food van.

She'd assumed it was just a line, after he'd told Dominic they were going out for dinner. Anyone trained in covert ops would be good at dropping those sorts of ordinary, minor details that added credence to falsehoods. But they'd both been starving by the time they'd left Sugar Fair. It had seemed wise to get some food before she succumbed to temptation and ate the entire bag of sweets she'd bought after a battle of wills with Sylvie, who'd tried to give her everything for free.

The peace of the waterway was exactly what she needed in the aftermath of everything that had happened today. It felt like she'd been through an emotional hurricane, battered from all sides. Listening to the cheerful, homey sounds and the cheeping of birds, she could feel some of the tension draining from her tired muscles.

However, she was still having to remind herself, every few bloody minutes at this point as their hands occasionally brushed, that Matthias *was* experienced at professional subterfuge.

Maybe he'd even had a pretend lover before, on a previous assignment. Maybe he'd given *her* hours-long tingles from a kiss, as well.

She scowled into the distance, and a passing jogger looked at her, startled.

Biting into the chip, she grimaced. She'd never been remotely sexually jealous in the past, over people she'd *actually* dated and full-on fucked, and now she was getting territorial about her fake boyfriend and his other theoretical fauxmances.

She might need to put in a request for some personal time off after this. Try some sort of mental wellness spa.

Matthias could come with her, her hopeless mind suggested cheerfully. They probably had massage oils at a spa.

Slamming down a gate on *that* thought route, she watched as a woman in overalls and a headscarf dropped into the hammock she'd strung along the deck of her floating home. With a drink in one hand, the woman opened her book and began to read, totally oblivious to them and the rest of London as it passed her by. In the next boat, another woman sat with her bare feet dangling over the side, lost in thought and humming softly as she stroked the back of a sleeping baby.

Empty benches along this part of the canal were the proverbial hen's teeth, but one was waiting for them under a sweeping willowy tree, near a small bridge. Pet arched her back in a long stretch as they sat down, enjoying the mildness of the breeze against her legs.

Matthias set the tray of food and sauces between them and handed her a paper napkin, and they watched a few hopeful gulls alight nearby as they ate.

He tossed the end of a chip and caused a small frenzy. "Could you live here?"

Pet tore off a bit of battered fish and threw it to the smallest bird. "I like the idea of it, but I think only because of a novel I read last year. A group of strangers and stray cats who created their own little neighborhood of houseboats."

He picked up another chip. "C. W. Tallen?"

"Yeah." She licked salt from her thumb, and his gaze dropped briefly to her mouth. Slowly, she lowered her hand. "I feel like the reality is probably less midnight feasts and love in the moonlight, and more moldy fixtures, septic tanks, and astronomical council tax." Crossing her legs, she swung one foot. "Anyway, I briefly experimented with a waterbed when I got my first flat. I felt sick every time I turned over, and the mattress burst during an intimate moment. Once you've had a night of, um, self-care suddenly turn into an amateur recreation of *Deluge*, the appeal of sleeping on water ironically dries up."

His flashing grin put a groove next to his mouth. She could see it even through the beard.

They looked at each other, until Pet had to lower her gaze to her food, her own smile playing around her mouth.

She sensed him still watching her. Setting aside the remains of her fish, she wiped her fingers on her napkin. "I'm sorry," she said, "that things got a bit—intense back there."

She was so attuned to the smallest of his movements that she heard the change in his breathing, felt the muscles in his thigh going rigid, just as she realized how that statement would be interpreted.

"The photo, I mean." Renewed heat flooded her cheeks as their eyes met. "Dragging you into my minor existential crisis, on top of—everything else."

He shook his head. In the waning light, she could see faint shadows under his lashes; the scar over his ear was a similar faded mauve, and she was caught by the impulse to lean up and touch her lips to it. Unlike the explosion of heat outside the bakery, this was a soft, gentle instinct, wrapping around her like a velvet ribbon, but again, that strange feeling of being in completely new territory.

Obviously, she *didn't* start randomly kissing his head without consent. Give her another week of this and she wouldn't hedge her bets, but she hadn't *yet* lost her mind.

"I get it." He *was* tired, too. His usually precise elocution was just slightly . . . smudged. Blurred and velvety. But his expression was clear, in every way. Far-sighted, straight to her inner turmoil and private thoughts, in a way that ought to have been uncomfortable and confronting, but felt—right. "Family," he said succinctly.

Yes. Family. She knew Dominic didn't share her feelings on this subject, even though they'd sprung from near identical roots. He'd genuinely never cared about the identity of his own father. And he was clearly worried what she might find if she turned over those particular stones. In his opinion, this was the quintessence of it being wiser not to rouse sleeping dogs from their decades-long nap.

Admittedly, if Gerald was anything to go by, their mother's taste in men didn't suggest that a storybook perfect papa was waiting in the wings.

"I don't need to look back," Dominic had told her last holiday season, when it had been late at night and they'd both had a lot of spiked eggnog. "I have Sylvie." He'd nudged her lightly. "You. The staff. The business. Humphrey."

He'd grinned at her expression at that last one, but sobered as he stared into the fire. At last, simply, he'd said, "It was a bleak road for a while there, but I'd walk it again to get where I am now."

He was happy. Truly, soul-deep content, and Pet was so glad for him that it made her heart physically hurt.

She remembered him turning his head, the flames flickering over his features. It had been a little jarring then, too, looking into eyes so similar to her mother's, but seeing love, affection, *peace* reflected back. "You're building your own happiness, too, Pet," he'd murmured. "You'll find the pieces of your own puzzle."

Before they'd left Sugar Fair, she'd told him about the diary she'd found in the box, tentatively, but his response had been calm and firm. He didn't want to read it. He didn't need to know. It would change nothing, excuse nothing, and he'd already found his closure where their past was concerned. It was today that mattered. Here. Now.

Shifting on the bench, she looked at Matthias. "It's not that I'm unhappy. Or feel like an incomplete person in myself. I've got the perfect career—even if Johnny *does* end up burning down the palace one day—and I love Dominic and Sylvie so much. I've got friends, a nice place to live, enough money. It's just—"

"The shadowy, frustrating hint of what could be," Matthias said, and the unexpected statement so entirely conveyed what she'd struggled to form in words. Her hair fell forward, brushing her cheek when she turned her head to look at him. "Like looking at a perfectly good picture, a scene that's almost right, that's . . . good enough, but seeing this elusive outline of what else there could be, that's never quite in focus enough to realize—"

He cut himself off. Something in his tone . . .

His gaze shuttered with his own thoughts. Then absolutely, totally absently, he reached out and smoothed back her tousled bob.

As his fingers touched the slightly pointed tip of her ear, Pet caught her breath—and his eyes came into focus. He flinched.

She drew back as his hand lowered.

"Sorry," he said, and it was her turn to shake her head.

"Do you see your own family often?" The question was unplanned, slipping out abruptly. She knew from experience that the most seemingly basic facts, the everyday check boxes on a form, sometimes covered the most painful parts of a person's life. Her Miss Marple tendencies did not extend to poking at personal and potentially difficult memories of someone she . . . cared about.

A short pause, before he responded, without visible emotion, that he'd grown up in the foster care system. He'd moved amongst multiple households, but his longest stint had been with a Mancunian family who'd worked and lived for several years in Ireland, in Limerick.

He was very matter-of-fact about it all, leaning forward and resting his forearms on his knees, staring across the canal, but Pet's eyes stung as she listened.

Lone wolf, that was what she'd thought about Matthias at first. Obviously close with Benji and on good terms with all his team, but still the most self-contained and self-assured man she'd ever met. She hadn't been able to imagine him truly *needing* anyone.

She'd never really let herself see him at all.

Pet had only lived in one house until she was eighteen, but she understood what Matthias *didn't* say, the feeling of being tolerated at best, invisible, more a temporary lodger than a member of the family.

And thinking about him as a child, a teenager, passed from one family to another, and none of them caring enough to even fucking *phone* him once in a while now . . .

She gritted her teeth as she forced away the prickling at her lashes.

"What happened to your parents?" she asked softly, watching his wide chest move with his deep inhalation.

"Common enough story. Unfortunately. Car crash. I was only about eight months old, so I don't remember them. No other relatives to take me in." He looked down at his loosely interlocked fingers. "I have a locket that was my mother's, with their photos."

"Do you look like them?"

Without lifting his head, he watched from the corner of his eye as she fiddled with a paper napkin. "My father was small and wiry, and my mother looked a bit like Sophia Loren—so, no," he added dryly.

His faint, self-deprecating smile faded when she said, from some place deep inside, "In the system—" Her voice was quite husky. "I'm sorry you weren't treated the way you deserved to be treated."

His shoulders were tense, but when he straightened, his expression wasn't what she'd expected. Guarded, yes, but not—not closed, exactly. There was a sort of . . . searching light there, and she touched her throat, absently rubbing where a knot had gathered.

"I suspect your opinion on what I deserve differs, depending on whether I've just stopped Johnny from skydiving for his birthday, or hidden the laser tag set." The ironic note sounded a little strained.

She looked down at his hands, where he circled one thumb around the other.

"Initially, they weren't the best years of my life, but it could have been considerably worse." His lips tightened. "I've crossed professional paths with enough escapees of the care system to recognize exactly how much worse."

A gull ventured closer, and he tossed another chip. "And everything changed after the move to Limerick."

"You liked it there?" She lifted her heel to the lowest rung of the bench, hooking her arms around her raised knee, and he inclined his head.

"Ireland, yes; Limerick itself, not particularly. We lived in an inner-city flat. It was an old, converted warehouse with all the original fixtures, which an estate agent would use as an excuse to hike the price an extra fifty grand, but just meant no insulation and windows that rattled in the wind. It would have been cramped even if I hadn't been six-four and twice my foster father's size by fourteen." Another ghost of a smile. "The moment I arrived to stay with them, my foster mother went to the supermarket to double their food stores."

Over their heads, a tree branch moved in the increasing breeze, casting more shadows along his cheek, so she wasn't sure if a muscle there had jumped or if it was an illusion of the light. "I spent a lot of weekends with a school friend's family. They lived—still live, most of them—in the countryside, in a big, rambling old house. Acres of grass and woodland. Horses. Dogs." He lifted his brows. "For a kid who'd always lived in cities, I felt like I'd fallen into a fucking Blyton book."

"Sounds like it could only be more teenage-boy utopia if your friend had a pretty sister," she teased lightly, and that groove appeared next to his lips again.

"He did. Two. Niamh was ten years older than me and Padraig, and happily married, and Jonna was fifteen and infatuated with the postman's son. He was eighteen, looked like a Ken doll, and regularly pretended he owned his dad's motorbike." Wryly, he said, "Even Padraig's good-looking friends wouldn't have had a look-in."

She looked at him for a moment. Then, very deliberately, she murmured, "Silly Jonna."

Matthias's fingers flexed once, hard, against his thigh. It was a few taut seconds before he turned his head again. He was close enough that she could have reached up and cupped his cheek, and her palm prickled as if the rough-softness of his beard were warming her skin. His eyes moved, a fleeting touch over each of her features before one long penetrating look, pinning her to her seat.

His pupils dilated, just a little.

Her hands clenched on splintery-feeling wood when he stood, his motion similarly jerky. He picked up the bundle of cold chips and oily paper.

"Are you finished?" The question was even.

Silently, she nodded. She rose from the bench as he distributed the remaining chips amongst the fighting birds. Combing her fingers through her hair, she tilted her hand to hide her face from view as they started walking again, heading without consultation for the bridge. She was pretty sure there was a lane on the other bank that led to a taxi rank.

Her skin was warm and flushed under her fingers.

It was probably wise of him to deliberately break that spell between them, and dial down the atmosphere, but it had left her feeling self-conscious and uncertain.

She was grateful for the distraction when, halfway across the bridge, she caught sight of a boat covered in ivy and fairy lights. "Isn't that The Page Portal bookshop? It's usually berthed closer to Paddington." Mindful of her high heels, she stepped onto the bottom rung of the railing to get a better look. "I've wanted to go for ages, but I haven't had time. Or made time," she admitted. Momentarily forgetting both her discomfort and her precarious position, she turned spontaneously to Matthias. "Do you want to have a quick look at—?"

She'd caught him in a frown, strange darkness in his eyes as he looked over her shoulder. Despite his preoccupation, one hand came to rest on the railing next to her, probably a kneejerk reaction after she'd already almost taken a header into the royal pond.

"Or not. It *has* been a really long day." She stepped down, and he took her hand, his arm steady as a rock until both shoes were back on solid ground. "Thanks. I think there's a taxi rank over there. At this time of day, it'll be way quicker than the apps."

She purposefully didn't look in the direction of the floating bookstore again once they'd crossed to the left bank, but without a word, Matthias walked on the other side of her and obliquely steered her toward it.

"Ignoring the fact that you're herding me like a sheepdog," she said, "honestly, let's just go home. I've already got so many books in my bedroom that I constructed a seven-foot tower one night, sat my alarm clock on top, and if anyone asks, it's a conceptual reimagining of Big Ben, inspired by the genius of Brooklyn DeWitt. Next time he judges the Westminster Art Prize, I'm entering it. But any new book purchases right now and the model will be approaching life-sized."

The front of The Page Portal was in view, the boat's pretty

wooden doors framed by the additional tables of books set up on the bank.

Matthias angled his head toward a table marked London Fiction. "Come on," he said. "C. W. Tallen also wrote a book where strangers and stray cats ended up renovating a seventeenth-century pub in Seven Dials. Instead of a romanticized view of life on a canal boat that ignores mold and expense licenses, we can read a fairy tale where you don't need to be an oligarch to buy a Covent Garden mews house."

"Cynics united, party of two," Pet murmured, letting herself be persuaded. "Dominic would be so proud."

"I thought you were one of life's optimists."

"I was." She admired a display of notebooks printed with Virginia Woolf quotes. "But my last boyfriend was a dick, I haven't had sex in so long I may have forgotten how to do it, and when I went to the supermarket on Tuesday, a single watermelon was almost six pounds and an old lady in the checkout line called me an undergrown whore." She turned her favorite notebook over to check the price. "This city is breaking me."

And she'd broken his carefully enforced impassivity, at least twice during that serene commentary.

He'd stopped walking at the sex disclosure, or lack thereof, but his brows went all fierce at her last grievance. It was lucky the supermarket lady wasn't on the canal this evening or she might have ended up *in* the canal.

Obviously, Matthias was a good person and very gentle unless someone was in active danger, so he wouldn't really do it, nor would she condone anyone drop-kicking a small-minded pensioner into quite stagnant looking water, but she was perverse enough to be warmed by his extreme annoyance on her behalf.

She propped the notebook back in place. "I wouldn't have fully ranked you amongst the world's pessimists, either."

He looked at the world through opposing lenses, of violence and danger, and of art and culture, loyalty and generosity. Life on this planet in all its ugliness and all its beauty. And even though he'd taken more knocks than most people, and she suspected she didn't know the half of it, he'd retained his compassion.

She suddenly remembered an incident back in March. There'd been a poor, frightened mouse in one of the palace assembly rooms. It had prompted a ridiculous amount of screaming and pandemonium, and more than one demand from guests for it to be shot at once. With an antique bow and arrow, no less.

Matthias and Benji had managed to catch the tiny baby, and she'd heard later that Matthias had driven out to a field and released it after his shift. Not just in one of the London parks—he'd taken it all the way out into the proper countryside.

Where hopefully it was now living in a little mouse house and best mates with a friendly squirrel.

"Since I started working with you and Johnny, one of my chest hairs turned white." He ran a hand over his scalp. "If I let much grow on my head, it'd no doubt follow suit. Once you've developed bleached pecs in your early thirties, all optimism is gone."

Pet's heels tapped cozily on the uneven wood as she walked up the ramp and into the boat. Matthias had to bend almost in half to get through the doors, but his head just cleared the ceiling inside.

"Lots of fiction," she said approvingly, looking up and around to take in every detail of the interior. The shop's absent owner had packed every inch of shelf and table space with books and little knickknacks. It would be a tight squeeze with more than a handful of visitors at once, especially when one of them could turn sideways and just about touch the walls with each massive biceps.

"Jenny's biased toward fiction." He ran a hand lightly along a row of embossed spines. "It was almost the boat's official motto—open a newspaper if you want dismal reality; fall into a story and dream instead."

"Jenny?" Pet looked up from an old, tattered edition of *Winnie-the-Pooh* that smelled like must and dust, and libraries and happiness. "Do you know the owner?"

A woman pushed through the doors, holding a cup of ice cream. She had loads of light brown hair, flushed cheeks, and very pretty hazel eyes. She stopped dead when she saw Matthias—then a wide smile lit up her whole face and she was suddenly beautiful.

She pushed the ice cream cup onto the nearest shelf, took two steps forward, and wrapped her arms around his neck.

"Hello, *deartháir*," she said in a slightly thick voice.

His posture was rigid at first, seemingly little more comfortable than he'd been in Sylvie's hug, but when the stranger exhaled shakily, he ran his hand down her hair in a single reassuring stroke.

Her own hand tightening on the side of her book and her toes digging into the soles of her shoes again, Pet stood watching the embrace. Her heart had done a sickening little jump and was pattering away like she'd just sprinted the full length of the waterway. Tension coiled, slithering and hissing into every muscle.

It caught her breath, the innate, illogical, irrational . . . *passion* of it.

She'd been mostly joking earlier, about her first toe-dip into sexual jealousy, but there was nothing of light internal banter about this feeling. It was a swift and ugly education, and she didn't like any aspect of it, or herself much in that moment.

Matthias's eyes met hers over his . . . friend's shoulder, and she saw something flash in his eyes. Flicker between his brows. His shoulders flexed as he reached up and caught the woman's hands in his own. Gently, he unwound her arms from his neck and gave her fingers a small squeeze before he released her. "How are you, Jenny?"

Jenny's eyes were wet. "Sorry. I forgot you don't do hugs." Her Irish accent was a strong lilt. She swiped at her lashes. "Good," she said. "I'm . . . I'm doing good."

Matthias said nothing, but somehow the fractional tilt of his head was extremely communicative, and Jenny seemed to have the translation key for the Matthias Code. Her mouth twisted.

"It's his birthday tomorrow," she said, and he nodded, suddenly painfully expressionless. "In a few weeks, it's the anniversary of our first date. Endless reminders and ghosts of celebrations, you know? I'm glad to remember. I hope I always do. But on those days, it's still like being punched in the gut."

"I know." Matthias's voice was deep and very controlled, but a rasp was breaking through. "I'm sorry. I was going to come and see you tomorrow."

"I'm going back to Ireland in a couple of weeks to spend some time with my family. Both families." She paused. "Niamh said they haven't seen you for months."

Just perceptibly, his mouth tautened. "No. Things have been busy. I need to call Grace."

"Prepare for a lecture," she said, lifting her brows. "Grace expects all her fledglings to check in regularly. You know the McCarthys. Much nicer than a gang, but a similarly permanent deal. Once you're in, you're a lifer."

His lips turned up, but the smile didn't reach his eyes.

Jenny studied him with obvious worry.

"If we say it enough times, will it sink in?" she asked very softly. "Will it finally matter? They don't blame you, Matthias. They don't associate that—that night with you. They—" She swallowed. "*We* all look at you and remember him as he was. The good times. The *best* times."

Pet's heart was still beating too quickly, in hard thuds, but that fierce twist of senseless, unfounded jealousy had altered swiftly into sympathy and concern. The implications of the exchange were clear.

Matthias's darkened gaze returned to her face—and suddenly, he reached out his hand.

She didn't hesitate. Her breath drawing in and catching, she slipped her fingers into his. *Around* his. She squeezed tight in a probably futile attempt at comfort. Support. When he drew her against his side, she felt the incredible tautness of his body. His muscles were locked down so hard that his arm moved in a barely perceptible quiver; it was like lying against a big cat and feeling the low vibration of a deep, silent purr, but there was no contentment behind it.

Her caution and self-consciousness were wiped out in one stroke in that moment. She felt nothing but his emanating tension and pain. Looking up at him, at the rigidity of his jaw, she rubbed her thumb in slow circles over his fingers and dropped her shopping bag to curl her other hand around his wrist.

She didn't know if this was part of the charade, if he'd only reached for her as an afterthought, to play the game in front of his clearly bereaved friend.

Right now, she didn't care.

Jenny was looking at her closely. There was no dismay in the other woman's body language, not a trace of jealousy or resentment in her expression. All Pet saw was that deep sadness, overlaid with stirring curiosity and . . . perhaps pleasure.

She returned Jenny's hesitant smile, and Matthias's hand momentarily tightened on hers.

"Jenny, this is Pet De Vere," he said. "Pet, this is Jenny Byrne. Jenny owns The Page Portal. She opened it when she was just twenty-two, and obviously it's become a tourist hotspot."

For a second, he sounded like a proud dad.

"That's not De Vere like the patisserie, is it?" Jenny asked after a short pause, and her eyes lit up when Pet explained the connection. "I love your brother's chocolates. I buy a big box at the start of each month."

She nodded at the book in Pet's hands. "If you're interested, there's a really beautiful illustrated edition of *Cinderella* by the same publisher. It's on the shelf over there by the *Pride and Prejudice* dolls."

Pet was interested. She was also interested in the Elizabeth and Darcy dolls, and this was likely to prove an expensive "browse."

She walked over and bent down to look. There were several other books she fancied.

As she started making a little pile, Jenny spoke to Matthias in a low murmur. Pet tried not to listen, giving them some space, but it was a small boat. She couldn't help overhearing when Jenny said, so very quietly, "I've met someone."

There was so much in those three words. Hesitancy. Fear. Guilt. And a gentle thread of the most tentative happiness.

Pet found herself tensing, waiting for Matthias's reaction, but his profile had softened and there was firm certainty in his response. "I'm glad," he said, and more tears sprang to Jenny's eyes.

"So am I," she whispered. "But—"

One aching syllable. Pet felt a returning sting in her own eyes.

"It's been over three years, Jenny." Matthias's voice slowed as he spoke, as if it were really registering for him, as well. He cleared his throat roughly. "He wouldn't want you to be alone. He sure as hell wouldn't want you to be unhappy. If he—or she—is good to you and brings back some happiness, I promise you, it's exactly what he'd want."

A tear slid down the side of Jenny's nose. She pressed the side of her fingers hard above her mouth and looked up for a moment to regain some composure. "I know. I know he would." Fresh tears welled up and spilled over, and she tried to catch them with her hands, touching the tip of her tongue to the corner of her mouth. "God. I'm sorry. I just— Oh god, just then, for just a moment, it was like h-he was here."

He nodded again, a bare inch of movement. "I know."

In two words, Pet had the sense of days, months, years, a thousand moments.

There was a box of tissues on a back shelf, and Matthias pulled out several. Pushing back all her gorgeous thick hair, Jenny took them, scrubbing fiercely at her face.

"I am going to be happy again. I can see that and really believe that now. I'm . . . I'm getting there. And it is a 'she.'" She plucked at the tissues, tearing a shred from one. "We met last year. In some ways, they're complete opposites, which . . . makes it easier, somehow. But b-both so kind. Smiles that light up a room."

She released another breath through pursed lips, obviously trying not to cry again. Pet looked down blindly at the book in her hands, feeling as if she were intruding.

Not before she saw Jenny reach out and squeeze Matthias's

arm. "It's made my day, though, seeing *you* with someone special. He'd be so happy, too." Her laugh was a little watery, but genuine. "He was so sure that one day some girl was going to turn your life upside down, and wrap you around her little finger, and light you up like a Christmas tree. He couldn't wait to rip the shit out of you for it."

Heavy silence.

Beneath Pet's fingertips, the lovely illustration of Cinderella danced with her Prince Charming, the latter a stark reminder of Codename Charming and why she and Matthias were here right now.

It's temporary, it's not real.

It's not supposed to be real.

Even in her own mind, it sounded increasingly hollow and unconvincing.

When she brought her pile of purchases to the counter, Jenny took a peek at each title as she rang them up and slipped them into a pretty cloth bag. "A woman after my own heart."

Hunting through her bag for her wallet, Pet temporarily put a stack of flyers Sylvie had given her on the counter. They were advertising the Woodland Witch-Fest, the annual magic festival in Hannigan's Wood. Sylvie and Jay had apparently run a Sugar Fair pop-up there for the past few years to promote the Dark Forest, their basement bar where cocktails were mixed in steaming cauldrons. She'd asked if Pet could put a few flyers in the St. Giles staffrooms.

Jenny scanned the text on the topmost card with interest. "Oh, I've always meant to check this out. Leave some here if you like. Loads of my customers would love it."

When they left the boat, the dinnertime lull was ending. A large group stood waiting for them to exit the ramp, and more people were drifting over from the surrounding restaurant terraces to peruse the outdoor tables.

The sky was rapidly dimming, the night starting to come alive with streaks of pink and orange edging the clouds. Pet breathed in the scent of the sweet peas and orange blossom Jenny was growing.

Swinging the handles of her book bag, she reached for the book Matthias had bought. "I'll put that in with mine until we get home if you want."

He gave it to her, then stole both bags the moment she'd slipped it inside.

On a startled, laughing protest, she swiped for them as they moved to get out of the way of the increasing crowd. "As predicted, I went completely overboard on the books. That bag's quite heavy, and I don't expect you to act as my personal trolley."

He staggered under the weight in an exaggerated stoop, before straightening and continuing to carry the bags with perfect ease. On one finger.

"Now you're just rubbing it in for the rest of us puny mortals," she said, grinning. She was glad to see that some of the tense lines around his eyes and mouth had relaxed since they'd disembarked into the dusk.

"I could carry you as well as your bags and still wouldn't classify it as anything close to heavy," he said, and she bit back an enthusiastic acceptance of that non-offer.

She'd been walking on four-inch heels for hours, quite a bit of that time on cobblestones, and his hair-dusted arm looked extremely inviting. She would have no objections at all to perching against his shoulder like a lazy spider monkey flagging a lift.

As they turned toward the lane, a winding brick path between an architectural office block and a Japanese restaurant, Matthias swore under his breath. His arm slid behind her back, not quite touching her, and for a second, she wondered if she was going to be slung over his shoulder after all.

Fortunately, her brain cells weren't *all* swooning around in a tide of dopamine and lust. On a breath, she said close to his lowered jaw, "Paps?"

"Apparently, they don't have anything better to do tonight, although we did smooth the way by coming to Little Venice. We're only about two minutes from Araminta." The newest members' club, a celeb-spotter's paradise, which would be swarming with photographers at this hour. "Photographer hovering near the restaurant menu board."

They were angling into each other as they walked, movements that felt strangely smooth now, almost practiced, as if they'd been choreographing this routine for hours. When his lips unintentionally brushed her earlobe, she steadied herself against his chest. Her index finger accidentally slipped between the buttons of his shirt, grazing the warm skin of his chest.

The taxi rank was on the busy street directly at the end of the lane, and she could already see from the midway point that it was empty. In silent communication, they stopped, remaining within the dubious privacy of the lane, albeit with an entire wall of three-story windows behind them and potentially dozens of architects working late and watching them cuddle by the hedge.

Pet realized how much she was leaning into him and straightened a bit, but they remained close. She wasn't sure if the photographer would have the balls to openly walk down the lane after them; there'd be no question if it were the Bulldog, but at least some of the paps would balk at confronting Matthias directly. In this instance, it was quite handy that he scared them shitless.

Despite the prickles where their skin connected, she felt as if they were exchanging mutual, rueful amusement.

"Nice night," Matthias said, his hand on her waist and head dipped down to her own.

If she moved about half an inch, she could rub her nose against his.

"Mmm," she agreed. "Definitely starting to get darker earlier, though. Autumn on the way. My favorite season."

"Mine, too. Are your feet sore?"

She returned her raised foot to the cobblestones. She'd been subtly trying to lift one and then the other, giving each a little break. "I love these shoes, but after ten hours, the Cinderella enchantment wears off and they turn back into medieval torture instruments."

He shot a look around the lane, but if he was checking for a place to sit, she'd already glumly noted the lack of benches. There was a brick podium supporting a brass sculpture, but she'd dismissed it as too high. With the national tabloids skulking about the place, she had no intention of being caught doing some amateur rock-climbing in stilettos and probably flashing her bum in her fourth-best underwear.

Matthias scanned it. "Do you want a boost?"

Her nod was more taken aback than agreement, but he set down the bags. His other hand went around her waist, and he lifted her carefully onto the podium. It put them almost on eye-level, although she had to tilt her head downward, an extremely rare occurrence even when her companion was only average height.

She swung her feet, enjoying the blissful relief of pressure on her soles and toes. Her groan might have been slightly too orgasmic, because his lashes flickered, and his hand tightened on her waist before he let her go.

In the dying sunlight, his profile was a beautiful intricacy of hard lines and soft curves. When his dark lashes touched his cheek, she saw that the very tips were lighter, almost gold. There were emerging shadows beneath those gold flecks, carving fatigue into his face.

"Jenny seems nice," she said quietly, and watched his lashes sweep upward, netting her back in that intense green.

"She is. Very." Resting one arm against the podium, he hooked his hand around the back of his neck, rubbing at the muscles there. Gruffly, he said, "And gentle. Quiet. Nothing like Padraig in some ways, but he was—all in, right from the beginning."

His biceps flexed where his sleeve strained around his bent arm. "He said he knew she was it for him, that she was his and he was hers, the moment he met her." Their eyes held. "He was the last person you'd expect to believe in that."

When she'd heard the name Niamh, Pet had realized the McCarthys must be the family he'd talked about. His close school friend, with the idyllic, rambling country home and the pretty sisters. And the lover with beautiful hazel eyes and a shattered heart.

She leaned forward, her hands propped against the brickwork. Matthias's hand rested near hers. "Jenny was in love with your friend from Limerick. Your best friend."

Matthias's gaze turned inward. She didn't think he even noticed his thumb was lightly stroking the pearl bracelet around her wrist, a gift from Dominic and Sylvie on her last birthday. They'd joked that if she was going to live in a palace, she needed some real pearls. "Best mates at school, since we were fourteen. Still friends at twenty-four after we joined the King's Guard." His chest moved with his even breaths. "He'll never make it to thirty-four."

Pet's grip tightened on the edge of the podium. "How did he die?"

She spoke so softly that the question was almost carried away by the faint breeze.

Matthias's fingers closed into a fist against the bricks. "He was murdered."

The words fell between them like a cracking stone. In his eyes, buried deep within, she saw the terrible hollowness.

Wordlessly, carefully, she touched his shoulders, her palms resting in the dips of his underarms. They stayed there like that for a moment, looking at each other.

Then she wound her arms around his neck and held him tightly.

For a moment, he stood as still and upright as he had in Jenny's embrace, but as she started to draw away, his hand touched her back. His fingers spread against her ribs, his thumb moving in a small half-moon shape—and his other arm slipped around to enclose her in the warmest, safest circle. He was hard and solid, his body almost enveloping hers, and she breathed in the sunshine and soap and cedar scent of his skin. His chin rested against her temple, and his hand came up slowly to stroke her head. Pet closed her eyes.

Music turned on somewhere, a deep bass vibration that thrummed through her body like a heartbeat.

"I'm so sorry," she whispered, and his arm flexed against her.

The tempo of the music changed, slowing, melancholic and moody, a different song.

He held her as if she were made of the finest porcelain, something delicate and perfect—but with a palpable sense of restraint, the repeated faint press of his finger pads as if he . . . *coveted*. Like she was something he'd been told to handle carefully, to guard, when really, he wanted to snatch.

She lifted her head, pulling back to look searchingly down into his face, and her hands slipped back down to his chest. His fingers curled lightly around her wrist.

Pet's breathing quickened, her thigh muscles tensing, as she saw a reflection of her own confliction. His lips parted as if he were going to speak—and then his grip tightened on her.

Heart hammering, she made a tiny sound on a scrap of a sigh.

This was probably such a bad idea.

As she touched his jaw in a featherlight stroke, he tugged her arm back around his neck. She didn't know if she fell forward or he dragged her into him, but her wrists entwined behind his shoulders and her hair fell across his cheek as their mouths collided.

Her little half hiccup, half kind of . . . *moan* was just audible against his lips as the kiss deepened, tongues tangling—frantic silken wet—and in turn, he sort of *growled* low in his throat when she cupped his cheeks with both hands, curving her body over his.

They kissed—and kissed—and kissed, heads changing angle to explore each other's mouths, breaths snatched in bare millimeters of separation.

Their little fingers brushed and entwined for the space of a blink, and it spiraled out of control as quickly as that.

Her dress had ridden up as her legs moved restlessly against the podium, instinctively trying to wrap around him, pull him in, and his hand slipped under her knee, pulling it aside so he could press closer to her. She could feel the warmth of his palm through the rumpled silk, agitating the sensitive skin on her inner thigh, and her hips wriggled, trying to arch against him.

At this point, she'd fall straight off the podium if he suddenly drew back, but her mind was beyond caution, and he simply pulled her farther down onto him. He was obviously innately aware of his strength—still gentle, his body cradling hers as he supported her weight, but he no longer touched her like she might break. His lips and hands were as demanding as her own, and she loved it.

Under the pads of her thumbs, his beard was raspy, sending a shiver down the full length of her spine when he tore his mouth from hers long enough to kiss her cheek, her neck, lingering under her ear. A tiny bite that liquified her bones. She rolled her head against his, kissing his jaw, and met the renewed, urgent thrust of his tongue when his lips returned, her legs shifting again against the hard bricks.

She was increasingly uncomfortable, hot and flushed, and would have sacrificed a lot to have a king-sized bed within tumbling distance. Or at least a couch. And preferably no scandalized architects. She hadn't entirely forgotten where they were right now—just . . . mostly—and she didn't know what the hell had happened to her inhibitions. Apparently, they'd fled with every harsh snatch of breath.

At the sound of very close footsteps and light laughter, their mouths parted, her lower lip catching and tugging under his upper one, separating with a light *pop*. Pet drew in another shaky breath, drawing her wet lip between her teeth. She'd slid right forward, and Matthias was holding her up; as they stared into each other's dark, dilated eyes, he lifted her the rest of the way off the podium and lowered her until her heels touched the cobblestones.

Her legs were trembling, and she held on to him as she regained her balance. She had a feeling she'd soon be having quite a *lot* of thoughts, but at present, she'd gone into a kind of lust-hazed, sexually unsatisfied lizard-brain.

Basically, just a scrolling news banner of "Matthias Vaughn: Hero of the King's Guard. Absolute motherfucking champion kisser."

She was in a public lane in Little Venice, with only two layers of thin silk between the world and her hard nipples.

The sensible side of her mind was jumping up and down, all but waving placards to get her attention, but the romantic, masochistic side just nudged her impatiently, winked hornily, and projected an image of climbing Matthias's body like a fireman's pole and picking up where they'd left off.

"What shall we say? 'Cheese' or 'just get a room'?" a woman called with amusement, and Pet jerked around in time to have her photo taken.

Belatedly, she put her arm over her chest, and wondered why she'd bothered. She'd probably just been photographed with her tongue curled around Matthias's back molars. It was ridiculous to worry about modesty now.

The painfully young paparazzo grinned at them with dimples in her freckled cheeks. "Thanks," she said. "I was about to pack it in for the day, but this lot'll pay for next week's food shop. I've got half a dozen blogs looking for pics of you two, the more PDA the better." She slipped her camera into her bag, dropping the crossbody strap casually over her head, and pulled a business card from her pocket. Bending, she propped it against a rock. "I'll just leave this here. If you're planning to dry hump His Royalness in public as well, do a chick a favor and tip me off. *Those* shots would cover my rent for six months."

She flitted off like a little dragonfly, and Pet turned slowly back to Matthias. Whom she technically hadn't been *dry humping*. Possibly because she'd been perched on a huge pile of bricks and it had been logistically unfeasible, but still. These people ought to have *some* sense of journalistic ethics and accuracy. Running her fingers roughly through her hair, she rested her forearm against her head.

"God," she said huskily. "Is the *Digital Star* recruiting from schools now? She looked about twelve."

Matthias had tensed, as if intending to follow the girl, but he stopped after one step.

Probably remembering, as she was, that this was exactly what was supposed to happen. Technically, the tabloids were falling straight into the trap.

Because again, and louder for those in the back row, this was supposed to be a calculated deception.

She wasn't meant to have shaking knees.

Matthias had leaned back against the podium. He was *slouching* in public. Almost more monumental than the not-quite dry humping.

A slightly hysterical laugh was building in her chest, but any sense of humor about all this was long gone. The last light wisps had crumbled to dust, crushed in a gut-deep, tight fist, as she'd helplessly witnessed the lingering impact of his grief over his friend. His stolen family. That all-consuming feeling, that compulsion to touch, to comfort, none of that had been for the fucking papers. It made her feel a bit sick even thinking about it.

With one hand behind her, she found a stone beam between all the modern glass and dropped back against it.

A group of businessmen had just left the Japanese restaurant down the lane. Clearly filled with high spirits and sake, the men walked between them with plenty of back-slapping self-congratulation.

Pet touched her fingertips to her mouth, feeling a slight sting where she'd scored the inside of her bottom lip against her teeth. Her body still hummed from the touch of his hands and mouth—and as she watched, her stomach sinking, Matthias pushed away from the podium, his back and shoulders straightening.

The grim mantle of responsibility, of *duty*, dropping back into place.

But as he adjusted his tie, he couldn't hide the whisper-fine tremor in his thick fingers.

She had the very strong sensation that her own fingers were being pried off a metaphorical steering wheel, one by one, and she was heading onto a road where she had no tangible control. No idea where it would end.

Or how bad the collision might be.

Chapter Ten

It was unavoidable, when he lived at his job, that work/life boundaries would sometimes tangle.

By Saturday night, the boundaries were a fucking Gordian knot.

Matthias found it impossible to relax his guard as he sat in an unmarked palace car, for once a short distance behind the cavalcade transporting Johnny and Rosie to the West End, instead of having them in his direct line of sight. Surrounded by the usual trappings of an official outing, it was muscle-memory to scan the vicinity for threats—and his protective instincts were in hyperdrive, focused not only forward but on the woman at his side.

Who was technically his job tonight. And vice versa.

A fact that sat in his stomach like sour milk, no longer just a form of singularly unique self-flagellation but fundamentally *wrong.* As if, even though this whole thing was primarily to salvage her reputation, he *couldn't* mentally reduce her to the status of a professional pawn, a task to be ticked off, that it was somehow betraying her even to think that way.

He was losing his mind. And he was going to be ticked off with himself in an entirely different way if he fucked this and she suffered the consequences.

He shot her a sideways glance. He was obviously losing sight of the big picture here—but it was hard to keep it clear when they were crossing more lines than a scribbling toddler. When he'd been dressing tonight, he'd tried to salvage a few tattered shreds of self-preservation, drag this back into the realms of something remotely appropriate.

Slim fucking chance, when he couldn't even keep his eyes off her, let alone his hands.

He felt as if he were balancing on a tightrope, trying to be convincing enough to persuade outside eyes, while still protecting them both.

She shifted on the leather seat. Her skirts were fluffed around her, the layered black netting of her evening dress sparkling with an odd, scattered sequin, feet neatly crossed in her lethally high heels.

It was asking for trouble, balancing a precious human body on a pair of expensive toothpicks, and he was constantly worried about her ankles.

They'd be safe propped on his lap. *Or digging into his back.* He crushed that taunting inner voice.

And curled his hand against the impulse to touch his thigh, where another of her high heels had left a faint mark when her legs had hugged his waist, her hips seeking and rubbing against him, that husky little cry in her throat . . .

He'd tried to suppress the memories from the lane last night, although he'd eventually given up and allowed himself relief, removing an affronted Miriam from his room because he couldn't fuck even his own fist with his cat watching disapprovingly. It had been disturbingly hollow, unsatisfying pleasure.

Desire-hazed moments flooded back, rushing into his mind and blood.

Tingling electricity coiling around his spine. Instead of jarring him back to reality—to sanity—a growl rose low in his chest, breath broken, his body hardening.

Pet's mouth opening eagerly against his, her tongue a playful, satiny rub, electrifying every nerve ending. Fingers cupping his cheeks, sliding around his ear, stroking over his shaven hair. Gripping onto him as if he were her anchor, or she his, their hands and lips and bodies pressing closer.

As she fell forward onto him, warm, welcome pressure, his hand found the curve of her knee, tracing the knob of bone there—skin softer and silkier than her dress, which wrapped around their legs, entwining them like the cool, sensual sheets of a rumpled bed.

Fuck. Matthias purposefully dug his fist into the site of the small bruise now, hoping a bite of pain would offer some distraction. Even as a hormone-driven teen, he'd had more control over his body.

But the physical side, he could handle. No pun intended.

It was in everything else that he was adrift in unknown territory. He was both cherishing and loathing the sensation.

And dreading the aftermath, when all this was over, and they had to return to some semblance of their usual working dynamic. No more slick little tongue teasing his, or warm fingers squeezing his hand, or Pet's palm cradling his head against her, as if she were trying to absorb some of his lingering grief into her own body. Like she didn't have enough of her own past pain to deal with.

"We're eighty people over the max limit for the Rose Room," Pet said into her phone, thankfully unaware of the turn his thoughts had taken, "which would be a fire safety violation even if the Clarences' stodgy aides were prepared to bend protocol, but the neighboring ballroom has a removable wall—"

She paused, her pen scratching as she jotted down fast scribbles on the notepad she'd pulled from her bag. She'd been taking a series of calls since they'd left the palace, dealing with the latest admin crisis. By the sounds of it, half her team had come running to her in a panic.

Another quick scratch of her pen. "If we put up the marquee in the camellia gardens, we can open with drinks and music first, keep everyone outside until at least half eight."

She glanced at Matthias, with a sudden, irrepressible hint of mischief. "Although if there's dancing, we might have to ask Johnny's PPOs to stop him reattempting the Worm. He's got a heavy schedule for the rest of the year and really needs all his vertebrae intact."

He was glad to see that return of her natural flirty devilry. She'd been unusually solemn today whenever their paths had crossed, and no matter what happened between them, it was just—unacceptable, an unhappy Pet.

But as she ended her call, the amusement left her eyes, leaving their expression for once opaque and hard to read. In the past, she'd worn most of her emotions as transparently as if an invisible hand were writing them in ink across her face.

Her lashes flickered, and she sank her teeth into her upper lip. Started to say something. Hesitated.

Her hand had come down to rest on the seat, almost touching his own, and they both lowered their eyes. His fingers moved reflexively, and a tremor went through hers.

Clearing his throat, he inclined his head at her phone. "Crisis sorted?" His voice was rough.

She nodded slowly. "This one, at least. Apparently, there's a new story about me and Johnny in the *Digital Star* this afternoon. The Bulldog's convinced he's on the track of a massive cover-up." They glanced at each other, and neither of them pointed out that, for once, he wasn't entirely bullshitting. Although to be strictly accurate, it was a calculated diversion, not a cover-up. Pet rolled her eyes. "He fancies himself as a legit investigative journalist. Next, he'll be claiming the Duchess of Clarence is the Whitechapel cat burglar and trying to tie the whole thing to some sort of wider corruption. I bet he's already picked out who he wants to play him in the film adaptation, once he definitively proves that I'm secretly shagging Johnny, and that this thing between you and me—"

A flush crept up her neck. "His articles are running concurrently with the . . . video, which is on basically every other site, so—I think a lot of the people following this narrative are just confused at this point."

Matthias wasn't surprised.

The people *driving* the fucking narrative were confused.

Pet's cheeks deepened to a shade closer to scarlet. They hadn't yet discussed the video, although half the palace had been murmuring about it behind their hands all day.

They'd expected the infant photographer's spying snaps, which had dutifully appeared online before they'd even arrived home from Little Venice. Slightly more of a surprise to wake up today and find that someone in the architecture firm had filmed the whole thing in high definition, and obviously sold it to the gutter press once they'd realized it had cash value.

Nice that the wider community was getting involved.

Matthias had caught a few seconds of the video before he'd had to accompany Johnny to a meeting in Camden, and the amateur film editor had even added a backing soundtrack and special effects. They were writhing against each other behind a pinkish-purple haze that transferred a mottled cast to their skin, as if they'd turned blue from lack of oxygen, and for some reason, cartoon birds now circled Pet's head. It looked like she was under attack, while Matthias totally ignored her imminent demise by rabid budgie in order to suck on her neck, but presumably, their unknown pornographer had been going for the romantic fairy-tale angle. Playing up the "Beauty and the Beast" narrative that the bloggers had apparently locked on to hard.

They hadn't talked about anything that had happened yesterday. He'd been called back to work last night—not that they'd likely have lingered in Little Venice, regardless. After almost having a fully clothed orgasm in public, it would have been rather anticlimactic to drop by a café for a placid cup of herbal tea. They'd both been a bit beyond speech in the taxi, and this was the first time they'd been alone today.

Frankly, he'd never felt less inclined to talk, but this was an assignment, and when undertaking a task, he regularly debriefed. No pun intended. It was protocol.

At least *some* of his behavior ought to stick within professional lines. "I'm sorry," he said abruptly, and the atmosphere in the car immediately altered. It was as palpable as a physical change in temperature. Pet didn't move or look at him, but her fingers were tight around her phone. "Things are—"

Getting completely out of control. He'd always been acutely aware of his surroundings, but last night, there'd been a point when that damned photographer could have come and sat cross-legged within two feet of them without interrupting.

Pet lifted her head, catching his grimace. "I—" She cleared her throat. "I guess nobody on the team can say we aren't doing our part."

"No. Although I doubt they were expecting quite so much dedication to duty."

Her eyes suddenly met his directly, and he saw a hint of something searching and *wanting* and worried, that made him want to drag her onto his lap.

Christ.

"Any kind of—mission," he said, wrapping a mental fist around his rapidly fraying control, "comes with its own brand of adrenaline, and that can provoke feelings, reactions, that a person wouldn't experience under normal circumstances."

He could actually see the complete physical withdrawal in Pet, then. It was as if she'd slammed a door in his face that he hadn't been consciously aware was open.

"So, you—" She spoke with tangible reluctance, as if she didn't really want to hear the answer. "You *have* done this kind of thing before? K-kissed someone on an assignment and—"

What?

"No." His reaction was forceful, a gut-deep rejection. "Christ, no. I've never done anything remotely like this."

With a sudden snort, he added, "And if you're imagining my military years were like a misogynistic espionage film, nobody's casting me as some womanizing dickhead with a gun and badge. I'd probably be the villain's henchman, silently cracking my knuckles in the background."

Pet's shoulders had relaxed, and he even saw a small smile emerging, but he didn't miss the pale pink flush in her cheeks. Wryly, he wondered if she'd already had a similar thought.

Seriousness returned. "I'm meant to be protecting your interests. Not taking advantage of—"

"Your professional responsibility is to Johnny, not to me," Pet cut in resolutely. "Nobody with a brain would doubt your integrity, Matthias. There's no question of taking advantage." Her blush deepened, but she held his gaze. "I wasn't expecting any of this, and I don't—I don't know if . . ." She swallowed. "But it should be pretty clear that it's mutual."

He was silent. No—after the visceral honesty of those moments in the lane, he couldn't just put her side of it down to adrenaline and propinquity, not anymore.

He still didn't know what she was thinking—on several levels— but the physical desire, the sexual attraction, it was raw and real, and for now, mutually intense. Apparently, miraculously, they were scrambling about, in heady, cautious wonder, on the same page there.

In other respects, they weren't even in the same fucking book.

Pet's thumb jerked on her phone, and the music of their ironically not-safe-for-work video blared out. Jumping, she muted it and glanced at Michael, their driver, but he'd pointedly put up the privacy screen when he'd joined them in the car. Apparently, he'd been online today, as well.

Automatically, Matthias looked down at the screen, where the scene in the lane was somehow even more sexually charged in the total absence of sound.

Every time he breathed, he inhaled the scent of Pet's perfume—a different fragrance tonight from her usual, a deeper scent that made him think of moonlit paths, heady flowers. Sex. "Interesting choice of filter."

It was her turn to snort. "We look like horny Smurfs."

When she wasn't driving him mad in more ways than one, she could make laughter spike inside him even on his worst days, but the amusement died as he watched his hands slide up the curve of her waist, pull her into his body. Yesterday-Pet's lashes fluttered as his tongue teased her upper lip, her teeth catching his lower lip in a brief nip, and her hips moved on the stone podium, trying to arch into him.

Beside him, flesh-and-blood Pet was sitting very still again—but one of her feet started to move restlessly against the other, rubbing the stiletto heel against the thin leather straps over her red-painted toes. She released a short breath as her screen self moved a hand farther down his screen's self back than he actually remembered.

He'd never been remotely interested in incorporating a camera into his sex life, so it was more than a little surreal to watch this, almost dreamlike. Although more of a bloody nightmare to see the view count and realize how many *other* people had watched this.

It was a hell of a lot more intimate and invasive than the photos.

Especially when Pet scrolled down, and a comment section popped up.

Jesus, there were some weird people out there.

He noticed a bunch more of the odd, cooing comments, from people who looked old enough in their profile pics to know better, and a few appearances from the usual trolls.

Pet immediately tried to cut away from the poorly spelled vitriol, casually covering half the screen as she'd done once before. The gesture broke through the web of caution and lust that had entrapped them.

He looked at her, something in his body settling. Gentling. "Pet," he said, "I appreciate the intention, but whatever my other failings, I'm not vain enough or sensitive enough to care about a bunch of basement-dwellers on Twitter. And let's face it, we do look completely mismatched."

Again, her expression was inscrutable. Then her lashes lowered as she watched the video, still playing on a purple-tinged loop. "I don't think so," she said, very quietly. "I think we look quite—sexy."

The car swept around a corner, plunging them into a roar of noise and shouting. Dragging his gaze from hers with difficulty, he looked through the windshield, scanning the organized chaos farther down the street, outside the theater. They were close enough to see what was happening on the red carpet. The cast of this production included several stalwarts of British theater, a popular young Hollywood actor, and a Korean music idol. The ground outside the New Pantheon was swarming with press. He grimaced at both the sheer volume of noise and the potential for incidents. The crowd looked like it stretched backward a quarter of the block, members of the public pressed up against the fenced-off barriers with their phones stretched out, shrieking hysterically and taking photos of almost everyone.

The New Pantheon was amongst the wealthiest of the West End theaters, and it showed tonight. The entrance had been transformed into a two-carriage train to reflect the setting of the play, with the audience walking through to get into the foyer, passing a mechanical and holographic reproduction of the most famous scenes.

Pet had showed them all sneak-peek photos. Another of her many connections had helped install the whole setup.

The royal cavalcade had reached the front of the line, and the crowd noise increased in a long swoop when Rosie and Johnny got out of their car.

Despite the presence of Benji and their most trusted juniors on the red carpet, Matthias couldn't help making another sweeping surveillance of the crowd. Pet was also watching anxiously, and as their eyes caught, a thread of humor returned.

She smiled ruefully. "Why do I suddenly feel like anxious parents? Apparently, the insta-relationship comes with a disaster-prone twenty-six-year-old son. Obviously, we should have read the Codename Charming fine print."

Lowering the privacy screen, Michael gave a thankful whistle when he was able to swing a right out of the pandemonium, turning into the small side street along the building's western façade. A private entrance was halfway down the street, under a modest awning, utilized for more publicity-shy and discreet arrivals. Since it was a rare celebrity or public figure who didn't want the full blast of cameras, very few photographers haunted this entrance; however, there would inevitably be one or two, hoping to get a couple of good shots.

As arranged, Matthias and Pet would divert down the "private" route, while everyone else did the usual red-carpet chaos. They'd still be photographed together, Rosie had deduced with entirely too much enthusiasm, but without making it quite so obvious as suddenly appearing *with* the royals, clearly off duty. The unspoken and true implication being that palace staffers might conceivably date, they might even be offered theater tickets as an employment perk, but they didn't start acting like celebrities without rousing suspicion.

Thank Christ.

When Michael opened the door for them, the Bulldog popped up like a leering jack-in-the-box.

Moving to block his access to and view of Pet, Matthias automatically touched her back in a gesture of reassurance—again with the grim acknowledgment that very little was practiced or artificial in his reactions where she was concerned.

"Ah, it's Beauty and the Beast, my favorite decoy couple, out for another little jaunt," the journo baited in a sing-song trill, like some fucking bird of prey. He lifted his camera and snapped a cluster of photos, the rapid-fire clicking surprisingly loud in the comparative peace down here.

Pet's eye twitched, but she took Matthias's hand with ease, and neither of them looked in the Bulldog's direction as they handed their tickets and security passes to the guards at the door.

They were almost inside without incident when the prick resorted to an expletive-laden allusion to Pet's role in the palace. It was a transparent attempt at provoking a reaction, the sort of pathetic, sniveling behavior Matthias had told countless clients to ignore.

Professionally, he knew far better than to give the arsehole what he wanted.

But when he spat something that was so fucking vile, purely personal instinct overrode years of training.

The Bulldog barely had time to blink before Matthias had a hand fisted in his collar and was propelling him backward into the brick wall of the neighboring building. He was well-built, top-heavy with muscle, but his return punch against Matthias's chest had all the power of a wriggling rat.

For once, Matthias had no compunction about using the greater force of his own body.

"Two strikes," he murmured, his voice low and even despite the rush of fury in his blood. "Take your photos, type up your lies, but don't so much as breathe in her direction again, you piece of shit."

The man's face went purple above the scruffy stubble on his weak chin. "I hope you're watching this," he blustered at the theater's door security. Both were former bodyguards Matthias recognized from the private sector beat. "You can corroborate that the palace is running a thug ring."

"I don't know what you're talking about," one of them—Isobel, he thought—said blandly.

"All in it together, you corrupt fuckers." The Bulldog made another futile struggle, and Matthias simply tightened his fist and raised his arm higher. The guy squawked as his feet left the pavement, his legs kicking in the air and at Matthias's knees. Again, pathetic. Obviously the sort who built muscle for aesthetics, not strength.

"And you're a fuckin' prick, mate," the other guard said, and smiled at Pet. "Come through, miss. You don't want to miss the performance. Oliver Browning is excellent. My nan used to bring me to see him at the Old Vic when I was just a kiddie."

"Oh, lucky," Pet said, totally ignoring the squeaking paparazzo. "He was brilliant as Lear at the Pavilion last year. I'd love to have seen him when he was younger and doing the hero roles."

"Yeah, for sure, when he played Earnest—" the guard enthused, and the Bulldog gave a loud growl of disgust.

He sneered up at Matthias, but his beady eyes were darting and wary. "Assuming you haven't fried *every* brain cell, you know you can't touch me. I'll have you in court before you can say 'rampant 'roids.' Not a good look for Princess Goth."

"You can stop pissing yourself. In about twenty seconds, I'm going to put you down, and you'll scurry off back to the gutter, physically unscathed."

He opened his mouth, but shut it with a snap when Matthias's fist tightened against his collar.

Very calmly, Matthias said, "I've got a direct dial to some of the biggest corner offices in Whitehall and Scotland Yard. Almost took a bullet once for an occupant of Downing Street." He looked at Pet, who was watching them with a smile starting to light her eyes. "Pet has connections in every damn industry in Britain. Between the two of us, I strongly suspect we could make your life a total living hell, and still have time to go out for dinner afterward."

Lowering the Bulldog back to the pavement, he released him. "Enjoy your evening. Get a better job." He straightened the guy's collar with a swift jerk—then leaned close and lowered his voice to a level just audible in their tense bubble. "And stay the fuck away from my—"

His jaw clenched.

The Bulldog's eyes narrowed. The pap was fuming, breathing hard, but his brow lifted. "But she ain't yours, *mate*," he said, just as softly. Taunting. Sure. "Is she?" His lips turned up. "A year from now, we'll all be here again for the new season of premieres. She still 'yours' then? How about six months? Three? What's the deadline?"

Twisting out of Matthias's grip, he stalked down the alley. Matthias stood still, watching him go.

A light touch on his hand. He didn't move for a moment, then he looked down. Pet's laughter was gone. She'd been out of earshot for that last exchange, but she hadn't missed the swift change in body language and power dynamics.

Her body was close enough that he could feel the netting of her dress catch on his clothing and see the rise and fall of her chest as she breathed.

Aware of the watching guards, he turned his hand to take hers.

Wordlessly, they passed into the cool serenity of the theater.

Their footsteps were nearly silent on the thick pile of the navy-and-gold carpet as they walked through the winding corridor to catch up with the other guests in the foyer.

Stragglers were hanging around in groups, giggling and posing for photos, but most of the crowd were making their way up the massive historic staircase.

The royal box was accessed via a private lift, and they copped several pissed glances as they skipped the queue.

"A small taste of the high life." Pet leaned back against the golden railing as they made the swift journey to the third floor. "On balance, I think I prefer the anonymity of the low life, even if it does involve more stairs."

The third floor was even more opulent than the foyer, every inch of the walls painted with typically Renaissance scenes of feasts, beards, nudity, and dramatically angled streets, so the artists could show off how long they'd spent practicing mathematical perspective.

Pet eyed a marble statue of a bald guy with watermelon-sized biceps and an acorn dick.

"Speaking of 'rampant 'roids,'" she commented, transparently trying to lighten the mood.

When her gaze subsequently snuck sideways toward his own upper arm, he shook off his preoccupation and said sardonically, "Before you ask—no. I worked out from a young age, but I'm what Padraig's grandmother would have referred to as naturally big-boned. No pharmaceutical assistance required." He ran his hand over his head. "And I can't blame the hair loss on that, either."

"I thought you shaved your hair down for the King's Guard."

"I did. But I'm not kidding myself. Judging by the photo of my father and his hairline, it doubled as a preemptive strike."

She giggled, and something inside him twanged and released. He couldn't keep it solely within now; he could feel his face softening, and as they neared the entrance to the royal box, he was acutely aware that he was under close surveillance. By his own damn team.

Carlos, Angela, and Sam, three of his juniors, all inclined their heads respectfully, and all of them had fucking devils dancing in their eyes.

Angela suppressed a grin. "Evening, sir," she said, as solemn and pious as a nun in church. "Nice night for it."

Carlos opened the door for them with an exaggerated courtly bow, and Matthias lifted a brow as he followed Pet into the box. It was almost full inside. Rosie and Johnny had two of the prime seats, but they'd invited friends and representatives from their personal charities to join them tonight.

Pet slipped into her seat and leaned forward to say hello to a charity rep they knew, and Benji emerged out of the shadows. He joined Matthias against the midnight-velveteen wall. They stood shoulder to shoulder, both keeping a laser eye on the movements of the audience, within and outside the box.

"You're *almost* indispensable, mate, but somehow I do struggle on without you during my shifts," Benji said with lazy, pointed calm as Matthias surveyed the large, cavernous space, locating their team members stationed in the boxes directly opposite, and at the four and eight o'clock positions around the balustrade.

"Habit. Never doubted your capability and never will." He shot Benji a narrowed look. "As much as it pains me to say it, in some ways you're the stronger side of the team. When it comes to intuition alone, you could join forces with the Duchess of Clarence and open a fortune-telling bureau. Any predictions about this evening?" He was only half joking, and his friend's mouth turned up.

"Rosie will stop her husband from tumbling over the railing

when he insists on giving the cast a standing ovation whether they're good or absolute shite." Benji nodded toward a small family group. "That kid over there is too young to be dragged to this by his parents; he'll be playing a game on his phone within ten minutes. And as much as you appreciate good theater, you'd rather be at home in bed with your own costar."

Underneath Matthias's fingertips, the soft nap of the textured wallpaper reminded him of Pet's white velvet coat. "I take it you saw the latest installment."

"The Little Venice love scene? Impressive performance. RADA-level, even."

Benji's eyes had been directed ahead, but he turned his head, then, his gaze resting on Pet's smiling profile. After a moment, he said, "I asked her out once myself. Right after she moved in."

As Pet had joked earlier, and their behavior over the past few days clearly demonstrated, they hadn't thrashed out all the fine print when it came to elaborate ruses to fuck over the tabloids.

However, Matthias didn't need a signed contract to know that he didn't have a right in hell to be immediately pissed off about that disclosure. Whatever was happening between them, and however long it lasted—whatever the *deadline*—there were absolutely zero circumstances in which any human had the right to dictate the choices of another. Within the bounds of legality, Pet could do anything she damn well pleased, even if that included dating feckless idiots.

He fully acknowledged that fact. He also went as rigid as the statue outside, his hand fisting against the wall.

Benji's lips twitched again as he redirected his attention to the audience. "She said no. At the time, since I have a very healthy ego, and she's a consummate professional, our Petal, I assumed she didn't date coworkers." He hummed lightly under his breath. "As painful as it is for *me* to admit, my ego will have to take the hit that I just wasn't the *right* teammate."

Matthias was running on three hours of sleep, sexual frustration, and a cocktail of mixed emotions. Benji never meant any harm with the shit-stirring, but he had minimal patience for it tonight. He didn't conceal the edge when he said on a low breath, "You were at the fucking meeting, and you've been watching this play out so far like it's one of your damned soap operas. It's orchestrated redirection, and it's temporary."

That last came out too forcefully, with a slight, harsh crack that he'd have paid over a week's salary to retract, but Benji simply nudged him.

"Oh, yeah. I *have* been watching. Me, and thousands of other people today. The two of you just about melted my fucking phone screen. You *would* have to be a world-class actor to fake that kind of connection, and no offense, but neither of you are going to be recruited by Hollywood any time soon." He cocked his head. "Whatever the reason you got into this, why not explore it properly?"

As the droning hum of voices rose from the stalls below, Benji continued, tongue-in-cheek, "I mean, the girl clearly needs to take advantage of the palace's subsidized eye tests and prescription lenses, but apparently—obviously—she finds you attractive."

"Drop it," Matthias said evenly, but his friend pressed on relentlessly.

"And she was bound and determined to be besties at the beginning, before she realized it wasn't like trying to crack the composure of a secretly laid-back Beefeater and win a grin; that you really *are* just that serious. Not *grim*," Benji inserted reassuringly. "Just—you know, incredibly, unbelievably uptight. *Some*

might say a walking safety manual. But I"—magnanimously—
"say what's *wrong* with being a massive control freak? Or dating
one. She'd always get to shag in neatly ironed sheets, you could
organize her button collection for her, and who doesn't enjoy a
rousing lecture on adhering to use-by dates and warning signs?
Our girl loves her a to-do list. She'd probably find it verbal fore-
play."

Blithely ignoring several tangible warning signs in Matthias's
rigid profile, he prodded, "Come on, mate. Live a little. That level of
physical spark doesn't come along every day. Especially for Brother
Matthias, the St. Giles monk. Even if it burned out quickly, you
could have a hell of a good time together, and Pet's the type to stay
mates with her—"

"Benji." One word, two hard-bitten syllables, but when Matthias
turned his head, Benji didn't just look at him. He saw.

And as the house lights dimmed, plunging them into a welcome
darkness, his expression changed.

Leaving his miraculously silent friend to stand sentry, Matthias
crossed the box and sat down next to Pet, moving her skirts so he
didn't crush them under his thigh. The seat creaked as he shifted. It
wasn't the first time he'd been in this box, but never as a spectator,
and he'd expected—

"I thought the seats would be comfier," Pet whispered in his ear,
directly echoing his own thoughts. "I think the seats in the stalls
are actually more cushioned than this." Her hum was a low vibration. "Prince Frederick got the national theater patronage. Maybe
all the West End producers and contractors deliberately installed
arse-breaking chairs in the royal boxes as a subtle act of rebellion."

As the curtain rose, Rosie twisted in her seat and looked directly
at them.

A spotlight swept across the audience, briefly illuminating her profile, and Matthias caught a flash of that odd expression on the princess's face that he'd seen once before.

It was starting to feel like there was more fucking drama in his real life than there would be in the fake murders onstage.

The light swung to fix on the stage, a train whistle echoed through the theater, and the first actor entered from stage right.

As expected for a New Pantheon production, it was high quality, and even in these circumstances, he found himself temporarily distracted and pulled along with the story.

The Hollywood guest star was probably the weakest point, attempting to steal scenes and overacting every one of them. But the rest of the cast ranged from creditable to excellent, and as the lead detective, Oliver Browning smoothed over any rough edges from the younger players. The icon of the Royal Shakespeare Company was short in stature, but infamous for his charismatic presence and elastic features. In repose, his face was almost plain, but with the slightest change of expression, he could transform himself into the best-looking man on the stage if a role called for it.

When the curtain came down for intermission, Pet again managed to read his mind and said much the same about the actor's chameleon looks.

Matthias stretched, trying to ease his back—the seats were abominable, and he didn't discount it *hadn't* been a ploy just to piss off the Duke of Clarence, the most frequent occupant of this box. "He reminds me of you," he said without thinking, and after a startled blink, she giggled.

"Either a paragon of beauty or a complete hag depending on the light, mood, and how much sleep I've had? As compliments go, I've had worse."

Except for a bad bout of malaria on an overseas assignment, he didn't think he'd flushed in his life before this past year, but he definitely felt a burn across his cheekbones. "Not physically." That point was so obvious it felt like a waste of breath even saying so. "Professionally. You have a knack for adapting to whatever and whomever the job throws at you. Somehow, you manage to be a different person to every difficult diplomat or prick peer, without artifice or sacrificing anything of yourself."

She looked totally taken aback.

A series of waiters entered the box with more champagne and refreshments. Nobody in this section of the theater would need to brave the foyer chaos to buy an overpriced ice cream or queue for the bathroom.

"Anyone would think that in your eyes, I'm the picture of competence at my job," Pet said, with a lightness that didn't quite ring true, and he frowned.

"Of course I think you're competent at your job, if we're going to radically understate the case. As good as Ji-Hoon is, you're demonstrably the best PA at St. Giles. Your predecessor on Johnny's team was a comparative rank disaster."

She looked at him for a long time, still with that curious expression. Had she really thought he didn't appreciate her professional skill? They might have driven each other up the wall at times with their different approaches and priorities with Johnny, but he'd always recognized how good she was at what she did.

"Although he wasn't nearly as reckless and actually read the protocol manual," he added smoothly, and succeeded in making her smile.

"*I* read the protocol manual," she retorted, laughter threading through the words. "And I adhere faithfully to every rule written after the twentieth century, unless it's blatantly ridiculous, like Section K. There is absolutely *no* reason to live in a palace if you're not going to occasionally put on a long skirt and twirl through the empty ballrooms."

"It wasn't the twirling that bothered the housekeeper," he said, unclipping his personal phone from his belt when it vibrated against his hip. "Or Johnny deciding to join in. It was the curtain he used as his makeshift ballgown. It was three hundred and fifty years old."

His thumb stilled against the screen when he saw the message.

Pet's smile faded. "Is everything okay?"

Slowly, he began tapping out a reply. "It's Jonna. Padraig's sister. Jenny obviously didn't waste time in alerting the McCarthy grapevine that she'd seen us." He grimaced. "It's press-gang orders couched as a friendly invite to her birthday party next month, in Ireland. Addressed to both of us."

"Oh," Pet said softly, after a pause.

Jenny's concerned words played through his mind. The McCarthys—and Benji—had always been the closest thing he had to a family, but he *had* distanced himself since Padraig's death. Not because he thought they blamed him; he wouldn't do them that injustice.

It had been too painful in the beginning—the starkness of Padraig's absence at that first Christmas in Ireland after his death, the jagged wound and torn threads he'd left, like a fundamental square torn from one of Fionnuala's heirloom quilts. The piece that had linked Matthias with the rest.

The longer he'd stayed away, the wider that gap had seemed.

Pet watched him finish typing out a brief, evasive response, then moved restlessly. "They probably recycled these chairs from some hideous ancient torture chamber after the refurbishment of the White Tower. I need to stretch my legs. And my spine. And maybe pee. The play's great, but the script's not exactly feeling like an *abridged* version of the novel. Do you want to take a walk?"

He stood, flipping aside his suit jacket to reattach his phone, and saw that Rosie had disappeared with her PPOs. Benji stood watching over Johnny. He looked across as they left the box.

Matthias waited while Pet used the bathroom—the VIPs even got a posh loo; the seat was a literal work of art, she reported, impressed, with glass flowers and butterflies imbedded in the transparent plastic.

When they wandered down a winding corridor to stretch their legs, their hands brushed; Pet hesitated, then slipped her fingers into his.

Matthias glanced at the completely empty space around them, nothing but echoing privacy. No journalists would get past security up here. They'd have to be hiding in the ceiling grates.

His hand engulfed hers, holding her tightly.

The walls were lined with framed pictures, mostly artworks but also photographs. They charted the history of the theater, from its beginnings as the *old* Pantheon to the twentieth-century reconstruction after the original building had been destroyed in the Blitz.

They stopped idly in front of the photos of the opening celebrations of a far more recent wing, Pet exclaiming as she pointed out a massive, tiered cake with the distinctive curlicue signature of De Vere's. "I bet my grandfather made that," she said, with a hint of wistfulness. "He was still working right into his eighties."

Her fingers suddenly flexed on his. She released his hand and leaned forward to look closer. "The bunting," she said. "And the balloons."

Frowning, he bent—almost having to drop to a full crouch to see the low-mounted photograph properly—and looked where she was pointing. His brows lifted.

Over the table of party food, bunting had been strung every-where, interspersed with balloons—and they were all emblazoned with little crests.

With roses in the bottom left corner.

Pet was scanning the neighboring photos. They both saw it at the same time—the central image, featuring the guest of honor and clearly the point of the party.

Looking, as usual, as if he'd rather be at home with his horses and whisky cellar, Rosie's father, the Duke of Albany, stood with a ridiculous large pair of scissors, ready to cut the ribbon to officially open the new wing.

Pet opened her bag. Pulling out the photo of her mystery rela-tive, she held it beside the New Pantheon photos. The crests were identical.

"I know all the current royal crests," she said, "and that isn't one of them. But a rose—that's the emblem of the Albanys."

Matthias took the photo from her, studying it again. "A rea-sonable chance, then, that our anonymous gathering somehow involved Rosie's parents."

She took out her phone and snapped a few photos of the ribbon-cutting shot. "Considering how many engagements we at-tend with Johnny in just a *week*," she said, "it'll be a miracle if either of them remembers some random event from thirty years ago, but—"

But it was something. And he knew what this meant to her. So, if they could get her the answers she needed, even if it just turned out to be the final piece of closure for her past, he'd help for as long as she wanted it—despite his cynical concern that she might end up wishing they'd left it alone.

A discreet bell sounded in the distance, warning of the imminent end to the intermission.

When they returned to the corridor outside the royal box, Rosie was also heading in, her senior PPO close at her heels. She was a bit drawn but smiled when she saw them. "Hello, lovebirds," she teased, ignoring their respective eye rolls. "Are you enjoying the play?"

Pet's return smile was preoccupied, and Rosie's shrewd navy eyes sharpened. "Problems?"

Pet held out the photo. "Rosie—this photo, the crest on the bunting—"

Curiously, the princess took it from her and nodded after one glance. "Right, the old patronage crests. I haven't seen one of those since I was little." She turned the photo over, glancing at the back, then took a closer look at the gathering. "Is this— Oh!" She'd obviously just noticed the Pet Duplicate. "God, I thought *I* look a lot like some of my relatives. Is that your mother?"

"No. It's not," Pet said, but didn't elaborate. "I know it's a massive long shot, but I wondered if I might be able to arrange a meeting with your father. See if, by any unlikely chance, he remembers anything about this party."

Rosie frowned. "My father?"

Pet brought up the photo of the Duke of Albany on her phone. "This was taken at the opening of the new wing here. It's his crest, isn't it? The Albany rose."

The princess's expression cleared. Putting out her hand to silently ask for the phone, she scissored her fingers against the screen, zooming in. "My father probably had to step in that night. Uncle Frederick's always excelled at reaping the perks of his patronages, while skipping out on the boring bits."

She put her thumb against the crest. "That's not a rose. It's a begonia. The Clarence emblem."

Handing the phone back, she said, "If you want details on this photo, I'd say your best shot is the family Oracle. Aunt Lia's away until Wednesday, but I'd consult her sooner rather than later. Last night, I found her coming down from the attics with a set of antique scales. To weigh the gold content in my mother's favorite tiara." She snorted. "It's probably a good thing she won't be at the reception for the Spanish royals. There's already a known klepto on the guest list. Add Lia into the mix and there mightn't be any valuables left in the room by the end of the night. Although a major jewel heist would be one way to distract the tabloids."

Laughter vanquished the shadows of fatigue when Pet grinned suddenly. "You at least can't say things have been boring around here, since Team Marchmont arrived."

Chapter Eleven

The evening reception to welcome the king and queen of Spain and visiting international dignitaries was being held in the Princess Anna ballroom, named after one of Rosie's eighteenth-century ancestors and still decorated in Anna's favored shades of pink and gold. It was one of Pet's favorite rooms in the palace, but there were few opportunities to have a really good wander and peer at its contents. She'd just passed a cabinet full of gorgeous little antique mechanical toys—a perfect miniature carousel, a stretching cat, a bell tower with a swinging, tinkling bell in its belfry. In usual circumstances, she'd have paid an extortionate sum for the key to that cabinet and ten minutes to hold things and have a play.

Especially when she glanced into the next display and saw a huge bowl of vintage buttons, many of them encrusted with semifine jewels.

Pet loved buttons.

Some people might consider it an obsession and those people would be wrong. She just liked to collect them, always noticed them on people's clothing, and had once stolen one directly from a stranger's coat at the age of six, by crawling under a train seat with a pair of scissors.

"If you're planning a button heist," Benji said behind her, "I'm afraid we'll be duty-bound to apprehend you."

Her skirts flared out and resettled around her legs as she turned around, her heart giving that shivery little jump when Matthias also moved through the crowd, stopping at Benji's shoulder. Both men were in full security evening dress, their posture military straight, game faces on—although she looked for and saw the flare of heat in his green eyes as they swept over her favorite pink evening dress and the swing of her hair.

She also saw the way his lips firmed, the muscle in his cheek twitching.

He was still trying very hard to keep some professional boundaries between them. Which was the smart, sensible thing to do.

The safe thing to do.

And increasingly futile.

Like her, he was continually betrayed by his body. For such a closed-off man, he couldn't seem to stop touching her. Holding her hand, tucking her hair behind her ears, spreading his fingers against the small of her back.

Meanwhile, she'd found another clue to her past—to her beginnings—that could lead to something she'd never have even dreamed possible. Yet, when she'd got home from the theater, her mind racing and nerves jumping, all she'd wanted was to curl up on the lap of her fake boyfriend.

And this morning, the *Digital Star* had published a detailed timeline of her past relationships, underlined their shortness of duration, and painted a further picture of her as some avaricious femme fatale.

All in all, Codename Charming: going great.

"However, since it's you, my darling," Benji continued smoothly, "I feel an accidental stumble coming on, if you fancy a head start."

Matthias's eyes cut sideways. Benji pretended to shiver with cold, but his teasing almost seemed half-hearted, as if he were simply performing on autopilot while his mind was elsewhere. The other man was always incredibly elegant at the very formal events, a suave film-star figure in the black-on-black tux, but his irrepressible grin was missing tonight. When Pet looked at him, he stared back—and his eyes were searching, deeply speculative. Discomfortingly so.

Last time she'd spoken to Benji, before the premiere, he'd been talking shit as usual. Teasing her about the video, suggesting that she'd probably engineered this whole situation herself, the lengths she'd go to finally get Matthias along to a TV night and turn him into another K-drama addict.

She and Matthias *were* becoming friends now. That was undeniable, the growing closeness, a bond both entwined with and separate from this intense sexual riptide. It would already be a huge blow to lose that.

Not so long ago, she'd thought—told herself—it was all she wanted from him.

She was uncertain and raw right now, feeling like her inner self was becoming exposed and stripped bare, vulnerable, and she couldn't bear for Benji to make light of it.

Didn't want him to know how much deeper it was going for her.

Her head tilted pointedly at the grandfather clock against the nearby wall. "You've got about two minutes before you're officially on duty," she said. "Shouldn't you be wandering around, staring frostily at the guests in case anyone *is* thinking of nicking a few artifacts? Apparently, a member of the Spanish party is notoriously light-fingered. And I'll have you know that I acquire all my buttons through legitimate means."

Such as legitimately belly-sliding under somebody's seat and legitimately snipping a button off their coat. In weak defense of her short-lived crime streak, she'd slipped a 50p coin into the woman's handbag in payment, which had seemed like a fortune to her at the time.

"I know when I'm not wanted," Benji said with heavy martyrdom.

"Then you've just routinely failed to act on it?" Matthias murmured, and Pet couldn't help laughing.

She saw only glimpses of him through the crowd for the first part of the evening, as he faded as far as he could into the background. The security presence was heavy this evening, black-clad figures in every nook and corner, while the British royals mingled with their Spanish counterparts.

Rosie was engaged in a lively conversation with Queen Isabella of Spain, who was one of the most beautiful people Pet had ever seen. The Spanish king was a more inconspicuous figure next to his glowing wife, but he had a kind face. When they'd entered the room, Pet had seen him reach out and finger the sash falling from his spouse's gown, letting it stroke over his palm in an explicitly sensual movement. Living in St. Giles, where unfortunately Rosie and Johnny's mutual devotion was one of the exceptions rather than the rule, it was lovely to see another happy marriage surviving the pressures of public life.

Pet was technically on duty tonight, but after the royals had completed the lengthy preliminaries, greeting each guest—with their assistants discreetly on hand to make sure no names were forgotten or pronounced incorrectly, and remind their respective bosses of small personal details about each attendee—the senior team had been instructed to just enjoy the party.

Quite honestly, she'd prefer to be in her pajamas right now with a book, but there was at least a visual bonus tonight. The room was full of beautiful gowns, shimmering with silk and crystals and handmade lace, and it was sartorial porn for her.

And both the champagne and the music were excellent, although you knew you were bloody bougie as a family when your parties included a thirty-piece orchestra instead of a four-spotty-teenagers band or a phone and speaker. She watched the people politely shuffling around the dance floor. It was a sad fact that the rich and titled of the world tended to dance like well-dressed broomsticks. Upright, uptight, and sweeping others out of their path.

She managed to weave her way back to the cabinets of miniatures and was staring meditatively at the buttons when Johnny burst through the crowd out of nowhere and snagged her elbow.

Without a word, he hauled her unceremoniously back into the throngs, walking her right across the room and out through a side door.

When they finally stopped in the empty, hushed corridor, the music in the ballroom was almost fully muffled. The palace might have astronomical heating bills, but it was even more soundproof than the high-class sex club not far from her old flat. Or, you know, so she'd heard.

Pet counted to five in her head, until she could speak without too much exasperation. "Johnny," she said. "I consider you a friend as well as a boss. I like you a lot. But Matthias and I are currently going to pantomime-level extremes to help you, and the past thirty seconds have not aided the cause."

"The p-press pack aren't invited to the b-ball," Johnny assured her absently.

"No, but quite a few trouble-making dickheads were, and they all probably have their phones." After the week they'd had, she was beyond mincing her words.

"I'm s-sorry, I was p-panicking," he said, and it sank in how much he was stuttering and how badly rattled he was.

Oh hell.

"What's happened?" She was already thinking of a hundred potential disasters.

Johnny looked both ways up and down the corridor and leaned in close. His eyes were pools of despair. "I've p-pinched the Spanish ambassador's p-parrot."

And that had not been one of them.

Pet stared at him for a solid ten seconds. At last, she said, "If that's some sort of euphemism, I'm not sure I want to know. Perhaps you could expound in a note and I'll read it later, after I've fortified myself with champagne."

That at least broke through Johnny's panic spiral. He gave a reluctant snort, but the metaphorical hand-flapping resumed immediately. "The Spanish ambassador's h-husband is a known k-klepto-m-ma—"

"Stop. Breathe." Pet took hold of both his forearms and waited until he'd sucked in a long breath, then prompted, "Okay, the Spanish ambassador's husband is the infamous kleptomaniac."

She had a very strong foreboding about where the rest of this was leading.

Given how quickly her life seemed to be changing right now—on a heart-deep level—she really wouldn't have minded one quiet evening to just commune with the buttons, drink her weight in champagne, and pretend she wasn't peeking at her not-really boyfriend being all stoic and stern with his very tightly knotted tie.

With great effort, Johnny slowed down his speech and carefully formed each word. "Every time the Spanish ambassador and her h-husband have come to stay at the p-palace, Rosie said he's stolen something. He can't help it." Johnny sounded sympathetic, but he winced. "This evening, right b-before the press call, I was coming back from a meeting in the north wing, where the Spanish contingent are s-spending the night. When I passed the ambassador's suite door, I heard c-crying, so I knocked and when there w-was no answer, I stuck my head in."

Of course he had. Johnny was a walking marshmallow the moment he saw anyone in tears.

It was an endearing quality, even if they did need to have a word about *not* barging into strangers' rooms if they pointedly ignored a knock. But with enormous apprehension, she ventured, "And?"

"I thought it was a ch-child. It wasn't. It was a parrot." Briefly, Johnny looked annoyed. "And it mocked me."

"It mocked you," she repeated faintly. She really was considering staying in this job for potentially decades if given the chance, wasn't she?

"It p-pointed its foot at me and started screaming '*Mole-rat!*' over and over. That's not important," he muttered to the floor, although he still looked peeved.

"What's 'mole-rat' in Spanish?" Pet asked curiously.

"I have no idea. It said it in English. W-with a strong Scots accent."

"Why—"

"This isn't actually the part of the story I thought you'd b-balk at."

"Sorry. Continue."

"I thought it was Mikael's c-c-cockatoo."

Pet pushed her hair back from her temples with both hands. "You thought the Spanish ambassador's kleptomaniac husband had stolen your assistant private secretary's son's cockatoo."

"I thought m-maybe he saw it and h-had a sort of moment," Johnny defended himself, flushing, and added darkly, "Although he'd probably have ch-changed his mind pretty quickly, after five minutes with the insulting little sh-shit." He ran agitated fingers through his increasingly tousled blond curls. "I know how much Mikael loves his p-pet."

Although he didn't know what the bird actually looked like, obviously. As the person who was clearly going to have to deal with an abducted, verbally abusive parrot, Pet felt entitled to one small snide thought.

"Your heart was in the right place," she said soothingly, hopefully hiding the internal sobbing. She steeled herself. "Where is the parrot now?"

"I took the cage to Layla's suite. She wasn't home, but when her p-partner opened the door, I could hear *their* cockatoo in the lounge." Johnny looked absolutely miserable now. "And when I tried to t-take the other one back to the ambassador's room, there were p-people standing in the hallway. I was r-running late for the reception line, so I just left the cage in the first place I thought w-would stay empty all night. This is the first chance I've had to g-get away and I can't be gone much longer."

He turned pleading eyes on her.

"I'll deal with it," Pet said crisply. "Don't worry. It'll be back in their suite before they leave the party."

Johnny's relief was so intense that his entire body seemed to deflate. With the release of tension, she thought he was literally an inch shorter.

"I'll make sure a massive bonus goes into your next paycheck," he promised.

And she would accept it, too. "Where is the cage, exactly?"

He told her, thus completing the turn of the evening into full farce.

They split up the moment they returned to the ballroom, Johnny making a beeline for his wife, looking irritatingly pleased with the entire world now. Pet moved as quickly and normally as she could through the crowd, smiling at people.

She made it to the west-side exit, but almost bumped into Matthias, who was also about to leave the room via that door.

"Are you taking your break now?" She checked her watch. The security team adhered strictly to rest breaks at these events, so nobody grew careless through fatigue.

He made a grunt of assent, but looked at her sharply. "What's gone wrong?"

Not so successful in concealing the inner weeping, then.

She debated for about three seconds only. When tasked with ludicrous side missions with potential to cause a diplomatic incident: assemble your strongest team. Even if it was only two of you.

Chapter Twelve

Trying to silently communicate her apology in advance, she made a "please come with" gesture, and Matthias's frown grew as he followed her into the corridor.

He closed the door behind him, leaving them alone in the quiet space, which felt much more intimate than this exact same situation had with Johnny on the opposite side of the building.

She didn't beat around the bush. "Johnny has kidnapped the Spanish ambassador's parrot, under the mistaken impression that it was Bob the Builder, Mikael Woodward's pet cockatoo, and had already been stolen by the ambassador's kleptomaniac husband. He's left the parrot's cage on a piece of stray furniture, so it can chuck insults at the portraits on the walls. In the Throne Room."

Matthias deserved a new service medal for maintaining his cool impassivity after that one. He absorbed the rush of information without a blink. "There isn't any stray furniture in the Throne Room," he said, then immediately caught on. "Ah."

"Want to spend your break helping me remove a bullying bird from His Majesty's monarchial throne and somehow sneak it back to the Spanish party's guest quarters without a single person seeing us?"

"I suppose it's a bad idea to get any of this on film," he murmured, without even momentary hesitation—and a glint of humor she'd have found much more surprising a fortnight ago—and she felt a little of what Johnny had clearly felt in his own rush of relief.

There was a lot of ambiguity between them right now, but she completely trusted that Matthias would come through in a crisis—however ridiculous. It was an incomparable feeling, knowing you had someone at your back when trouble knocked.

Almost immediately, though, the second thoughts fell thick and fast.

The whole thing *was* incredibly silly, but they could get in legitimate trouble for it—probably not official-sanction trouble, but not a good look, either. Especially for a senior security officer. Her conscience didn't knock; it kicked the door open and barged in. "Actually, it might be better if you pretend you didn't hear or see any of—"

Matthias gave her one square look and started walking down the corridor.

"There's really no point in *both* of us becoming the mockery of the entire palace if we're caught taking the bird for an evening stroll," she muttered, jogging to catch up with him.

"Gives a whole new meaning to the phrase 'Budgie Smugglers,' doesn't it?"

"Your beloved protocol manual has been breached. And this is a very inconvenient time for you to develop a sense of humor about it."

"Pet." All traces of flippancy disappeared. Matthias put his hand on the door to the back hallways and looked at her. His voice and stance were uncompromising. "As I said, I have nothing but respect for you and your complete competence in every situation that's thrown at you, which in Johnny's employ comes with few limits, but I'm putting two options on the table here. A: we do this together, or B: you go back to the ballroom and let me sort it."

He probably sensed her incoming retort, because he added, "I took an oath to protect Johnny to the full extent of my ability, and now that I know about it, this situation technically falls under my job description." He shrugged. "Admittedly, we hadn't expected he'd start pinching parrots, but—let's be honest, we probably should have."

"If you don't take a proper break, you might be fatigued later."

"If I felt remotely suboptimal or at risk of becoming so, I'd rest. I don't. But thank you for your concern."

She might find him incredibly attractive, and more so every day, but in these circumstances, the light sarcasm knocked him back a solid notch.

Her attention suddenly caught on the movement above his head. A security camera was swiveling to follow their footsteps with a faint whirring sound. *Shit.* There were thousands of them all over the palace, and obviously her brain had never fully woken up after he'd snogged her senseless in the lane.

With a renewed blush in her cheeks, she ignored his lifted brow and rubbed at her nose. It shielded her mouth from view of the lens, although it was a bit late to worry about this now. "All of this *is* going to be caught on camera and there's already footage of Johnny's entire escapade. The CCTV team will be editing it into a short film by now. *The Prince and the Parrot.* It'll probably be nominated at Cannes."

"Johnny isn't technically a prince." Nice to know Matthias hadn't abandoned *all* pedantry. She was starting to take a certain sense of comfort from the side of him that cinched his ties so very neatly.

He flicked back the side of his black jacket and removed the black security phone from its clip on his belt. It was a very naturally suave, 007-esque moment. Pet had never found anything remotely sexy about Bond—take away all the gadgets supplied by Q, the real hero of the franchise, and he was the posturing, womanizing twat you'd find in every bar in the city. Relying on cheesy pickup lines that had consistently failed to get men laid since the first caveman grunted something about Paleolithic earthquakes and rocking his world.

When Matthias did his stuff, though, it was much more interesting.

He pressed two numbers on the phone and held it to his ear. "Melinda, it's Matthias . . ." He paused, that visible wryness deepening as the head of the CCTV security branch spoke in response. "Yes, I am taking my break in sector five." Twisting to look up at the camera, he touched his temple in a mocking salute. "I thought I'd mix things up. According to my . . . one of our colleagues"—his eyes turned pointedly back to Pet—"people who never deviate from fixed schedules are at statistically significant risk of turning into tedious old bastards."

Pet pressed a hand to her chest. "You remember our conversations word for word. That's so gratifying."

That definite hint of amusement deepened, and it struck her that even when they clashed, everything kind of *clicked* when they worked together, and could feel incredibly natural.

"Lin, for classified reasons I'm going ghost for approximately fifteen minutes," Matthias said, "and I'm requesting a code 60 on a specific piece of footage from earlier this evening." Pause. "Yes. I do mean the footage of 4A traipsing around the property with a birdcage and leaving it to shit on the king's throne." The next unknown comment brought out a flicker of another smile. "Thanks."

He ended the call and calmly returned the phone to his belt.

Pet wrinkled her nose. "As simple as that? You just ring up and tell them to turn a blind eye for a bit, and withhold information from their debrief, and it's done in ten seconds? Jesus. No wonder powerful people get away with murder."

"People get away with nothing on Melinda's watch. She's a walking moral compass, with eagle-eyesight. Incidents of serious harm would be reported without exception, but unless the parrot has fallen off its perch from sheer boredom, this doesn't fall under that category. And if Johnny ever murders someone—either on purpose or because he accidentally knocks them off the palace balcony—her team will immediately pass the footage to Scotland Yard." Matthias was the soul of blandness as he held the door open for her. "Unless the victim was really, really irritating."

She *was* grateful that he'd just cleared a significant obstacle from this jolly little caper, but considering the metaphorical backflips she sometimes had to turn, it was a bit peeving that Matthias could erase Johnny's scrapes at the push of a button. "And where did '4A' come from?"

"All members of the family are given codenames for ease in communications, simply numbers in order of the succession. Their partners are assigned their number, followed by 'A' for a current spouse, 'B' for a former spouse, and 'C' for a romantic partner outside of marriage," he said. "Which includes acknowledged boyfriends and girlfriends, but not illicit affairs, for which there's an entirely separate section in the protection codebook." She looked up, assuming he was joking, and he shook his head. Honestly, multiple times a day in this job, she was grateful to be an assistant and not a princess. "Therefore, Rosie is '4' and Johnny was once '4C'; now '4A.' Extremely unlikely to ever be '4B.'"

"As long as she's 4, he'll be 4A."

The back corridors in this section of the palace were used primarily by staff, and everything was currently very quiet. Most people who didn't live-in would have gone home by now, and quite a few people were at the party. When they reached the secure Brancaster wing, Matthias set his thumb to the touchpad, unlocking the first access door.

"We'll go via the eastern side," he said. "Far less likelihood of awkward encounters after we've retrieved the birdcage."

The eastern route to the Throne Room was a journey back into the Jacobean era, as much of this section was original. Wooden floors, walls, and low ceilings, with glorious stained glass windows. It was dark outside, but the lights on the exterior of the palace were reflecting through the glass, casting a low, colorful glow. Beautiful, but the air was a little musty. Pet put up her hand to muffle a sneeze. She kept finding herself tiptoeing with exaggerated and currently totally unnecessary stealth, and it was difficult to stop.

There were four entrances into the Throne Room, three of them suitably grand. They were using the small poky door behind the monarchial dais. If you were in the room, it was usually hidden by a painted screen, which was all Pet initially saw when they quietly opened the door.

She *heard* plenty, however, most of it in language that would raise brows in a back-alley pub.

The Spanish ambassador's parrot did have a very strong Scottish accent. Specifically, Glaswegian. It was chattering and trilling nonstop, apparently very cross with a nonresponsive painting. A series of sounds like someone clucking their tongue was followed by a distinct "Bile yer heid, bile yer heid." A whistling tune that sounded uncannily like the first notes of "Head, Shoulders, Knees, and Toes." "Ya fackin' eejit."

Matthias's phone buzzed. He closed the door behind them and checked the message. "Melinda says the ambassador's parrot is named Ailsa. She was a gift from the Scottish Embassy for the ambassador's child, but has become a family member and lucky mascot. She's picked up a lot of vocab from watching TV. Her preferred genre is films, the bloodier the better." Another buzz. "She bites." *Buzz.* "But probably isn't carrying some sort of 'bird rabies.' If you want to put much faith in that expert veterinary diagnosis."

Pet rubbed her temples. "I suggest you also request a very large bonus from Johnny."

On the other side of the screen, a stream of invective cut off abruptly.

There was a long silence, broken by a few wary, high-pitched whistles from Ailsa, before the parrot decided that attack was the best defense. "Fackin' bastards! *Click-clock.* Wheeee!"

"I used to live a fairly normal life," Matthias commented as he quickly typed in a reply to Melinda.

Pet peeked around the edge of the gold-flecked screen. Johnny had left the large birdcage dead-center on the throne, and the parrot sat on a perch within, cocking her head and occasionally bobbing it like an '80s teen in a mosh pit.

"It's a Kirkby Grey parrot," she hissed. "They look nothing like cockatoos. How the hell did Johnny think she was Bob?"

When she spoke, Ailsa's beady eyes shot toward her. Pet took a hasty step back. That was a murder bird if she'd ever seen one. She could see a glimpse of something lying in the bottom of the cage. Possibly a toy. Probably a weapon carved from the bone of the parrot's last victim.

Ailsa bobbled closer across her perch, eyes locked on Pet. She leaned her head forward and opened her beak. A deep voice emerged like a possessed demon. "Pick a windae, yer leavin', wee lassie."

Two firsts in Pet's life: her mouth literally dropped open, and Matthias started to openly laugh in her company.

She couldn't fully appreciate it, as she was busy glaring at a moshing parrot. Who was also fucking *laughing* now. Proper chortling to itself. The little dick. "Did that bird just threaten to throw me out the window?"

Matthias had reclipped his phone and come to stand at her side. There were laughter lines around his eyes and his voice still contained an unsteady vibration. "It's a quote from *Red Governor*. Ailsa's been watching gangster films."

"She strongly emphasized the word *wee*."

"She's a parrot, Button. She's mimicking, not mocking."

Pet started to make a dire reply, but— Had he just called her "Button"? She twisted to look up at him. He was looking at the bird, his face still alight with amusement. He didn't seem to have noticed what he'd said, and she wasn't sure if she'd misheard.

Ailsa was still laughing to herself, and because she'd obviously picked up the human laughter sound from the child in her family, it was like *The Birds* crossed with *The Omen*.

The parrot spotted Matthias, then—and visibly preened. Shifting from one clawed foot to another, she ruffled her back feathers, and briefly covered her face with a foot, peeking around it.

She trilled a series of clucks and coos, a few bars of "Head, Shoulders, Knees, and Toes" again, and then said, "*Braw*."

It sounded like someone saying *phwoah*, which would have been funny enough.

But when she extended it to "*Y'er a braw jimmy, son*," it was Pet's turn to snort-laugh, the fizzing sensation in her tummy over that possible "Button" momentarily supplanted.

This time, Matthias hadn't got the reference.

"She called you a 'braw jimmy.'" Still no recognition yet. "Fit, Matthias. She thinks you're fit. Ailsa has a *wee*"—she copied the bird's emphasis—"crush. Aww. Look, she's hiding her face again. The homicidal murder-bird fancies you."

"She's just quoting films," he said again, but his cheeks were ruddy, not helped when he approached to pick up the cage and Ailsa started bobbing so excitedly that she became a feathery blur.

She made a series of *bob-bob-bob* sounds, and Matthias glanced at Pet. "Maybe Johnny heard that and thought she was introducing herself."

He was being sarcastic again, but it wasn't beyond the realms of possibility.

He carefully lifted the cage by the top handle. Pet reached to help, but stepped back hurriedly when Ailsa lifted her wings and shrieked at her.

"Sorry. I think you might have to carry her on your own. If I come near her 'braw jimmy,' I suspect I'll be found unresponsive in my bed tomorrow with several feathers floating mysteriously in the breeze."

The braw jimmy cast her a dark look as they left the Throne Room.

Until tonight, if she'd been asked to rate the single tensest moment of her job so far, the honors would have gone to the time Johnny had been asked to fire a ceremonial flaming arrow, in a sacred historical village where every single building was made of wood and thatch. That was now overtaken by walking through the halls of the palace at nine p.m. with the world's loudest and foulest-mouthed parrot.

They made it through an entire wing without meeting anyone, but when they were heading into the danger zone, where several corridors converged near an atrium, Ailsa decided to start belting out "The Bonnie Banks o' Loch Lomond."

"She's got a decent voice," Matthias observed, but halted at the sound of footsteps.

"I'm sure she's chuffed to hear that, Simon Cowell, but this isn't exactly—*Shhh!*" she hissed at the chattering bird, who started vigorously moshing again.

"*Shhh!*" Ailsa repeated in a high-pitched nasally tone. "*Shhh, shhh, shhh, SHHHHHH!*"

"She's definitely mocking."

"At least she's stopped sing—"

Another long belt of "The Bonnie Banks."

Voices came from around the corner, and Matthias swung the cage into the shadow of a column, then held out an arm. Pet slipped under it immediately, tucking herself against his body and trying to ignore Ailsa's jealous, plotting glare.

An unknown woman made a scornful huffing sound. "Only nine o'clock and they're at the singing stage of pissed already. Why are posh people such fucking lightweights?"

The footsteps came closer, and Pet reached up to wrap her hand around Matthias's wrist. He moved, turning so that his body fully blocked all view of hers. With his head lowered, she could see reluctant laughter creeping back into his eyes as she tried to stop her lips twitching—but his visible amusement died as quickly as her own when the women rounded the corner and Pet reflexively went up on her tiptoes, pressing her body to his.

Their breath mingled before their mouths brushed—first in an accidental bump, then, as they searched each other's eyes, Matthias slowly nudged her lower lip with his own. Her fingers clenched, one hand holding tightly to the cool fabric of his jacket, the other convulsing around hair-roughened skin, her thumb shaping the bony joint in his wrist.

Unable to stop herself, she caught his lip in a reciprocal soft mini-kiss. Drawing in a breath, Matthias tightened his arm across her back, lifting her fully off her feet for a moment. She slipped her arms around his neck to steady herself, swallowing hard as his hips moved to cradle hers, supporting her against the wall behind her.

They stayed like that, lips just touching, his forehead resting on hers.

"Are you—oops!" The first woman cut herself off with a snicker when she saw them, and Pet retained just enough lucid thought to hope Ailsa remained silent.

Matthias and the column were blocking the women's view of the cage, and she suspected the bird was sulking.

That optimistic hope was crushed when Ailsa suddenly let out a long, uncannily human moan.

Matthias abruptly buried his face in Pet's neck, his shoulders starting to shake. She had to move one of the arms wrapped around his head and hide her own face against her forearm.

"Sorry, don't mind us." The second woman's voice was vibrating with her own laughter as the staffers hurriedly backed away.

"Awkward," Number One hissed through another giggle.

Number Two replied with a shrug in her voice, "Eh, they're

from Team Marchmont. The Albany staff are always shagging each other." She sighed. "Maybe I should ask for a transfer. Total waste of perfectly romantic surroundings when you can't even have one little fuck in a ballroom. Although it is a violation of Section M of the manual."

As their footsteps and laughter faded away, Pet wiped her eyes with her wrist, taking a long, shaky breath. Her hips were still cradled against Matthias's, he was warm and hard around her, and his beard tickled the fine hairs under her ear.

Her fingers were itching to trace the outline of his ear, stroke over that scar. She blinked. "Who on our team is always shagging?"

Matthias lifted his head, as they remained there like it was perfectly normal to be standing in a back corridor, their pelvic bones pressed together, Pet's feet hooked around his legs, and a stolen birdcage beside them. "Benji's probably making up most of the numbers."

"I imagine Ji-Hoon could fill me in, in excruciating detail." Pet swallowed again as he carefully lowered her back to the ground, with that painstaking gentleness he always used with her—until they got completely lost to their surroundings and each other.

The silence around them suddenly seemed echoing. Her hands were still resting against his abdomen, her fingers lightly curled, feeling the slightly-too-fast rhythm of his breathing; and despite the tension in his jaw, he hadn't stepped back, as if he were reluctant to part from her.

"Matthias," she said, and his darkened gaze returned to hers.

Right before something smacked her in the face, hitting her under her left eye.

She continued to stare at him for a second—two . . . three—

before her head lowered to study the small, mangled green object that had landed near her foot.

When this month had begun, she hadn't even been casually dating *one* person. Now, she appeared to be involved in an intense love triangle.

And the other woman had just tried to blind her with a half-chewed grape.

When she turned a narrowed glance on Ailsa, the parrot had a piece of straw in her mouth. She tried to hurl it in Pet's direction, as well, and looked frosty when it barely moved.

Pet opened her mouth—and Ailsa trilled something.

"She just called me a tart. Between the tabloids, that old lady at the supermarket, and your feathery girlfriend, I could develop a complex."

Matthias said with suspicious blandness, "Sounded like normal parrot noise to me. We'd better get her home before we outrun our luck and my break."

Ailsa head-bopped her way along her perch. "Tar*t*," she repeated, very emphatically, stressing the last letter.

Pet looked at Matthias for a single beat more.

"I hate this bird," she said conversationally, as they recommenced the evening stroll from hell.

Conversely, this was probably the best night shift Melinda's team had ever had. Pet hoped nobody *was* attempting a major jewel heist or surprise attack in any other part of the building, because she'd bet almost every eye in the surveillance and recon team was glued on the camera feed currently whirring above her head.

"I thought you liked animals." Matthias scanned his key card again to get them into the next stairwell. They both stepped back to let the other pass and momentarily collided. Pet muttered an apology as she steadied herself. Voice very slightly strained, he added, "What about those hundreds of guinea pigs you want?"

"My guinea pigs will not belt out Scottish ballads like a drunken pub crawler and transparently plot my murder," Pet muttered, as Ailsa turned to face her and whispered in a very sweet tone, "*Maggot.*" She cast a meaningful glance out the closest window, speaking to the stars to make sure the universe heard. "They will either be cuddly bundles of unconditional love or a well-organized team of small furry assassins, ready and enthused to dispatch my enemies. I'm karmically owed nothing in between for not shoving Ailsa into Prince Frederick's room while he's sleeping tonight and locking the door."

She was so relieved when they finally reached the correct guest wing that her knees felt weak. They hadn't been able to avoid another two staff members she didn't recognize, but Matthias had worn his most "approach me at your own peril" face this time, and Pet had chirped, "Evening!" as if they weren't escorting a large bird who was currently stuck on a vocal loop of disdainful "*Eejits!*" interspersed with cooing at Matthias.

Both staffers had stared at their unlikely trio in astonishment, but as Pet had surmised in the past, few people questioned Matthias on anything. And apparently, she just appeared the type to do things like this, because the pair shrugged and walked on.

"The ambassador is in Suite 56." She was scanning door numbers as they moved quickly through the winding corridors. The carpet was impractically winter-white and so plush her heels were sinking into it. "There. That one."

She tried the handle, but someone had locked it since Johnny had barged in uninvited earlier. She really hoped that wasn't because the Ailsa-abduction had been discovered, but presumably Melinda would have messaged Matthias if it had been reported.

Anyway, the parrot might be a beloved *family* pet, but if the ambassador's household staff had discovered Ailsa's disappearance, she suspected they'd be extremely disappointed with her subsequent return.

"Locked," she confirmed, and Matthias slipped his phone from his belt.

He sent a short message to Melinda, and they stood waiting.

"Bile yer heid," Ailsa advised Pet rudely.

"Bile yer own."

Matthias coughed on another low laugh.

The parrot did an eerily accurate impression of a dripping tap.

"It's like being trapped with a horrifying sound effects box," Pet said, but fortunately the electronic door lock beeped then, the lights turning green. Ailsa added that sound to her repertoire. "Melinda's like the all-powerful St. Giles wizard. Can she cast her all-seeing eyes farther and say if there's anyone in there?"

"The ambassador and her husband are still at the party. Unsure on their staff. There are no cameras in the suites themselves. Or in family or staff apartments, in case you were wondering."

She hadn't been but was profoundly relieved to hear it. Not that anyone spying on a Pet-Cam would currently see anything more interesting than her stress-cutting about five hundred silhouette portraits, and one attempt at morning yoga that had ended after ten minutes, when she'd fallen asleep in Child's Pose and drooled all over her new mat.

Very quietly and slowly, she turned the handle of the suite door. The room within was dark and silent.

She opened the door a bit farther, listening closely. The VIP guest suites were spacious and usually contained multiple bedrooms, but with the light from the hall she could see that all doors were open, and there were no internal lights on anywhere.

"I think we're good." Standing back, she held the door so Matthias could maneuver the birdcage inside, leaving it open so they could see.

He lifted it higher, once more as if it weighed no more than tissue paper. "Where did Johnny find her?"

"Over there," she said, pointing as she looked with avid curiosity around the large space.

He walked over to set the large cage down on a table that was probably worth about five thousand pounds. "Home sweet home, darling," he said to the bird in the deep, resonant voice that unfailingly gave Pet a little shiver, deep inside.

"Don't encourage her," she muttered, as the bird bobbed frantically and preened her feathers again.

"Braw," Ailsa complimented him, before she started stropping way too loudly, "*Corn, corn, corn*. Meep. *Corn!*"

There was a small chiller bag on the chair by the table. Pet opened it and found a container of chopped corn and carrots, and a handful of Ailsa's lethal grapes. When she offered a piece of corn, the bird just about took her fingers off. She shoved a few grapes in through the bars as well, keeping a safe distance this time.

"Bye, Ailsa," she said to the chomping parrot. "May you live a long, happy, and diabolical life, and may we never meet again."

"Bye," Ailsa repeated through a mouthful. "Bye-bye-bye."

As she turned away, ready to get the hell out of there, the parrot swallowed her corn and finished, "*Maggot*."

Pet was almost at the door, Matthias a few steps behind her, when she heard voices that sounded far too close.

Speaking in Spanish.

Chapter Thirteen

Oh, Christ. *Mierda,* in fact. Pet might fancy doing a bit of a Miss Marple in her golden years, but she was definitely not cut out for the Agent 99 stuff at any age.

Her breath slamming into her throat, she looked wildly up at Matthias. She always liked looking at Matthias, but right now, he was a vision, absolute performance art in motion. He barely hesitated. He took literally one second to scan the room and weigh up their best options, then he closed the door and locked it from the inside, leaving them almost completely in the dark.

"FACK!" remarked the parrot, briefly becoming the narrator of Pet's internal monologue.

Matthias activated the flashlight app on his phone, and reached for and found her hand, even taking time to give her fingers a quick, reassuring squeeze before he went to the farthermost door and tugged her with him into . . . God knew where.

She was seriously concerned that she might be having a heart attack.

He closed the door and started typing rapidly into his phone with one thumb. Putting his free arm around her, he hugged her tightly against him. "Hang in there, sweetheart," he said against her ear. "Unfortunate but temporary blip. Just think of it as par for the course this month."

Her heart gave a more pleasurable little squeeze then.

That was—possibly—the second time an endearment had slipped out tonight, but she supposed she shouldn't get too excited about it, considering she'd just heard him call the world's most odious parrot "darling."

With the cast of light from his phone screen, she could now see that they were in . . . What the hell sort of space was this?

Her eyes widened.

After taking in the empty racks of metal bars, some sort of archaic wooden contraption, and several straps hanging from the ceiling, she whispered back in Matthias's ear, "Is there a sex room in *every* VIP suite?"

She thought she'd felt a tremble run through him, but it could have been laughter rather than overwhelming lust this time, because there was barely suppressed amusement in his low response. "Pet. It's for luggage storage and garment-steaming."

She was *not* blushing this time, and if she was, he couldn't see it in this lighting.

"Their bags were on the bed in the spare bedroom, so they've obviously opted not to use it. Slightly belated warning from Melinda—" he added, switching subjects in his more usual manner. It was impressive how quietly he could speak when he needed to. He managed to hit at a lower decibel than a whisper. "Three people incoming—the ambassador's husband, one of the family's aides, and for some ungodly reason, Abigail Kingsley, the Chancellor of the Exchequer."

Cuddled into the comforting warmth of his body and slightly reassured by his sheer calm, Pet's brain was ticking back into gear, although she couldn't help staring tensely at the door, waiting for it to be yanked open at any moment.

"Abigail Kingsley and Señor Serrano are both patrons for the same marine-life charity," she said. Rosie was also working with the charity, and Pet had recently done some background research for her on possible corporate donors. She'd also spent an afternoon with Rosie and the chancellor on the East Sussex coastline back in April, helping with a reservoir cleanup while Johnny had been off sick with a tummy bug. She'd been genuinely impressed that there'd been no press at all there; Abigail Kingsley worked in the highest levels of government, and she'd picked up discarded plastic for hours, for no media clout, simply to help. It had taken a team of hundreds to fully clear the nesting area for an endangered species of pink-billed gulls.

Pet didn't have a high opinion of most politicians and certainly not the current bunch, but it was nice to know there was one good egg. She'd admired the other woman's efficiency, too. "They work together regularly, but halfway through the party is extreme dedication. Sounds about right for the chancellor, though." She was struggling to breathe steadily while keeping her voice hushed. "My Spanish is rusty, but I heard something about documents."

"Signing documents, is what I got. The aide said she'd see them in the Augustine library tomorrow morning for 'the meeting,' and she hoped they enjoyed the rest of the party, because they deserve to play as well as work. I think. I haven't used my Spanish for a while, either." The blueish light from Matthias's phone cast unfamiliar shadows and hollows into his craggy face, but his solid strength remained comforting. "Hopefully they'll be in and out."

She strained her ears, but still couldn't hear anything beyond the heavy door.

"Maybe they've set up a makeshift office in another suite?" she suggested hopefully. "It should have taken them about twenty seconds, tops, to reach this one, so unless the chancellor's heels are stuck in that carpet, or they've decided to crawl the length of it for drunken giggles . . ." A realization had been nagging since he'd shut them in here, and it finally sank in. "Uh—unless Ailsa fell into a snoring coma the moment you plunged her into darkness, she's gone *awfully* quiet out there. How soundproof is this room?"

Matthias tilted his phone screen. "According to Melinda, who's getting way too much of a kick out of all this, the aide is currently heading upstairs, and Ms. Kingsley is still deep in conversation with Señor Serrano in the corridor." He released Pet and moved closer to the door, running his hand over it. "But you're right about the soundproofing," he murmured. "Despite the cosmetic renovation, this part of the building is at least three hundred years old. The walls are solid stone beneath that cladding and this door must be several inches thick." His big fingers were moving with care as he traced the panels. The delicacy of his touch was making her think thoughts that were totally inappropriate for this situation.

"What are you looking for?" She moved closer as well, trying to see clearly in the dim light.

"These rooms would have been used by ladies' maids in earlier eras, and if they were sometimes steaming clothes in enclosed spaces—" As he bent to the lowest panel of the door, there was a sudden click. He slid a panel aside to reveal a small grate. "And we have sound."

Immediately, the noise from the lounge drifted through the narrow space.

"Donder th' plank, ye scurvy lubbers!" Ailsa had commenced on a pirate phase. "*Meep.*"

The parrot started whistling "Head, Shoulders, Knees, and Toes" for the third time, and Pet heard two *beeps*, one after the after, as the electronic lock on their own door clicked into place—who even needed Q when they had Melinda?—and the outer suite door was unlocked and opened.

"We have turned a spare bedroom into an office for the duration of our stay," Señor Serrano said as he walked into the suite, having switched to English now. "But the contracts are on the table here, Madam Chancellor."

Listening to the rustling of clothing as the pair entered the lounge, Pet drew instinctively back and ended up nestled against Matthias again.

If the Señor noticed this door was now closed, he wouldn't be able to get in even with his key card if Melinda had initiated the secondary security locking. Regardless, her heart was almost in her throat, and it didn't help that their only light source was now a thin strip from the grate, as Matthias had silenced his phone.

She tried to shift her weight discreetly and silently swore when her high heel twisted awkwardly; she would have fallen if he hadn't caught her, holding her against him. Her foot was bent at an unnatural angle, and she had to sit fully on his lap to prevent it snapping off like a plastic doll.

His fingers slid against her stomach as he steadied her, and her abs clenched at the accidental tickle; she automatically put her hand over his to still the movement. Looking down in the dim light, she sat, just breathing. She watched as their hands turned very slowly into each other's hold, her thumb creeping up to curl around his.

Exhaling, she let her head fall back to rest against his shoulder.

Footsteps in the lounge, flat soles and a heavier tread, then

Señor Serrano's voice: "If you could just sign on the third and fifth pages, please, ma'am."

More rustling of heavy silk and a faint clattering of beads—Pet knew her fabric noises—and then the turning of pages, as the ambassador's husband continued to speak in a mixture of English and Spanish on various facts and legalese associated with the charity.

Eventually, the chancellor signed. Pet had listened to entire ASMR YouTube videos on the scratching sounds of fountain pens; it always made her throat tingle.

"Could you repeat that last, thank you, Eduardo?"

Señor Serrano dutifully repeated a report statement on a recent fund-raising drive.

"No," Ms. Kingsley said crisply. "The very last."

A slight pause, and then: "Ma'am."

"Again."

In what could not be described as anything but a purr, the ambassador's husband said with more emphasis, "*Ma'am.*"

Oh.

Oh *no*.

"Good boy." Also an unmistakable purr.

Pet lifted her head and twisted to look up at Matthias. Even in this darkness, she could see the change that came over those well-controlled features. Their expressions must be identical right now.

Sheer, unrelenting oh-fuck.

At the sounds of very wet snogging, she pressed her free thumb between her brows and idly wondered if—in very, *very* dire circumstances—teleportation might after all be possible.

When she heard words which her brain translated entirely against her will as "God, you're wetter than a sponge," she almost stuffed both thumbs into her ears then and there.

The chancellor spoke with the snap of command Pet remembered from when a group of volunteers had been mucking about at the reservoir. "Take off your belt and give it to me."

After the distinct sound of a belt buckle coming undone, they were back to the world's loudest and slurpiest kissing. It sounded like an octopus engaged in mortal combat with a vacuum cleaner.

Fortunately, it stopped abruptly when a familiar voice started doing exaggerated Darth Vader heavy breathing and then snort-chuckling to herself. "Heeheehee."

One of the most powerful women in the UK was involved in this utterly surreal situation. If Pet and Matthias were discovered now, it was very likely they would both be on the chopping block, and the two out there would come through with little to no consequences. The unending immunity of wealth and power.

Despite the very real problems here, Pet could feel another fit of the giggles rising.

She hadn't been so at the mercy of external forces for a long time, her life and her mind and her heart were all in absolute turmoil, but she also couldn't remember maybe *ever* having such a constant bubble of laughter and smiles trying to rise to the surface.

She almost lost it completely when Ailsa decided to recite the first words of "Wee Willie Winkie." A tiny squeak made it out of her throat, and Matthias turned his head into hers and put a warning thumb over her lips. Their faces were very, very close, and she could see how close he was to the edge, as well.

One more cackling laugh from the parrot, and she felt Matthias's chest expand on a shuddering breath. Quickly, she placed two fingers against his own lips, and they sat there, hunched together, eyes locked, touching each other's mouths, both trying desperately not to laugh.

The chancellor's next words shriveled the giggles in her throat.

"I think perhaps we'd better move things into this makeshift office," Abigail murmured dryly. "Your wife definitely won't return until after midnight?"

Their hands fell away, and Matthias swore very faintly against Pet's hair.

"She won't be back at all tonight," assured the adulterous twat, sending her heart plummeting straight into the pit of her stomach. "She's leaving directly from the party to fly to Newcastle, for a meeting in the morning. Her bags are already in the helicopter." His voice lowered to a thick brogue of arousal. "We have all night if need be, *mi pequeña erizo*."

"My staff know I intended to finish these contracts this evening, but I can't possibly be seen leaving the palace in the morning." The chancellor's own voice was husky as a slurpy noise indicated probable neck-sucking. "One must maintain at least an *appearance* of discretion, especially since we're already suffering from others' selfish carelessness of late—"

If she was referring to the half-dozen other members of her party who'd recently been caught out in extramarital affairs, she had the sheer balls to sound morally disapproving.

"—but I imagine I can eke out an hour or three . . ."

"Foooooooookin' 'ell." Ailsa's accent took a sudden detour via Manchester, but pretty much summed up Pet's feelings.

"As delightful as I'm sure your pet usually is, perhaps you could cover her cage first," the chancellor said pointedly, as the parrot launched into an old folk tune.

An hour. Or three. Trapped in a glorified cupboard, listening to the Chancellor of the Exchequer smack the Spanish ambassador's bastard husband on the arse with his own belt, while a parrot sang bawdy Scottish pub songs.

If Johnny ever knew about this, he'd never have to feel embarrassed again by his propensity for winding up in absurd situations. She and Matthias had now blown him out of the water. This was the royal flush of "how is this even my life right now."

And—oh god. Matthias was due back on duty soon, probably in mere minutes by this point.

There was only one last hope . . .

. . . that was dashed when Señor Serrano and his hypocritical "little hedgehog" tumbled across the room and presumably into the spare bedroom-turned-office.

And didn't close the door.

At the first moan, Matthias reached across and slid the panel closed, leaving them in blessed, blessed silence.

He activated his phone light, and Pet released his hand to press her palms against her cheeks.

"Matthias, I'm so sorry," she whispered, her mind working rapidly and failing to come up with any solution except to hope that the cheating duo were into a sort of kink that involved both blindfolds and earplugs, giving her and Matthias a chance to make a bolt for it. "When are you due back on shift?"

"Eight minutes." He was already typing. There was grimness in his tone, but he wasn't the sort of man to rail against situations that couldn't be changed. He was very much the "this is what we have to work with, so we'll make it work" type. So was she, usually, but she did have her limits. "Melinda's team will already have seen that we're temporarily trapped. We always have extra staff on standby in case of emergency or sudden illness, so I'll have to bring one of the subs off the bench. God knows how long this is going to take."

She chewed on her lip as she sat sideways on his lap, watching him organize an extremely last-minute replacement for the rest of his shift. It occurred to her that she probably ought to move now that they couldn't be overheard, but she—didn't want to interrupt him.

Obviously, it wasn't because she was increasingly tempted to take up permanent residence.

It would make it difficult to do their jobs.

He glanced up when he'd finished the silent communications, and his eyes visibly softened when he saw the guilt she couldn't hide. She'd dragged him into this.

"Pet, it's okay," he said, and despite the matter-of-fact tone, there was gentleness there. Even a renewed hint of humor. "And possibly worthwhile just for Ailsa's epic trolling. Don't worry. We rarely have to pull in the subs." She bet he'd personally *never* had to skip out of an important shift partway through. "It's all training for the team. We always need to be prepared for curveballs."

"True for every member of Team Marchmont, but I sincerely hope *this* curveball is a one-off." Releasing a sigh, she did slip off his lap to sit on the floor, then, leaning against the wall and tucking her silk skirts around her calves.

His hand moved automatically, probably to help her. Not to instinctively hold on to her. Even if that was what it looked like.

"Think of the bonus material when we eventually write our Team Marchmont memoirs." He was making a valiant attempt to keep her spirits up, and she did appreciate it.

She exhaled again as she wrapped her hands around her ankles, partly because her limbs felt like spaghetti, and mostly to stop herself from reaching back out for him.

"The chancellor has been at the palace multiple times," she said softly. "She must be aware of the level of interior surveillance. How blindly arrogant do you have to be, in her position, to assume you can skive off in the middle of a royal reception, disappear into a married guest's suite for 'an hour or three' at this time of night, and expect everyone to believe you're 'working'?"

Matthias shrugged out of his jacket. He laid it over her legs like a blanket, then moved to sit at her side, stretching out one long leg and resting his arm across the other knee. There was more than a little cynicism in the words when he replied, "She's probably got away with similar incidents in the past, and no doubt will again. Unfortunately, it's likely happening in every government across the planet."

Pet traced a pattern with her fingertip over the soft, fine weave of the fabric. "I thought the chancellor was quite an admirable person," she said in low tones. "Is there a single turn at which our government fails to be disappointing?" After a moment, she added with a little too much force, "Maybe the Serranos have an open marriage and his wife wouldn't care what's going on out there, but it didn't sound like it, did it? And the way she was looking at him when they arrived . . . I hate infidelity so much."

Matthias had turned his head. They were sitting in a small orb of light from his phone, and it created a strange sense of intimacy. Back in their bubble. "Because of your mother?" he asked bluntly, but a scowl immediately darkened his brow. "Or did some fucker cheat on you?"

His voice was as quiet as her own but charged with obvious anger on her behalf. The element of sheer disbelief in that growly "*you*" broke her out of her reverie.

The flush of warmth was so—glow-y, she was surprised she

wasn't lighting up the apparently non-sex room like a human lantern, but self-consciousness followed hard on its heels. She looked down at his jacket, the way he'd tucked it carefully over her cold feet. "The *Digital Star* wasn't wrong about one thing. My relationships don't last long enough for cheating to be a factor."

When he didn't immediately respond, odd nerves tightened their grip and she found herself saying more than she'd meant to. "I've dated quite a bit, but it's never serious. Fun for a while, and I'm still friendly with most of them, but—"

But she'd never experienced—in a single one of those relationships—even a scrap of what Sylvie and Dominic, or Rosie and Johnny, had found in each other. She'd always been more of a temporary novelty to most people, including the boyfriends who told her she was pretty and funny and a good laugh, but didn't really know anything about her.

Everyone's first choice for a party date and the last person they'd turn to if they needed help or nonsexual comfort. Ironically, when she'd made a successful career out of problem-solving and metaphorical handholding. Of course, people—even Dominic, at one time—did tend to reduce the profession she loved to mindless fetching and carrying for the overly indulged. Her brother had initially dismissed the entire PA field as a waste of her intelligence and education.

Her job drew on every skill she possessed, and—usually—it made her happy.

When it came to her life choices, the only approval she needed was her own. But when Matthias spoke of her ability with such candid simplicity . . . That mattered.

After Pet cut herself off, Matthias's arm flexed against her, but he didn't say anything.

Her heartbeats thudding so heavily that she was worried he might hear it, she crossed her own arm over her chest to muffle it. Hold it in.

Sitting there, listening to his slightly harsh breathing in the dim bluish light, emotion caught in her throat, her chest, her trembling fingertips.

She loved her brother and sister-in-law, and even Mabel and Jay, and their whole patchwork bunch of eccentric, loyal weirdoes so fiercely, but she'd never felt—or *inspired*—anything remotely as genuine in her romantic relationships. Or, to call a spade a spade, her situationships and one-to-three-night stands.

Something mutually true and deep and *real*, instead of superficial passion and fleeting feelings.

Once, over a drunken night of cocktails and way too many crisps with an old flatmate, she'd blurted that maybe she just wasn't meant for the whole "love to the very core even when they're pissing you off, and hold hands on the Tube, and listen after a shit day, and fuck loads, and nuzzle each other's wrinkles, and cuddle in the bath when we get arthritis from all the shagging" kind of deal.

Looking at her blearily over a massive Mai Tai, her flatmate had shrugged. "Maybe you aren't. Don't *have* to be. Loads of different kinds of love and happy out there."

She'd twirled her cherry stem thoughtfully between her teeth. "But in your case, sweetie, I don't think it's a case of *never*. Maybe it's just—not now, not yet, and not them." Frowning through the booze-haze, she'd said carefully, "Honestly, I reckon you're just not ready for it. And the right person hasn't come along yet. When you are, and they do—you'll know it."

Wiggling her foot in its fluffy, super-soft sock to encourage more of Pet's absent-minded petting, she'd added, "They'd better be big into snuggling."

At her side now, Matthias leaned his head against the wall, observing her in silence, then, reaching for the jacket she still had over her lap, he took something from the internal pocket. A small notebook and a little plastic object.

He gave her the notebook, then, as she blinked, unsnapped the plastic circle. It unfolded into a tiny pair of craft scissors, which he also held out to her.

She took them automatically and stared wordlessly from the scissors to the notebook.

"It seems to give you comfort," he said, gruffly. "Making your art."

Had he . . . started carrying these around specifically for her? So she could cut her silhouette portraits when she needed to? Even the way he'd referred to it, as her *art*, when so many people dismissed it as a silly party trick that she'd started thinking of it that way herself.

His cheekbones were darkening.

Her heart squeezed, hard.

They skimmed over the basics of all this pretty well in fiction, and from what she'd observed secondhand in real life. In her safety net, her sort of perpetual supporting actor role. The invisible daughter, the happy-go-lucky sister, the flirt who harmlessly dated the main character before they found the real thing.

She'd seen and read about breathtaking shivers, head-spinning kisses, the constant driving desire to press somebody against a wall and suck on their short, thick, rugby-player-ish neck.

Maybe that last one was situation specific.

Nobody had come close to adequately portraying how *scary* it was, feeling all these *feelings*, these countless, multiplying, golden threads linking her to somebody else, and the total lack of control. Her mind and her body and her hormones all arbitrarily reaching out for him, and not knowing if or when he was going to step back and sever the growing bonds with one stroke.

His flush had spread to the tips of his lovely, generous ears. She'd never not be enamored with how all his features were so substantial, like his physicality was a direct reflection of his inner self and integrity, vast from his feet to his heart.

With the memory of stirring hardness pushing against her middle also looming . . . large in her mind, she managed to keep her gaze from drifting downward.

Instinctively, she wrapped her hand around his biceps, giving him a squeezing mini-hug on his arm and touching her forehead to his shoulder bone in a nuzzling movement, before she carefully pulled a sheet from the notebook and started snipping. From the first cut, even as her mind still raced, her shoulders relaxed a little. This really was like meditation for her. And he knew that.

He didn't move for a beat or two, then he inhaled deeply and removed another two objects from the jacket. A small folding knife this time, and a polished fragment of wood.

As she'd thought on multiple occasions, a veritable magician with those pockets of preparedness.

She turned the piece of paper, carefully making a series of small snips, and Matthias opened the knife and began whittling the wood. She'd seen him before, on his breaks, producing tiny intricate sculptures in a very short time. Mikael had a series of them on his bedside table, mostly the little boy's favorite cartoon characters and cars. It never failed to intrigue Pet, how such large hands could produce such minuscule features—even down to miniature fingernails and barely noticeable whorls in ears.

The sheer absurdity of this scene—the two of them sitting on the floor, calmly cutting and slicing at their paper and wood, while on the other side of the door, people were having loud and quite . . . *slurpy*-sounding sex—it all added to the sense of being in a bubble outside of real time and place.

Carving out a slice of wood with a careful flick, Matthias lifted a brow and gestured at the knife. "Any requests?"

For some reason, Pet thought again of that terrified field mouse he'd held so carefully. "A mouse?"

He looked a little quizzical, but set his thumb against the wood and moved the knife. The first curve of a rounded ear appeared.

She couldn't help another grimace at the closed grate, and he shot her another long, piercing glance. "Do you want to talk about her?" Quiet. Serious. "Your mother?"

Not really. But—

"I suppose it's a bit hypocritical in some ways, to completely condemn adultery." She did, however. "When I literally wouldn't exist without it. I just don't understand why people don't end their relationships first, if they're so unhappy."

And Lana and Gerald had never been happy.

"Pure selfishness. I've guarded plenty of people who expect everything delivered to them on a platter without putting in the work, and don't give a damn who they hurt." His response was uncompromising, and she wasn't surprised. There were an awful lot of people in this city—including amongst her friend groups—who had lenient views about cheating, although only if they weren't on the receiving end, but she couldn't imagine Matthias ever hurting an innocent person. Not deliberately.

Was that why he was still periodically whacking bricks into that invisible wall between them, despite the constant battering of their mutual lust and just plain *liking of* each other? In some ways, they were very different, but she also sensed a kindred spirit in ways that mattered. Right from the beginning, really, Pet had felt that.

But maybe he sensed exactly how much she was beginning to want, and he instinctively didn't want to hurt her if it was a lot simpler on his end. Just sex and growing friendship, both of which had obviously caught him off guard.

The thought made her want to retreat into the shadows behind those leather straps she still wasn't convinced weren't for acrobatic sex, but it *would* be very Matthias. The man's protective streak was a mile wide—in fact, sometimes that seemed to be *all* he expected someone might want from him, which was so—

"At Sugar Fair," he said jarringly, as he scraped out another piece of wood, "I didn't want to further flip the lid on obviously painful history. But—you and Dominic are *both* children of your mother's affairs?"

She moved her scissors in a twisting turn, shaping a corner of the paper into a small, jutting beak. "More than a decade apart, so the odds of it being the same bloke are nonexistent. Lana was not the type to form lasting attachments. Even her favorite foods changed every other week." She made an infinitesimal snip. "In Dominic's case, he always knew. Gerald never let him or any of us forget it. But it wasn't until I was a teenager that I realized it hadn't been a one-off . . . *indiscretion*, that my mother was serially unfaithful." She lifted one shoulder, not looking away from the emerging art. "Gerald may have been, as well, for all I know. Their marriage was a joke."

That had been the *real* charade of a relationship.

Matthias was watching her closely. "You mentioned his attitude toward you. That he treated you differently than your sister," he said, very low. "Pet, was he—?"

"He wasn't physically abusive," she said, understanding that dangerous flicker in his expression. "But—"

But he *had* been abusive. It had taken her a long time to recognize and admit that, that every slighting comment, every bit of emotional blackmail, the impossible standards, the constant criticisms, it had been more than just shit parenting.

She hadn't intended to go into detail. She'd never talked about this in full with anyone, not even Dominic, but she found herself telling Matthias—not all of it, but enough, and by the time her voice trailed away, he'd set down his knife and the partly finished mouse sculpture, and both her hands were entwined tightly with his.

Her throat and her eyes felt very dry, and his features were set and tight.

"Very rarely am I glad someone's dead," he said, incredibly quietly. His fingers flexed around hers. "Although part of me wishes I could meet him after all."

Quite explicitly, Gerald wouldn't have enjoyed that family get-together.

"The guy was a piece of shit." Every word had jagged edges, as if he'd carved them out with his knife. "Not just once but *twice* he took his own dysfunctional relationship out on innocent kids. And the fact that it happened to *you*—" He was patently furious, but when he released one of her hands to tuck a stray piece of hair behind her ear, his touch was conversely light, almost cradling. "I'm sorry, Button."

No mistaking the nickname that time, but she was too caught on the warmth of his palm, briefly cupping her cheek, and the way that one short, husky sentence said so much.

He dropped his hand, but they didn't look away from each other.

"Pet," he said. "The photo. Your unknown doppelgänger. Usually, I'd caution that it's very likely to be a dead end. But—"

She knew what he was going to say, managed a slight smile despite the immediate clutch of anxiety at the reminder. "But if the Duchess of Clarence is part of the equation, *anything* is possible."

Matthias was giving her a bit of the cyborg-scanning treatment, but for all the impersonality of that particular expression, she knew he was worried for her. Trying to ascertain how she felt about that mystery bio dad suddenly becoming—to misquote Pinocchio—a real life boy.

Or to be accurate, a real life middle-aged to elderly man.

And honestly—she didn't know herself.

It was like contemplating and trying to grasp at fog. It just ran through her fingers. They all joked about Lia being a cross between a clairvoyant and an MI6 informant, but she was a human being, and the event in the photo was potentially three decades ago. If she didn't remember a thing about it, Pet had no further steps planned yet. And certainly, there was no concrete picture in her head of some anonymous man. He was as much a part of the mist. Right now, nebulous. Nothing. An unknown fragment of the past.

Matthias's hold was gentle as he cradled her fingers on his palm; she didn't think he realized he was stroking circles on her skin. Venn diagrams, to be precise. "Even if we can find out who he is, he could be a disappointment, Pet," he said bluntly.

"I know," she said, and she did. Her father could be anyone—a criminal, a deadbeat. Or actually dead. "I'm not expecting a fairy tale, Matthias."

But—aren't you? The soft whisper in her head was unwelcome and hard to ignore. *Isn't part of you still hoping for a happy-ever-after?*

And hadn't she learned, repeatedly, that life could be good—great, even—but it was never a fairy tale? She wasn't one of Matthias's rock stars and bankers who expected the world on a plate—and sometimes, even when you wanted something really badly, it wasn't meant to be.

Silently, she placed the finished silhouette portrait on Matthias's lap. He'd still been searching her face with uncomfortable shrewdness, but his expression lightened as he picked it up.

"Amazing," he said, turning over the detailed outline of Ailsa. For better or worse, the parrot was the star of the show tonight. "May I keep it?"

"I made it for you." She watched as he slipped it into the side of his phone case, with the care a curator might afford an original Da Vinci. "A little reminder of your devoted fan."

Rolling his eyes, he reached over and opened the grate to see if they were clear to leave yet.

And closed it again, emphatically.

Bloody hell.

"Is it just me," she mused, "or is a bit of dirty talk really sexy in the moment, yet gobsmackingly awful when it's coming through a wall?"

"This building might be structurally sound"—he placed a palm against the wall, as if he were actually double-checking—"but it sounds like they're proposing to violate several laws of gravity and physics."

"At least if they bring the whole thing down, we should be able to make a run for it in the chaos."

Matthias picked up his whittling again. Wiggling his knife, he drew it out in a curling stroke, and she watched with fascination as whiskers emerged.

After maybe twenty minutes—and another horrifying grate-check—tiredness finally caught up with her. Her mind started drifting. When her head began to nod, she shook herself, trying to wake up. It would be disastrous to still be here in the morning. At some point, a completely sober, out-of-the-sex-haze Señor Serrano *was* surely going to wonder why an empty room in his suite was suddenly closed and locked.

"It's all right." Matthias looked up from his whittling. The little mouse was going to be smaller than his thumb when it was finished. His voice was so rumbly and soothing it almost sent her straight into a nap there and then. "Sleep, if you need to. I'll wake you when we're clear to go."

"I am not going to sleep," Pet said piously, with great determination and only a little slurring, and almost immediately dropped into semi-consciousness.

She was dozily half-aware when Matthias pulled his jacket higher around her neck, and she instinctively cuddled in closer against his bulky warmth.

"Nice," she mumbled, nuzzling her cheek on his arm again.

After warm, wandering seconds, she felt a butterfly-tickling sensation near her temple, as if the fine hairs there had stirred in a breeze—or been smoothed by a callused thumb. She slipped into full sleep and was completely disorientated when he gently shook her awake a while later.

"Pet," he said against her ear. "We have to go. Serrano's escorting Ms. Kingsley to the side stairwell and coming back. Melinda's unlocked the door. She's stayed two hours past her shift to see us safely out. I owe her enough Baileys to fill a bathtub for this one."

She was groggy and even more tired than earlier, but the renewed rush of adrenaline propelled her upward, and he made her slip on his jacket for warmth, stating that the older sections of the palace would be colder this late at night. Using Matthias's phone for light, they checked the floor for any scraps of wood or paper, then cautiously opened the door. Señor Serrano had left the light on in the lounge, but Ailsa's cage was covered with a dark sheet. The faintest snoring mumbles were coming from beneath it, and she felt a single spike of bizarre affection for the murder bird.

Matthias extended his hand, and she slipped hers into it, both actions automatic and natural as they let themselves out of the suite. The corridor was dimly lit and empty, but she had to force herself to walk normally and not sprint all the way back to the staff wing. They took a circuitous route that would bypass the side stairwell completely. She had no desire to see either Serrano or the chancellor again, and she certainly didn't want to make small talk with the latter.

Matthias let go of her once they were clear of the guest suites, but she was so loopy that she almost fell over getting into the staff lift, and he tucked her hand around his forearm for support.

When they finally made it home to her suite, he stood waiting patiently while she fumbled with the key. Stifling a yawn, she had just enough energy left to feel slightly self-conscious when she turned in the doorway.

After spending hours locked in a luggage room listening to other people having sex and not being at all sure where this was going between them—well, she *had* read the protocol manual, from cover to boring cover, but if there was an etiquette section that covered these circumstances, she'd missed it.

He saved the day by reaching into his pocket and holding out a perfect object on the palm of his hand.

She stared at the finished mouse sculpture before she reached out for it, turning it over to examine every detail. It was *adorable*, and in its tiny paws, it was clutching a teddy bear—a perfect miniature of Hercule, down to the pocket square.

She held it reverently. "Thank you so much."

He moved his head in that typical dismissive gesture, but a faint smile flickered through his eyes.

"Oh! That reminds me. Just a second." She turned and crossed the lounge to her kitchenette, where she'd left her paper bag of purchases from Sugar Fair. They'd been so busy she'd almost forgotten about it—a sign of highly unusual times, when Sylvie's truffles went uneaten for more than a couple of hours. Digging into it, she pulled out the white chocolate mice she'd added to her order at the till. "It's the day for mice. You know, as well as parrots."

Matthias took the ribboned box from her and turned it over, reading the handwritten label. He looked up, a frown deepening the faint lines between his brows, and she shrugged with a small smile of her own. "When I was filling in for Dominic's executive assistant last year, I got in the habit of watching people gravitate toward their favorite sweets. I thought those might be yours."

"They are." He ran his thumb over the box. He was obviously taken aback—beyond what was merited by a few sweets, however good. Pet's stomach clenched. Did people never give him even silly little gifts? "Thank you."

Normally, she'd brush it off with a light remark and a flirty smile, but as they stood there, searching each other's expressions, she took a small step forward. They both reacted to distant voices at the end of the corridor, flinching slightly, but didn't look away from each other.

Pet tilted her head, gesturing in the direction of the unseen staffers heading home. "Could be a photographer," she murmured, tucking her tongue into her cheek, and his mouth tipped up.

"I haven't given the Bulldog nearly enough credit," he said, setting the chocolate box carefully down on the table beside her door, "if he can get into this wing at this time of night and disguise his voice to exactly mimic Andrew from the Comms team."

Despite the heavy irony, his eyes were dark in the shadows. When he stepped forward and their bodies collided, she felt the echo of her reactive shudder run through his wide torso. As his hands went to the curve of her waist, pulling her up on her tiptoes in one smooth, sensual movement, she seized his tie, tugging his head down.

With his breath against her lips, she whispered, "Can never underestimate the cunning of the tabloids."

Their mouths brushed, then immediately parted at that first tingling contact, his tongue tracing the inner curve of her lip before flirting, tangling with her own.

The playfulness died a swift death. The second kiss met, clung—exploded. It was like being flung headfirst into a whirlpool, crashing over her and pulling her under. She made a noise of both need and anxiety, even as she hooked an arm right around his neck, almost climbing his body to get closer.

He lifted her, pressing her up against the open door, one hand slipping down to cradle her thigh as her legs went around his waist. The sound deep in his own chest was both protective, instinctively reassuring, and reciprocal driving desire. Without breaking the kiss, Pet moved her head before her neck gave out, and he held her higher, supporting her full weight with apparent ease. The new position rubbed her directly against his stirring erection, and she tore her mouth from his to drag in a shaky breath.

Her hips moved in a sinuous arch, seeking more of that friction, and they both groaned, Matthias's teeth nipping lightly at her earlobe before he pressed an open-mouthed kiss against her neck. Pet's entire body was shivering, convulsive little tingles, and her inner muscles clenched hard when she pushed against him. Her head rolling against the door as he nuzzled her throat, she was beyond conscious thought, uncaring how precarious her position was—in every meaning of the word.

Craving his kiss, she pushed forward, wrapping her arms tightly around his neck as his mouth returned to hers. His thumb moved in those delicious light circles against her thigh, under her dress, and she touched her tongue to his, then sucked on him hard. He grunted, pushing her harder into the door.

A spike of lucidity penetrated.

Mostly because with the change of angle, the physical evidence of his arousal seemed to have doubled in size.

Quite literally, doubled in size.

She was suddenly rather less rousingly enthusiastic about anything *else* penetrating.

There wasn't a single moment, in all these months with Matthias, that she'd *ever* found him intimidating.

Gruff. Sexy. Irritating. Wonderful. Never intimidating.

Right now, as their lips parted and he rested his forehead on hers, their breaths harsh and broken, his pupils dilated to full black, she was intimidated.

The proportions of what she felt against her stomach as he shifted her weight were straight-up alarming. After years of recurring pelvic issues, she was no stranger to occasionally uncomfortable sex, and frankly, even *reading* about tree-trunk cocks made her want to glue her legs together.

This was Mr. Prepared, who usually had everything but the kitchen sink on hand, she recollected hopefully, smoothing his tie and trying to get her breath back. He'd been carrying fucking *handcuffs* at one point. Maybe he was also concealing a literal cudgel in his pocket. Or some sort of sizeable vegetable. Portable snack.

Pet. He's a vegetarian. Not a guinea pig.

Someone cleared their throat.

Probably not for the first time, she realized, given the loud, exaggerated quality of the sound.

Matthias jolted, and they tore their eyes from each other.

Benji, also still in his work suit, was leaning against the door of another suite. Carefully expressionless, he lifted a casual hand to them. "Sorry to interrupt," he said, oh-so-politely. "But Melinda gave me the bare bones of why my incredibly reliable co-lead suddenly scarpered midshift. And I really need your signature on these"—he held up the pile of papers under his arm—"because you told me explicitly that they have to be emailed through by midnight."

Matthias's arms had tightened reflexively around Pet—and her legs had locked harder around his waist, she realized with a flush, her muscles cramping as he lowered her to her feet.

He swore very creatively.

"Your mind was on other things," Benji soothed. His face was still a deliberate façade of nothing. "Codename Charming making favorable progress, I see."

Pet rubbed her nose. She was holding on to Matthias's arm, and he held her waist, supporting her with his body, which was doing the dual service of steadying her wobbly knees and modestly concealing his arousal.

After they'd writhed and moaned, and she'd come very close to having an orgasm against her fully open door.

Apparently in the fine print of the nonexistent Codename Charming contract, there'd been a clause that she was going to turn into an accidental exhibitionist.

"We thought you were a journalist," she said virtuously, and Benji nodded with great understanding.

"Good to be on the ball. Notable tabloid hotspot, the second-floor staff wing. After eleven o'clock at night. Behind four consecutive locked gates."

"Wait for me at the stairwell," Matthias said crisply. "I'll come with you to the office."

Pet expected another dig, but Benji looked at her for a moment and simply murmured, "Night, gorgeous. See you tomorrow. And thanks for the invite to the magic festival, by the way. Looking forward to it. Always fancied meeting a sexy witch or sorcerer."

They all had a rare simultaneous night off on Wednesday, since Rosie and Johnny were having a date night at home, which gave the junior members of the team a chance to practice leading operations in a protected environment.

After Rosie had heard Pet was going to the Woodland Witch-Fest to support Sylvie, she'd made another of her sweet-voiced "suggestions" that Matthias accompany her.

He'd agreed, albeit rather skeptically, and suggested Benji might want to tag along, too. Pet hoped they weren't going to regret it, because she'd had an ominous text last night from Sylvie, telling her to wear clothes that she wouldn't mind being permanently stained.

Considering that Suave and Meticulous here were always pressed and starched within an inch of their lives, she wasn't sure Witch-Fest was going to be their cup of tea. Or cauldron of potion.

When Benji had gone, after a last glance back, she wordlessly slipped off Matthias's suit jacket and handed it back to him.

He shrugged into it. His gaze remained locked on her face, the expression on his own conflicted. His lips parted—then he simply tilted up her chin with one knuckle and brushed his lips lightly over her own. "Goodnight."

It was a low, sexy murmur, and she found herself swaying into him.

Their bodies touched at that same angle as before—and she went still.

When she frowned, he said questioningly, "What—?"

Cocking her head, she very gently bumped him with her hip.

"If we're performing some sort of dance," Matthias said, in a much more normal tone, "I should warn you that I do a decent waltz, but my abilities end there."

She filed away that tidbit of info. "Matthias. May I ask you a very personal question?"

Immediate inscrutability. If he was even half decent at poker, she was recruiting him to form a competition duo. "Go on."

"Do you have something in your right trouser pocket?"

He continued to look at her, then lifted one eyebrow, reached into his pocket and withdrew a metal tube decorated with vintage drawings of Regency carriages. Sylvie's famous chocolate breath mints. "Johnny's mints. They were in Ailsa's cage."

"Oh, thank *God*."

Chapter Fourteen

School visits were always an extra headache for the security team, as adolescents were often overly enthusiastic and unpredictable. However, those attributes were par for the course on Team Marchmont anyway, and Johnny did genuinely enjoy kids.

Wednesday morning's engagement, the opening of the new science wing at Evelyn Pennington College, was in a former stately home. Prattlings, once the aptly named country pad for prime ministers.

A lot of plotting and deals would have taken place within the palatial stone walls, a tradition likely being continued with glee now that the building was occupied by about six hundred teenagers.

Many of whom were now plastered against the floor-to-ceiling windows, gaping down at Johnny and his entourage as he greeted their headteacher, Alexandra Brentwood, a tall Black woman with a kind, very shrewd face. She turned to welcome his aides, shaking hands with Pet.

Matthias stood with Benji, scanning the front of the school. He genuinely enjoyed his job, took pride in it, but he couldn't deny that from a purely personal perspective and for the first time in his life, work was slipping to second-priority status when it came to where he most appreciated spending his time. With a strong probability of soon falling to a very *distant* second place.

His body was under no illusions as to *its* priority. Pet was hiding it well—she had a better poker face than he did today—but she was palpably nervous about the meeting she'd arranged with the Duchess of Clarence this afternoon. And every muscle, sinew, and cell were drawn to her. Wanted to *go* to her. Hold her until that tautness left her mouth. Fucking *cuddle* her.

He'd become a cuddler. Highly situation and person specific, but still.

Maybe he'd stop making his juniors attend the personal development seminars recommended by the protocol manual. Personal development was proving extremely unsettling.

Pet had always been an indomitable force, but he was mentally upgrading her to the status of a mine in the games of *Battleship* they sometimes played with Johnny to help him decompress after minor calamities. Small and lethal, knocking down more defenses with every moment together. Months—years—of vital shields were cracking and toppling, and it had left him feeling as vulnerable as a fucking newborn lamb. From day one of this supposed "fake" coupling, he'd done the emotional equivalent of ripping his fingernail down to the quick, leaving himself continually exposed to further damage, but there was no turning back now.

Even if he was heading for absolute internal carnage.

Benji cleared his throat. "I thought we might have to fend off some ardent teenage fangirls, all atwitter over Johnny's big baby blues, but looking at that terrifying army of young 'uns plastered against the windows, they seem to be more interested in *you*, mate. Evidently, they're real big into muscles if they don't mind that the monster biceps are attached to zero charm and a face like a smashed-in Rubik's cube."

Matthias's reluctant amusement vanished when he realized that wasn't just a joke. He *was* under a lot of scrutiny from the five floors of large windows.

"That's your youthful fanbase." Layla had broken away from the group around Johnny. She addressed them with a twitching mouth. "Apparently most of the senior class are fascinated with the romance *behind* the royals."

He could see that. He'd never seen so many teenage girls in his life—and he'd faced down armed offenders who were less alarming en masse. Jesus, some of them were *pointing* at him.

They all went very quiet and bashful, however, when the procession of aides and press arrived in the refurbed, high-tech science wing Johnny was opening, although the stares continued.

While Johnny and Pet went to admire a child's experiment, Benji said at his shoulder, out of earshot of the media and the kids, "You seem to have pissed off the Bulldog. His attacks have taken an ugly swing into the extremely personal. He's ripped into Pet's full dating history, making her out to be some sort of heartless, promiscuous honeybee, who flits from flower to flower." His voice was heavy with disgust, but there was barely veiled concern there. "And you've been painted as a violent brute, who's still dealing with anger issues after your colleague's murder and will go to any lengths to protect your charges."

With a scornful snort, Benji added, "There's a scattering of truth in that last bit, but anyone who'd call you violent and un-fucking-controlled has never spent more than five seconds in your company. But there'll be people who'll buy it."

Fuck, Matthias despised that guy. A bottom-crawling piece of shit whom he didn't want anywhere near Pet, even verbally.

Across the room, she was laughing with a group of girls. As they all exchanged conspiratorial glances, she took a pen and corrected something in their workbook.

When she raised her head and saw him watching her, she tucked the tip of her tongue between her teeth in a guilty look, her eyes dancing.

Familiar emotion sledgehammered him in the chest.

"That prick will never pull her down to his level," he said, "but she shouldn't have had to deal with it in the first place."

Benji looked at him for a long moment, then returned his gaze to where Johnny was charming another group of kids. Their shyness had dissipated completely as soon as he rolled up his sleeves and asked to participate in an experiment extracting bismuth from an indigestion syrup, joking that he was getting addicted to antacids after too many family dinners, thanks to the king's abysmal tastes in food.

"Another sign the Bulldog knows fuck all about any of us," Benji murmured. "Going after Pet was a two-fold sign of rampant idiocy. She's more than capable of taking care of herself and could be impressively vengeful if she wanted. And from the moment she stepped foot in St. Giles Palace, she's had unconditional backup. You've been incredibly protective of her since the beginning."

As if the universe wanted to underline that fact, it was less than thirty seconds later that a small explosion shattered the low hum of laughter in the room, the sound echoing from wall to wall.

They reacted immediately. As most people froze, their full team went into action. Benji and one of their juniors, Francesca, were closest to Johnny. They pushed in front of him, covering his position as he reared back, hands against the workbench. Pet was at his side, with a little girl, and Matthias pulled them behind him, angling his torso and arm to protect their heads. A maneuver he'd performed dozens of times, both in training and in the field. Usually, his heart wasn't pounding into his damn throat. The rest of the team secured the remaining children.

It was all over quickly.

An easy threat clearance, only a momentary blip. A combustion experiment in the corner had gone out with a literal bang. Purple and blue smoke was pouring from a beaker, flanked by a clearly mortified child with two thick plaits, freckled brown skin, and very wide eyes.

"Sorry! Oh, fuck," she said, earning herself a reprimand from her headteacher.

Johnny recovered a lot more quickly than he had with the sword incident at the museum. With a genuine-sounding chuckle, he squeezed out from behind Benji to go speak to the embarrassed student.

Matthias watched him closely, then looked down at Pet, belatedly realizing he was still shielding her. From the chilling threat of dripping purple slime. The kid with her had darted off to giggle with her friends.

"You all right?" he asked, hearing the abrasive rasp in his voice. "I didn't hurt you?"

"As if you'd ever do that," she murmured, once more just casually knocking him off guard, reaching in and giving his heart a subtle twist.

The ceiling lights were reflected in her eyes, casting a deceptive tinge of blue amidst the brown. They were close enough that he could see the smooth haze where her pink eyeshadow blended into gold and white. It reminded him of mixing watercolors. Hand of an artist, even in her makeup. When the tip of her tongue touched the center of her upper lip, in that little habitual gesture, the muscles in his abdomen flexed.

"Four," she said softly after another second's pause, and his frown was a questioning flicker. "Tiny freckles. On your left cheek. Just four. Just the left."

The sexual awareness between them was electric. His heartbeat quickened again, a hard, thudding rhythm.

Silent tension seemed to be settling over them once more like storm clouds, but a few kids' laughs rang out then, a happy sound that shattered some of the invisible barriers.

"Cheers." Johnny grinned as he and one of the teens clinked glasses, and they both took a large gulp of a foaming pink liquid.

Benji moved forward, frowning, but the science teacher said hastily, "It's okay. We cleared it ahead of time. All protocols followed. We've been experimenting with flavor extractions from fruits, but everything is completely edible."

The rest of the visit in the science wing continued uneventfully, Johnny dutifully signing a visitor's book and having his handprints taken in clay for a plaque.

They left the kids to their work and exited the lab, heading through an atrium toward the arts block, led by Ms. Brentwood and trailed by the bored journalists. Everyone paused in the atrium to dutifully admire the arcing ceiling, stained glass windows, and enormous murals of ancient mythology. There was an almost spiritual aura to it.

Matthias automatically catalogued the exit points, then—in a move that had become just as instinctive—did a rapid check that both Johnny and Pet were secure and comfortable.

Out of the awed quiet, echoing around the central dome, came a little giggle. Unlike the kids' laughter, this was much deeper in tone and accompanied by a humming sound. He turned his head sharply.

Three seconds ago, Johnny had been standing near a large potted tree, looking at a golden fresco on the ceiling. He was now coming back toward Pet and Benji . . . or rather, *undulating* back toward them.

He'd somehow produced a gait previously unknown to mankind, but likely familiar to marijuana-munching caterpillars. In quite a physical feat, he was moving sideways and appeared to be rising up on the left side of his body, sinking toward the floor with the right, then vice versa, all while keeping a perfectly straight head. Anyone who looked directly at him for too long was going to end up seasick.

As he bobbled past, he pushed his head forward in a smooth movement and smiled—eyebrows pulled taut, lips parted, not a single tooth visible. With no disrespect intended, Matthias suddenly had a very strong childhood flashback of helping a foster father make dinner, and idly carving a hollow grin into a peeled potato.

Nobody else was moving. Even the press pit was still, everyone watching in total silence as a member of the royal family boogied his way past.

Looking high as hell.

Johnny paused to look Matthias up and down, failed to contain the motion to simply his neck muscles, and fell forward. Matthias caught him by the arms, and Johnny turned that increasingly disturbing smile on him. "Hello."

"Hello," he returned grimly, removing one hand to see if the other man was going to stand up straight on his own.

Right. That would be a no.

Johnny reached up and patted one of Matthias's wrists. Peering up with the glazed eyes of an apocalyptic zombie, he mused, "D'you ever look at p-people in the street and think 'I could just pick you up and squash you between my enormous thumbs'?"

Behind him, Pet's expression succinctly summarized the widespread emotion throughout the atrium.

An absolutely massive "what the fuck is going on right now."

"No," Matthias said matter-of-factly, and set Johnny back on his feet again, holding him until he seemed steady. Ish.

"Oh." Johnny looked disappointed.

He cheered up when he noticed Pet. That creepy-arse smile swung from her to Matthias. He pointed between them with all his fingers, as he addressed the press grandiosely. "They've been wanting to bang for absolutely *ages*, you know." He tapped the side of his nose. "It's quite remiss it took you this long to notice."

His words echoed through the room, crystal clear. The acoustics in here were excellent. What a boon for the more musical amongst the students. None of whom were in earshot anymore, thank Christ.

Matthias exchanged one glance with Pet, who looked slightly dazed, like Alice midtumble into Wonderland.

A fragment of thought went through his mind that at least it couldn't get much worse. Always fatal. He took full karmic responsibility for the next twenty seconds, as Johnny turned to wave cheerily at a bewildered reporter, who automatically waved cheerily back, before announcing, "*I* do not need to b-bang. I have banged. I am a banger. Three t-times this morning." His tone evolved into immense satisfaction. "And I'm bloody good at it, too. Ask my wife."

Pet's hands had moved to her cheeks, angled outward as if she were adding a couple of jazz hands to the performance, but her initial confusion was dissipating into action. There were exactly two more seconds of obvious silent swearing before she went straight into calm crisis mode. The moment anything went awry at these things, she was ready for it—and apparently that now included Johnny wafting about, smiling like an intoxicated blobfish and massively oversharing in front of three different media outlets.

Making eye contact with Matthias again, she very subtly curled her thumb against her other arm. He nodded once, touching his earpiece and flicking the concealed microphone around to his mouth. He murmured a few terse codewords to summon the on-call medic.

"Ms. Brentwood," Pet said quietly, after another hard stare at Johnny's face. Probably at his eyes, because Matthias had just done the same thing. His pupils were pinpricks. "I think we need to double-check what was in the pink concoction in the science lab, because unless it was 190 proof vodka, he might be having an allergic reaction." Even with her attention on Johnny, she hadn't missed the headteacher's growing horror and purposefully kept her tone light.

As one of the other teachers raced off back to the lab, Pet lifted her voice. "I'm sorry, I'm afraid we'll have to cut this short." Johnny was staring blankly into space. "Mr. Marchmont's been taken unwell."

"Mr. Marchmont's off his fucking face," a cameraman muttered from near the back of the pack.

The royal correspondents were starting to shake off the collective confusion, and tangible excitement was creeping in. A routine school visit had suddenly turned into a potential goldmine for page views. Despite the recent gossip-mongering, they weren't *all* vultures—Johnny had never been anything but kind to them, and the ones who obviously liked him were watching with concern. Several asked if they should call for medical assistance. At least two-thirds, however, were blatantly composing their headlines already. Matthias turned his body to block as much of Johnny from view as he could, ignoring the demands that he move.

Johnny didn't aid the cause by cocking his head like a bird and peering around Matthias's biceps. He half expected him to chirp a fucking "peek-a-boo."

"Jesus, is he having a really belated reaction to Ailsa's bite or something?" Pet muttered at his side. "Step one of his metamorphoses into Parrot-Man, the world's chattiest superhero. Johnny? Are you feeling sick? Dizzy?"

"Feathery?" Benji suggested sardonically. He signaled to the rest of the security team, who moved to start clearing out the press pack. The incessant, annoying sound of the camera shutters picked up speed. As expected, most of them resisted expulsion, claiming this probable medical episode was somehow news "in the public's interest." Layla was over there, too, making a preemptive attempt at a PR save.

Johnny drew a deep breath and raised a finger, as if he were about to make a grand pronouncement.

And then just stood there.

He eyed his finger with great interest from all angles.

"Is he . . . all right? Have you called a doctor?" Ms. Brentwood looked understandably appalled and not sure what to do, almost certainly a rarity for her.

"The medic is on her way. You don't know what was in that drink?" Pet asked her, and the headteacher shook her head.

"Absolutely nothing *dangerous*. This is a school. The safety of

our students—and visitors—is always paramount." Ms. Brentwood looked worriedly at Johnny. "A reaction to an ingredient, you
think?"

Johnny stumbled slightly, and Pet's hand shot out to steady him.

"I've got him," Matthias said, and Benji jerked his thumb toward
a bench under an indoor tree. It was covered with donors' plaques,
and it was the only seat in the space.

"Reckon he'd better sit down," he advised crisply. "Johnny, mate,
pull up a pew, yeah?"

None of them were bothering much with formality at this
point, but they still couldn't just shove him toward the bench,
so getting him to sit down proved a mammoth task. He'd suddenly regained his voice and was adamant that the lines in the
patterned floor tiles were structural cracks. He was convinced
he'd fall through the floor if he moved and was extremely vocal
about it.

Finally, when Pet glanced at the lingering members of the press
pit and ran her hand from her forehead over her hair, her control
fracturing just enough to glimpse leashed panic, Matthias had had
enough.

"Johnny." It was a deep, uncompromising command, and Johnny's glazed eyes jolted toward him. "We won't let you fall through
the floor. Will you let me help you across?"

He didn't think Johnny had a bloody clue what was going on
now, but when the other man nodded, he carefully swung him up,
and piggy-backed Rosie's very tall, surprisingly heavy husband
across the room.

When he'd signed his St. Giles contract, they had warned him it
would bring a different set of experiences and logistical challenges
to his previous roles, and yes, this would qualify.

Johnny started swinging his long legs, like a kid riding a donkey at the beach.

When they finally got him seated on the bench, he leaned forward with his forearms resting on his knees. He was pale, with red splotches beginning to mottle his cheeks.

Hell.

Matthias activated his mic. "ETA on the medic?"

Five minutes.

"I d-do have a lot of sex," Johnny informed them. He considered. "Not while we're working, of c-course. Sometimes on the royal train, though."

There were still cameras pointed their way, the more stubborn journalists whining at his team, who continued to fence them out.

Benji cleared his throat. "Good for you, mate. Maybe you should just rest a bit—"

"But in the end, it's n-not about the chains and all that," Johnny said, and Pet double-blinked.

"Trains?" Benji double-checked after a pause, stressing the word, and Johnny looked at him blankly.

"No." His face softened as he went on more emphatically, "It's not just about good sex. When it's *her*, and you're looking into her eyes, and f-feeling her breath on your skin, and her hands on your face, it's like . . . the world just goes. Just you t-two. Forever." He looked down at his hands, his fingers interlocking. "And nothing else really matters."

Complete silence throughout the atrium.

Even the camera shutters had stopped.

Matthias was very aware of the smallest sensations of his body, as if he could physically feel the blood pumping through his veins.

Pet's lashes flickered as her head turned slightly in his direction. He could see the unevenness of her own breaths.

Johnny suddenly sat up straighter and lifted his finger again, but this time, he followed through on the promise of an announcement. "I f-feel a bit weird."

Before anyone could catch him, he tipped forward and hit the floor.

"On the bright side, that should put an emphatic nail in the coffin where the me-and-Johnny rumors are concerned," Pet said, as she continued to wear a path in the large fluffy rug on the floor.

The Duchess of Clarence's personal office was surprisingly sparse on decorative detail—maybe she'd already pawned most of her belongings—but the walls were lined with packed bookcases. As Matthias watched Pet walking back and forth, trying to pace out her nerves, he noted absently that many of the books were very uniform in appearance, their spines almost too perfectly matched and upright.

Pet's Miss Marple streak was apparently contagious, because it took every scrap of his severely battered willpower not to experimentally tug on a few of those books and see if a bookcase swung open. They were living in the palace, not a *Famous Five* book, but at this point, the duchess having a concealed underground lair would be the least surprising part of the month. And unless she was transporting everything straight to a high-end dealer, she had to be hoarding her stolen goods somewhere before she sold them off.

She'd only returned to the palace today from an overseas

engagement, but on receiving Pet's request for a short audience, she'd invited them to her office this afternoon, before they headed to Hannigan's Wood for this magic festival. He'd been firmly instructed to wear his cheapest, least sentimental clothing. It was probably a bit concerning how off-balance he felt without a tie.

When he'd fingered his bare throat for the fourth time on the way here, Pet had informed him sweetly that—although she'd wondered in the past—it apparently wasn't a *The Girl with the Green Ribbon* situation, and his head wasn't actually going to roll right off without the tie.

"It's headline news that Rosie and Johnny spend their commutes boning. The memes are already going viral," Pet said. "Social media's taking the piss, the armchair prudes are outraged, but I think most people are getting a genuine kick out of it that their relationship is so passionate." She coughed. "Chains and all. Although the Bulldog's probably composing a blind item suggesting I went all 'woman scorned' and poisoned him."

"Don't give him ideas," he said. "Today's effort was fucked-up enough."

She grimaced. "At least Johnny's all right."

The medic treating him had taken one look at the list of ingredients in the kids' concoction and tapped her finger against item number five.

"Utterly innocuous," she'd said, as she took Johnny's blood pressure. He'd regained consciousness by that point but had vomited twice. "For almost everyone. Unfortunately, it's a literal one in a million response—like a lightning bolt straight into the central nervous system. The equivalent of downing five bottles of wine in ten seconds and chucking in a whacking load of recreational drugs for good measure. No lasting effects once it's excreted from the system." Matthias wouldn't have been surprised if Alexandra Brentwood had been the next to collapse at that point, so great was her obvious relief. "I'm afraid you'll be a bit miserable for a few hours, but ultimately just fine, Your Highness."

"That's m'wife," Johnny had muttered, his hand cupped near his mouth. "I'm just a m-mister."

"It was more of a physical description than an honorific," the medic had responded with a deadpan expression, managing to get a small smile out of him.

He'd regained more of his cheer after a phone call with Rosie. The human rubber ball struck again. Matthias had never envied that impervious resilience more.

Pet paced in front of him again, her fists opening and closing.

Her increasing agitation acted on him like a razor blade scraping over raw skin, and he wasn't exactly sanguine about this, himself.

He was experiencing that insidious sense of premonition, that this meeting *would* turn up some answers for her. They'd skimmed the surface of the potential risks in that, but he hadn't wanted to flatten her hopes any further with his cynicism. However, his concern had deepened with her casual disclosure earlier that she'd invested her unwanted inheritance from her mother into De Vere's. As a major shareholder in her brother's very lucrative business, she was in possession of both financial assets and an empathetic heart, both of which were a draw to unscrupulous personalities.

And if the unknown branch of her family tree turned out to bear more rotting fruit like her arsehole stepfather—

Christ, he was physically unable to just stand here when she was so anxious. He reached out and snagged her fidgeting hand, hooking a finger around one of hers. She stopped pacing and exhaled a long breath.

He looked down at their linked index fingers, curled tightly around each other.

He was so sure that one day some girl was going to turn your life upside down, and wrap you around her little finger, and light you up like a Christmas tree.

Pet squeezed his finger, swinging their hands. "What is it? Your face looks weird."

"Blunt," he said. "But true."

Her brow lift was a delightful study in exasperation. "Your *expression* was weird. Your face is lovely."

Alarming. Evidently, she *did* need to take advantage of the staff subsidy for prescription lenses, and she was regularly behind the wheel of a car.

Diverting the subject, he nodded at the bookcases and voiced his suspicions about hidden mechanisms.

"Not that I'm trying to tell you how to do your job," she said, "but as senior security, shouldn't you be, you know, concerned about a campaign of systematic theft?"

He shrugged. "I'm personal protection division. People are my concern, not property. And truthfully—"

"It's fucking hilarious?"

Neither of them could hold back their grins.

They were standing there like that when the door was flung open.

The duchess sailed in and headed straight for the small bar trolley in the corner of the room. "Terribly sorry to keep you waiting," she said breezily, pouring herself a few fingers of whisky. She glanced at the clock, considered, then topped it up to a full glass. "Drink?"

As they politely declined, she peered at them over her glass, the ice cubes rattling as she seated herself in an armchair, waving them to the small couch. "No need to censor yourselves."

Pet had pulled her hand from Matthias's immediately, an act of professional discretion that he should approve, not want to firmly retrieve it. Lia watched with interest as Pet sat down and he took up his usual stance behind her seat. He didn't anticipate an imminent attack from the duchess, but habit died hard.

"You could ravish one another on the chaise longue for all I care. Although I wouldn't recommend it. There's a particular loose spring that does not encourage carnal activity. How can I help?"

Pet blinked, but she hadn't spent months around Johnny's equally chaotic thought processes for nothing. She rallied quickly and didn't beat around the bush. Taking out the photo, she passed it to the duchess, who flicked it straight with a dramatic flourish.

"We're trying to identify someone in this photo," Pet said, "and Rosie says that was the old Clarence patronage crest, on the bunting. It may have been an event for one of the duke's or your own patron charities. I know it's a very slim chance, but do you possibly recognize where—"

"It's the function room at Rosaline Abbey," Lia replied calmly, sipping from her drink. With her pinkie finger, she pointed at a shadowy shape in the background. "That's the Perigioni clock. Centuries old and a court jester still pops out on the hour. It reminded me of Frederick." She cocked her head. "That cake was excellent. One of your grandfather's, I believe."

Pet leaned forward, gripping the edge of the couch. "You remember that party?"

"Well, *party* is an optimistic term. It was the opening of the Windsor Literary Arts Circle. You've never met such a tedious group. Absolutely *endless* speeches. They're still just as bad." Her hovering pinkie finger moved to their anonymous Pet-alike. "I always thought it wasn't a coincidence that Carlisle refused any further public appearances after that evening, even when her books became more popular. But then, if you can afford to be a recluse, I'm a devout advocate. Most people are dreadful."

The duchess's attention had still been mostly on her whisky, but now fixed on Pet. "The resemblance is really quite remarkable, isn't it? You gave me quite a surprise when you first turned up at the palace." Her tone became very dry. "Like most of the population, I haven't seen Carlisle in person for years, and for a fleeting second, I thought she'd either tapped the fountain of youth or found a far better cosmetic surgeon than mine. But your cheeks are rounder, and the eyes aren't quite right."

Pet's inhalation was audible, but her voice barely perceptible. "Carlisle?"

"Carlisle Tallen, the woman with *almost* your face, darling. And judging by what's happened to your face now, I presume you didn't know she existed."

"No. Not until I saw the photo. I—" Pet twisted to look up at Matthias.

One look into her eyes and he moved around the couch, sitting beside her and taking her hand.

"Carlisle Tallen. A reclusive author," she said slowly. "Wait—C. W. Tallen? She of the idyllic houseboats and historic pubs?"

Matthias lifted his brows. He still emphatically dismissed the concept of fate—but the universe had really decided to front up and make a case for it lately.

"She regretted not choosing a pen name," Lia mused. "She's never reached the grandest heights of publishing, and would probably be horrified to do so, but even well before the social media age, I believe the odd reader would track her down. And she doesn't even like visits from friends." Well, that boded well. "She still refuses to have a phone."

"It'll be easy enough to find her now, regardless," he murmured, seeing Pet catch at her upper lip, and the duchess returned to her drink.

"Yes, it will," the duchess agreed, after swallowing a mouthful. "She lives at Fable Cottage, Upper Hanley Road, Windsor."

Silence.

Pet gripped him hard.

They were going to be in Windsor tomorrow morning. Johnny had a meeting at the castle.

And they both had the afternoon off, because they were on duty in the evening for an event in the palace gardens.

Those twangs of nonexistent fate.

Before they left the office, Matthias fixed the duchess with a penetrating stare. "You've had periodic interactions with Pet for months now." He made *some* effort at keeping the exasperation at bay and his tone respectful. "It never occurred to you to mention the obvious connection?"

Lia considered. "No," she said, wonderingly. "Isn't that odd?"

At which point, she finished her drink, walked to the bookcase, turned her back, pulled on a book, and disappeared through a hidden door.

Chapter Fifteen

When the taxi dropped them off close to Hannigan's Wood, Pet was still balancing multiple different emotions—including the simmering annoyance of knowing she'd wonder for the rest of her life what was behind the Duchess of Clarence's bookcases.

It said a lot when even the revelation that she was probably related to a semi-well-known author wasn't the most pressing issue on her mind, but she'd made the decision in the car to just—set everything aside tonight. Try to relax for a few hours. And enjoy being with Matthias. Before they eventually drew a line under Codename Charming and he still very possibly withdrew to a safe, horrible professional distance.

She reached out and grabbed his hand, and he automatically squeezed hers, looking down at her. He was weirdly unfamiliar in his casual clothing, but she kept sneaking peeks at the way the fabric of his shirt stretched across his shoulders. She did actually miss his tie, though.

"Pap?" he asked under his breath, sending a skewering glance around the entrance to the park.

She opted for an enigmatic smile that he could interpret any way he liked. Anyway, there probably were photographers around somewhere. The *Digital Star*, at least, hadn't given up, even though most of the tabloids seemed to be losing interest in her, thank God.

Releasing a breath through her mouth, she gazed at their surroundings. Across the expanse of green grass and spreading right up to thick woodland was a veritable fantasyland. Probably fifty different tents, selling everything from glittering, bottled potions to replica armor and fluttering wings. There were pop-up food stalls constructed to look like hollowed-out trees, and a string quartet dressed as trolls. Pet could see Sugar Fair's tent from here; it was Sylvie's signature pink, lavender, and gold, with fairy-lit ivy strung around the entrance.

Fantastical cosplay, iridescent potions with legally questionable promises of shinier hair and better sex, boozy cauldrons, and her favorite face glowering at it all? What an inexplicable oversight that she'd never been to Witch-Fest before, when this was clearly her spiritual home.

His mind obviously still on the meeting with Lia, Matthias said abruptly, "Even I didn't expect we'd come out of that office with a fucking *postcode*. The whole thing's gone from zero to sixty."

And didn't *that* sum up both their lives right now.

She looked up at him. She wasn't sure what her face was doing, but the concern in his own was suddenly shot through with something fiercer.

With a slightly jerky movement, he kissed her palm. His body was curved over hers, and she couldn't stop herself from cuddling in closer.

Their heads bumped in a little sliding nuzzle, then he said into her ear, "If you do want to go and see her, we'll go. If you're not ready—if you're *never* ready to reopen that chapter, you can put the photo in a drawer, or in the bin, and none of this will touch you again."

It was a low growl of a promise. Matthias, prepared to do battle even with her memories.

A stray coil of desire wound tight at the near brush of their lips, the feel of his fingers at the curve of her waist.

As per the growing norm, someone took a picture of them.

The sights and sounds of the festival returned as a teenager a few feet away lowered her phone and turned red.

"Sorry," the girl squeaked, wincing as she encountered Matthias's glare. "I should have asked. I love you guys. Oh, wow, you're *so* cute. I bought you these."

Amidst that fluster of embarrassment, she thrust a pair of very beautiful, delicate lilac fairy wings at Pet—and ran off to rejoin her giggling friends before either of them could say anything.

Or thank her for what looked to be a very expensive gift.

"Oh my god," Pet said, turning the wings over to admire the glowing shimmer of hand-painted feathers. "We really do have shippers. They're actual people. This is so weird." She smoothed the feathers, enjoying the softness against her fingers. Her cheeks were hot.

Matthias nodded at the wings. "Do you want me to get rid—" Pet clutched them protectively to her chest, wide-eyed, and he redirected midsentence. "—put them on for you?"

A ribbon of humor twined between them, and she looked measuringly from the wings to his wide torso, then fluttered her lashes at him, temporarily hiding again in light flirtation. "Absolutely, but as open-minded as I'm sure Witch-Fest is, I think Oberon role-play is best reserved for the bedroom."

He gave her his most poker-faced, cyborg look of disapproval—but he couldn't hide the flashing smile in his eyes. Silently, he made a twirling motion with his finger, and she obligingly spun around. He looped the ribbons of the fairy wings under her arms, securing them with painstaking care.

Holding her hair out of the way as his fingers fumbled with the fiddly hooks, Pet looked up and realized they were under close surveillance again—of a more personal variety this time.

Sylvie, Dominic, and his sous chef Liam stood nearby, in front of a stall selling cosplay armor. Benji had arrived, too, and was just turning away from a coffee wagon. He handed a steaming cup to a pretty woman with glasses and beaded braids, presumably this week's love of his life. And Jay had just left the Sugar Fair tent, holding hands with his girlfriend, Emma.

With identically raised brows, every one of them stood and watched big, brawny Matthias fluff out her wings for her.

Sylvie moved first, barely repressing her grin. She gave Pet a quick hug and waved at Matthias in greeting. "I'm so glad you could come. Love the wings, too. Maybe we should have gone fairy instead of elf." She touched her pointed costume ears and pretty tiara.

"*We?*" Pet repeated, relieved her voice sounded mostly normal. She scanned her brother from head to foot. "Last time I checked, Resting-Haughty-Face doesn't count as elven cosplay. He just looks like that."

Dominic's epic case of RHF intensified. Very pointedly, with a martyred air, he touched his sternum. "As agreed, I'm wearing a fucking Elf King necklace."

Pet peered at a tiny gold amulet almost hidden by his collar.

His eyes glinting with amusement, Benji introduced his date, Jerrica, and Jay rubbed his hands together.

"Good timing, team. The first heat of Wands starts in ten minutes."

"Wands?" Pet repeated—and, in the space of a one-syllable word, went from curious to severe apprehension as Mabel appeared through the crowd.

Her thin arms were laden with a stack of giant magical wands, each probably half a meter long and an inch thick, attached to paint canisters.

"I thought we agreed Sugar Fair would sit out any future Wands battles," Sylvie said, groaning. "There have probably been actual hostage situations less tense than last year's disaster."

"I already signed us up." Blithely, Jay produced a stack of what appeared to be armbands, some purple, the rest red. "I was going to suggest Sugar Fair versus De Vere's, but for at least one god-damn year, I'd like to make it to the second heat, and I have no intention of being disqualified by Mabel again." He cast a specu-lative look at Matthias, whom he'd met several times when Sugar Fair and De Vere's had collaborated on Rosie and Johnny's wed-ding cake. "Bags Vaughn for our team."

He and Mabel began dispersing armor, and it probably wasn't a good sign that this game required more protective gear than the average stormtrooper.

Pointedly slapping a purple armband into Matthias's hand, Jay gave him a brief tutorial on correct magical-weapon-operation and glitter warfare. As Pet watched, a smile growing, Matthias studied the wand with the intensity and care he'd award an actual gun. His lips moved, and she'd bet half a week's salary he was asking about the rulebook.

Sylvie came over to secure a red armband around Pet's biceps. Following the direction of her gaze, she murmured, "I was going to lightly complain about my membership in the 'behind the snazzy suit, my man's sometimes an overprotective, territorial caveman' club, but I suspect *you're* currently eye-fucking the founder, president, and enforcer, all in one."

Pet wrenched her eyes away. "You'd be hard-pressed to find someone more naturally protective than Matthias," she said, aware of her deepening blush. "He was born for his job."

"He's certainly a superlative bodyguard to Johnny. Which clearly isn't the easiest of assignments." Sylvie picked up a Wand and demonstrated the trigger mechanisms for Pet, how to activate each separate canister. "But when it comes to Matthias's protective instincts, there's obviously the professional and the personal. There's nothing professionally detached about the way that man watches you. And watches *over* you."

With a huge effort, Pet kept her head turned away from him.

"I suspect that if he gave into the *extent* of those instincts," Sylvie added, "you'd find yourself wrapped snugly in cotton wool, probably a thick layer of bubble wrap as well, and permanently tucked under his arm."

Her sister-in-law was suppressing a grin, but her face was acutely perceptive, as always. She hesitated, then said, close to Pet's ear, "When you told us about Matthias, I believed you initially, because—I wanted to. And I couldn't see you being part of deliberate deception. You live your life more honestly and openhearted than anyone I've ever met."

Pet's hands tightened on the Wand.

The curve of Sylvie's mouth deepened. "Dominic didn't buy it."

"I noticed." Pet's momentary wryness faded. "I didn't want to lie to you," she said on a bare breath, fiddling with the triggers, and Sylvie shook her head.

"We know the tabloids," she said, just as softly. "Through bitter experience of our own. That situation would have spiraled way out of control if you hadn't done something to check it. I know you'd have wanted to help Rosie, too." Moving Pet's fingers, she gently repositioned her grip on the controls before she could accidentally glitter-missile someone. "And—ultimately, it's *not* a lie, is it?"

Pet was unable to resist the invisible pull this time, as if warm fingertips were reaching out to turn her chin toward him. She watched as he fired a practice shot at a paper target, purple glitter exploding in the center. At his side, Jay steepled his fingers gleefully, like a plotting warlord.

Without lowering the wand, Matthias angled his head, looking back at her over the bunched muscles of his shoulder. He'd pushed up his sleeves, and she saw his arm flex compulsively as his grip tightened.

Slowly, she exhaled.

When she met Sylvie's watchful, sparkling gaze, her sister-in-law's small smile had grown.

"We're . . . attracted to each other," she said, in the absolute understatement of the millennium.

They were keeping their voices hushed, but Sylvie's snort was likely heard in the next county. "Thank you, Captain Obvious. I *had* gathered. Apart from that weirdo at the *Digital Star* who seems to have a personal vendetta about it, I think everyone is well aware by this point that you'd like to climb that man like a tree." She held up one hand and wiggled her callused fingertips, scarred from years of molten-hot sugarwork. "I got scalded from the iPad screen with that last round of stalker photos."

Pet winced. "Dominic didn't see the video, did he?"

"About two seconds of it. I've never seen him shut down a tab so fast. He stopped muttering direly about you being coerced into sordid arrangements by the palace PR team after that. And threatened to throttle Matthias instead."

When Pet cast her eyes upward, Sylvie added cheerfully, "We had a short, pointed conversation about the fact that his 'baby' sister is a fully grown woman who makes her own choices and knows what she's doing—"

Unpreventable additional grimace at that one.

"—and would undoubtedly prefer her beloved big brother to remain intact. As would his adoring wife," Sylvie finished. "Dom is not a small man—and neither is Jay, but the two of them just moved behind Matthias and they've disappeared completely."

She was right. All Pet could see of the other men was the edge of Jay's shoe.

They observed that interesting phenomenon for a moment.

"He really is massive." Sylvie sounded like an intrigued professor making an anthropological discovery.

Pet glanced sideways. Her sister-in-law's very curious, wide eyes were darting back and forth between Pet and Matthias, obviously cataloguing the extent of their size difference. She could almost *see* the fascinated speculation scrolling across Sylvie's forehead.

"Face-sitting, cowgirl, and the Upstanding Citizen position," Mabel reminded her, popping in like the chorus of an extremely horny Greek play. She picked up a handful of Wands from the pile. "Or you're going to be crushed like a can compressor. We're quite fond of you around here and would prefer you remain three-dimensional."

Sylvie made a sort of squeaking noise. "*Mab*—"

Calmly, Pet lifted her Wand and shot Mabel in the chest.

"Pet!" Sylvie couldn't control her giggles now.

Mabel blinked down at the pink glitter splattered over her shirt.

"Dead center," she said admiringly. "However, I'm obliged to state that we may be on the same team, but I value vengeance over victory."

"Don't retaliate until the gong goes," Sylvie said warningly, still grinning, and Mabel cocked her head.

"I'm not wasting my shots until it counts." She raised her brows at Pet. "She can watch out for me later, though." Her shrewd gaze flicked over to Matthias. All the men had seen the rogue assassination, with varying degrees of amusement. "Although I doubt I'll get near her. Jay's single brain cell is working more sluggishly than usual today, putting Pet and the Hulk on opposing teams. There's no chance in a zillion years that dude is aiming a weapon at her, and he'll be more focused on watching her back than taking out the opposition."

Pet shook her head. "We've never played anything but board and video games at the palace, since Matthias keeps vetoing anything more exciting, but I'm sure he'll want to win."

As she said it, though, she realized that Matthias *wasn't* particularly competitive when they played games with Johnny. Highly analytical and focused, but he didn't care that much about winning.

In fact . . . She frowned, and Mabel looked at her with that characteristic, knowing expression.

"I bet he engineers it so that you win most of those games," she said, almost tauntingly. Her eyes were both cynical and affectionate.

Pet *did* win a lot of the time. And there'd been several occasions when she'd been almost out of the game, or at risk of being killed, only to find more money in her bank or her path suddenly cleared of enemies in their multi-player quests.

Her lips parted. Matthias was talking to Dominic, Jay, and Benji, and smiling just a little, and it struck her for the first time that he was looking—not exactly *relaxed*, this was ever-alert Matthias and they were in a crowd of strangers with weird weapons, but . . . It was hard to define. As if *something* in him had started to settle, just a little, even if he weren't quite aware of it. When he let himself, he looked—

"He looks happy. Brooding and pessimistic, as usual, but much happier."

For a moment, it was like her mind had gained an external voice, and Pet jumped as a newcomer with a glorious cloud of soft hair stepped closer, smiling a bit anxiously.

"Jenny," she said, and shook herself internally, managing to return the smile sincerely. "I'm so glad you came."

"I can't stay long," Jenny said, gesturing behind her, where a small group of people were browsing a potions stall. "We're going out for dinner with Sarita's family, but we thought we'd stop by for a quick peek since we were in the area."

At the edge of the group, a tall, striking woman with short black hair and large, thickly lashed eyes kept looking at Jenny, her expression both soft and fervent.

"Matthias will be really glad," Pet said, as she turned to introduce Jenny to Sylvie and Mabel.

They shook hands, Sylvie and Jenny exclaiming over how much they each loved the other's business, then Sylvie tactfully moved Mabel away a few steps, probably also seeing the faint lines of tension on Jenny's face.

Jenny glanced over at Matthias, who hadn't noticed her arrival yet. Biting her lip, she studied Pet before she said, very frankly, "Jonna McCarthy said he gave his usual noncommittal response to her party invite. I was hoping he might be convinced to go. He used to be really close to Padraig's family. Almost another son and brother to them, although I don't know if he's ever really realized, deep down, how much they love him for himself. Not just as an adjunct of Padraig." She stopped, wetting her lips and obviously steeling her spine against the sudden thrust of memory. "He's pulled away since Padraig was killed. I know that Matthias has *never* been very . . . open. Padraig said it was like sieging a castle, becoming friends with him, but that once the drawbridge was down, you were in for life. You'd never have a more loyal mate."

She frowned. "I like him very much for himself, as well, but I've always felt like I owe it to Padraig to—to keep an eye on him, I guess." Her head moved in a short, self-conscious gesture. "I know that sounds ridiculous. He's an ex-military bodyguard built like a tank."

But he had a heart just as big. And he felt very deeply.

One of Sylvie's pastry chefs had just come over to give Sylvie a message—Kate, Pet thought her name was—and the young woman held up a small object that glinted under the overhead lights. "This isn't your button, is it?" she asked, her voice carrying over the crowd noise. "I found it in the kitchen prep area."

Sylvie took it, turning it over. "Not mine. It's pretty. If you can't find the owner, Pet might like it. She collects buttons."

Jenny had stopped to collect her thoughts, but she cocked her head at that, looking at Pet curiously. A smile grew in her eyes. "Of course," she said. "You're Button. I should have realized."

Pet was still clutching her Wand. She almost fired another shot, accidentally this time, at the unexpectedness of hearing that from someone else—Button with a capital "B," unmistakably a nickname. A pet name. "I—what?"

"Matthias has always been just as tight-lipped as Padraig about their work. I know they have to be discreet. But he did his best to make small talk, poor guy, when he'd come around every week to check on me in those first days. Months. It's all a bit of a blur now. Back then, it felt somehow endless *and* as if time was standing still." Jenny's eyes clouded at the recollection. Pet couldn't even imagine what those days must have been like. Couldn't bear to imagine it. "Once he started his assignment at the palace, he'd give me a few bare-bone scraps of anecdotes to cheer me up, but he'd codename everyone. I know a few of your colleagues as Cupcake, Domino, and Farquaad."

An unexpected spike of laughter shot through Pet's body. She was guessing "Cupcake" was Ji-Hoon, who faithfully produced dozens of them for every staff birthday. And she'd put money on Farquaad being Prince Frederick. Domino? She wasn't sure, unless it was poor Johnny, constantly toppling everyone else over.

"I haven't seen him as much this year," Jenny said, "but every time, when I'd ask about work, the common denominator in each scrap of information was 'Button.' I don't know if he realized how much he talked about her. About you." Those traces of sadness lingered in her eyes, but a mischievous smile touched her mouth. "Button was obviously driving him up the wall, with her propensity for running into trouble, but he was *not* a happy bodyguard when someone blamed her for their mistake, and Ebenezer yelled at her."

Pet's heart was beating hard, her mind skimming over the surface of everything, almost afraid to delve deeper, but she absently translated that one. Ebenezer. Rosie's Scrooge-like private secretary, Edward, before he'd retired. She remembered that incident.

Jenny let out a sigh, the lines easing around her mouth. There was a strange poignancy in the way she looked at Sarita, then, and her shoulders relaxed, her hands unclasping. Her eyes returned to

Pet for another long moment. She reached out to touch her fingers. "I should have put two and two together," she said, "and realized that I can probably stop worrying about him now."

Matthias saw her, then, and she went over to speak to him.

Pet stood there for more than a minute, not turning until Sylvie and Mabel reclaimed her attention, summoning her to get her armor before the battle began.

"Surely we don't actually need *armor*," she protested absently. "I'm obviously going to be shaking glitter out of my ears for weeks, but I don't anticipate actual bullet wounds."

She hadn't even finished speaking before Matthias appeared with a padded vest in his hands.

"Jay's demonstrated the shot mechanism," he said. "You could easily be bruised without protective gear."

Both his tone and his expression were uncompromising, and over his shoulder, Pet saw Sylvie's eyes starting to dance very pointedly.

"I could also be attacked by a rabid squirrel or blinded by paint in my retina . . ." She trailed off as he produced a pair of goggles. "Oh, for God's sake."

When a group of kids started taking practice shots at nearby trees and she saw how hard some of the glitter bombs hit, however, she retrieved the largest vest from the armor stall. He lifted his brows, but after a moment of heavy conversation—held entirely with their eyes, in utter silence—he lowered his head. Firm lips twitching, he remained still as she tugged the vest into place and fastened the straps under his arms.

"Is Jenny gone?" She couldn't see the other woman or her friends in the crowd now.

"They're having a look around, then heading out for dinner. It's her girlfriend's birthday."

He spoke perfectly normally, but she wanted to be sure— "Are you okay? I know you said you were glad that she's found someone else, but it must be difficult, too."

When she lifted her head, she caught a flash of something deep and painful, but it was fleeting.

"She's a good person, who deserves a good life. Ultimately, it doesn't matter what Padraig would have wanted where she's concerned, it's what she wants and needs herself—but he *would* have wanted this for her. If she's happy, I'm happy for her."

Pet's palms were resting against the vest, feeling the movement of his breaths. Her fingertips momentarily dug into padded nylon and steely muscle.

Then, realizing how much of his chest *wasn't* covered by the now very inadequate-looking body armor, she took a step back, surveying him from head to foot with a frown.

The smile returned to his eyes, and he unexpectedly bent to drop a kiss on her forehead. She moved simultaneously, looking up, and his lips landed squarely on hers.

They both made a slight sound, their eyes open, close enough that the sweep of her lashes almost fanned his own.

Neither of them moved. Pet wasn't breathing. Her toes curled hard in her depressingly sensible shoes. Matthias's chest moved with a rough inhalation, and his hands closed hard on her waist when—without breaking that shared gaze—she darted the tip of her tongue in a fleeting touch to his.

With a loud screech of static, a voice crackled through hidden speakers. "The first Wands heat will begin in five minutes. If you're not participating"—a thread of staticky laughter—"we suggest you keep clear of the woods or you're likely to find yourself unexpectedly bright, sparkling, and sticky."

"That sounds promising," she murmured against Matthias's mouth.

She was discovering many favorite new sensations right now, but the best of them all might be the vibration of his silent laughter.

Chapter Sixteen

Pet didn't know what tortuous mind had invented Wands, but they couldn't have made it more difficult—or suggestive—to use the damned things if they'd tried. When the first reserves ran out, various buttons and levers had to be pushed simultaneously to activate secondary canisters, which required a lot more concentration than most people had when they were running around the woods being shot at by other wand-bearing nutters. To fire a "spell," a.k.a. a massive wad of gelatinous sparkles that exploded on impact, the wand stick had to be flicked in just the right way. Adding tricks like a half turn of the wrist either sent two spells at once or shot it off in different directions. To triple-barrel it, the tube had to be pumped in an extremely phallic manner, and a very difficult maneuver called a "mortifer" activated the death canister, containing gold glitter. If you were hit with a golden death spell, you were out of the battle instantly; otherwise, you could take three strikes before elimination.

This was going to be chaos.

It was also bloody hilarious, she discovered as she dashed through the undergrowth, darting from tree to tree, ducking to avoid flying spells from teams whose armbands spanned the full rainbow and kept going into pink, turquoise, brown, and—

Pet swore as a stranger with an aquamarine band popped out from behind a massive oak and got her right in the chest with a pink spell. Her assailant grinned and blew imaginary smoke from the end of her wand, disappearing in a flash before Pet could fire one back.

Crouching down in the soft grass to catch her breath, she whipped her head around at a flash of movement in nearby brush. Crab-crawling backward, she dove to the side as a glitter bomb sailed over her head and exploded in a massive *whoosh* of golden glitter.

Sneaky, but not quite fast enough . . .

Quiet as a prowling cat, she crept around the bushes and flicked her wand, twisting her wrist so two spells flew out. The first lost momentum and rolled along the ground without detonating; the second caught Jay on the shoulder.

"Shit," he grumbled, and flung his wand back, but Pet was already away running.

A shadow moved to her left, and she instinctively veered right and entered a small clearing just as Matthias appeared on the other side of it.

His chest was rising and falling quickly, and he'd taken a hit as well; a trail of blue glitter dusted his ribs. They looked at each other in the increasingly gray light, wands held at the ready—then, simultaneously, without turning their heads, they both fired a shot sideways.

"Damn it," a member of the yellow team groused, coming to a stop and looking down at his stomach, where their spells had landed almost on top of each other. "I'm out."

Matthias lifted his brows at her, his eyes laughing, and they went their separate ways.

She knocked out three more players in the next half hour, but took a second spell-hit, from a smirking Mabel.

When she edged past Burnham's Cottage, a seventeenth-century, one-room structure *mostly* still standing in the center of the woodland, she eyed it warily. There was only one door and no windows, so she didn't think anyone would trap themselves in there. But alternatively, there'd be no way anyone could sneak up from behind, so there were *worse* positions for a magical sniper. And the door was ajar.

She was so busy watching the doorway—and admiring the fairy lights and lanterns someone had strung through all the trees—that she first got stuck in a vine and had to wrench her hair free, and then almost missed the flash of movement to her left. A glittering ball came barreling directly toward her face, and she ducked and rolled with a muttered curse.

Coming up on her haunches, she caught her brother scowling at his Wand. His secondary canisters weren't loading; she'd had the same problem earlier with a jam in the mechanism. Dominic had flatly refused to participate in the game at all, until he'd realized people would be firing bombs at his wife's head, at which point he'd plucked a weapon from the pile without another word. Annoyingly, there wasn't a scrap of glitter on him; so far, he'd managed to come through the battle without even mussing his silver-streaked hair.

She thought she'd kept her evil giggle internal, but Dominic's head came up like a jaguar scenting prey—and he swiftly moved behind the stone wall as he continued fiddling with the controls. It was too tall for Pet to get at him, unless she tried some inelegant schoolyard acrobatics and probably got herself shot in the arse if anyone else was prowling this part of the woods.

"As the resident Hobbit," she said, "I cry unfair disadvantage. And what kind of cretinous brother glitter-missiles his sister?"

"As fond as this cretin is of his baby sister," Dominic's voice returned from the other side of the wall, "he's also fond of winning. But I'll give you a five-second warning that I've almost got this fixed."

Matthias moved so silently behind her that she didn't hear him coming; she jumped violently when he crouched at her side, and he touched a finger to his mouth. Wordlessly, he extended an arm. She blinked at him, then started to grin. Taking his hand, she put one foot on his thigh, and with swift ease, he lifted her to sit on his shoulder, then straightened to his full height.

Still holding his fingers, crossing her feet elegantly at the ankles against his body, she extended her Wand over the wall and performed a graceful, twisting flick-shake. The canister fired, and clouds of golden glitter drifted prettily through the air.

There was ominous quiet, before Dominic stalked into sight, eyes narrowed. From his formerly immaculate head to his waist, he looked like a Christmas ornament.

"Well," Pet said thoughtfully from her comfortable perch, as Matthias casually played with her foot. "The *Times* did call you the gold-standard chocolatier."

Her brother reached up and flicked a golden glob off his dark eyebrow. "I currently despise you both."

Another twenty minutes in, she'd had a few more near-misses and was moving very edgily through the darkest depths of the woods when she heard a branch cracking. Holding her breath, she pressed against the closest tree and slipped her hand along the bark as she crept sideways. Under cover of thick, low-hanging branches, she peered around the trunk.

Matthias was barely visible, crouched by the fallen carcass of a dead tree, his wand aimed through the thick foliage. She took a moment to admire the bulge of muscle in his thick thighs and the steady deadliness of his stance, with a very proprietary feeling. He flicked his wrist with barely any visible effort and a glitter ball fired from his mortifer canister.

From deeper in the underbrush, Pet heard a muffled and very vehement "Oh, *fuck*."

Another twig snapped a few feet from her. Holding herself very still, she stretched on her tiptoes—and saw Benji, who still only had one spell-blast on his armor, sneaking up on Matthias, who'd now taken two.

Matthias was ducking and returning fire from the other direction. He hadn't seen Benji, who adjusted his red armband and raised his wand with a dramatic flourish.

Pet pressed her lips together as she considered.

Then she raised her wand and fired.

"*Ungh.*" Benji made a squawking noise as his torso erupted in a ball of pink glitter. Swishing his wand down, he spun around, and his mouth dropped open in outrage when he saw her. "*Petunia De Vere.* You're on *my* team. You unholy traitor."

"Sorry," she said penitently, lowering her wand and holding it in both hands. "I missed."

Matthias had turned with tiger swiftness, and she heard him laugh aloud.

She grinned.

Benji looked from her to Matthias, trying and failing to keep scowling. He rolled his eyes. "Jay really should have put you on the same team."

With no warning, he brought his wand slamming down, sending spells firing in opposite directions.

One smacked into Pet's belly; the other clipped Matthias's shoulder.

They looked down at the kill shots, then lifted their heads to look at Benji.

He shrugged. "All's fair in love and war."

Neither of their teams made it to the second heat, and Jay was still sulking into a flagon of Sylvie's lethally alcoholic Witch's Brew as they all sat near a gorgeous bonfire outside the Sugar Fair tent. It was swirling out flames of deep blue, purple, and emerald, reacting with different types of wood sap. People kept browsing the stalls and playing games, but the atmosphere changed with the sinking sun. The string quartet had been replaced by a rock band, new food trucks had arrived with various dinner options, and there were cauldrons teetering with booze all over the place.

Jay's girlfriend, Emma, rested her chin on his shoulder, grinning up at him as she wiggled her feet to the bass beat that rolled across the grass, and he reluctantly smiled. His hand came up to cup her cheek.

Pet was sitting on a tipped-over tree trunk with lights threaded through its branches, her hands wrapped around her flagon of Witch's Brew. She looked up, smiling faintly, as Dominic dropped down to sit beside her. He groaned as his joints cracked.

"I don't think I was ever young enough for wand combat," he said crisply, resting his own drink against his raised knee, "but at almost forty, the time has emphatically passed." He looked around. "Where's Matthias?"

"Taking a work call with Benji." She took a mouthful of the drink Sylvie had made for her, rolling the bursting berry flavor over her tongue. "It's rare they're off-duty at the same time, and I think it's a palace law, that things go wrong as soon as you clock out."

"Problems?"

"On the scale of Johnny disasters, barely a blink," she said ruefully. "But Benji's heading back shortly to check in. Matthias'll probably want to go, too."

"I doubt it," Dominic said, calmly. "Not if you're staying here."

"He's very dedicated to his job. It takes priority over—"

"Over a mocked-up facsimile of a relationship and complete violation of employment laws? No doubt." Her brother raised his glass to his mouth. "But how long did the playacting last? Twenty-four hours? Less?"

Pet looked down into the swirling depths of her flagon and didn't immediately reply. She could feel Dominic watching her with a characteristic mix of cool calculation and genuine concern. He wasn't quite used to the family-man mantle yet; it suited him, but sat on his shoulders a little self-consciously.

After a moment, he said, in a different voice, "May I ask a favor?"

"Yes," she said without hesitation, and lifted her head to see his eyes soften.

"Always ready to jump in head-first." He ran his hand over his hair, still damp from the hosing-down they'd all had after the Wands battle. At least the water had been warm. Ish. "Between you and Sylvie, I'm going to be fully gray by forty-five."

His expression sobered to seriousness. "Take Matthias with you, when you go looking for this woman in Berkshire. Don't go alone."

She'd given him the bare bones of what they'd discovered about Carlisle Tallen, and she'd known he'd be concerned, on multiple levels.

Her hands tightened around the glass. "I'm not even sure if I'm going."

"Of course you are," he said bluntly, and yes. Of course she was.

"I'm not going to pretend I don't have qualms about this. Whoever this woman is to you, there's every chance you'll find her as much a disappointment as the rest of our relatives. I don't want you to be hurt, and I certainly don't want you opening a potential can of worms." He paused. "The potential pitfalls magnify significantly if it turns out this woman *is* a paternal connection."

She drew in a deep breath, and his eyes gentled. He even smiled a little. "But you're never going to be someone who'll hide from the truth forever, no matter how scared you are."

That statement stabbed home, in more ways than one.

"If it goes wrong," Dominic said, "you—"

"I've got you. And Sylvie." She touched his arm. "I know."

"You do. Always." He held her gaze steadily. "You've also got yourself. I hope you give yourself enough credit, Pet. Life's thrown a lot of shit at you. Yet you're still a person who stops a car whenever she sees a bluebell wood, just to spend ten minutes sitting with your favorite flowers. Brutally stabbed by a total stranger, and the first thing you asked when you regained consciousness was if the person who attacked you was all right. Despite the way you came into the world and your first experiences of it, you still see the beauty in it, and the good in people. You're a survivor. And darling, I'm so bloody proud to be your brother."

Tears stung behind Pet's lashes. She tried to speak and couldn't.

Dominic cleared his throat, his own voice a bit rough as he added, "But for the love of God, please don't go viral with any more videos."

Sylvie came stumbling over. She was slightly tipsy, giggling and happy, her pink-and-lavender streaked hair slipping loose from her plait. She wound her arms around Pet's neck, planted a kiss on her cheek, then tumbled into her husband's arms. Dominic caught her, cradling her on his lap. Foreseeing imminent PDA of his own, Pet accepted with alacrity when Jay jogged over to ask her to dance.

As they moved onto the dance floor, she saw his girlfriend, Emma, dancing with Liam. It was almost fully dark now, but the park was lit up with thousands of lanterns. Jay gave her an obligatory twirl, then they did a sort of slow shuffle. It was quite a fast song, but he was a self-confessed shite dancer.

"Quite an honor, though, dancing with a real-life hero," he said, winking at her.

"Hero?" she said blankly, her mind still in other places.

"You and Vaughn single-handedly tackling London's mugging problem. Literally tackling. Sylvie was totally horrified, and so proud she bought a newspaper and pinned the clipping to our office noticeboard."

"Oh, that." Pet hadn't been surprised when that incident had belatedly hit the news—although hopefully her cash value to the press was dropping by the hour—but God, it seemed like a million years ago.

Jay snorted. "Yes, *that*, Miss Casual. The crime-busting duo. Pretty impressive, Pet, especially when you turned yourself into a human rocket launcher. Seems to be a multifunctional technique of yours—I remember a similar maneuver in your viral video." He cleared his throat. "Um, your *first* viral video, I mean." She was *not* blushing again. He grinned. "Foil a mugging and land your man, all with one simple starfish-swoop. Or to be strictly accurate, land *on* your man, in that first instance. Your poor boss really does need a hazard light at times."

Behind him, she saw Matthias and Benji had reappeared under a string of lights, Matthias reclipping his phone to his belt. He was scanning their little group. His gaze moved to the dance floor. She lifted her hand. He was too far away to see his face properly, but she thought the set of his shoulders relaxed a little. Inclining his head to listen to what Benji was saying, he leaned back against a tree, his eyes on her.

For a second, she let go of Jay, resting the heel of her hand against her chest. Her thumb rested lightly against the hollow of her throat, and she felt the rapid skittering of her pulse.

After a minute or two, the music changed, the band launching into a song that she recognized after taut seconds as the rock adaptation of a Kovalenko symphony; it had been playing the night of Rosie's ball, when she'd first seen Matthias. Her dark angel that night. Pure safety from the beginning; later, provocation, temptation, desire.

Much more. Maybe everything.

They performed another clumsy turn, and Jay noticed Matthias, as well. Jay's dark eyes—which always had that melancholic romantic poet look, even when he was in a reasonably upbeat mood—rested on him, then returned speculatively to Pet.

"You make a slightly comical couple," he commented.

Her fingers tightened involuntarily on his. "Comical?"

Jay didn't seem bothered by her most dangerous tone.

Admittedly, few people were.

Maybe the odd baby in a passing pram.

"I mean, the physical disparity speaks for itself. Height-wise alone. He must have to hang a ladder around his neck just so you can give him a casual kiss." He'd had more drinks than she had, and his voice was becoming a bit slurred.

With a total lack of survival instincts, he went on, "I think you're respectively the least and most intimidating people I've ever seen in my life. Purely from a visual perspective." A hasty addendum. "I've seen hi-res footage of you almost breaking a man's ribs with your thighs; I'm not likely to underestimate your lethal streak. It always is the Bambi-eyed ones who'd literally nail someone to the wall if their lover was threatened."

As he glanced again at Matthias, he made a wondering sound. "I guess beauty really is in the eye of the beholder, huh?"

Pet's body felt very stiff, as if he were trying to maneuver a rusty marionette doll around the floor. "Whatever else you're going to say—*don't.*"

Their eyes met and they stopped moving completely, although bodies continued to swirl around them.

Jay's hands fell to hold her wrists lightly. His expression—all of him—was suddenly very sober. "I'm sorry."

The words were thick.

"I've had too much to drink," he whispered, "and I'm taking my own shit out on you and him, but that's no excuse."

She was still angry. She *hated* it—God, she *hated* it, every time someone looked at Matthias like that. Every time they so entirely and wholly failed to really see him. And she was so damn tired of the world in general always prioritizing the things that mattered least. But at that note in Jay's voice, she said reluctantly, "Are you okay?"

His mouth twisted, his shoulder half lifting, and a thread of concern wove through her protective fury.

"It's not Emma, is it?" She looked over at where his girlfriend was dancing with another of the Sugar Fair staffers now. "I thought things were going well. Sylvie said—" At a hint of a wince, she stopped. "Oh. Is it—" Her glance went involuntarily to where Sylvie and Dominic were still curled up together, totally engrossed in each other.

Dominic's lips moved, curving, and Sylvie reached to brush back a strand of hair from his forehead in a revealing gesture. Her hand cupped his cheek, and she rubbed her thumb over his smile.

Pet didn't miss the deeper flicker that went through Jay's eyes.

Sylvie had never said anything, but it had been obvious, from the moment she'd seen the best friends together last year, that his feelings for Sylvie had gone well beyond platonic devotion.

Both Sylvie and Dominic had been transparently relieved when Jay had started seeing Emma.

"My feelings for Emma are genuine," Jay said with unexpected starkness, the admission probably lubricated by multiple flagons of Witch's Brew. "I'd never have continued with the relationship if I didn't see a real future there. It wouldn't be fair to her."

There was an unspoken, looming "but" there.

"Do you . . . still love Sylvie?" Pet asked hesitantly, not sure she really wanted to know if the answer was yes.

"I'll always love Sylvie." Simple. Warm. "She's family. That's unconditional. Forever." A muscle flexed in his lean jaw. "Unpicking the . . . romantic side of it has been the most difficult experience of my life, but the threads are mostly snipped. I'm getting there. It helps that I do know, in my gut, that we are, now, exactly what we were meant to be. Honestly, I don't think I ever really believed we'd be anything else." With an ironic turn of his mouth, he added, "I even quite like Dominic. In a lot of ways, it's been *easier* than I thought, to accept, and welcome what I'm finding with Emma, but—"

He exhaled, long and hard. "Have you ever felt so much like the secondary character in everyone else's stories that it's absolutely fucking terrifying to suddenly become the hero of your own?" The sound he made was derisive. "Does that even make sense?"

The music and light continued to swirl around them.

"Yes," Pet said, her voice cracking. "It does."

Jay looked at her, really focused on her. "Secondary characters unite." He released another breath through his taut mouth. "I suppose it's time to be brave and reach out for *our* futures now."

Benji stood at Matthias's side, watching Pet dancing with Jay. The co-founder of Sugar Fair wasn't that much shorter than Matthias, yet from a purely superficial perspective he and Pet were a well-matched pair. Physically, the guy was similar to the dates she'd occasionally brought to staff events. Conventionally handsome in a sort of romantic, literary way.

But it'd been obvious even at the now infamous birthday ball that Jay wasn't remotely on Pet's radar in that way, and vice versa. His eyes had been solidly fixed in another direction. Head over heels for his best friend, and blatantly heading for heartache.

Benji was still studying Pet contemplatively. "There's been *something* between you two all along, hasn't there?"

He didn't immediately respond, but he didn't deny it. It was true, no matter how much he'd tried to ignore it. There'd been a weirdly instinctual connection there from day one.

Once, when Matthias had been a kid, the foster parents du jour had sent him to a day-long holiday program during a school break. Most of the other kids there had given him a wide berth, but he still remembered one shy, lonely little girl with messy bunches of hair beneath her ears peeking at him for a while, then coming over and declaring, "We're going to be friends." She'd turned bright red immediately after, and neither of them had said much more to each other, but he'd played dolls with her and she'd given him half her sandwich, and for that day, they'd been friends. In the easy, simple way most kids did.

He'd never seen that girl again, but that stout, firm *"We're going to be friends"*—that was exactly what he'd felt when Pet had held Hercule to her chest in that hospital bed and looked into his eyes. That this was a person he'd like. A person who was going to mean something to him.

It wasn't the sort of thing that happened to him, this kind of *pull*, like he was being drawn toward someone. Hell, he saw most people as possible security threats, until they proved otherwise—and even then, he was still prepared for them to go rogue. He'd seen the bleakest edges of the human psyche, what most people were capable of, if their own unique trigger was pulled.

There were very, very few people he gut-deep trusted, and it usually took years to build that level of bond.

"I'm sorry," Benji said unexpectedly, somberly, and Matthias turned his head. "I know I don't say it, and I should. Especially after what happened to Padraig. You never know when—" His lips tightened. "You're like a damn brother to me, and I never realized . . . I thought you found her attractive, but—" He shrugged slightly, near dismissively. Pet was beautiful. That was simple fact, and a lot of people would be attracted to her physically. Nothing earth-shattering in that. "I never saw it. That—"

That the physical side of it was almost incidental. Matthias had taken good care that nobody saw it. Until the bloody tabloids had started stalking her, he'd successfully suppressed it himself for the most part—the full extent of it, that hard tug of awareness. The strange, primal sort of knowledge of how deep it could go, on his side, if he let it. If he didn't keep his distance from her.

For quite a few years, he'd wondered if he even had a heart, in the metaphorical sense. Since it lodged in his damn throat every time she decided to chuck herself into danger, he clearly did, but as unpracticed as it was, it functioned best in one piece.

As he didn't harbor a hidden masochistic streak, he'd had zero interest in having it cracked in half—by someone who could end up doing it unintentionally, unknowingly, and with a huge amount of guilt if she ever realized, because—that was Pet. She'd been treated like shit, like *nothing*, by the people who should have loved her unconditionally, yet she'd still grown into an incredibly empathetic human being. He'd once found her trying to build a wing-splint out of ice lolly sticks for a bird that had flown into a palace window, for God's sake.

It seemed incredibly naïve now that he'd ever thought he could control this.

"It—doesn't matter," he said tautly. "The priority right now is still making sure that Pet's career and reputation are definitely secure."

And doing everything he could to help her fill in the gaps of her past, find the missing piece of the puzzle, whatever that end picture looked like. She'd be all right whatever happened; she was strong. But *her* priority was her family, and it'd be impossible in her position to fully quell the optimistic possibility that she might uncover a whole new part of her life and future. When pitting caution and harsh experience against hope, the latter could be a powerful opponent.

"With one embittered exception, the press interest in Pet is peaking," Benji said bluntly. "The excuse of this media racket is rapidly running out. At some point soon, you're going to have to acknowledge that this is obviously real, and has fuck-all now to do with anyone but you two."

"Says the guy systematically sticking his nose in," Matthias said, but the sarcasm rang hollow.

In the silence between them, the music stopped, and a new song began.

That Kovalenko symphony remix again.

Benji's eyes were searching, the expression in his own still drastically unlike his usual persona. "Why?" he said after a moment. "Why have you obviously thought this is something that could definitely never work long-term, if that's the level of—*caring* we're talking about?" He ran his hand through his hair, dislodging flakes of dried glitter at his hairline. "I know we take the piss out of each other, but—"

Even with Padraig, Matthias had never stripped layers off himself, laid himself bare. There'd never been a reason to; nothing—nobody—to challenge the necessary armor he'd built. By the age of six, he'd known that survival and self-sufficiency were inextricably entwined.

Ingrained self-defense died hard. He found himself automatically reverting to the surface answer, the easiest of the truths. "Pet's said herself that she prefers to keep things short-term, that lust always burns out back into the platonic. And Christ, that's when the guys she dated—"

"Looked like cheery clones from the same toothpaste ad," Benji filled in calmly. "So what? I never saw her look at any of them the way she often looks at you." He cocked his head. "So, it's *Pet's* looks that're the big draw to you after all, then, is it? If she weren't conventionally pretty, or if she got sick, or scarred—"

"It wouldn't change a fucking thing." The words were a gutteral bite, a visceral reaction straight from his heart. "Pet isn't her looks. That's the fucking least of her."

"And of you," Benji said, very pointedly. In a drawl, he added, "Pet's many things, but shallow ain't one of them, mate, and you know it. Neither of you care about appearances, but for the record and to drastically understate the case—having copped more of an eyeful of your 'pretend' snogs than I'd like—the woman likes the way you look. Which again, you must know by now." He held up a hand, checking the points off on his fingers with obnoxious exaggeration. "You have more in common than otherwise. I suspect she even secretly likes your protective streak—and going nose to nose with you over it. Next objection?"

At that careful flippancy, it tore free, low and raw. "Even in the miracle scenario where she wants this to be something . . . lasting, I don't know how to be that for someone. What she needs. Deserves."

Benji looked at him in silence, as the lights from the dance floor traced patterns across the grass, the field of green rippling like a night sea. Pet and Jay had stopped dancing. With a jump of concern, Matthias saw she had a strange look on her face. If he'd upset her—

At his side, Benji said softly, "Don't you?"

With a little tugging movement, Jay twirled Pet neatly around, and she stood facing Matthias.

He'd cut through the dancers and was looking down at her, those rough-hewn features fierce and uncompromising. Around them, a few people gave him wary glances.

If he noticed, he gave no sign, his attention focused solely on her. He frowned. "Are you all right?" He shot a glance over his shoulder to where Jay was heading back to the group. "Did he—"

Pet's fingertips were dovetailed against her stomach. She pressed them tightly together, then silently reached out her hands. Tilting her head at the dancers, she lifted her brows.

He blinked, then grimaced.

"There are probably still photographers floating around," she murmured innocently. "And you told me you do a decent waltz." Even when everything inside her was gripped with the unknown, she couldn't help smiling. "Or were you joking?"

"As you've pointed out on several occasions, I rarely joke." But as if he couldn't resist those electric strings between them any more than she could, he was already wrapping his big hands around hers, tugging her into his arms. "I was flat-out lying."

The music had changed to a slow song, one she'd disliked for years, but she was barely aware of either the tune or the words. She and Matthias had proved to be bloody amazing partners in a lot of ways, but they weren't well matched on the dance floor. As Jay had snidely but truthfully pointed out, she couldn't wrap her arms properly around his neck unless he lifted her or bent himself in half; they compromised with his lowered head and her palms against his chest, his arm locked around her back.

Perfect.

Resting her cheek against the softness of his shirt, feeling the residual streaks of dried glitter, she closed her eyes.

His fingers touched her hair, smoothing the fluffing mess. She'd straightened it this morning, but she'd since been murdered with glitter and sprayed with a hose.

When his thumb brushed her ear, she drew in a quick breath, enjoying the tight shiver.

He cleared his throat, a deep, tactile rumble. "Did you take your earrings out or have you lost one?"

She jerked, reaching up to touch her naked right earlobe. "Oh, shit. Oh—damn it, I love these earrings." They were her birthday pearls from Dominic and Sylvie, to match the bracelet she'd thankfully *not* worn today.

"We'll look—" Matthias cut off, echoing her skeptical expression as he looked around the still busy and now only light-lit park, with the fairy-light-studded woodland beyond.

The chances of finding the earring were almost nonexistent.

Although—she suddenly remembered that embarrassing tumble straight into the vines outside Burnham's Cottage, the impatient wrenching free of her hair.

"During the Wands game, my hair got tangled in the shrubbery outside the old cottage. It might have come out then."

They exchanged another doubtful look—then headed for the cottage.

She was not intimately—or at all—acquainted with the world's other fake boyfriends, and she'd bet anything he'd come across at least one in his celeb assignments, but she really did have the best one. Ten million stars. Unlike the night sky above them. Only the moon was beating the light pollution. She looked forward to the day she moved into her Miss Marple cottage and sat outside at midnight to enjoy the proper stars. And use her night goggles to monitor nefarious activity.

After half a glass of Witch's Brew, it was even harder not to imagine Matthias out there with her. Sitting on his lap while he lectured her about the village privacy laws and nibbled on her neck.

A light-art installation had been set up in the woods, and the Witch-Fest organizers were handing out lanterns for anyone who wanted to follow the Sculpture Walk.

They each took one, leaves and woodchips crackling beneath

their feet as they started down the path. They'd have to branch off shortly to get to the cottage, but Pet was fascinated with the artworks placed sporadically through—and *in*—the trees.

Matthias nodded at a shimmering LED-lit parrot in an oak tree. "An homage to Ailsa." It moved mechanical wings, sending out shimmering shafts of light like bioluminescence in the dark.

She could hear voices ahead and behind them, but the night was otherwise still, and beautiful.

At a flash of light, they both looked to see another installation—a depiction of *real* warfare this time, sculptural soldiers lurking in the underbrush, their guns shooting out occasional bolts of ice-blue light.

A few steps on, they came across a wounded officer, sprawled next to a tree, his fellow soldier kneeling beside him. Their hands were clasped in a gesture of loyalty, support, promise, holding each other's wrists.

She was studying the poignant scene, and for a second didn't notice Matthias's unnatural stillness.

Glancing up at him, her breath caught at the look on his face, stark and revealing in the flickering glow of her lantern as she lifted it higher.

"Matthias?" A whispering splinter of sound.

She saw him swallow, his lips tightening, then he tore his eyes away. "Sorry," he said, hoarsely.

She looked again at the fallen figure, the crouching friend. In the moving, artificial lights and the rustling *shush-shush* of the trees, she had a sudden flashing memory, as if her own body was superimposed over that motionless sculpture, Matthias taking the place of the worried guardian, his hand wrapped around hers.

But she didn't think that was where his own mind had gone.

Grief was an unpredictable, vicious bastard that hit hard and didn't go down lightly. It lurked in the shadows, looking for any opportunity to bite. Matthias stared at the technically skillful, powerful art that had just unexpectedly grabbed him by the throat. After an emotional bulldozer of a night already, his defenses were down.

"Matthias?" Pet said very quietly, but it wasn't until her soft fingertips touched his that he was able to drag his eyes away from those metal soldiers, gripping each other's wrists.

He looked down at her. The light from the lantern flickered over her face.

She held on to him. "Matthias, what actually happened to Padraig? Was he killed on assignment?"

She hadn't asked in Little Venice. For all her inquisitiveness, she seemed to know instinctively when someone wasn't ready to talk yet. And he'd rarely spoken about the actual night of Padraig's death these past years, since the sheer hell of having to call the McCarthys and turn up on Jenny's doorstep with a police officer.

It felt right to tell Pet. To—turn to Pet, their bodies physically drawn together in a way that wasn't in the slightest bit sexual. The weight of that settled over him, deep and encircling—but in that moment, it was warmth. Comfort. In a way he'd never experienced. "Yes," he said, "but not technically on duty." He ran his thumb over her wrist, feeling the whisper-fine hairs on her arm and the faint thrum of her pulse. "On our dinner break. We were guarding this absolute prick—"

As he told her about that evening, in the mist and fog of the spires of Cambridge, she set down her lantern and wrapped her free fingers around his forearm. He recited the facts on automatic at first, almost as if he were giving the police statement again. His seemingly endless run to find Padraig after the eruption of screams. Arriving without caution or planning straight into the scene of a thwarted mugging and assault, where Padraig had put himself between a group of gang members and a sobbing woman, distracting them long enough that she'd been able to run, find help, summon the police.

He'd been trained and strong, but fatally outnumbered.

He'd been stabbed seven times. By the time Matthias had found him, he'd lain sprawled across the cobblestones, his blood trickling into the grouting.

"He was already dead." His gaze returned to the soldier sculpture, but it was torn flesh and coagulating blood he saw, not metal. Lifeless, either way. An outer shell with no inner spirit. No flashing grin and shite jokes. That big heart motionless. Silent. Its job done. "I knew he was dead. But I had to try. I had to—I had to try."

His voice cracked then, and Pet made a tiny sound. She stretched up, tugging him down to her; he held back for only a moment, then let her cradle his head against her neck, support more of his weight as he leaned into her. When she put her hand over the thick, twisting scar that scored across his scalp, he reluctantly answered her silent question about how it had happened.

The bastards had got in several blows and slashes before the police had arrived. It would have been impossible to fend off every strike with that many, and his movements had been hindered, trying to shield Padraig. He'd have been killed as well if the reinforcements hadn't arrived. He owed those officers his life.

She gripped him so hard that her fingernails dug into his skin. Her cheeks had blanched a ghostly white in the night.

As the trees whispered to each other above them, he managed a faint smile. With his thumb, he traced a jutting, once-broken bone in his cheek. "It didn't really matter physically. Not sure most people noticed any difference."

Pet shook her head viciously. With trembling fingers, she ran a light touch over the scar. "I'm so sorry."

Something else fractured inside him then.

He wasn't sure if she pulled him farther down, or he pulled her up, but their mouths locked in a short, fierce, hard kiss.

Pet was breathing hard when she slowly lowered down from her tiptoes. She touched her lower lip as if it were tingling like his own.

The voices behind them were getting louder. Her hands still shaking, she picked up her lantern, and without a word, they moved down the path, diverting off through the trees to find the abandoned cottage.

The Witch-Fest decorating committee must have bought out every store in London that sold fairy lights, because almost every tree was dotted with pinpoint twinkles, like thousands of watching, hopefully benevolent little beings.

"You blamed yourself," Pet whispered in the darkness. "For not getting there in time." It was a statement, not a question.

And he knew she understood it, had walked a parallel path of regret and guilt herself more than once.

"Yes." He held an encroaching branch out of the way, so it didn't scratch her. "For a long time."

"Not anymore?" she asked hesitantly.

He stopped under the sweeping branches of an oak, twigs cracking under his boots. Starkly, he said, "I know, logically, that there was nothing I could have done. He was gone before I even got there. And once he walked in on that attack, there was no going back. No question he'd act. He'd never have waited for assistance, left her there alone, even knowing how badly he was outnumbered."

"It must have brought it all back," she said grimly. "The night of the museum opening, when we walked in on the mugging."

The macabre similarities still preyed in his nightmares. The cobblestones, the blood on the ground, the knives, the flat, dead eyes of the human trash who preyed on the vulnerable. The evil.

And caught up in it—one of the people who mattered to him the most.

Pet caught at her lip. "And I—"

"Rushed in without a single thought for your own safety, and just about gave me a coronary." As he turned, the lights of their lanterns met and blended. "Not for the first time. Very much doubt it'll be the last."

She wrinkled her nose at him, and against all odds, he felt that trace of a smile return.

When they reached Burnham's Cottage, it was quiet and pretty, twinkling with its own lights, although this part of the woods was so deserted that Pet would have found it more creepy than charming if she'd come by herself.

She pointed out where the vines grew, and they lowered their lanterns, scanning the ground.

As they hunted, she said carefully, "Jenny said you'd pulled away from the McCarthys after what happened to Padraig."

Matthias got down on his haunches and ran his fingers through a patch of thick grass. "They never blamed me."

"I should fucking hope not." She saw his brows lift at her emphatic reaction, but something had changed in his stance, relaxed a little in the rigidity of his shoulders, since he'd told her the full horror of what had happened to Padraig. And to him.

He'd sacrificed his ability to defend himself to protect his friend's body. If the police hadn't arrived—

She couldn't even think about it.

"It was hard to be around them at first," he said slowly. "And then it had been so long, I didn't know how to broach the distance. I'm . . . not used to—*having* people."

"No," she said. "I know."

He looked at her for a long moment in silence, then— "You *shouldn't* know." The words were unexpected and harsh. "You should never have known what that feels like. And I hate that the people who should have had your back from the beginning failed you so completely."

Pet's breaths were light and quick as he said, "I don't know how you came through that and still managed to be—" He cut himself off.

Her heart twisted. What remained of it, because she was pretty sure that he held most of it in his big, scarred-up hands.

Hoarsely, she said, "Accept the invitation, Matthias. Go to Ireland and see your family."

Matthias looked at her in the lantern light. He nodded once.

The atmosphere was crackling and flickering with building heat, as if they were back standing by the campfire. Abruptly, he grimaced. "Honestly, I'm surprised Jonna wants me anywhere near her birthdays after my misfire with her present a few years ago."

She swallowed twice to make sure her voice was clear. "Why? What did you get her?"

"An irritating-as-piss children's toy that bleeped incessant random shit, had no apparent off button, and eventually started chasing her around the house, going for her legs like some deranged, rabid rodent. By the time we'd had the birthday cake, I had to literally snap the thing in half to get it away from her, and then she was woken up at two in the morning when the legs crawled out of the rubbish bin and ran under her bed."

She stared at him in total silence.

"I did apologize," he said, a shade defensively. "More than once." He snorted. "I didn't have much choice after she rang me in the middle of the night. She can give an impressively bloodthirsty rant on little sleep, after being jolted awake by the rhythmic footsteps of tiny, disembodied legs. I remember a particularly detailed description of how she was going to submerge my entire body in liquid gold and solder me to a podium in County Clare, as a monument to rank bastards."

From the moment they'd agreed to Codename Charming, life had become a tenuous balance of shattering emotion, intense feeling, and just plain fun. Laughter was the last thing Pet had expected after the past few minutes, but she started to giggle. "I think I'd like Jonna. May I politely ask *why* you gifted your honorary sister with an interactive nightmare?"

"She always used to send out a mass text with what she wanted for Christmas and her birthdays. In my defense, there was only one letter difference between the brand names of the demonic toy and what she actually wanted."

"Which was?"

"Some sort of enormous, hooded wearable blanket. And before you ask, yes, I did end up buying her one." He observed her, probably seeing her acquisitive gleam. "You want one, too, don't you?"

"Want. Need. Will have located and ordered one before I go

to sleep tonight. Po-tay-to, po-tah-to. And by potato, I mean the happy, cozy, couch variety."

Something glinted under the moonlight, a tiny pearlescent sheen in the grass. "Oh!" She knelt to look. "I've found it."

She rubbed the earring against her shirt to clean it and tried to loop it back through her ear, but it had an unusual, fiddly mechanism, and she usually needed a mirror to get them in. Her compact was in her bag, back at the Sugar Fair tent with Sylvie's things for safekeeping.

When she swore lightly as the hook pinched a sensitive patch of skin, Matthias took the earring from her, briefly examined the mechanism, and bent to reattach it for her.

His fingers touched the incredibly sensitive skin on her neck, his thumb under her jaw, and her "Thanks" was embarrassingly breathless.

Under the sheltering canopy of the glowing tree, his head was still close to hers. She could hear the *cack-cack-cack* of a nearby bird, and the hopeful chirping of an amorous insect, but the festival seemed distant. Unreal.

It felt as if they were the only people in the world.

Her eyes followed along the line of his throat, watching it move as he swallowed, down to where a scattering of dark hair peeked out from the neckline of his shirt.

Amusement fading away, her solemn gaze returned to his.

Saw the rapidity of passing emotions there.

Without looking away from each other, their hands came up and entwined. Just for a moment, she leaned her cheek against his raised wrist, and saw a transitory softening amidst the heat that tightened his jaw.

His chest expanded with a deep breath—and then his fingers

were sliding around her neck to the back of her head, holding her as his mouth came down on hers.

She made a soft sound—of relief, desire, overwhelmed, as she slipped her arm under his, running her nails up his back, pulling him hard into her.

It was that tidal wave of sensation, almost shocking in its intensity, and her knees actually buckled. He caught her against him with an arm around her back, but his own legs couldn't have been all that steady, either, because they ended up on the ground.

Pet landed on his lap, her thighs splayed over his own, and they both grunted as their hips rocked involuntarily together. With a hand on his jaw, gasping for breath as their lips parted, she looked cloudily into his equally dazed eyes.

"Pet." Her name was such a rough growl she barely recognized it. Matthias shook his head as if he'd sustained a hard blow. "Are you su—"

She pulled his face back to hers, kissing him hard, and he groaned into her mouth. His hands drove back into her hair, cradling her head as his tongue thrust against hers.

Then, with a huge effort, he tore his lips away, a sound resonating deep in his chest when she instinctively tried to follow him, her lips seeking his. With his palms still against her cheeks, his fingers tangled in her hair, he rested his forehead against her temple. He was breathing as fast and heavily as she was.

"Sweetheart, it would fucking kill me if you ever regret—"

Through the fog of emotion, something hot and almost angry spiked. She brought her hand down and fisted it in his shirt. "I would never," she whispered fiercely. "No matter what, Matthias. I would never."

His eyes were so dilated with desire that they were black in the flickering light. "How much have you had to drink?"

In the midst of her own desire, without breaking the connection of their eyes, she extended her arm to its full length, pointed her finger, and smoothly booped herself on the tip of her nose.

He considered her for a few more seconds—then he caught her mouth again with his, their tongues sliding together, and dragged her closer into the warm shelter of his body. She arched up, rubbing into him, and he groaned again, low in his throat, kissing her cheek, her jaw, her neck. She turned her head and nipped at his earlobe with her teeth, loving the way she could make his whole big body shake.

Another bird's cry shattered the stillness of the night. She was almost beyond conscious thought, but—they couldn't do this here. It might feel like they were in a warm, passionate bubble, but eyes—and cameras—could peer through the undergrowth at any time. The internet had scored quite enough of a look into her sex life already.

This was them alone now. It was private.

She should have trusted that, even in the grips of pure arousal, Matthias wouldn't risk her safety. Without taking his mouth from hers, he stood in an impressively fluid, swift movement. She wrapped her legs around his waist and shuddered when his erection ground against her as he walked.

Lost in the kiss, she was only vaguely aware that he'd scooped up both lanterns with one finger and was walking them into the cottage. She'd never actually been inside before, and at any other time, she'd have been curious to explore the small dwelling. As he kicked the door shut behind them, and spun to press her up against it, however, there was nothing but him. His body, his breaths, his husky voice.

Pet loved his heavy weight, the feel of his skin, the rasp of his beard—the sensation of being entirely surrounded by him. Even as frantic desire gripped every muscle, she'd never felt so safe.

He unclipped her belt with her work phone and lowered it to the ground, careful not to drop it before his attention returned entirely, deliciously, to her.

As he pinned her with a thrust of his hips, she tipped her head against the wood, closing her eyes, and he kissed her throat. With an inaudible murmur, she brought his mouth back to hers, and their lips parted against each other in almost desperate urgency.

His fingers trailed down her throat, tracing over her collarbone, and she drew in a shaky breath when his hand cupped her breast. Blindly, she tugged at her buttons with one hand, parting the shirt, pulling it fretfully from the waistband of her short skirt—she was hot, aching; she needed . . . With that incredible, sexy ease, he lifted her, so that his mouth could fasten on her nipple, rubbing her with his tongue, sucking hard over the fragile lace.

She cried out. Her hips moving in involuntary circles, she gripped his shoulders, her head arching back into the door.

Time was blurring into nothing, and she didn't know how many seconds or minutes passed before he propped her even higher. She suddenly realized how high up she was. Much higher and she'd be just about sitting on his head, recreating the scalp-balancing act of the Green Eighty Conference. He pressed a reassuring kiss to her bare tummy.

"Put your legs over my shoulders," he rasped against her skin.

Her skirt was already caught up, and his hand pushed it out

of the way as he moved her thighs over his shoulders. Pet's eyes opened as she gripped his head, and she stared at the opposite wall of the cottage as his breath fanned her most intimate flesh, sparkling across incredibly sensitive nerve endings. Her neck arched again, and her knees drew up reflexively, her heels digging into his back.

Matthias had one arm up, holding her hip, her waist, keeping her secure on her precarious perch, although she didn't have the slightest fear that he'd ever let her fall.

Whether he'd let her *go* was another question, still a prickling uncertainty in her gut, but he'd never let her fall.

He'd moved the lace of her knickers aside with his thumb, the calluses on his skin a delicious abrasion against the slight prickliness of her own skin. She hadn't shaved for a few days, but there was no space for self-consciousness as he lightly nuzzled her, an almost . . . adoring gesture that stopped her breath, as if a ghostly hand had closed around her throat.

When he parted her with his fingers, his mouth closing over her, his tongue swirling over her clit, she arched back so far that her gaze was fixed on the ceiling. In the flickering lantern light, she was pretty sure there was a mouse moving up in the wooden beams. She felt as if she were getting fucking amazing head in Cinderella's bloody attic or something.

Idly, she wondered if it might be the same mouse Matthias had rescued from the palace.

Then there were no delirious thoughts at all, just spiraling sensation and tickling, clenching, unbearable anticipation.

She brought her hand down to grip Matthias's where he held her waist, unable to stop wiggling and rubbing against him, trying to increase the friction. He was taut with tension and arousal beneath her, against her; as he withdrew two pumping fingers from her, he replaced them with the hook of his thumb, stroking deep inside her, playing his tongue around her clit.

Sucking hard.

Her internal muscles were gripping onto him, constantly flexing, releasing, flexing . . .

Pet flung her head back again, her breaths coming so fast she felt light-headed, her eyes blind, her thighs squeezing around his head, and she cried out loud as she came. Her body hunched forward, wrapping over him, as the contractions pulsed through her.

They stayed like that for long seconds, as she huffed out one breath after another, then she fell back against the door, forcing her jelly-legs to loosen their grip before she suffocated him.

He lifted his head, their eyes meeting in the dim, dancing light, and she moved her shaking hand to touch his mouth. His beard was wet.

His gaze was—everything.

She was already reaching for his buckle when he lifted her down—and for the first time in her life, she truly appreciated her lack of height, because it was so unexpectedly sexy, sliding down his body. Trying to set his belt and devices aside with the same care he'd taken with her own phone, she went right to the floor, glorying in the deep tremble that went through his thighs and gripped the muscles of his stomach, as she unzipped him and drew his erection out into her hand.

His deep voice cut with a strangled hiss as she admiringly stroked the length of him, leaning in to kiss the swollen head, catching a drop of precum on the tip of her tongue. She was relieved to see he wasn't as daunting in size as she'd feared, just a bit bigger than average.

But from a purely aesthetic point of view, the toughest looking man she'd ever known had the prettiest penis she'd ever seen.

It was his turn to brace himself against the door, his fingers digging into the wood as he looked down at her. Despite the glaze of lust in his eyes, his head cocked as he registered her expression. His chest heaving, he said huskily, "What are you thinking?"

Thoughtfully, she curled her tongue around the head, and his breath expelled in a broken rush. Holding his shaft against her cheek with an affectionate nuzzle that made his hands fist again, she murmured, "That it would probably be inappropriate if I cut a silhouette portrait of your dick."

His thigh jerked, both with surprised amusement and in reaction to the second sweep of her tongue.

"It wouldn't really do it justice." She sucked him deep, then released him with a wet *pop*. "But I'm guessing you wouldn't want to whittle me a life-size sculpture."

There'd been a time when she'd thought she'd never hear him laugh aloud at all.

Let alone partway through a blowjob.

He held out for several long minutes while she thoroughly enjoyed herself, then he drew back with a harsh curse. He extracted a thin wallet from his trouser pocket and drew out a condom. She took it from him, carefully tearing it open, and smoothed it up his length with another fond stroke for her new best friend, before she found herself scooped up and spun back around against the door. His palm cradled her head, protecting her from the hard wood, and he hitched her thigh high up on his hip.

Their mouths sought each other, licking into each other, sucking, nipping.

When he reached between them to move himself into position,

Pet's hands tightened on his shoulders, and he hesitated, searching her eyes.

One last silent question.

In answer, she slipped her arm around his head, drawing his mouth to her throat, and her breath left her on a high-pitched cry as he pushed inside. His first thrusts were slow, gentle, his hips rocking against hers as he worked into her, but she was soon wordlessly demanding more, drawing her knees up, clenching down on him, pushing back against him.

Her hand fisted in the air above his head as her arm tightened, her eyes squeezed closed and her mouth open, panting, as each thrust pushed her farther up the wood. It turned fast and frantic, each of them trying to prolong the other's pleasure, straining for release.

Matthias cupped her cheek, turned her face into his, their lips open and damp, dragging against each other. Golden sensation was building and gripping inside her again, even more intense this time, every thick rub of him inside her pushing the friction higher, like a deep, terrible, wonderful itch, tingling from her clenching vaginal muscles through her belly, and down to her toes and fingertips.

She shattered moments before he followed her under, their limbs entwined so tightly around each other . . .

Her heart was thundering so hard it physically hurt. She let her head drop to his broad shoulder, her eyes still closed, and felt him kiss the curve of her neck.

That lingering kiss was so utterly gentle that her lashes stung, and she tucked her face tighter into him.

She didn't know how long they stayed there like that, collapsed against the door, Matthias keeping one arm propped behind her to avoid crushing her.

Beep-beep-beep.

She flinched at the insistent trill of his phone.

For what felt like extensive seconds and not nearly long enough, he didn't move. Then, very carefully, he withdrew, her thighs flexing around him at the tug as he pulled out, her intimate muscles still clenched up around him. Slowly, Pet unwound her legs, letting them drop back toward the floor. She was shaking.

They looked at each other. Matthias's throat moved with another swallow.

Well. Suffice to say that if there were a protocol manual for verbally contracted fauxmances to rescue the reputations of hapless royals, they'd officially crossed every line in it.

Neither of them spoke. She didn't want him to speak if he was going to— She felt desperately, terribly protective of what had just happened, what they'd experienced. What they'd shared.

Despite the surface efficiency of his movements as he took care of the condom with a tissue from his pocket and unclipped his phone, his breathing was very unsteady.

She touched her own raw-feeling throat and rubbed the side of her hand against her hairline, feeling the dampness there. "Benji?"

Ack, instead of the hoarseness she'd expected, she'd gone all high and breathy. Orgasms didn't usually turn her into Marilyn Monroe, but very little about this experience fell under the heading of *usually*.

At least a simple text was an improvement when it came to the unwelcome intrusion of reality. Since they were *usually* interrupted by rogue photographers and amateur videographers.

"Yes." His hands not steady either, Matthias tapped out a response. "He's heading back. Asks if I can check in as well when we get back. Our newest recruit mixed up the alarm codes and created accidental havoc this evening. Poor kid's apparently ready to quit."

She was very conscious of the thick cloak of tension in the air, but even when his mind clearly wasn't on work for once, she heard the note of empathy in his voice. For all Benji's affability, it didn't surprise her at all that Matthias was the one summoned to offer commonsense comfort.

He ran his hand over his brow. They were both still damp with their own and each other's sweat. "He's also asking if we've seen the news about the Serranos."

"The Serranos?" Pet was momentarily brought out of her own preoccupation. She'd been feeling guilty about Señora Serrano since the other night, unsure if she ought to do something, anonymously, or if it wasn't her place. Obviously, it *wasn't* her place to tell a stranger that her husband was an unfaithful slimeball, but—

"Apparently, the Spanish royals attended a ball last night, and Ailsa decided to put on a one-bird play in a crowded hotel foyer, which we'll give the working title *Karma*. It included a dramatic recreation involving graphic sound effects, a lot of moaning, and a crystal clear 'Madam Kingsley.'" He reclipped his phone to his belt. "Señora Serrano has put out a carefully worded statement through her rep. She's kicked him out on his arse."

"Oh my god. The poor woman. She'll be happier in the end, but—Jesus. Ailsa gets shit done, but that was brutal. I'm starting to think she and Mabel have a lot in common."

They were standing here having a normal conversation—if adulterous cabinet ministers and scheming, amorous Kirkby Greys ever fell into that category—but it was like a whole other conversation was going on silently beneath.

The insides of her thighs were so slick that if she made any sudden movements, she was going to end up doing the splits for the first time in twenty years.

And all she wanted to do was slip back into his arms, pretend the rest of the world didn't exist, and make love to him until she couldn't even walk.

Because that was the only possible term for it. She finally got the difference between great sex and—communicating, sharing, and adoring someone through physical touch and mutual pleasure.

Beep-beep-beep.

Her own phone this time. She bent to pick it up, because sure. Of course both their phones would go off right now, but if this were Johnny texting because he'd thrown his game controller into a medieval stained glass window again—

Her hand tightened around the plastic case.

"What is it?" He'd obviously seen something tighten in her face.

She didn't look up immediately. "It's Layla." *Now*, her voice was husky. "She's been working late doing press releases and is giving us an update. Her media moles have indicated that almost all major outlets are officially abandoning the line of speculation on me and Johnny."

She hesitated, then read out the rest of the text. "'No matter how beguiling a scandal, or shocking a headline, thankfully life and the news moves on. Currently, to a major infidelity scandal involving the Chancellor of the Exchequer and a parrot.'" She couldn't even hear the comforting rhythm of Matthias's breathing now. "We can't cut off Codename Charming too quickly or we'll undo all our 'hard work'—but we should give ourselves a pat on the back."

In this dark little old room where they'd been more intimate than she'd ever been with another human soul, she finally looked at him. "For being reasonably convincing."

Chapter Seventeen

The day of reckoning.

Maybe in every respect.

The sky over Berkshire was blue and clear, beautifully serene, not a cloud in sight. A picture-perfect afternoon. As Matthias drew the car to a stop outside the gates of an almost surreally pretty cottage, like something out of a period film, Pet was a tiny bit afraid she was going to be sick.

That sense of constraint between them had deepened every hour since they'd had to part last night—Matthias having been caught up with Benji and the unfortunate recruit for far longer than expected—and arrived separately at the castle this morning.

The text from Layla had thrown down the gauntlet. Obviously, she'd known that Codename Charming wasn't going to last forever, but she hadn't acknowledged the full extent of how much she'd been hiding behind it. So long as she and Matthias *had* to keep spending time together, were *supposed* to be affectionate and touchy-feely, and look like—like two people falling head over heels in love with each other, she didn't have to put everything on the line.

Right now, everything in her life seemed to be culminating in a moment when she'd have to step forward, heart in hand, open herself up to the truth—to *herself*, as well—and hope it didn't all end up in pieces.

She glanced out the window again at Fable Cottage, her abdomen tightening.

Matthias's expression had taken on an increasing implacability, a grim undertone that only heightened her uncertainty, but as he unbuckled his belt and twisted in his seat, a shaft of pure concern broke through like a bit of sunlight breaching heavy cloud. He reached out and touched her cheek, and she closed her eyes as the warmth sank into her skin. She just managed not to rub against him like a kitten.

"It's not too late," he said softly—and her lashes parted. His jaw ticked. "We can still turn back."

She looked into turbulent pools of green—his eyes were a stormy sea today—and slowly, she shook her head.

"No," she said. "We can't."

It was much colder outside than it had looked through the window, and Pet shivered as they walked up the path to a pink-painted front door, pulling her light coat around her.

Extending her hand toward the bell, she hesitated.

"Whatever happens," Matthias said, as their eyes met again and held, "it'll be all right."

God, she hoped so.

She rang the bell.

They stood wordlessly, waiting, the only sounds the rustling of the trees in the breeze and the faint shuffling of her feet on the mat.

Nobody answered her second ring, either, and she couldn't hear any sound within.

She twisted her hands together. "I mean—it *is* rude to turn up without calling first." Carlisle not having a phone had made it rather difficult to contact her in advance, and by the sound of it, she was the sort who'd dismiss that kind of phone call as a potential scam. Pet could've sent a letter, she supposed, but it had felt— *meant*, somehow, when they were already coming to Berkshire. "I guess we'll just—"

Without warning, a woman appeared around the side of the cottage, holding an armful of firewood.

"Ridiculous to be lighting the fire in summer," she said, and Pet's breath caught in her throat. Even their *voices* were similar.

Although in person, several decades on, she and Carlisle weren't quite as physically alike as it had appeared in the photo, and it wasn't simply the age difference. Experiences reflected on a person's face, and the other woman's expressions, the way she held herself, were so foreign to Pet's own mannerisms that it caused a surprising amount of differentiation.

As bizarre as it had been to see a near doppelgänger of herself, the sudden sense of unfamiliarity was strangely even more disorientating. Her stomach was churning into anxious knots.

There was a slight hardness in Carlisle's eyes and around her mouth. Not nastiness, but definite cynicism.

"Whatever you're selling, I'm not interested," the woman said abruptly. Then, as she reached them, her gaze fell on Pet, who'd previously been hidden beside Matthias.

She stopped dead.

A piece of wood fell to the ground.

None of them said anything.

At last, Matthias bent to pick up the fallen bit of wood. "Can I help you with those?"

The practical question broke Carlisle out of her frozen silence. She shook her head without looking at him, her eyes still fixed on Pet. "Christ Almighty," she said, her tone unreadable. "Confronted with the ghost of Christmas past. Unseasonably early, and my younger self seems to have shrunk."

The seconds ticked by as she continued to stare hard, her face totally expressionless now. Then, very coolly, she said, "Pardon my candor. But who in the sweet Lord might you be, and where did you get my face?"

The inside of the cottage was a surprise. Almost startlingly modern in contrast to the historical exterior, fitted out in stark shades of black, gray, and white. Carlisle showed them into a lounge and waved them imperiously toward a black leather couch, then walked over to a small home bar.

Pet had a strong sense of déjà vu. So far, this was playing out very similarly to the meeting with the duchess. If that continued, things were about to get starkly illuminating.

"I'd offer you the obligatory cup of tea," Carlisle said over her shoulder, "but I rather feel like something stronger. It's five o'clock somewhere, isn't it?"

She made herself a gin and tonic, then poured the two glasses of sparkling water they'd requested.

Bringing the drinks over on a small tray, she set it on the coffee table, and sank gracefully down on a gray armchair. Her eyes—a lighter shade of brown than Pet's, she saw now—watched them shrewdly over her glass. "I don't generally let *anyone* into my home," she said bluntly. "Let alone strangers. But it's not every day that a young clone turns up on my doorstep. And my curiosity is easily piqued at the best of times."

Matthias had actually sat down beside Pet for once, but his body language was as alert and watchful as always. At that last comment, however, his gaze slid sideways. She could almost *hear* the pointed observation that she obviously shared more than simply appearance genes with this woman.

She leveled her brows at him, but both their mouths twitched.

Carlisle's interest had sharpened. Her eyes didn't dart between them; she took her time, focusing on them in turn. A visual dissection.

"Well, you are an author," Pet offered, speaking for the first time since her initial awkward greeting. "Authors are meant to be curious, aren't they? Plotting must be sort of—literary detective work."

Thin brows lifted. "A well-informed doppelgänger. Where did you get this address?"

"We work at the palace. And the Duchess of Clarence is a law unto herself," Pet said ruefully, and the other woman smiled slightly.

"She has to be, with that husband." She leaned back in her chair. "Well. Under usual circumstances, I'd be furious at Lia for giving out my personal information willy-nilly, but I'm assuming you're not here to talk your way into an interview. Perhaps you'd kindly fill in the blanks behind your extremely unexpected appearance— and I mean that in both usages of the word. If I were a man, I'd think my youthful indiscretions were coming home to roost. However, while a good deal of my twenties and thirties is an admitted blur, I think I'd remember giving birth to a child."

She moved her glass, the ice cubes inside clinking together. "But as I don't believe in extraordinary coincidences, we've clearly sprung from some branch of the same tree. Goodness knows it's a tangled thicket. I think the last cousin who took up amateur genealogy gave up after a week."

Pet set down her own drink after a hasty sip. "I was hoping *you* could fill in the blanks." She opened her bag and withdrew the photograph. "I recently received some belongings from my mother's estate. We found this amongst her things."

Carlisle took the photo, and Pet continued, her throat dry despite the water, "My mother—she didn't have any relatives we don't know about. I'm almost certain of that. So—so if we are related, it's probably not on the maternal side. I think it must be—paternally." She set her jaw. "And I'm hoping you might be able to tell me who that is. The unknown paternal side. Who *he* is."

The other woman's brows lifted. "I see." Her narrowed gaze lowered to the snapshot.

"If she took that photo," Pet said, "you must have known her? Her married name was Hunt, not De Vere. I changed my name to my grandfather's after my—my stepfather died." She gestured anxiously. "The duchess said that was taken at the opening of an arts society in Windsor, at Rosaline Abbey. You—"

"Lana?" Carlisle asked sharply. Her own expression had changed. Dramatically. "Your mother was Lana Hunt?"

Without a word or even a prior glance this time, Matthias took Pet's hand. When his fingers closed around hers, yet another bit of her heart chipped off and fell into his curled palm.

She held her breath. "You *did* know her?"

Carlisle looked at her without comment for long seconds, her face becoming so inscrutable that Matthias's old bosses in covert ops would probably have hired her on the spot.

She was completely motionless, and the silence stretched into uncomfortable lengths.

Then, raising the photo, she looked down at it again. "I do remember that night." Her voice was equally enigmatic. "My work was part of a successful anthology at the time, and I was invited as a local guest speaker. I'd known your mother for some time, however. Lana was going through a literary phase at the time. We met at a writing group. She had no talent whatsoever," she added sardonically, "but I suspected she cultivated multiple hobbies just to avoid spending time with her family."

The sophisticated coolness fractured momentarily, as she shot a glance at Pet. "I apologize. That was—"

"True," Pet said. The snarky comment didn't leave so much as a pinprick of pain. Her mother's neglect, her selfishness . . . it couldn't hurt her anymore. Because she was strong, and she was a decent person, and Dominic was right. She would build her own happiness, regardless of the past.

The knowledge washed over her with an incredibly calm, *clean* sort of feeling, like the emotional equivalent of fresh linen and sea breezes.

Carlisle swept Pet with another calculated look. "How old are you?"

"Twenty-seven."

The other woman's nod was unsurprised and abrupt. "This photo would have been taken a year or so before your birth. It was a month or two after this event that I attended another function. My brother was staying with me that weekend, and I invited him along. He'd recently gone through a very ugly relationship break-down, and I thought a night's diversion would take his mind off it. A decision I came to regret, since it was there that he met Lana."

With pinched lips, she said, "It was several weeks before I re-alized where he was going at night. Until I informed him of the fact, he'd been unaware that she was married. He ended the affair at once." Her smile was tight and unamused. "As a family, we've never followed social conventions, but we at least draw the line at willing adultery."

Pet's breath left her in a rush.

"I fell out of contact with Lana after that. As far as I'm aware, my brother never saw her again, either. At least—I *presume* he didn't know about the evident result of that month of madness," Carlisle added, with a shade of deeper grimness. "He never told the family, if so. But we haven't been close for some years. He strongly disliked my second husband, and our own relationship never recovered." A sudden, frank snort. "Although as it transpired, he was quite right where that bastard was concerned. When it comes to sexual entanglements, we're not always a family of good choosers. Hopefully you've broken the mold in that respect."

She had. Emphatically. Pet was now an *excellent* chooser. The world's finest, in her opinion.

Carlisle swallowed another mouthful of gin and tonic, her gaze unwavering from Pet's face. "Admittedly, I wouldn't be his first choice of confidante, to confess his little secrets, if it turns out you're not quite such a surprise to him."

Pet absorbed that deliberate shot in silence. Matthias's grip tightened on her.

"So . . . your brother is my . . . is my . . ."

"I don't claim to be a geneticist," Carlisle supplied, that irony heavy and layered, "or, despite my authorial status, a detective, but given the dates and circumstances—and the fact that you and I are both dead ringers for my late grandmother—the logical conclusion would seem to be that you're my brother's daughter. My long-lost niece. I didn't expect to wake up this morning in a soap opera."

Despite the inherent melodrama of the statement, she wasn't exactly jumping for joy at her potential newfound aunt status.

"Did you?" Carlisle asked. She spoke with apparent indifference, but her eyes were extremely watchful.

And there was no mistaking the cynicism now.

"What?" Pet's mind was running in multiple circles at once, her response half-absent, but at Carlisle's next words, her eyes snapped back to her maybe-aunt's face.

"This *seems* to be a surprise, but was it really?" Carlisle was still lightly bobbing one foot; otherwise, she sat as still as Pet. "Or were you well armed with the facts when you arrived? If it's money you're after—"

Matthias moved abruptly, and Pet put her other hand over their clasped fingers. In reassurance, rather than seeking support. When their eyes met, she could see the deep anger there. The outrage on her behalf.

For just a moment, she'd felt as if she were encased in ice— all that newfound, wondrous peace undermined by a knee-jerk instinct from the past—but she shook her head, as if she were physically sloughing it from her body.

Matthias's hard gaze turned on Carlisle. "As Pet said, authors are supposed to be observant." He didn't raise his voice, but all the ice she'd thrown off had attached itself to his vocal cords. "Adept judges of human nature and character," he said, bitingly sardonic. "If you can't see that she has more integrity in her little finger than many people display in their entire life spans—"

He prudently left the rest unsaid, but the inference of "you're a fucking fool" was so bright and shining that he might as well have written in the air between them with a sparkler.

Perversely, the rudeness seemed to relax their reluctant host. Carlisle's mouth quirked. "I suspect you might be somewhat bi-ased."

"Extremely," Matthias said, and Pet's heart pinged again. "Changes nothing."

"To be fair," Pet murmured, "you did think *they* might be after *my* money."

"Totally different," he growled, more like a big, grouchy bear than the starchy soldier, and she had to press her lips together. It occurred to her suddenly that he was sometimes a bit like a giant version of Hercule, a thought she would not be sharing.

Carlisle leaned back in her chair, steepling her fingers. "You have to realize that in his profession, at his level, when fame and that much cash is on the table, there have always been people who'll try to take advantage. We might not be the living example of Happy Families, but at the end of the day, he's still my brother."

Pet's attention jerked back to her. She blinked. "Fame?" she repeated.

Her confusion must have been so transparently honest that a reciprocal frown fluttered over Carlisle's features.

Pet's lips parted. "Who—" she began huskily, and had to clear her throat before she could ask slowly, "Who is your brother?"

Carlisle stood swiftly and went to a small dresser in the corner. From a drawer, she withdrew a framed photo of her own. "His first agent was an unrepentant snob who thought 'Oliver Tallen' sounded like a nineteenth-century Cockney chimney sweep."

She turned the photo around.

In the posed studio shot, a younger Carlisle stood unsmilingly next to a man with a dimpled grin. He was—naturally—younger as well, but the famously elastic features were much the same. A few less lines around his eyes, a more limber look to his body, but unmistakably the same figure they'd seen only days ago, stalking around the stage of the New Pantheon.

The icon of the Royal Shakespeare Company. A veteran of the West End stage.

Her biological father was Oliver Browning.

The halls of the palace were unusually deserted. This evening's party in the gardens was a big event, full of VIPs, and most of the staff were involved in some capacity. Matthias had been forced to report in as soon as they arrived home, but he'd left her with palpable reluctance. He was still furious on her behalf at Carlisle's insinuations. Pet had known he was an incredibly loyal friend to the very few he let into that privileged sphere, but she'd felt the full force of that today.

Sylvie's words came back to her—that he'd probably wrap her in cotton wool and bubble wrap if she'd let him.

Even at the festival, she hadn't let herself truly believe— She'd been terrified to hope. She was *still* terrified to hope, but meeting Carlisle had at last clarified things, in an entirely different way than she'd expected.

She had to talk to him, as soon as they were off duty tonight.

Smoothing her sparkly pink cocktail dress as she walked quickly down the stairs, she halted midstride and diverted into the nearest bathroom. She needed a minute, to get her thoughts together before she had to put her professional face on for a few hours.

She also needed an anxious wee.

This was one of the luxe bathrooms used by official guests, so it was all marble floors and expensive fittings. She stood at the sink washing her hands, looking into a gold mirror. The blusher on her cheekbones was standing out too much on her pale face, and she tried to wipe some of it off with wet fingertips, only succeeding in streaking her foundation.

At the unmistakable sound of retching, she turned. She hadn't realized the far end stall was occupied. "Hello?" she called. "Are you okay? Do you need help?"

There was a muffled grunt, a shuffling sound, then the toilet flushed, and the door opened. Rosie came out, wiping her mouth with the back of her hand, and Pet looked at her, completely taken aback. The princess was dressed for the party, her hair a perfect shiny coil at the nape of her neck, her navy dress sleek. Her makeup probably *had* been immaculate, but her watering eyes had smeared her mascara.

"What on earth are you doing up here by yourself?" Pet was momentarily distracted from her own problems. She didn't want to sound like a Mother Hen, but the grounds were crawling with strangers, and she hadn't seen any sign of Rosie's PPOs outside. "And why aren't you in bed, if you're sick?"

Clacking to the mirrors on her high heels, Rosie peered at herself in the glass and screwed up her nose. She swiped under her eyes with a tissue from her purse. Despite her lingering green tinge, she raised an ironic eyebrow at Pet. "You and Matthias really are rubbing off on each other." A tiny smirk crossed her face as she leaned forward to pick off a stray fleck of mascara. "In more ways than one, obviously."

Fumbling in her bag, she muttered, "Damn, I've left my powder compact upstairs. I don't suppose you—?"

Pet opened her own bag and pulled out her compact, but she was still watching Rosie with narrowed-eyed concern, and the princess rolled her eyes as she dabbed powder under her eyes.

"I didn't purposefully ditch my security. I promised Johnny ages ago I'd stop doing that." A blithe aside. "I was just caught off guard on my way downstairs. It's highly inconvenient to be more than ten feet from a bathroom at this time of the day." She snapped the compact closed. "*Morning* sickness, my arse."

It took about one point five seconds to register, then Pet caught her breath. "Oh my god. You're—"

Rosie caught her smile between her teeth, her expression unusually, endearingly bashful for a moment. When she nodded, Pet couldn't help it—she squeaked and threw her arms around the other woman's neck.

"Rosie! Oh my god! I'm so happy for you." She realized what she was doing and stepped back hastily. "Sorry!"

Firmly, Rosie reached out and hugged her again. "Pet. You saved my husband's life. You've upturned your own to help us. You sit through countless hours of Battleship and Monopoly and charades to keep Johnny's mind off his nerves, and you've helped him find his feet this year. Even when he's consistently knocked you off yours. You and I are friends for life."

Pet felt the sting of threatening tears. The maelstrom of emotions from the past few days were catching up to her, her composure starting to splinter.

Rosie looked at her hard. "Are *you* okay? What happened this afternoon?"

She'd asked about the photograph this morning, if they'd found out what they needed to know from Lia, and Pet had given her the bare outline of their plans. She found herself spilling it all out now and saw Rosie scowl when she got to the gold-digging accusations.

"It—doesn't matter," she said slowly, leaning back against the sink. "I know I'm not like that, and the people who matter know I'm not like that. It can't touch me." She shook her head. "It's weird.

The way it played out, in some ways it was exactly what I'd most worried would happen. Carlisle wasn't happy about the connection. She was very wary. Suspicious. Probably understandably so. Her life is set and established, she clearly isn't interested in any upheavals, and they're a family that would easily be targeted by people with bad intentions." She stopped. Exhaled. "There's also a good possibility that my real father knew about me all along and just didn't give a shit."

Rosie touched her hand, and she moved her head in another swift shake. "A few years ago," Pet said through the growing lump in her throat, "that would have crushed me. Even a few damn *days* ago, I was incredibly apprehensive about digging further into this. But I was sitting there in that cottage, looking at her and listening to her, and I thought—" She bit her upper lip. "I thought—I'm okay. If Oliver Browning doesn't want to know, if I never hear from Carlisle again, I'll be disappointed. It'll hurt a little. But I'll be okay."

Her voice cracked as she said, to herself as much as to Rosie, "I've grown up. And despite the way it began, my life now is pretty fucking great. It's full, and it's happy, and it's bursting with love. And I *have* a family. Dominic. Sylvie. Mabel, Benji, Jay, you and Johnny, and—"

"And Matthias," Rosie finished softly, leaning her hand on the edge of her own sink, her eyes fixed on Pet's face. There was nothing but empathy there now. "You want him, don't you? Without the artifice. Without the pretense. For good."

"More than I've ever wanted anything in my life." The lump in Pet's throat was hard and painful. "And when we're together, I can't believe that he doesn't— That this isn't—" She looked down, watching the soft, expensive lighting glow on the surface of the compact Rosie held so carefully. "Even though I feel closer to him than I've ever felt to anyone, there's still this last bit of distance between us. I just can't shake the feeling that he doesn't really . . . *want* to want me. And if that's the case—"

Then she was going to have to let him go. Because they both deserved full happiness.

Rosie was silent. When she did speak, her words were unexpected. "We trust our security personnel with our lives and our family's lives. We have to run extremely extensive background checks on every new hire."

Pet lifted her head, pressing her thumb under her lashes.

Rosie hesitated, with another long pause. Then— "A man who was passed from foster family to foster family as a child. Who never really belonged to anyone, or had anyone who was truly his," she said quietly. "Whose experience with romantic relationships seems to largely boil down to one-night stands, and in a few instances, being used for his body and discarded, even laughed at, for his face."

Pet stiffened. The sudden fury in the pit of her stomach was so strong that she could have gone out in sympathy with Rosie and vomited right there.

"He finally lets his guard down enough to form a close friendship. Almost brothers, apparently," Rosie continued, noting her reaction without comment. "His friend dies violently."

Her steady gaze didn't leave Pet's. "And then one day, he sees this hopelessly pretty, happy, bright spark of a woman." She was still speaking levelly. "Within seconds, she's been badly hurt on his watch, too. He holds her hand on a cold wooden floor, and he brings her a tiny teddy bear in the hospital."

She held up Pet's powder compact. Her fingernails were midnight blue and painted with tiny silver stars, and they sparkled under the light.

The compact was one of the most beautiful gifts Pet had ever been given, an antique piece that she'd had dated to approximately 1921. Whoever it had originally belonged to, they'd taken very good care of it. More than a hundred years old and it barely had a scratch. She polished it every month, and she'd wished fervently that she knew who'd given it to her. On her twenty-seventh birthday, she'd had a ridiculous number of presents piled on a table, and a few of them had lost their tags.

"He buys her an expensive antique compact for her birthday," Rosie said softly, and Pet's eyes jumped to hers from the compact. "Not because he cares about the cost—or thinks she will—but because she'll love it, and he knows that, and he wants her to smile. He doesn't put his name on it. He'd never tell her," the princess finished slowly, "because it's ridiculous, isn't it, it's impossible. He doesn't know that she *sees* him, the way he sees her."

The combined rustle of their silk dresses was loud in the thick silence.

"They're both used to being alone. They're both afraid."

Pet was breathing quickly, her chest aching. She looked again at the compact. A tear slipped down the side of her nose, and she caught it on shaking fingertips.

"Life isn't always easy, Pet," Rosie said. "Neither is love. But they're sure as hell worth fighting for."

Matthias and Benji were escorting Johnny to find his missing wife when a figure pushed through the mingling press pack.

The Bulldog was red-faced, his eyes glinting a bit feverishly. "Thought you were home free, didn't you, you fucks?" His hands fisted at his sides. "You know I won't give up, that I'll throw open your sordid little mess. Need to shut me up, so you issue a few threats. Call in your corrupt mates in the force, tell them to start poking into my business—"

As Benji moved with deliberate coolness and lack of haste to secure Johnny, Matthias spoke into his headset, his gaze calmly on the pap, whose body was vibrating with coiling rage. "Francesca and Carlos, we've got an unregistered guest in the press pen. Escort him out, please."

The Bulldog took another step forward, his fingers clenching and unclenching. "Or just a funny coincidence, is it? I don't buy the pathetic attempt to cover up this prick's filthy affair, and suddenly bloody lawsuits are bursting out of the fucking woodwork left and right. I could lose everything—and the rats aren't just in the palace. Fifteen years I've given that paper and they don't even let me clean out my desk."

His voice was rising steadily.

Hordes of fancily dressed people in the party marquees had lowered their glasses of champagne and were staring across the grass, murmuring with growing interest.

The journalists from the registered press rota were on high alert, ears perked, cameras emerging.

Gesturing against his thigh for Benji to remove Johnny from the situation, Matthias said levelly, "After the complete trash you've written about someone very important to me, I applaud whoever else has had enough of your bullshit and complete lack of ethics, but I haven't spared you a single brain cell since you last wormed your way into our presence. It must have been one of your other admirers. That's the problem with stalking and making up shit about half the city. You tend to piss off a lot of people."

"Liars." The pap looked from Matthias to Johnny, who wasn't entirely cooperating with Benji's attempts to steer him away. In his peripheral vision, Matthias could see Johnny's anxious eyes darting between him and the Bulldog. Tension was building in his muscles. His instinct was twanging hard again. On the scale of physical threats, this prick would usually barely scrape into level one. But the man was functioning on irrational fury, adrenaline, and by the smell of him, a fuck-ton of booze, a volatile combination.

Matthias kept still and outwardly relaxed, aware of every single vulnerable body in the vicinity, but his muscles were bracing.

The already turbulent situation amped into the stratosphere when Pet and Rosie appeared, both women running. And where the fuck was Rosie's team? Matthias had a split second in which his eyes met Pet's—and his heart slammed against his ribs when he saw the way she was looking at him, what was shining true and clear amidst the anxiety.

Benji's final words to him at the festival rang in his head.

"There aren't any guarantees," his friend had said, simply. "Maybe she'll break your heart. Maybe she'll end up being your best friend. And maybe she'll be the love of your goddamn life, you lucky bastard." Benji had held his gaze squarely. *"Maybe,* when you're old and gray, she'll be the best friend who's holding your hand, still driving you mutually mad, having incredible sex, and looking at you like she'd stand between you and an advancing army. And you'll be looking back at her the same way. So, ultimately, you're going to have to decide—is it worth the risk? Is *she* worth the risk?"

And in the end, it was as simple as that.

The Bulldog had also seen the women. His eyes flickered—and something in him obviously snapped. He lunged at them. God knew what the fuck he was planning to do, but Matthias was already moving.

In his so-called "work," the pap had repeatedly proven himself a sniveling coward and a misogynist to his core. The guy usually targeted women with his filth, and he was a classic bully when it came to physical altercations. It was entirely predictable that when his rage bubbled over and he lost control, he went for the two people who were smallest in stature.

However, as he'd also consistently underlined, he was not the brightest or sharpest crayon in the box.

Even as Matthias—and Benji, *and* Johnny—lunged at the bastard, Matthias's blood a hard, pumping rush in his ears, his own fury hazing his vision, he was aware that he was witnessing a singularly catastrophic error of judgment.

Sure enough, before the pap got within six feet of Pet and Rosie, the princess grabbed an umbrella from the nearby bucket standing at the ready in case of rain. England's shite summers to the rescue. She opened it with a snap, and the Bulldog reared back a step, understandably startled at having a pink parasol swoop at his face like a hostile stingray—putting him neatly in the path of Pet, who slammed the heel of her hand under his chin.

His head snapped up, his teeth clattering together with a painful rattle they probably heard right across at the marquees.

As he reeled, the Duchess of Clarence emerged from absolutely fucking nowhere with an ugly gray vase under her arm. Supremely casually, she smashed it down on the precise spot under the man's scapula that would temporarily numb the nerves in his legs.

From Bulldog to fainting goat, in less than five seconds.

Echoing silence fell across them all, broken only by multiple heaving, jagged breaths, then—

"Drat." Ignoring the pap on the ground at her feet, the duchess looked crossly at the shattered halves of the vase. "I was going to get five thousand pounds for that."

Pet was still shivering with residual adrenaline, the shock of seeing Matthias facing a clearly unhinged paparazzo, before the guy had charged straight at a pregnant Rosie. Everyone and everything seemed frozen, but when the dazed Bulldog stirred enough to grasp frantically at his splayed legs and spit out a vile epithet against them all, she looked down into his bloodshot eyes.

He glared up at her, also quivering, with reaction or hate. Probably both. "You couldn't even come up with a convincing cover," he hissed, into a resonant sort of quietness broken only by clicking cameras. "Expect—" He was slurring; it sounded like "'spect." "Expect anyone to believe that ugly bast—"

"Stop." Pet didn't raise her voice, but the word cut clearly through the invective, carrying across the grass to where Matthias had halted a short distance away, his whole body taut. His arrested gaze full of—everything. "Just—stop."

Amazingly, the Bulldog did stop, his cracked lips parted, but she barely glanced at him. She continued to look directly into Matthias's eyes. She hadn't planned for any of this. Hadn't intended to lay her soul bare in front of the entire bloody press pack. But the words tumbled free, as if they'd been pent up too long, as if she'd been holding on to something that belonged to him, that wanted to fly to him. "I adore him," she said, so simply, and watched Matthias's chest move as he drew in a long breath. Watched his lashes briefly close. Saw the tremor that ran right through him.

And she at last let herself believe.

As his green gaze pierced hers again, his jaw clenching down so very hard, she continued, enunciating every word, "He's the most beautiful person I've ever known. The bravest. The most honorable. I'm proud just to know him." She swallowed. "I went looking for family." Her eyes stung. "I'd already found it."

More tears rose in her throat at what that did to him.

It was like he'd been turned to stone—but his eyes were alive, on fire.

Wrenching her gaze from his, just for a moment, she jerked her head down. The Bulldog was breathing heavily, staring up at her. "It's real," she said. "It was always real."

And then, as if someone had picked up an invisible remote control and pressed "play" on a paused, frozen scene, everything went into motion.

Security officers pulled the pap to his feet, steering him away as he redirected his grievances and started hollering that he couldn't move his legs—demonstrably untrue—and that he was going to sue the duchess.

Lia didn't even look up. She was still staring with great annoyance at her broken vase.

Around the lawn, gossiping politicians and various members of the press corps rolled their eyes. Pet saw more than one open grin. Evidently, the Bulldog had rendered himself rather unpopular.

He was swept out of her mind for good when Matthias snatched her up, scooping her into his arms. She was still trembling, but his hold was sheltering. Unbreakable. As his big hand cupped her head, his closed eyes resting against her temple, she wrapped her legs about him without hesitation.

They stood there, time vanishing into irrelevance. Pet didn't realize she was properly crying until he caught a few tears with his lips.

He was holding her to him as if someone might try to rip her out of his arms.

Like he never wanted to let her go.

Feeling his heart thudding hard against her palm, Pet moved her hand to clasp his neck, nuzzling in so she could dust feather-soft kisses across his throat.

Another hard shiver went through his body, and his grip tightened on her.

When he kissed her ear, her cheek, her neck, his chest worked as he tried to breathe out his own adrenaline. Their foreheads rolled together, and they looked at each other.

"I'm in love with you." They said it at the same time, stark and unsteady and truthful, and even as she absorbed his words into her, felt the incredible relief of it, felt them sink deep and settle into her heart until she felt as if she were shining brighter than the fairy lights around them, she saw the renewed impact of her own words on him.

She had to lean her forehead back against him for a minute. She'd never felt like this before, as if there were so much rising happiness inside her that she wouldn't be able to contain it, and it would spill out and light the world.

"I'm in love with you," she said again, softly, and he pressed his mouth to the bare curve of her shoulder. "I think I fell halfway on that first night in the hospital. But if I'd been prepared to admit it, I was probably a complete goner after you saved the mouse. Whole heart gone. Yours. For good."

It was a moment before he spoke, was able to swallow over the deep hoarseness in his throat. "For good." He said it with that very

Matthias-coolness, but his muscles were so taut and tight that she could feel his abs and his biceps all flexing compulsively.

"In the beginning, you obviously didn't even want to be friends, so I didn't let myself think about it." She cleared her own throat, which was still clogged with tears. "And to be honest, I was getting a bit pissed off about the protocol manual."

For the first time, some of his tension relaxed. His half laugh was quiet and rusty sounding. She was vaguely aware that other aides were getting the music going, trying to restart the party, and that scattered guests and journalists continued to peer their way.

Pet didn't give a damn. Matthias was looking at her as if she were the only other person in the world, and that was how it felt right now. He walked with her a short distance, however, moving into the semi-privacy of a shadowed alcove. They were at least out of earshot of the press, and she was cuddled close enough to hear Benji's voice in his earpiece before he flicked it off, the other man stating that he had everything covered for as long as they needed.

"You have no idea how bloody hard it was to keep that distance between us." Matthias's voice was still very low, as if he were struggling to register that this was real, that it had really happened for them. She entirely understood. The tips of their noses touched. "From the beginning, it was like—"

When he hesitated, she said softly, "Like I already knew you."

The moment they'd looked at each other across that hospital room, it had been like something inside her had recognized him.

His mouth nuzzled back against hers. "The friendship was almost there without us having to do a damn thing. But once you started working here, it took about three days before I realized how easily I could get in way too deep, if we got close." He stroked her lower back with his thumb as he said bluntly, "I didn't think there was a hope in hell you'd ever see me that way."

"But you must have felt it these past days." Pet caught her lip between her teeth, biting down, and he kissed her again, his tongue flicking over the minuscule hurt. "When I touched you. When I looked at you." She wrinkled her nose. "I don't think I've exactly been subtle. I've basically crawled all over you from the moment we left that staff meeting."

His throat moved under her drifting fingers. "It was like being hit by a fucking two-by-four, just realizing that the sexual pull went both ways," he said. "But to even imagine you might want—for good—"

"I used to wonder, sometimes, if I just . . . wasn't capable of loving someone like this, if not having someone to love when I was little had somehow—" She saw the shift in his expression, felt the way his hands flexed on her. "That's how you felt, too."

He nodded once.

"It's not true," she said. "For either of us." She searched for the right words. "I've never felt like this about anyone. It makes me feel—it makes *everything* feel beautiful. You know?"

"Yes." Another deep rasp. "I know."

"I don't have a clue what I'm doing." She twined her arms about his neck. "But I want you, and you want me, and we'll learn the rest as we go."

The smile slowly crept into his eyes, warming and deepening the green color she loved. "Our new private mission?"

"Mmm." She tugged his mouth down to hers. "Permanent assignment this time."

As his teeth gently nipped her lower lip, she pulled back just long enough to ask, "Are you, by any chance, likely to be even more overprotective now?"

He grimaced.

And didn't bother to deny it.

"That's okay," she murmured. "Me too."

When they finally remembered that they were technically still on duty, they reluctantly left the alcove, and found Rosie and Johnny coming their way, hand in hand. Benji was keeping a discreet distance behind them, but his eyes were dancing as he looked at them.

Johnny grinned at them. "Well. F-final report on Codename Charming, comrades?"

Matthias's fingers were playing with Pet's. "Which objective would that be? The openly stated point, to avert press attention, or Rosie's underlying motive in suggesting this particular course of action?"

Blinking, Pet followed his pointed gaze to Rosie's face—and saw the princess flush slightly. "*Rosie*. Did you—"

Rosie rallied, her nose lifting in the air. "We *did* need to suppress the rumors about you and Johnny, for all our sakes, and especially yours." She exchanged glances with Johnny, who'd slipped his palm protectively over her middle. "*If*, simultaneously, you two were clearly meant for each other and weren't doing a damn thing about it, and it was getting extremely aggravating—it's really just a bonus, isn't it?"

Pet opened her mouth. Closed it again.

Rosie's lips quirked. "Either way," she said, and her eyes softened as her gaze rested on their entwined hands. "Mission resoundingly successful."

Epilogue

Happy.

Pet stood outside the door to the Bluebell Room. Rosie had offered the sunny little drawing room at the front of the palace as a place to meet on neutral territory, in privacy and comfort.

Oliver Browning was already inside with his husband, the playwright Nishan Rao. According to the household aide who'd showed them in, the couple had arrived over twenty minutes early. Anxious. Apprehensive. And excited.

Oliver *hadn't* known Lana was pregnant. According to Carlisle's succinct call last night when she'd grudgingly located a phone, barely five hours after Pet and Matthias had left Berkshire, her brother had been understandably surprised to hear from her when she'd phoned him—and speechless for over a minute once she'd baldly explained why they were speaking for the first time in years.

After that extremely rare silence, he'd been full of questions, Carlisle had told her, but with a thread of affection behind her sardonic impatience. No practical, *cautious* questions; nothing about DNA tests, meeting with witnesses and security present, and so on. Just—who; when; where was she? What was her name? Was she all right? Did she—did she want to meet him?

He'd wanted to come to the palace last night. The moment he'd heard.

His sister had informed him crisply that he might want to give himself at least a twenty-four-hour breather, to let it sink in before he rocked up to a stranger's doorstep. And, with a sensitivity that would have been surprising if Pet didn't suspect a decent-sized heart existed beneath the other woman's acerbic exterior, Carlisle had thought Pet might also need time to prepare herself.

For the sudden transformation of a far-fetched possibility into a living, breathing human.

And the chance of a real-life happy *beginning* in every way.

Before she'd unceremoniously hung up, Carlisle had said abruptly, as if she'd come to a decision, "He and Nishan wanted a child. They tried different routes with surrogacy and adoption, but they didn't have much money early in their careers, and it was all ultimately difficult, painful, and unsuccessful. They gave up a long time ago. But they always wanted to be parents."

Exhaling, Pet tightened her grip on Matthias's hand. She looked up at him—then blinked, and with a sudden grin, reached up with her free hand to wipe a trace of red lipstick from his mouth. "Not sure it's your color."

That very private smile was still in his tired eyes as he squeezed her hand in silent reassurance—and she'd do everything she could to make sure he never lost it. Although she wouldn't say no to a shared nap soon. They were walking around with identical purple smudges under their lashes. Last night had involved a little bit of bonding with Miriam—immediately undone when they'd booted the affronted cat out of his bedroom—and almost no sleep whatsoever.

He tilted his head at the door. "Ready?"

Yes. She was ready. For all of this.

When she opened the door, the two men standing in front of the fireplace swung around immediately. Oliver Browning was much smaller in person than he looked on the stage—and he hadn't exactly looked tall even from the royal box. She could see where she'd got the short genes from.

As Matthias stepped closer to stand at her back, she drew in another unsteady breath—and so did Oliver.

Without looking away from her, apparently unable to tear his gaze from her face, where he seemed to be tracing every feature with transparent wonder, the actor felt behind him for his husband's hand. Nishan immediately gripped his palm. The playwright was the significantly taller half of the couple, a broad-shouldered man with warm brown skin and graying black hair, cut in a stylish sweep over his wide forehead. With a wisp of amusement, Pet realized he was hovering protectively over his husband in a very familiar fashion.

Nishan's face was harder than Oliver's in every respect, sharply chiseled with an aquiline nose and guarded eyes. That discerning gaze moved over her, from her carefully straightened bob to her lucky heels, cataloguing every detail.

Pet's eyes returned to Oliver, whose free hand had gone to his mouth, his fingers resting against his lips. That slim, elegant hand was shaking, she realized with a hard pang.

Almost simultaneously, they each took a step forward.

"Hello, darling." Oliver spoke for the first time, that familiar, resonant baritone cracking. She'd never heard him anything but entirely vocally confident, performing his lines with ease. This wasn't Oliver Browning the actor; it was Oliver, the man. Uncertain. Emotional. Overwhelmed. "I'm very pleased to meet you." He had to clear his throat, but the words fractured again. "You have no idea how much."

There was a wet sheen in his dark brown eyes.

They were her eyes. Down to the flecks of caramel near his pupils.

That fine tremor was shivering right through her body. Matthias brought her hand to his mouth, pressing a reassuring kiss to her wrist.

"Hello." Her voice was a husky whisper.

Oliver took another long breath, his chest expanding and falling with a shudder. He closed his eyes for a moment. Then, letting go of Nishan's hand with a hard squeeze, he came over to her. "Lord," he murmured. "You look so much like photos of my grandmother when she was young."

"She also looks like Carlisle *now*," Nishan said dryly, his stance still watchful. "If either of us read the tabloids or used social media, we'd have spotted the resemblance weeks ago, by the sound of it."

Oliver grimaced at the very idea of the gutter press—and possibly his sister. Pet imagined he'd copped his own share of unwanted attention and outright lies over the years. Something else they had in common. "But you have my eyes," he said thickly, his attention still fully on her. "And you're entirely your own person. The best PA in the palace, according to the young lady who showed us in here."

He sounded absurdly proud. Pet had to swallow over another lump in her throat.

Oliver lifted his trembling hand. "May I—"

She nodded slowly, and tentatively, incredibly gently, he touched his fingertips to the hair at her temple, then briefly cupped her cheek. A tear slipped down his clean-shaven cheek. "Oh my god," he said. "I'm a father. We have a daughter."

Pet was fighting tears of her own. Over his shoulder, she saw Nishan's face soften.

Oliver pressed his lips together. "I want—" He cleared his throat. "We talked about this all night, and we want to be very clear that there's no pressure on you here. You're a grown woman, with your own life, and we have a lot to learn about each other. I have many questions, and I'm sure you do, too. This must be incredibly overwhelming for you. And ultimately, whatever decision you make, now or ever, I'll abide by it. But—I very badly want the chance to know you, Pet. If you allow us to be a part of your life, we—we're here."

The room was so quiet she could hear all their individual breaths.

Nishan walked to stand by his husband's side, resting a comforting hand on his shoulder. When she looked at him, he nodded—and his eyes were suddenly glittering.

She couldn't speak—but when she dipped her head, her own lashes wet, it wasn't an acknowledgment.

It was an answer.

Forever.

Matthias could hear Pet's voice as he unlocked and opened the front door. Hanging his key next to hers on the hooks on the side cabinet, he stood for a moment, inhaling the mingled scents of her favorite candles and the lingering traces of her perfume. It was less than a fortnight since they'd moved into a shared suite, but he wasn't sure he'd ever get used to it, having a real home, for the first time in his life.

He wouldn't ever take it for granted.

The two-bedroom suites were generally reserved for staff couples with at least one kid, but Pet was an unabashed favorite of Rosie's. They'd turned the second bedroom into a combined library/silhouette-cutting/whittling room and spent most of their free evenings curled on the couch in there.

The lounge was getting increasingly cluttered with their favorite artwork, mementoes they picked up on overseas engagements and dates in London, books, and photos. On one shelf, a tiny wooden mouse clutching a teddy bear sat in his own little pink armchair, next to minuscule bookcases. Matthias's gaze rested on the blown-up shot someone had snapped for them in Ireland, at Jonna's birthday party. Jonna was laughing up at him, teasing about the gift they'd bought her, reminding him of the infamous demonic-toy incident. Her mother, Grace, had an arm tightly around Pet, whom she'd instantly adopted into the fold, while Niamh stood by, smiling.

And next to it, an official work headshot of Padraig, taken not long after he'd met Jenny. Pet had found it and framed it. His friend's eyes were crinkled with his smile and seemed to look straight into Matthias's. Happy. At peace.

Family.

But the heart of it—*his* heart and home—sat cross-legged on the rug, holding an earnest conversation with a besotted Miriam. Pet was holding out a photo of an absolutely enormous, surly-looking cat. "This is Humphrey," she said to Miriam, with great seriousness. "It's always important to know the enemy."

Miriam did her slow-blink of love at Pet again. "*Mrrp,*" she agreed.

His moody cat had taken one look at Pet and fallen into a state of instant, abiding adoration. She'd become a purring bundle of unconditional affection whenever Pet was around, had started sneaking off to nap in her suite before they'd moved in together, and didn't make a peep at night now, lest her goddess's sleep be disturbed.

As Pet was also his favorite human, Matthias fully empathized with the sentiment.

He also found it more than a little aggravating, after the number of times he'd been kneaded like bread dough at two in the morning, and scratched when Miriam decided she no longer wanted the stomach rub she'd been demanding nonstop.

Pet lowered the photo, her eyes sparkling up at him. He stood, looking at her as she sat there in a shaft of sunlight. The strap of her dress was slipping off her shoulder, and the locket with his parents' photos rested against her chest. She'd worn it every day since he'd given it to her. One of her hands rested on Miriam's head, stroking the purring cat, and she was biting on her lip.

Out of nowhere, an image that had always been blurred by the passage of time, important but indistinct, seemed to glide out and settle over the scene, like a sort of sensory echo.

The smile in her expression slipped into concern. "Are you okay?"

It was almost certainly bullshit, probably a twist of memory. Like Pet's aunt, he didn't believe in extraordinary coincidence. But—

He saw her again. A tiny girl with lonely eyes and short black hair. Declaring they were going to be friends—as she nervously caught her upper lip between baby teeth.

"A long time ago," he said, "did your parents ever put you in a school holiday program?"

Pet's frown deepened. She tilted her head. "Yeah. A few times, especially when I was very young. Lana and Gerald weren't big on looking after us themselves. Why?"

He shook his head, dropping to a crouch to kiss her. Their lips touched, then clung. Pet's hands came up to clasp his jaw as his tongue drove against hers. They were both breathing hard when he pulled back.

Her hands were sliding down to his shoulders when her fingers tightened on him. She went very still. Very slowly, as if she were testing each word and his reaction to it, she said, "*We're going to be friends.*"

His forearm coming to rest on his raised knee, he exhaled.

"You were that boy," Pet said, barely audible.

"You were that girl."

They were staring at each other. When he reached out, she slid her fingers between his.

"My first real friend. Even if it was just for that one day." Pet looked at their interlocked hands, then lifted her gaze back to his. "Still don't believe in fate?"

After . . .

Under the moonlight, the lights strung through the trees glittered, the bluebells carpeting the ground just visible in the soft glow. It wasn't the most conventional place for a wedding, a random bluebell woodland in the middle of nowhere, but Pet and Matthias had found this place on a day in the countryside together. She'd loved it so much they'd stayed here all afternoon.

And fucked like bunnies all over the spot where their St. Giles colleagues were seated right now, which was somewhat awkward.

The liquid satin of her slip dress moved against her legs. Sylvie reached to adjust the simple white roses pinned in Pet's hair and the chain of her locket, then squeezed her hand, her eyes gentle and happy, before she ducked around the side of the aisle to take her seat next to Mabel.

Releasing a breath through her mouth, Pet stepped up to the edge of the flower-scattered aisle, where Dominic, Oliver, and Nishan were waiting for her, all equally smart in their morning suits.

Carefully positioning his phone, Nishan took yet another photo of her. Her dads were making up for lost time with a vengeance, but she was surprised they had any wall space left in their house, they'd framed so many shots of her, of Matthias, of all of them together.

Dominic and Oliver each crooked an elbow, and she slid her arms through theirs.

Oliver blinked hard, his eyes wet, as Nishan took his free hand.

Dominic smiled at her. "Ready?"

She looked across the sea of smiling heads to the other wide aisle, where Matthias stood, his own arms occupied. Grace McCarthy and Jenny stood with him on one side; Niamh and Jonna on the other.

Their eyes locked.

"Always," she said.

To the gorgeous strains of a Kovalenko symphony, they walked up the aisle. She passed everyone, all her family, all their friends, but their gazes held each other the whole way.

When the aisles converged and met, their escorts stepped back, and Matthias held out his hand to her. His jaw was locked hard against a surge of emotion, but that look had said everything.

Pet stepped forward, reaching for him.

Just as Johnny leaned forward to get a better look at them, lost his balance, and managed to catapult off his own chair. He slammed into Matthias's back—and for once, by some combination of physics and sheer surprise, dislodged the immoveable object.

Matthias stumbled forward, twisted to try to break his fall, and landed straight in Pet's arms.

She caught him.

She was within about an eighth of an inch from landing on her arse in her beloved bluebells, but she managed to stay standing, laughter springing helplessly into her eyes as she looked down into his face.

As the guests chattered loudly, inevitable cameras clicked, and Rosie hid her face to smother her giggles, Johnny apologized with an audible groan.

Grinning, Matthias pushed back upright and tugged Pet against him with a hand at the small of her back. He shook his head. "Doesn't matter," he said, ignoring protocol and kissing her, straight on her smile. "We never let each other fall."

Acknowledgments

Thank you so much to my new editor, Nicole Fischer, for being so welcoming, kind, and encouraging, to all the team at Avon for your hard work, and to Liza Rusalskaya, for lending your considerable talents to yet another gorgeous cover.

I'm forever grateful to my agent, Elaine Spencer, for believing in me from the beginning, and for your expertise and support—and for happily wrangling international time differences and being prepared to FaceTime before the crack of dawn!

To my friends both in and outside of the book community: I couldn't do this without you. Huge thanks and hugs especially to Emma, Tamara, Stephanie, Olivia, Madeline, and Holly.

To my family: you're everything, and I love you so much. (And a million thank-yous to my mum for being a sympathetic ear when I was thrashing out plot problems and needed to talk in minute detail about a story you hadn't yet read.)

As always, to the people who give up your time to read my books and let them be part of your lives for a little while, and the bloggers, Instagrammers, YouTubers, and TikTokkers who work so tirelessly in the book community: I honestly can't thank you enough. I appreciate you all more than I can ever say.

And to my incredible Nana, to my endlessly kind Uncle Ken, and to my beautiful, talented friend Kate—you all made the world a better, brighter place. I love you, and I miss you terribly.

About the Author

Lucy Parker is an award-winning romance author who lives in New Zealand. A romance reader from a young age, she loves to write about people pursuing their dreams and falling hopelessly in love along the way—often with the last person they would expect! Her previous titles have been featured in *Entertainment Weekly*, *Cosmopolitan*, and *Oprah Magazine*, and were included in NPR's Book Concierge for four consecutive years.